Deadly Lover

Charlee Allden

ACKNOWLEDGMENTS

With all my heart, I thank my mother who has always encouraged me, read my books, and urged me to get them published. You mean the world to me and inspire me more than you know.

This book has been made better through the encouragement and generosity of many author friends and readers. Special thanks to first readers Eden Glenn, Pam Wells, and Donna McAteer and most recent readers Shelby Reed, Lis'Anne Harris, and Abigail Sharpe. I'd also like to thank the members of Sandra McDonald's SF&F Critique Group and in particular Bridges Del Ponte and Jean Osborn. To my sisters in spirit, the members of the Inkplots critique group, you're instrumental in my writing life and your insight on this book was invaluable. To FCRW, your support and encouragement helped me stay strong through the ups and downs of publishing. To the Jolaj and the Gang group, you are all crazy-wonderful. This book also owes much to Margie Lawson, a gifted teacher with a special vision of writing craft. I look forward to learning more from her in the years ahead. Any deficiencies are entirely my own.

CHAPTER 1

Lily Rowan stood on the roof of her apartment building. The city spread around her like a menacing maze, a childhood friend whose grown-up face didn't quite fit her memories. Or maybe it was her that didn't yet fit.

Her doctors said, *give yourself time.*

Her therapists said, *give yourself time.*

Her brother said, *give yourself time.*

Hell, in the beginning, even her unit director had told her to take some time before going back to her position on the special tactics squad.

Time was up.

One last psych evaluation to prove she could cope with the memories of a training op gone terribly wrong, with the panic attacks that followed, with a job that left no room for hesitation, no room for indecision, no room for fear.

Lily stepped to the roof's edge—the toes of her boots jutting over the precipice. Standing there, four stories up, wasn't the dumbest thing she'd ever done. Not even close.

Face your fears.

She owed that bit of advice to her father.

The enormous alloy barrier a dozen blocks east ringed The Zone and kept the Ormney settlement out of view. It might hide the unfamiliar structures and keep the Ormney sequestered during the night hours, but it couldn't wall away her memories.

Face your fears.

That's what she'd been trying to do when she decided to live in The Mixer—so close to The Zone and one of a handful of places where Ormney and Earth natives worked side-by-side.

Face your fears.

"Lily!"

Her brother's voice in her ear jerked her out of her thoughts. She traced a finger over the slender com-link wrapped over her right lobe. The missed call signal flashed in one corner of her com-lens.

Her love for her brother gave her the will to push a little cheer into her voice. "You're supposed to wait for me to answer the call."

Brian chuckled. "What good is it to be a hacker if you can't use the skills when your sister is being a pain?"

A grin tugged at her cheeks as she stepped back from the edge. "You're not a hacker. You're an electronic security expert. There's supposed to be a difference."

"Yeah, yeah. And you're supposed to be easier to reach now that you're on medical leave."

The message indicator still blinked urgent at the edge of the lens in her right eye—code STU. Special Tactics Unit. Deepwater Security and Protection Services. Her employer. And it could only be about her appointment. She let the message scroll across her com-lens as text.

"Oh damn. Bri, I promise I'm not trying to avoid you, but I've got to go." She ran through her mental checklist for anything she might need then engaged her apartment security remotely. "They just changed my evaluation appointment and now I'm late."

"Don't sound so worried, Lil. You're going to do fine."

"Love you, baby brother." Lily disconnected the call and jogged across the catwalk stretching across the narrow alley between the buildings. If she kept to the rooftops, she could make it to the glide-rail station faster than if she went down to the ground.

Halfway across the second catwalk she heard the scream.

She froze. Unable to move.

For three sickening seconds she stood on the narrow walkway, trembling, trapped in memories of blood and pain and death.

The last time she'd heard a voice that full of agony she'd

been the one doing the screaming. But that was in the past. After months of rehab and hard work she'd learned to push through the fear, use the adrenalin.

She sucked in a breath, held it, then started the measured breathing she'd been taught. Oh, she'd been dosed with the appropriate drugs to prevent the stress of the trauma, but too many transfusions equaled not enough of it staying in her system in the critical hours after...

Another scream tumbled from a broken window on the third floor of the next building—this one mixed with the shouts and crashing thuds of a herd of wildebeest trapped in a tea shop. Her brain screamed in protest when she tried for a better explanation of the sound that crackled across her nerves, fueling her memories and raising goose bumps along her flesh.

Lily activated her multi-com and linked to the emergency response net. A cool artificial voice responded. "State the nature of your emergency."

"A woman screaming. Being attacked." It didn't say enough, but no more words bubbled up.

"Acknowledged. JAX Metro Domestic Dispute Resolution and Medical Emergency Units en route." Emotionless, efficient, cold. "Please stay clear of the area. Estimated time to scene is ten minutes."

Too long. Her heart gave a thud. Far too long.

Lily sprinted across the catwalk and headed for the building's rooftop entrance. Already reaching for the mini-pulser in the pocket of her well-worn leather coat, she wished for something with range and accepted that she was going to miss her fitness evaluation. Whatever coil of fate had caused the psych team to change her appointment at the last minute had made the testing redundant. Fit or not, she was it. "Inform Metro units, off-duty civilian contractor on scene. Deepwater International ID Tango-Lima-One-One-Three."

She yanked open the door and pounded down the stairwell. She could see residents filing into the stairwell below. As she got to the third floor landing, Lily shouted out a warning to clear a path as she hugged the wall and eased into the hallway. She stopped at the first corner and listened. A guttural growl rumbled from somewhere around the corner. A resounding thunk and a hoarse groan followed close behind. Different victim. This one sounded male and hurt, but not yet dying.

Wrapping her hand firmly around the slim cylinder of her pulser, she eased around the corner. A woman leaned against the bare polyplast wall, blood dripping from her busted lip. Crimson streaks splashed across her lemon yellow jumpsuit.

Lily met the woman's eyes briefly before edging past her.

"He's a *stringer*," the woman warned, her words liquid with her own blood.

Shock hit Lily like a blow, low to her belly. A *stringer*. An Ormney.

A holo-perfect image of Kiq, the first Ormney she'd ever met, flashed through her thoughts. *His tall, broad frame towering over her, his features almost human. Almost. His Ormney eyes nearly hidden in the striped bands of his face. Elliptical pupils wide, eyes wild. Claws razor sharp and slashing.*

She couldn't get air past the crushing band of panic that tightened around her chest. Lily fought past the fright, past the memories, past the fear. Fear of the damage an Ormney could inflict. Fear of freezing up and being less than she'd once been. Fear of facing Kiq's dead eyes again.

"Stop, *couyon*! You *killin'* her." The voice, angry and desperate, echoed down the hall and jolted Lily back to the present danger.

She needed to think. She knew as much about Ormney abilities as any Earth native. She licked her suddenly dry lips, keyed in the safety override on her pulser, and boosted the power.

A man, early twenties, chest and feet bare, sprawled across the hallway floor in the shadows at the end of the hall. The flesh of his arms was shredded. He struggled to get his feet under him, to stand, but one leg lay limp and useless. His efforts smeared the plastile floor with blood.

Lily forced her own legs to carry her forward, pushing into a jog and picking her way around the injured man. She lunged into the room—an efficiency with no cover, no place out of reach, nowhere to hide. The Ormney stood steps away, his back to the door. A thick mane of dark hair bushed wildly around his head. He stooped over a still figure stretched across a multi-platform bed. One arm hung low as if the chore of his grim work had fatigued him. His clawed hands dripped with blood. Angry red streaks painted the room as he struck the woman again.

Lily's muscles burned with the need to run.

She couldn't. She was stronger than that.

Ignore the blood. Ignore the woman. Focus on the threat.

With his Ormney physiology, a stun pulse from across the room would never take him down. She strode forward and reached for the center of his broad back, but he was already turning. She adjusted her angle, going lower to avoid his shoulder as he spun around.

She discharged the pulser, but the Ormney managed to slip toward out-of-sync. He blurred into a hazy ghost-like image, but he didn't disappear completely. Something made him think better of attempting the slip in the too small space.

He snapped back to in-sync before the charge had fully dissipated, catching only a fraction of the effect and leaving him strong enough to take a swing at her. Instinct overrode training and she put an arm up to block him. The scratch of his claws against the leather of her coat wound her tighter as the force of the blow knocked her off her feet.

She braced for his attack, for debilitating pain, but the massive male went for the open window. He crashed through the too-small gap, smashing the frame, heedless of the scrape of mangled metal and glass against his thick Ormney hide.

Lily grabbed for the edge of the platform bed and pulled herself up, trying to ignore the wet, sticky gore beneath her palm.

Damn. Damn. Damn. Her breath shuttered as she batted her bloody hand against her pants leg. She spared only a glance for the woman lying silent and broken. She wasn't moving and her still form was drenched in crimson. It coated her ruined flesh, soaked the carpet, arced across the walls. Not good. Not good at all.

Lily headed for the window and leaned carefully through the battered frame. The Ormney had made it a block down the alley. She had little hope of catching him, but she could keep him in sight. Make sure Metro would have a chance of catching the bastard.

She shoved the pulser into her pocket, climbed through, and reached for the emergency glide-pole attached to the side of the building. Damn thing looked a year behind any sort of maintenance. With a shiver, she stepped off the ledge then activated the glide. The aging mechanism clattered against the building as it dropped her in a controlled fall.

Seconds later her feet hit the ground. The jarring impact radiated upward, forcing the air out of her lungs. Momentarily unable to breathe, she forced herself into a protective crouch. An angry roar jerked her attention to the end of the alley. The Ormney swung around and headed back toward her. His bellow died abruptly as he blurred, then disappeared.

Damn.

She hadn't anticipated that.

Why would he run, then come back at her?

Damn his Ormney hearing. A human would never have heard her on the glide from that distance.

Lily shoved to her feet and sprinted. Kiq had taught her that any *slip* followed a pattern with a semi-predictable set of outcomes. While the bastard could reappear anywhere, there were three most likely positions. She chose instinctively, stopping an arm's reach from where—if she'd chosen right—he'd reappear.

A subtle disturbance rippled in the air in front of her. Lily tightened her fingers on the pulser's trigger pad. As the Ormney *slipped* back to *in-sync* he got the full force of the charge. His body jerked, and his bowels released, sending a foul odor wafting from him. Somehow he managed to maintain some muscle control. He struck her hard, throwing her against the alley wall. The impact robbed Lily of her senses. Her knees crumpled. She landed hard on the pavement. The certainty that she would die if she didn't get a second charge off formed in her thoughts as everything around her dimmed.

She wasn't dying. Not today. Lily tapped every scrap of strength left in her body and thrust the pulser out in front of her. He slammed into her. Her arm buckled.

Too close.

He was too close.

His smothering weight forced the pulser too close to her own body.

No way to avoid getting transfer from the pulse.

No choice.

She gripped the weapon tight and braced for the jolt as she squeezed the trigger pad.

Lightning flashed through her, setting fire to her nerve endings. The world outside her body ceased to exist. A moment later it snapped back in place with a flash of agony.

She blinked hard, trying to focus. Where was he? She could no longer feel the weight of him crushing her down. She struggled to sit up, dull pain lashing her senses. The hum in her ears made her want to shake her head. She knew from experience that would be a bad move. When her vision cleared, the Ormney lay in front of her in an unmoving heap.

The welcome shrill of sirens ringing down the alley drove Lily to her feet to wait for Metro. She kept her breath shallow determined to push away the ache in her ribs.

She couldn't push away the consequences of her actions so easily. Lily looked down at the body.

Dead.

No longer a threat.

She studied the faint pattern of light and dark bands decorating the Ormney's face and decided he was fully mature, middle aged even.

Six months ago she hadn't known those patterns were unique to each individual Ormney or that the bands faded with maturity. Six months ago she hadn't known how to counter their ability to *slip*. Six months ago she hadn't known the agony of those claws digging into the soft flesh beneath her ribs, carving out a path to her vital organs.

Kiq had taught her well. This time she knew. And this time she hadn't hesitated to go for the kill.

The rush. He gloried in it. The sweet, addictive pleasure. So...unexpected.

He studied the alley below, admiring his handy work. This kill had been necessarily hands-off. A means to an end.

He'd been prepared to accept the lesser gratification of a well-executed plan. *She* had been meant to serve a purpose. With her family connections to the police and her personal history with one of the animals, she'd been meant only to be a witness. Someone to help the idiot Metro cops see his brilliance—the service he was doing for the community. They needed to wake up and see what was happening behind closed doors.

He rolled his shoulders to shake off the anger. How could they be so oblivious?

In the alley below *she* moved, tried to straighten, then stilled. He could see pain etched on her face. A weighty pleasure settled in his chest as he remembered the thud of her slim body hitting the wall. The sound reminded him of the day he'd been strong enough to throw a rat against the wall with enough force to smash its filthy head. But the Ormney animal's blow hadn't broken *her.* No, she'd surprised him. Not the uninteresting girl he remembered. Not merely the damaged woman he'd expected.

No. She was exquisite.

Strong. Fierce. Pale and blonde, subtly pretty. He pressed a hand to the cool glass, wanting to touch her creamy skin.

No, he didn't mind sharing the kill with her. She'd brought down the big ugly animal with nothing but a pulser. She'd done it where he'd been able to see every glorious detail. With the others, he'd had to let his kill go off to meet its inescapable fate alone. But she'd brought the animal down, right there, in plain sight.

He envied her the freedom to kill out in the open. But his way was more of a challenge. She'd never be able to match his cleverness. Last time, the cops hadn't been able to understand his kills, let alone trace them back to him.

She might not be as clever as him, but she was smarter than the cops. She'd figure out exactly what he wanted her to know and no more.

She was perfect in every respect. Perfect because he'd made her what she was. And he deserved perfection.

He deserved her.

CHAPTER 2

Facing her cousin across a dead body wasn't exactly the best way for Lily to reconnect with the O'Leary side of her family. Even before Metro had set up the bright mobile lights in the narrow alley, she'd had no trouble seeing the distance in Sean's familiar green eyes. When he'd assigned Detective Newman to question her, she hadn't expected he'd let her return to the alley. She'd been wrong.

Now, she stood out of the way and watched Sean work the scene. She'd heard he was a good cop, a good detective, but she'd never seen him on the job before. She soaked up the sight of her kin. With his cropped blond hair, a shade darker than most of the O'Learys, he looked so much like her memories of her dad that it hurt to look at him. It hurt, but she craved the sweet pain.

Lily smiled grimly. Sean would make Captain soon. He took in everything and his body language broadcast calm discipline as he instructed the patrol officers and evidence technicians. Experience and responsibility sat easily on his shoulders.

One of the med units had already transported the female victim. Lily had been grateful to be in the alley when she heard them come and go. She didn't want to see the victim. To remember herself torn and bleeding.

"Lily?" Sean's voice pushed away the dark memories. Eyebrows raised, he waited for the answer to a question she hadn't heard. That he expected her to answer was a welcome bridge across the expanse between them.

The Deepwater duty officer had already been on her com-link, ordering her to avoid the local authorities and get clear of the scene as quickly as possible. But this time she couldn't avoid them. Metro employed way too many members of her family. Might as well get the questions over with and on the record.

Sean stepped closer and leaned in, subtly blocking her from the view of the officers and techs. "You sure you don't need the medics?"

She probably did. The pain in her lower back throbbed and she'd had enough concussions to know what her dizziness and nausea meant, but she could get medical aid on her own when this business was done and there weren't a dozen cop eyes watching. "You have no idea how sick I am of being poked and prodded." She grinned in an attempt to sell the non-answer.

"I heard you were in a training accident." His back to the others, he let his concern show on his face, but he kept his tone light and casual. "That's what the military says when the incident is black ops."

Lily clenched one fist behind her back and straightened her posture. "I'm not military," she reassured. "It really was a training accident." Fatigue and pain ate at her, but she kept her breathing shallow and even, avoiding the sharper stab of what might well be broken ribs. Despite her injuries, she hadn't reached her body's limits. She could and would push through.

Sean hesitated. "This was a clean kill, Lil. You're in the clear here."

It was the use of the nickname more than his reassurance that chased away some of her worry. "Thanks, Sean."

He slipped back into his cop face. "I hadn't heard you were in town. Are you on the job here?"

Her family knew she worked for Deepwater, but they had no idea she'd been in the Special Tactics Unit. STU rarely worked in the US. She spent most of her time doing hostage recovery in countries most people couldn't place on a map.

Lily shook her head. "I haven't been cleared for duty. I was on the way to an evaluation appointment when I heard her scream."

Eyebrows that matched his hair drew together. "Your appointment was in The Mixer?"

"No." Lily kept her answer brief by rote. "The appointment was downtown at the regional office."

Sean let her statement hang in the space between them, letting silence ask for more than she wanted to give. He was good, but she knew all the interrogation techniques and how to resist them. Still, she wasn't on the job here. This was Sean. Family.

And if there was a chance that she could have her family back...

"I was on my way to the Clinton Street rail station." Lily took a moment to breathe and brace for his reaction. "I have an apartment a few blocks down."

"Shit, Lily. An apartment? How long...?" He fired the questions at her like bullets then stopped, putting up a hand. "No, wait. Don't answer that. I want plausible deniability when Mom finds out you've been living in town without coming to see her." Sean shook his head and met her gaze directly. "Damn, Lily, you sure know how to pick a neighborhood."

Lily shrugged. She had no intention of trying to explain her reasons for being back in the city or what had drawn her to The Mixer—a neighborhood plagued by street gangs, home to the good folks too poor to move up or out, and the one neighborhood where Earthers and Ormney mixed on a daily basis.

Sean hesitated. "We thought you were staying up in DC with your mom."

Lily shook her head, then fought down the resulting wave of nausea. She tried to keep her tone light. "She hasn't forgiven me for my career choices, Brian has roommates, and no way would I stay with Rose and Bradley."

"Yeah, Bradley's been in town a lot lately, I thought maybe he was here..."

"Avoiding me?"

Sean nodded. By any rights, when her longtime boyfriend dumped her, he should have been given the cold shoulder by the whole O'Leary clan. But Bradley Rubiero had married her twin sister and that made him part of the family. What choice did any of them have? Lily had made it easier on everyone and made herself scarce, courtesy of Deepwater.

Lily brushed past Sean and the techs to get closer to the corpse. Splattered in blood, death stealing the color from his skin, the dead Ormney looked every bit the monster. What had he looked like before? Before he'd turned murderous? And why…or when…had that been?

Sean followed Lily, signaling the others to clear the area. He stood by her side and waited until she met his penetrating green stare. "Do you want to add anything to the statement you gave Detective Newman?"

Lily squatted next to the body, thinking. "Yeah. There was something off about the Ormney's behavior."

"You mean other than him ripping up an unarmed woman?" There was no humor in the question.

"Yeah." She remembered the Ormney's eyes. They'd been wild. Like Kiq's had been that day. Wild, then empty and dead. But she couldn't tell Sean about that. "He ran when he should've fought. Fought when he should've run." She met Sean's intent stare. "Have them check him for chemical influence."

"Street drugs don't work on stringers the way they do on us." He used the street slur for the Ormney without any apparent malice. Maybe he didn't realize the disrespect of using it while crouched over the corpse.

"No," Lily agreed. "Not street drugs."

"Then what?"

Lily weighed the backlash she'd weather from Deepwater for what she needed to tell him. It didn't measure up to the dead man at her feet. "There are things that mess them up. I'll get you a list."

Jolaj stopped in the shadows just inside the alley and watched the two Earthers crouched over Lanyak's body. He'd met Detective Sean O'Leary several times and judged the man to be honorable and fair, but trapped by the strictures of a system that was seldom fair to the Ormney people. The woman didn't wear Metro ID, but she seemed at ease with the detective. Their knees brushed against each other as they talked and leaned into one another like allies.

Her slim legs were encased in denim but her hips were hidden by an ill-fitting black leather coat that hung low to the curve of her bottom. It did nothing, however, to hide the swell of her breasts. Her wrists and neck were almost delicate in their thinness—cream skin wrapped over bone and sinew. Her golden hair lay in silken sheets against her head, ending in a knot at her neck. Her frowning lips were wide and full. Her eyes, a piercing green, shone with sharp intelligence.

As they pushed to stand and stepped around his dead friend, he noticed the stiffness of her movements. Barely discernible, but clear in the careful way she breathed, the rigidity of her posture, the subtle hesitation before each move. His hunter's instincts screamed she was either weak prey to hunt or an injured member of the flock to be protected—instincts better suited to survival on a primitive planet. It was what his people had expected when they'd left behind their dying world in search of a new home. They'd planned and worked, sacrificed and engineered themselves to give their descendants the best chance of coming into being.

Now any chance for Lanyak's descendants was lost. They would never be born. Never exist. The ache of the loss touched a familiar cord and roused a grief that had become thick and layered like an earthy strata of rock and silt.

Lanyak lay dead in an alley, and Jolaj had to find a way to keep the others who'd made the same choice from coming to the same fate.

CHAPTER 3

The smell of waste, blood, and burnt flesh threatened to bring up the Ready-Meal Lily had eaten for lunch. She swallowed slowly, deliberately, as if focusing her attention on the movement of tongue and throat could force down the guilt that had been building as she thought about the drug angle. She let the sickly, wet ball of emotion settle in her belly then caught Sean's eye and coughed up the more useful bits of hard-won knowledge. "You know that list?"

Sean's face stayed calm, but curiosity crept into his green eyes like a cat slinking through tall grass. "The list of drugs that might have made this guy go Frankenstein?"

Lily dipped her chin. "Nothing on that list is something he'd be exposed to accidentally."

Sean's jaw tightened as he absorbed the information and Lily knew he understood the implication. Someone had drugged the Ormney intentionally.

"Who else would know about this list?" Sean spat the words out as if the criminal intent left a vile residue in his mouth.

"Ormney med researchers. A handful of people at Deepwater. Beyond that? Hard to say." Lily considered the reasons she'd chosen to live in the Mixer. "You've been working cases in this neighborhood awhile, right?"

"Sure." Sean shot her a look that reminded her she'd confessed to living down the block. "Not exactly a low crime neighborhood."

She suspected she'd get a call from Aunt Jane. Sean was too smart to lecture her himself.

"Yeah, we have our share of trouble. We have property crimes and even violence more than other neighborhoods." She let her gaze slip down to the body lying on the ground. "The other thing we have more of is Ormney. If someone wanted to start trouble with them, this would be a damn fine place to start."

The Ormney's natural ability to slip out of phase by changing the rate at which the tiniest particles of their bodies vibrated hadn't earned them any friends. It made people nervous and insecure behind their locked doors. Ormney were said to walk through walls and that had kept them living in a restricted area and earned them the stringers slur, a reference to the outdated physics of string theory. For some people, the restrictions didn't go far enough.

Sean straightened and gave her a hand up. A muscle in his jaw twitched as he considered her comment, then his lips tightened for an instant, a brief flash of a smile. "Everyone in the family says your father was born with cop instincts. Right from the crib. He'd have been proud to know he passed that on to you."

Longing rushed up and dragged her back to a thousand hugs and a million smiles. Would he be proud?

Sean's attention shifted to a point over her shoulder and Lily turned to follow his line of sight. Panic tightened her muscles with a jolt.

An Ormney male approaching them.

Big and getting closer.

Seconds ticked by like miniature explosions. Her heart raced, dizziness a danger hovering just out of sight.

She was better than this, damn it. She just needed to breathe. A gasp for air cleared her head, but reminded her why she'd been breathing shallowly. The pain she'd been careful to keep at bay flashed through her and only sheer force of will kept her knees from buckling.

The Ormney stopped within touching distance. He seemed torn between reaching out to steady her and stepping back. He had no way of knowing that his presence acted like a flame on kindling, igniting the lingering fear, bringing the panic back to crackling, explosive life.

She forced herself to still, not to run, not to fight.

Sean stepped forward, clearly at ease with the Ormney. "Law Keeper Jolaj."

The words, Sean's calm voice, his nod of recognition, edged away the panic.

"Law Keeper," Lily acknowledged. She wanted to step back, need more space, but stubbornness wouldn't allow retreat.

"Jolaj, this is Agent Lily Rowan." Sean finished the introductions with a hesitation that hadn't been there in his earlier greeting.

She wanted to explain to them that her own discomfort didn't come from any sane objection to the Law Keeper's arrival. Her panic didn't work on rationality.

He was close enough that she had to crane her neck to see his face. He didn't, thank God, extend a hand for shaking.

"I regret we meet under these circumstances." The low bass of his voice rumbled through Lily with the lush resonance of a well-played cello.

He stood at least two meters tall and his shoulders strained against a traditional Ormney cotton tunic. They always wore natural fiber, something that allowed them to take their clothes with them when they slipped. An Ormney symbol had been stitched onto his tunic, giving it the look of a primitive uniform.

The name clicked for Lily. "Father Jo?"

He accepted the name with a nod. Faint bands of color painted his face in shades of tan and rust. The subtle patterns drew attention to his eyes and hinted at a masculine beauty that surprised her. His deep auburn hair had been pulled into a single heavy braid that hung across his shoulder and nearly to his hip.

"You have quite a reputation in the local community centers. Father Jo." Law Keepers were something like a cross between a cop and a chaplain. They had jurisdiction in The Zone but they weren't often found in The Mixer.

He stood motionless as he spoke. "Many of the young adults in my quadrant volunteer in the centers to promote understanding between our people."

And Ormney and Earther volunteers alike sang his praises for the programs he helped put in place.

His gaze slid beyond her to take in the crime scene and the dead man then returned to her. "Your title is Agent?"

"I'm a civilian security contractor."

He frowned, tiny lines appearing on his forehead as he turned to Sean for clarification. "Civilian security?"

Sean laid a hand on the Law Keeper's shoulder. "Agent Rowan is on scene because... Jolaj... Lanyak attacked a woman and she's the one who stopped him."

The dead Ormney on the ground behind them made it clear that Lily had stopped him in a terribly permanent way. She watched Jolaj carefully for a reaction, but he was difficult to read. He was nothing like Kiq had been—before the accident. Kiq had been easygoing and sweet and brotherly. He'd also been at least twenty years younger and Earth born. She had no idea if the differences were generational or individual. How could they have been on Earth so long and still be such a mystery?

Sean leaned in closer to Jolaj in an I'm-your-buddy stance that she knew meant he was trying to interrogate without making the other man aware of what he was doing. "Did you know Lanyak, personally?"

Jolaj nodded, but didn't elaborate. "How is the injured woman?"

"She's been taken to South Regional Med Facility. She's in critical condition. Was Lanyak under any stress—"

"There is nothing." Jolaj's voice sharpened. "No reason less than self-defense, that he would ever harm a human."

Lily understood denial. She kept her arms at her sides—not closed off, not confrontational. "The victim wasn't much larger than me and unarmed. She wasn't a threat to him."

His gaze snapped to hers. "And yet you killed him."

She'd wanted the Law Keeper to focus on her. She'd wanted a better look into his face, those eyes. To see his reaction. Now that she had his full attention, she regretted the stupidity. There was anger in his Ormney eyes, but also sadness. A deep, devastating sadness.

Sean grimly tried to take back control of the conversation, probably trying to divert Jolaj's anger away from her. "Agent Rowan believes he might have been drugged."

The Law Keeper's eyes widened, but the rest of his face remained still, placid. "If you believed him innocent of malice or the will to harm anyone, why did you kill him?"

Sean opened his mouth to intervene, but Lily put up a

hand to stop him. "He has a right to some answers." She lowered her hand and met the Law Keeper's gaze. "I had to defend myself. He attacked me."

"He attacked you, yet you aren't injured badly enough to seek treatment at the med facility?"

"No." Lily slid her hands into the pockets of her coat, trying to look more relaxed.

His eyes narrowed. "The fact that he died here, in the alley, seems to indicate he tried to flee."

"Yes, and I followed to try to give Metro his direction. When he heard me, he turned back." She could hear patience wearing thin in her own voice.

"And your only option was lethal force?"

"Yes. Damn it." Her voice had edged up in volume against her will. "The only thing I had on me was a pulser. It didn't give me a lot of options."

"A pulser need not be lethal," he said. "They are in fact designed to stun the attacker, are they not?"

Sean shifted, trying to put himself between them. "Law Keeper—"

"Yes." Lily had no reason to explain herself, but she couldn't seem to stop. "That's right, the pulser is meant to stun a human. But that wouldn't have stopped him."

"No." Jolaj's one-word response hit her like a fleeting blow, enough to leave her reeling without knocking her down.

"No?" What did he mean by no?

"I agree." All trace of anger had disappeared. He could have been discussing city ordinances.

"You do?"

"Yes. The question remains, if you had no options, why do you feel guilty about your actions?"

Through the whole exchange his voice hadn't changed in volume or tone. It gave away nothing and left Lily confused and off balance.

"I don't. I...why would you think that?"

"It's obvious to see when you look at him." The relentless Law Keeper just wouldn't ease up. "Perhaps you believe you could have used a lesser force?"

Regret, guilt, and anger churned around inside her. "No. A standard stun blast wouldn't have done enough to stop his charge.

If he'd have had more time, he would have ripped me up like he did the woman upstairs. As it was, I took a goddamned solid blow to the chest that sent me flying into a goddamned wall."

"But you don't require medical attention?" That rich voice delivered the question with grating calm.

"No!" She could only stand there with her mouth clamped shut. Why had he circled back to that? Then he slipped, disappearing like a specter. She recognized the telltale disturbance in the air as he slipped back to in-sync behind her. She started to spin on her left foot, only to be defeated by a sharp pain under her ribs and a debilitating spasm in her lower back.

The world spun and she lost her footing. He caught her, lifted her in his arms, and pulled her against his chest. "You need a med facility, Agent Rowan."

Sean and the Law Keeper were arguing but they sounded muted and beyond her comprehension. She wanted to fight, to flail and scream, but instead she choked back the panic, the rush of memories. The tension that gripped her only intensified the pain. She focused inward, on her breathing, on her heart rate.

A quick glance at Sean revealed a scowl, but he'd stopped arguing. He spoke through clinched teeth. "Jolaj is going to carry you to the medics."

"Yeah, okay." She managed the two words, but couldn't push anything more past the fear-squeezed muscles of her throat.

"Breathe, Agent Rowan." The Law Keeper's words were low, meant only for her. He hefted her easily and carried her toward the med unit in the street.

"I can walk." The words were small and ragged.

"No."

She had fast come to hate that word on his lips. She clamped her jaw shut.

He made a gruff noise at the back of his throat. "Almost there."

Struggling to relax enough to get air into her lungs, she concentrated on the steady rhythm of his breathing, counted his strides, cursed the embarrassment that made her cheeks heat. He'd seen her fear and she hated that even more than the thought of going to the med center.

She blinked away the threat of tears and forced her eyes wide open. She had to face the fear or she would never overcome it. The firm line of his wide jaw and the rust-tinged streak lining his eyes like a faded mask filled her vision. Kiq's markings had been bright, crisp…terrifying in his fury.

The rational part of her brain knew she was safe. Her pounding heart wouldn't kill her. The counselor had promised her it wouldn't, but damn if it didn't feel like it could.

The tops of the building along the alley leaned in on her as they went past. Faces peered down from the windows like scientists watching rats in a maze. He carried her past the techs, the cops, the crowd of civilians. Ormney faces dotted among the human. They accused her with their cat eyes, seemed to see her fear and find her pathetic, weak.

The Law Keeper shifted her weight in his arms, lifting her onto a gurney. The sharp press of his claws tugged at the thick denim of her pants.

Oh, God—Kiq's claws had shredded her skin so fast and then the feeling of being ripped open… No! She wasn't there. She was in The Mixer, on the gurney, safe. Nausea twisted her gut with a violent grip.

Lily swung one arm at the med tech standing there, shoving him hard, as she rolled to her side and spilled the contents of her stomach on the toes of his shoes.

The Law Keeper showed sense enough to step back out of her reach as she let the techs help her lie back. She ignored them as they began their scans. Pushed it all away and instead focused on the Ormney male who watched her as if she might bolt and run. Those blue-green eyes saw everything. Their eyes were better than any humans, but that wasn't it. Holding her, he must have felt her fear as it gripped her body.

He knew she was terrified. That his touch had bothered her far more than the broken rib the med techs would mend before the day was over. But her fear of his kind, those claws—she'd been trying to overcome it for months and it sure as hell wouldn't be gone by morning. It pissed her off, him knowing her fear when she knew nothing about him.

She'd thought she'd understood the Ormney abilities. But she didn't understand his. His slip hadn't fit any of the patterns. To make the kind of slip that put him directly behind her, that kind of precision and ease should have been impossible. And that meant she didn't really know the Ormney at all.

CHAPTER 4

Lily hated med facilities. She felt too exposed, too vulnerable. She'd slept in far less secure places in the field, but at least she'd been able to choose her spot, a spot she could control, a place no one expected.

She twisted the white sheet in her hands, cursing the damn Ormney do-gooder who'd poked his broad nose into her business. She would've gone to the Deepwater Med Center in her own time. At least there she could be in and out without her family knowing about her injuries. And it was a hell of a lot more secure.

Her chest tightened as a man in scrubs walked into her room. If she'd let them dose her with meds she'd never have heard him. How was she supposed to get any rest, sleep, when anyone off the street could look her up on the lobby kiosk, walk in and slip something deadly in her IV? How many drug cartels, pirate crews, and petty dictators had she pissed off?

Paranoia.

Most of Deepwater's STU agents suffered from it to one degree or another. A laugh bubbled to the surface and escaped on a huff of air. At least she was normal in that respect. Reality was she had little to worry about back home.

The man who'd entered her room wore scrubs that were tailored to his leanly athletic frame and his dark hair had been styled to perfection. He looked to be late thirties with aristocratic features and a confident stride. She had no reason to think he was anything other than what he appeared to be.

At her small laugh, he met her gaze with a wide, friendly smile and sat on the edge of her bed, hip to hip. Lily resisted her need to move away. She could feel the heat of the man through the thin sheet. With warm fingers, he lifted her hand from the soft, twisted cloth of the bed covering and adjusted his position, ending with more of his thigh pressed against her. She worked to remain relaxed and slipped into the silent meditation exercises she'd learned to help her cope with the invasive environment of med facilities.

"You don't recognize me," he said. "Not that you should. You were only, let's see, about eight last time I saw you." His voice sparkled with the overt exuberance strangers use when speaking to small children and his eyes shone with enthusiasm.

He moved his fingers to rest against the inside of her wrist. It was an old fashioned way to check her heart rate and it drew her attention to the fact that he wasn't wearing the standard ear-receiver that would have fed him her vitals as he walked into the room. Her earlier thoughts echoed back to her. *Anyone could walk in off the street...*

"Timothy," he said. "Timothy Perry from New Duval Drive."

The mention of the street she'd lived on in what she thought of as the golden age of her childhood—before her father died—readjusted her expectations and the memories clicked into place.

"Timmy, from the end of the block?"

"Now you remember." He squeezed her hand gently, beaming like a man watching his kid take her first steps.

A shiver of relief fired along her nerves before her heart rate settled back to normal.

She nodded and, still fighting the urge to shy away from his touch, watched as he relaxed his hand on her wrist but didn't let her go.

"I saw your name come up on the rotation log and knew I had to stop in to see you. Little Lily all grown up and still getting into scrapes."

Lily forced her lips into a semblance of a smile. He must have been about Sean's age back then, just a few years older than her. Regardless, he was right. She'd always been in a scrape back then. Her father had praised her fearlessness and her mother had scolded him for encouraging her. "I never learned to accept when people told me I couldn't or shouldn't do something," she said. "I always have to find out for myself."

"Did you just move back into town? I see your cousins getting mended in the ER on a regular basis, but this is the first you've been in."

"I've been back about six months."

"Six months without an ER trip, you must be good at what you do."

He probably thought she was a cop like her O'Leary cousins. Like her father. She shrugged and let it stand. "And you're in medicine now?"

"Tissue regeneration," he said. His hand slipped up her arm and he fingered the white scars that wrapped around her bicep, barely visible at the edge of the hospital gown's sleeve. "I could get rid of these for you."

"Thanks, but I've had more than my share of regeneration therapy." She made an effort to sound light, like it was a joke.

"Side effects from regeneration therapy are rare these days."

Lily dipped her chin in agreement. "But the odds increase with exposure."

"True," he said. He kept his smile in place, but his lips tightened.

She really had been exposed to the therapy more than was recommended. When Kiq had ripped her up she'd suffered massive tissue damage, much of it internal. The company doctors hadn't risked using the therapy on external damage and scars when she had organ and muscle tissue to regenerate. They'd even let her bones heal naturally.

A flicker of movement caught her eye and drew her attention to the figure hovering in the doorway. Bradley... for all the world as if he'd never turned his back on her, betrayed her in the worst possible way.

He was as beautiful as ever. Full sensual lips, dark coffee complexion, and mink brown hair that hugged his skull. Mischievous gray eyes set off the striking features and called attention to his mixed heritage. People thought being an Ambassador's son had given him legs in DC despite several missteps, but Lily knew it was his easy charm that made him perfect for his position as a Liaison in the Ormney Affairs Office.

His charm would carry him past any small misdeed. It had always been that way. In school, he'd charmed the teachers into letting him retake tests or overlook his tardiness. He'd charmed her mother into overlooking her curfew. He'd charmed Lily out of her pretty pink dress after the graduation dance. He might have eventually been able to charm her into forgiving him for their break-up, but no amount of charm could make her forgive him for marrying her sister.

Bradley wrapped a hand around the doorframe and lifted his voice. "Am I interrupting something?"

Timothy's grip loosened and his hand trailed down her arm as if he would pull away. She caught it and pressed it in place on her forearm. Moments earlier she would have been glad for him to go, but she didn't want to be left alone with Bradley. Timothy seemed to get the hint and stayed put, ignoring the dictates of courtesy that would implore him to stand and face the newcomer.

"Yeah, you are," she answered. "I'm catching up with a friend."

Bradley ignored the obvious hostility in her voice and stepped into the room. "Oh?"

She'd hoped he'd take the hint and leave. Resigned, Lily made the introductions.

"Bradley Rubiero, Timothy Perry."

Bradley moved around the bed and put out his hand, forcing Timothy to let go of Lily's arm. Timothy didn't budge from his seat on the edge of the bed, though. Ignoring the room's single chair, Bradley edged back to the wall and leaned against it, keeping the high ground. It was a private room, but small, leaving them all too close for comfort.

Bradley folded his arms across his chest and eyed Timothy with an edge of resentment. "So you've known Lily long?"

His proprietary air annoyed her, but Timothy seemed unaffected so she relaxed back into the pillows and watched Timothy's face, doing her best to ignore Bradley.

Timothy's eyes were cool and assessing as he spoke. "Yes. A very long time. We practically lived in each other's pockets." Lily registered the exaggeration. He'd recaptured Lily's hand as he spoke. She didn't see Bradley's reaction to the suggestive answer, but she watched satisfaction flash across Timothy's features at whatever that reaction had been.

Lily decided she'd had enough and pulled away.

"Timothy and I lived in the same neighborhood before Mom moved us to DC."

"I see. So you were friends as kids." Bradley sounded smug and satisfied, which made no sense to Lily.

"Bradley is married to my sister Rose. You remember her, right, Timmy?"

He nodded. "I'm afraid I teased you both about being the flower twins. Can you ever forgive me?"

"Of course." She pasted on a smile because for once the past didn't matter. His teasing hadn't hurt her or if it had she couldn't remember.

Bradley pushed away from the wall. "Their mother gave them feminine names to discourage them from following in their father's footsteps."

"I know," said Timothy, turning back to Lily. "All the Rowans and O'Learys have been in law enforcement for generations."

Her family had also been neo-traditionalists, with women staying home to raise kids, for generations. She'd believed Bradley had more mainstream notions of family and gender roles, but in the end Bradley had married her neo-trad sister.

Lily leaned her head back and spoke more to herself than to either of them. "Mom was never cut out to be a cop's wife, she was determined her children wouldn't serve."

"Well," Timothy said. "Nothing so simple as a name could stop you, could it?" He squeezed her hand. "I guess this is my cue to go. Is there anything I can do for you before I do?"

The approval in his eyes left Lily feeling a little embarrassed. Uncomfortable. "There is one thing. A woman, late twenties, brought in this afternoon. Serious trauma, beaten and cut-up. I don't know her name."

"The one from The Mixer?"

"Yeah. Do you happen to know…"

Timothy's smile slipped into a more sedate curve. "Critical but stable, last I heard."

The woman was still alive. Relief washed over Lily like a wave crashing over the sand. Cool and fresh then gone, leaving her raw and exposed. Even if the woman survived, Lily knew she would have to fight a lethal reaction to the toxin secreted from the gland beneath the Ormney claws. But that bit of knowledge wasn't public.

"Thanks, Timothy." Lily watched as he left the room.

Bradley paced over to the small window ledge crowded with bouquets. Sean must have com-linked the whole clan. When she'd come back to her room after the bone mending the flowers had been waiting.

"The O'Learys," he said, shaping a hand in the air around the synthetic blooms as if they were too delicate to touch.

"Family," she said.

He stuffed his hands in his pockets, but kept his eyes fixed firmly on the flowers as he spoke. "I suppose there's one in here with my name on the card."

"Yes," she said. "You and Rose. The big bunch of yellow carnations." The silly things were stuffed into a container covered in smiley faces. Sunny. Cheerful. No doubt the perfect thing for a relative confined to a med facility bed.

Bradley nodded. "Rose always knows the right thing for any occasion." He waved one hand toward the slender vase of calla lilies, so deeply purple they appeared black. "These must be from—"

"Sara," she confirmed. Her favorite O'Leary cousin and the one closest to her in age. Sara was Sean's younger sister and he must have called her while Lily was on the way to the med facility. Sara's floral arrangement had been the first to arrive. "The card says, 'you picked a crappy day to get hurt. Don't die before I have a chance to come over there and kill you.'"

"That woman has a morbid sense of humor."

"Appropriate for a Medical Examiner." Lead ME for one of the largest metropolitan areas in the country. All the O'Learys were strong, smart, capable, but Sara was Einstein-smart. She could have been head of any lab at any University or Institution she chose, and yet she'd chosen to stick close to the family business— law enforcement, crime fighting. The O'Learys were public servants down to their toes. Lily loved that about them.

Bradley continued to study the flowers, his back to her. "She still won't speak to me without snarling or threatening me with bodily harm, you know."

She hadn't known. The thought that one of the O'Learys had taken Lily's side warmed her in a way she should no doubt feel guilty over. They'd all supported her at first, but they'd all gone Switzerland when Bradley married Rose. Lily understood. Rose was family too.

"Can't blame her," said Bradley, finally turning to face her. "Sara's right," he said. "What I did was unforgiveable. Stupid. After you and I broke up, she called me. Told me I was an idiot and someday I'd see that and be eaten up with regret."

He crossed the small room in two graceful strides that brought him to her bedside, so close his thighs brushed the blanket. She could smell the subtle spiciness of his cologne. "She was right," he said, reaching for Lily's hand. His fingers wrapped firmly around hers. "God, Lily. She was so right."

Anguish lashed his features. Lily thought she should have rejoiced. She couldn't count the times she'd wished him miserable.

More than that, he'd said what she'd longed to hear. She should be happy or at least satisfied, but the shock of it sat coldly in her belly.

"Damn, Bradley." Lily jerked her hand free. "Sara is right. You are an idiot. You can't say shit like that to me. Get the hell out of my room before I break your pretty face."

Bradley took a quick step back out of reach, but a grin tugged at those sensual lips. "Rose never yells at me, you know. Never calls me names." There was a wistful note in his voice.

Lily didn't want to think about Rose. Her sister. Her twin. They'd been as close as any two people could be...and then they weren't. Weren't close. Weren't anything at all.

He looked down to his toes then back up, his grin wider than before. "You still like my face, huh?"

Lily met his gaze coolly. "You know how easy it would be to rearrange your features?" Even in her own ears her voice sounded lethally calm. "I wouldn't even break a sweat."

His grin slipped, his expression turning repentant, earnest. "Damn it, Lily. I wish you would. I deserve it and it would at least prove you've still got feelings for me. Anything is better than apathy."

Frustration bubbled up over the cold anger. This is why he did so well in the diplomatic core, she thought. If she hit him now he'd see it as proof she gave a damn. One way or the other.

"Just go, Bradley."

"I can't do that." His shoulders straightened and his chin lifted. The difference was subtle, but unmistakable. "I'm actually here on official business."

"What?"

"It's about the woman who was attacked today and the Ormney male you terminated."

CHAPTER 5

Jolaj watched the machines pump air into the woman's lungs. His own breathing slowed, weighted down with sorrow. Surrounded by the noisy equipment and plastic tubing, she looked small and frail. Nothing like the sturdy human female he remembered. He'd never met her, but he'd seen her. With her big brown eyes, broad nose, and short black hair styled to spike wildly around her head, she'd resembled Lanyak's lost mate as much as any Earther could. Jolaj understood why his old friend had been drawn to her even if he hadn't approved.

"You shouldn't be in here." There was an edge to O'Leary's voice.

His presence didn't surprise Jolaj. He'd been expecting him. But he didn't know what had brought on the animosity.

"Detective," he acknowledged.

O'Leary leaned against the door frame and folded his arms across his chest. "You're making the staff nervous. People are bound to be a bit touchy for a while."

Jolaj didn't want to make things worse, but he'd owed it to Lanyak to look in on the woman. "She was attacked by an Ormney male and here I am, standing over her and out of The Zone after curfew. No need to explain."

The curfew required all Ormney to return to The Zone by seven each night, one of the many conditions of the treaty between the Earthers and his people. With time they'd taken what had once been a fenced area containing a few cramped barracks and built it into a small town tucked behind a four-stories-high and meters-thick alloy wall. It had become home, but it could be taken away any time the Earthers chose. The treaty allowed the Ormney to stay on Earth in exchange for technical knowledge the Earthers hadn't yet developed. But it gave them few rights and made it impossible to move beyond refugee status.

Jolaj stepped forward to leave, but the detective straightened and stood firmly in his way.

"You said you knew the attacker." The detective spoke with uncharacteristic anger simmering beneath his words. He'd always been sympathetic in the past. If they'd lost a supporter because of this attack, the response from their detractors would be much worse.

"Yes. I knew Lanyak from before The Crossing."

The detective indicated the woman on the bed with a jerk of his chin. "She's a licensed sex worker. Do you have any idea why Lanyak might have been visiting this woman?"

Jolaj had more than an idea, but he didn't think the detective was ready to hear the truth.

"If Lanyak had been an Earther," said O'Leary, "the answer would be obvious, but—"

"We don't do sex with humans," Jolaj finished. "I can't help you, Detective. I have no idea if Lanyak even knew the woman." He managed the lies without blinking, but lying to this man he respected didn't sit well.

O'Leary studied him as an architect studies a dwelling, looking for cracks or stress points. "I suppose the victim could have been coincidental. Lily was right about the drugs."

Jolaj tripped on the name. Lily Rowan, the Agent at the scene. "Lanyak would not have taken any drugs knowingly." Jolaj thought of his friend. The man had had no enemies.

"I know." Detective O'Leary nodded, but his mouth twisted, settling into a frown. "You don't do drugs either."

Jolaj wanted to know how Agent Lily Rowan had known about the drugs, but asking would prolong a discussion he badly needed to avoid. "I should go."

As he tried to step around the detective, the man put a hand up to stop him. "Is it true the victim might get sick from some kind of toxin in the claw wounds?"

That question stopped him, freezing his soft leather shoes to the cold, tile floor. He didn't want to answer, but could see little choice. "It's true. The toxin is secreted when our claws are extended."

"Shit." Tightly leashed anger thinned O'Leary's voice and his face hardened as he spoke. "And you were going to leave without telling me?"

Jolaj hadn't mentioned it because there was really no danger. Lanyak would have made sure the woman had the anti-toxin in her system before they'd ever had sex. Mating could damage any male's control and it would have been irresponsible to have sex with her without first protecting her.

Jolaj glanced at the woman who couldn't even breathe for herself, then turned back to O'Leary. "Do you really think she'll live long enough to become sick?"

O'Leary burst into motion, pacing the length of the small room. "That isn't the point. Shit. How is something like this not common knowledge?"

Jolaj watched the man pace. He was lean and almost graceful, O'Leary's refined features set him apart from many lawmen. It was the green eyes that provided the clue of his relationship with Lily Rowan. It had to be a family connection, but the similarities only went so far. "The knowledge would only make your people fear mine more."

"But surely something like this would have to come out. It's been twenty years." O'Leary's voice rose in pitch.

The man's disbelief reminded Jolaj of the years between them. "We try very hard to avoid harming Earthers. One of many reasons I knew Lanyak would never have done this. In his right mind he would never have endangered our people this way."

O'Leary barked an unpleasant laugh. "Well, I'm glad avoiding assaulting us is to *your* benefit." Sarcasm didn't suit O'Leary. "Is there anything we can do for her, to help her fight the toxin?"

An interesting question. It meant that O'Leary hadn't gotten his information from his own government or from the Ormney council. He wanted to tell the detective that this information had been passed on to the Earther government before the treaty had been signed, but he'd be breaking that treaty to do so. He couldn't do that, not even to salvage his relationship with the detective. But he had to give some answer so he spoke very carefully. "Perhaps, this is a question better asked through more formal channels."

The detective didn't respond immediately. The moment stretched as they measured each other.

Finally, O'Leary stepped back. "Come on. I'll escort you back to The Zone."

As Jolaj followed, he couldn't help but wonder how the detective had learned about the toxin. . . and that brought his thoughts back around to Lily Rowan with her lush curves and intelligent eyes. The woman who seemed to know far too much. Could she be the one?

Jolaj would go back to The Zone with Detective O'Leary, but then he'd see what more he could learn about Lily Rowan.

CHAPTER 6

Lily fought fatigue as Bradley lingered in front of the darkened windows. Light shone in from the hallway. Med Centers never seemed to sleep, but for Lily it had been one hell of a long day.

"It's late, Bradley, get to the point or get out."

He wrapped his hands around the bar at the foot of her bed, frowning.

"Ormney Affairs is concerned." He stood posture stiff. He'd gone from conciliatory ex-boyfriend to diplomat as easily as a hostage-taker turns from holy terror to shrewd negotiator at the mention of money. Typical Bradley. If one tactic isn't working, switch things up. But she wasn't buying his crap this time, no matter how he packaged it.

"Does the OA think there'll be retaliation for the attack?"

"That's one concern." His fists tightened on the bed-frame, then, as if he realized what he might be giving away, he shoved his hands in his pockets.

"The Ormney is dead." Lily could hope that would satisfy people, however unlikely.

Bradley shook his head. "People like to spread blame and there are always radicals like *Earthers Before Ormney* and *Indigenous Life* waiting for an excuse to rally the public to their cause."

Lily had to concede the point. She'd spent most of the last five years overseas, but that didn't mean she hadn't kept up with current events back home. "Okay. But I don't see how I fit in, unless you're worried about the press."

"They'll be waiting for you when you're cleared out of here tomorrow. We can't give them anything they can use."

Lily had no intention of speaking to the media. "Consider me on board with the need for discretion. Now, if that's all—"

"No. That's only the surface," said Bradley. "Lily, this wasn't the first Ormney attack." Grim frustration darkened his features. "Two weeks ago, a patrol found a woman floating in the St. Johns River. We think she may have been killed down by the docks."

"I didn't hear—"

"We buried the case and it's still unresolved."

She hesitated, contemplating the pull Ormney Affairs must have to bury a murder. "You think the Ormney man I took down today might have been responsible for the earlier attack?"

"Maybe." His mouth tightened for an instant, a quick flicker that let her know he didn't really think so. "It would be convenient if he were."

She tried and failed to shut down her curiosity. "But killers get better at their crimes, smarter not dumber. The docks are busy, but noisy and full of rat holes and unattended containers, warehouses even. Why go from there to an apartment building with neighbors likely to hear a scream and call Metro? Damn, I heard her clear down the street."

Bradley wrapped his fists around her bed-frame again. "This guy wasn't planning. You were right about the drugs. But the fact that he didn't plan this one doesn't exclude him as a suspect. Maybe first time he got lucky. Went bat-crazy in a more convenient place."

It didn't seem as likely to her way of thinking, but she wasn't getting involved regardless. "Again, what has this got to do with me?"

"OA wants an investigator looking at these crimes as related. Right now Metro isn't tying them together."

"How can they if you buried the first murder? Does Sean know?"

"No. Detective Jasper was on call for the last incident."

The *incident*. Lily didn't like the term. It seemed to be used to sanitize all manner of ugly things and it sounded way too clean for violence. The memory of her own *incident* twisted in her belly like an angry boa constrictor. "So, you tell them and let them figure this out."

"Even if we do that, they don't know the Ormney like you do."

Lily felt the blood drain from her face. How much did he know about her work with an Ormney? "One encounter doesn't equal knowledge."

His full lips pressed into a thin line. "I know about the Ormney trainee. That whole program had to be cleared through our offices. I've kept up with you."

But he hadn't gone to see her when she was in recovery. Hadn't called or brought her sister to visit her. "You haven't told—"

"No," he said. "Not my place."

"Thanks, but I can't help you. I'm not an investigator. Metro—"

"There's anti-Ormney sentiment at Metro," He spoke over her. Determined. "We don't want someone on this who might have their own agenda."

"Metro isn't anti-Ormney, and in case it's slipped your mind, I'm still working for Deepwater." Lily eyed the water on the side table, but wouldn't ask him to get it.

"We don't have a problem with Deepwater getting involved, and your call on the drugs thing makes it clear you're not anti-Ormney." Switching tactics again, his tone softened as he released the footboard and came around the bed to pass the water to her. "We need someone who'll appeal to the Ormney Continuation Council if we need their cooperation to resolve this."

Lily sipped drawing in the cool liquid to sooth her throat. "You think the drug thing will negate me killing one of their people today?"

"Yes, I do. They're fair and reasonable."

"Saints. I know." She couldn't stop her eyes from rolling. Lily knew the Ormney were probably more ethical than Earthers as a whole, but worshiping them like they were all good was just as dumb as demonizing them.

Bradley's jaw twitched. "I didn't say that." Soft and subtle hadn't lasted long.

"I'm not even active." The thought managed to heap on

more fatigue. She could feel it pressing her into the mattress.

"I understand your final evaluation was today."

Lily huffed out a breath. "Yeah, well I didn't exactly make it to that."

"You're cleared," he said.

"No, I—"

"It's been taken care of."

Lily stared him down, but he met her gaze with steady confidence. After seconds ticked by, his black eyebrows drew together as if her doubt perturbed him.

"Well, damn." Lily shook her head. "You can do that?"

"OA can do that. We've got a good working relationship with Deepwater at the top level." Bradley's determination sat between them, as undeniable as the moon in the sky. "Lily, you could consider this a transition to a local position. You wouldn't be back in town if you weren't considering a transfer request."

Let Bradley think what he liked about her choice of local for her rehab. "I'm not sure fat-fingering a case like this would be a great way to win friends at Metro or in the regional Deepwater offices. Bradley, I'm not trained for this sort of thing."

He stretched and all his annoyance slid off as he relaxed. "I want you..."

Lily's muscles tensed to rigidity.

Bradley sat tentatively on the edge of the bed, near her thighs. "I want you on this assignment. I won't take a no on this."

She pressed her lips together and narrowed her eyes, giving him her best eat-dirt-and-die face.

He reached out and tucked a lock of hair behind her ear, face softening. "How can any woman look so beautiful in a med facility bed?" His hand lingered, knuckles skimming her jaw line. His wedding ring glinted on his other hand.

Lily's jaw clenched tight as she bit out a response. "How's Rose?"

He sighed then withdrew his hand and leaned back out of swinging distance. Smart man. "Healthy. I can't say either of us has been happy in a long while." He met her glare directly. "Our marriage is all but over, Lily."

"Does Rose know that?"

"Yes. She doesn't want to rock the boat, but that's the only thing keeping it together now." He shrugged as if he weren't ringing the death toll on his marriage. His sister's marriage.

"You're a jerk, Bradley. You know that?"

"Yeah. I know."

"I hate you." Her voice felt small and cutting in her mouth as she ground out the words.

"Hate." A melancholy look settled into his eyes. "That's a strong emotion. I have strong feelings for you too."

"Hate?"

"Of course." He laced the whispered words with a wistful note and a hint of humor.

The moment stretched thin then faded.

"Right, then." Lily wasn't letting fatigue get the best of her. She shifted her hips, sitting up straighter. "I have an idea about how I can deal with the press tomorrow."

"How's that?"

She pushed down the thin blanket, adjust the med gown and swung her legs over the edge of the bed. "You help me get out of here tonight. I want to go home." She bent her head to study the IV in her arm.

"You want me to take you home?

"Don't get any ideas." She lifted her head. "I want you to drop me off at my place."

"Of course."

"And I'm not getting involved in your damn investigation." No way would she get involved in anything that meant dealing with Bradley on a daily basis.

"Of course."

CHAPTER 7

Lily pressed her forehead to her apartment door and smiled. She'd enjoyed the look on Bradley's face when he realized he wasn't getting into her apartment...or anything else. It felt good for all of thirty seconds. Then the thought of Rose married to the jerk stole the smile away.

Despite the late hour, light from the street streamed through her privacy glass windows, painting her open-plan living space in stripes of mellow-amber and leaving a lace-work of shadows that suited her mood. She shrugged out of her coat and winced at the twinge of pain in her lower back. She'd be sore for a day, but she'd rather be in pain at home than trapped in the med facility.

Carefully, she hung the coat on the hook by the door and ran a hand down the aged leather. It had been her father's. The only memento she'd managed to save before her mother had tossed away all her painful memories. Weary to her bones, Lily reset the security and navigated her way through the familiar shadows to the shower.

She scrubbed the blood from beneath her fingernails and washed the sticky residue of the alley from her hair. Soap and steam and shampoo mixed in a floral bouquet that did wonders to erase the day. Rinsing away the soap, she watched the bubbles circle the drain. But instead of relaxing, her muscles tightened again.

She couldn't say if she'd heard a noise or if some cursory visual cue had surfaced in her brain, but every breath she took solidified her certainty that someone was in her apartment. Silently, she cursed her own carelessness then she cursed the audacity of the intruder. If the bastard had waited for her to get naked, thinking it would make her more vulnerable, he'd be disappointed. It had been a bad day and getting caught naked only made Lily angry, it didn't make her unarmed.

She reached for the hunting knife she kept on the high ledge to her right then peeked carefully around the edge of the shower screen. She couldn't see anything, but that didn't mean he wasn't there.

She left the shower running and stepped clear of the frosted screen, adjusting her grip on the blade. A chill rippled across her wet skin as she surveyed the room. A set of strategically placed partitions hid the lav. Another obscured her view of the door. With lights on, she'd have a clear view of everything else.

The lav was only two meters away. She didn't think he'd gotten that close, but she didn't think he'd be hiding by the door either. How had he been able to bypass her security in the short time she'd been home…and without her hearing anything? He had to have been in the apartment when she'd arrived.

She stood still, watching for movement in the darker corners of the room.

Nothing.

He was there. She was sure of it. To hell with the damn shadows.

"Lights full."

The immediate response of the environmental controls banished the darkness, leaving nowhere to hide.

Jolaj, the Ormney Law Keeper, stood just beyond the far window, narrowing his eyes against the sudden brightness of the lights. "Forgive my intrusion, Agent Rowan."

Her heart pounded loudly in her ears as she adjusted her stance. Sean had vouched for this guy, but she couldn't come up with any good reason he'd be in her apartment, let alone out of The Zone at midnight.

"I meant no harm," he said, "but I must speak with you. Privately." He stood motionless, hands relaxed at his sides. "I'm unarmed. There is no need for your weapon."

"I'll decide what I need." She could handle most men, but he was easily over two meters tall and muscled. If he meant her harm she'd be in trouble. He could probably snap her in two.

Lily worked at keeping her grip on the blade light and ready. "You'd better explain why you're in my apartment. I could shove this blade through your heart just because you're outside The Zone past curfew."

He angled his broad-featured face like a curious hound. "You could try."

He spoke as if it were a sop to her ego. They both knew he could *slip* toward *out-of-sync* and the blade would never connect. Against her will, Lily's hand tightened around the knife's hilt.

"I truly wish you no harm, Agent Rowan. I'm here to ask you for your help."

Help? She couldn't imagine any scenario where she could help him. He met her gaze levelly. Cool, calm, determined.

"How long have you been in here?"

"Only a moment," he said.

He hadn't been in the apartment when she'd gotten home. He'd *slipped* from the hallway into an unfamiliar room? No, he stood near the window, not the door. If an Ormney was going to *slip* blind into a room, they would *slip* back on the other side of the door where they weren't likely to end up mangled by a piece of furniture or a wall. At least that's what Kiq had taught her.

From the street, then? From street level to a second-story apartment? She considered the precision required. Even more than his *slip* in the alley. His skills must be crazy good, but so far he hadn't pressed his advantage. He'd been upset by the loss of the Ormney male that afternoon, but he'd only insisted on getting her medical attention. Lily took a deep breath and released it slowly through her nose then lightened her grip on the blade.

She suppressed a shiver as the effects of the adrenalin dumped into her system began to fade and the cool air of the apartment made it impossible to ignore that she stood naked and dripping. Her modesty had died an awkward death within a month of being assigned to a roving remote access search and rescue team. No one did anything alone when they were deep in bandit controlled hill country. But being naked in front of him suddenly made her feel vulnerable.

"Sit," she said. "You are too damn big standing."

She waved him toward a chair. He might not be a threat, but she'd feel a lot better knowing that seated he'd be at a disadvantage.

His expression unruffled, he sat.

She reached for the robe she'd left out that morning and shrugged into it awkwardly. His eyes followed her movements as she fought the material clinging to her damp skin, twisting and shimmying her way into the garment.

She wondered if he enjoyed the show. Most people would have politely looked away or ogled, but he wasn't most people. He simply watched, closed-faced, hard to read. If the scars that formed a tangled web across her abdomen and arms disturbed him, he wasn't letting it show.

Ormney and Earth natives were similar in many ways, but she had no idea if the Ormney found Earthers attractive or even interesting in an animal-in-the-zoo kind of way. The similarities had made it easier to accept them when they turned up on Earth, but the broad, not quite normal shape of their faces made them too different to blend in completely. Lily had never considered the question before, but she had to admit, at least to herself, that she found his wide cheekbones, broad nose, and square jaw line oddly attractive.

Wrapped in her robe, she moved over to the chair opposite where he sat and leaned a hip against the arm. She waited for him to speak, but he said nothing, his gaze lingering on her bare feet.

"You had something to say," she prompted.

His attention shifted and his jaw tightened. In the bright light of the apartment, the elliptical pupils of his eyes had closed to mere slits. The irises were the color of a Mediterranean sea and just as deep. "I've come to ask you to help me protect my people."

Lily was too tired to laugh at that. "Protect them from what? The backlash over the attack?"

He seemed to weigh his answer. "That's a part of it. If we can find the one responsible for the deaths, maybe we can alleviate some of the…backlash. But that's not the most pressing part. I fear more of my people will be targeted."

"Drugged, you mean?"

"Drugged, yes." His gaze slid to the noise of the shower.

Lily went over and turned it off then returned to her spot,

propped against the chair. "You don't think this was an isolated incident."

"I know it wasn't. This is the second such offense against one of my men. Two humans have been lost, two of our men lost, and their descendants with them." Anger and sadness laced together in his deep voice.

Confused, Lily frowned. "You mean someone is killing their children?"

He shook his head. "I mean only that with them dead, there will be no descendants."

She knew the Ormney religion centered on the descendants they hoped to have. Kiq had explained how knowing their planet was dying had forced his people to focus on securing a future for their race. It had shaped their culture. He'd carried two figurines in a small pouch to represent the children he'd one day have. He'd hand carved them and painted them with an intricate pattern of blue and gold to represent his family line. She didn't know what had happened to those carvings after his death.

"The first man was drugged?"

"He was a dock worker. Two of his coworkers found him locked in a cargo container with a woman. They were both dead."

"A woman?"

"An Earth woman."

Lily could picture the scene too damned easily. Flashes of memory filled her head with bright red blood and lethally sharp claws. She swallowed the lump of fear and pulled her lip between her teeth, biting hard enough to focus her thoughts. "Two Ormney men, two human women. That's a pattern, then." A pattern might mean serial killer.

"The one who did this won't stop at two," he said.

"No," Lily agreed, but she was no murder investigator. "You didn't report this."

It wasn't a question. Bradley had said a woman was murdered, but he hadn't said anything about a dead Ormney being found.

"The men who found the bodies panicked." Jolaj fisted his hands against his thighs. "They took them from the container and brought the male home for our death rite."

"And tossed the woman in the river."

Surprise flickered across his features, but he didn't try to deny it or ask how she knew. "It was a terrible thing, but by the time I learned of it, there was nothing I could do."

"You have to tell Metro about this."

"During the death rite the body is incinerated. I can't produce Fresna's body and I have no evidence he was drugged. I will tell you all I know. Assist you in any way I can." His stoicism dimmed as he leaned forward and braced his forearms on his thighs. "But you must understand, I'm not here in an official capacity. I will only provide this information to you. You must agree to help me, Agent Rowan."

If he hadn't looked so earnest and the situation wasn't so serious, she would've laughed. That made two men in one night, asking her to investigate the same crime. "Why me? If we're talking about a serial killer, I'm totally unqualified to handle this."

"There are many reasons why it must be you. You have contacts in Metro, Ormney Affairs, and Deepwater." He slid further forward in the chair and Lily knew whatever he was about to say, it would be the real reason he'd come to her. "And I believe I can trust you with information I would not share with other investigators."

"Why?" She huffed out her confusion and tugged her robe tighter around her. "Why do you trust me? You don't know me. Why would you trust me with your secrets?"

He got to his feet and stepped toward her. "I believe you know something about secrets, Agent Rowan. When they can be told and when they must be kept. That sometimes discretion is essential to accomplishing a mission."

A chill rippled through her at his words. She focused on her breathing, her pulse. Calm. He was guessing. He didn't know anything about her work for Deepwater. There were lots of contractors with countless roles. He couldn't know she'd been STU. Or that she'd been assigned to help develop their pilot program for Ormney agents.

It had almost been inevitable that Deepwater would recruit Ormney into the agency. Their abilities were too useful tactically for the suits to allow such a valuable resource to go untapped. It had taken years to get federal approval for the program and more years until a new generation of Ormney had shown a willingness to serve.

Kiq had been the first. Lily had no idea if they'd started

working with another Ormney.

Jolaj got to his feet. "I trust you because you owe us, Agent Rowan. You owe Lanyak."

He reached into a pouch on a cord slung low on his hips then moved closer.

Lily stepped back, cursing her weakness. His movement, the sight of his claws as his hand reached out to her, triggered the panic. Her chest tightened like an invisible rope had been cinched across her breasts.

He hesitated, then, slowly, reached for her as if he had no fear of the blade still clutched tightly in one hand.

Lily held herself still, despite her pulse accelerating and the flight-or-fight response dumping adrenalin into her system, and stood her ground as he wrapped one claw tipped hand around her wrist. He lifted her empty hand to chest height and with his free hand pressed something into her palm.

Two carved figures rested there. She recognized the shapes and intricately painted blue-and-gold design. Her hand trembled. It couldn't be. She lifted her eyes to his.

He held her gaze. "You owe Kiq."

Lily couldn't breathe. There didn't seem to be a single molecule of oxygen left. In the vacuum, her pulse thrummed loudly in her ears. The room seemed to spin around her. Her chest ached and her limbs shook. She used the last bit of air in her lungs to speak. "You knew Kiq?"

Jolaj nodded, face solemn. "I know his family and I brought his body back to his parents."

Lily watched his next words form on his lips. Her vision flashed in and out, giving the moment a time-lapse effect.

"After. You. Killed him."

CHAPTER 8

Lily reached out blindly. Using the soft brush of the chair under her fingertips, she eased into it. It seemed no amount of meditation and training could banish the memories and the guilt. She couldn't fight them. The sharp ache of regret rolled over her.

She cradled the knife in her lap and fisted her free hand in the fabric at the edge of her robe. She tugged it tighter across her waist as she tried to pull her control back together.

When the wave receded Jolaj had stepped closer. Something, compassion or pity, filled his eyes.

"I can buy that you know about Kiq." Her voice came out threadier than she liked. She swallowed, trying to wet her dry throat before she continued. "But, h-how much do you know?"

"Everything."

He somehow managed to bring that bass voice of his to soft murmur. "The Continuation Council received a full briefing. I learned of it from one of the councilors."

He crouched in front of her chair, so she no longer had to look up to meet his eyes. His big, clawed hands pressed against his thighs as he found his balance and settled there like an immovable boulder. "I didn't know you were the one involved until tonight. When Detective O'Leary told me you'd alerted him to the toxin in the claw wounds as well as the possibility that Lanyak had been drugged, I knew of only one way you could have such knowledge." His eyes searched her face. The pupils had gone a wider, making his eyes look more human. "You still carry the scars."

He hovered on the razor-thin line between threatening and soothing. His stance wasn't overtly aggressive. His expression seemed almost tender and protective. In a lesser man his position might even be vulnerable, balanced on the balls of his feet. Thighs slightly apart, leaving his body open. She still had the blade in one hand.

But he was anything but defenseless. He was solid, agile, confident, and very male. His stance conveyed that maleness in a potent way and reminded her she was female. That his masculine strength was there, available, calling her to move closer and be sheltered.

God, she was losing it. Imagining things that weren't possible.

Lily had to remind herself he was, by nature, a predator. Their genetic engineering at work. She didn't believe he meant her harm, but everything inside her screamed danger. And she'd let him get close enough that she could see the tiny striations in his blue-green eyes, smell the clean masculine scent of him. Too close.

She wrapped her arm more tightly around her middle, wanting to retreat and hide, but determined not to let her fear or her ghosts get to her.

"If you're so damn clever," she said. Self-preservation had provided a back bone for her shaky voice. "You don't need my help. Go to Sean. Work with him."

"I can't." He kept his voice low. Calm. "The Council would never allow me to be involved officially. Our jurisdiction is limited to The Zone. Both crimes occurred outside."

Lily shook her head. "Surely they want this over. It'll be difficult to convince the public you're not a threat with this kind of thing going on."

"I fear they'll be convinced to restrict all of our people to The Zone as the solution."

"It might prevent any further attacks." She didn't like the idea, but it couldn't be dismissed.

"And how long should we stay behind the walls?" He leaned in for a moment, pressing against her own private boundaries, then stood in an explosion of pent-up emotion. "Should we wait the length of the killer's life span?" He paced away, giving her the breathing room she desperately needed and leaving her feeling terribly alone.

Lily carefully rebuilt the walls of her composure, then stood and laid the knife on the table. "Metro will come up with something. Give them a chance to work the physical evidence."

Jolaj pinned her with a hard stare. "And will they be able to pursue the investigation if it leads them to Deepwater?"

"You think Deepwater is responsible?" She didn't want to believe they would use what had happened to Kiq to do something like this.

"I don't know. But who else would know what toxins cause us to react this way? A secret we've managed to keep away from the public for twenty years."

Lily considered the possibilities. "Maybe one of your people."

"All of the attacks have occurred outside The Zone."

"That doesn't mean it couldn't have been an Ormney." She took note he didn't directly deny one of his people could be capable of the crime.

"If your investigation leads you to look at us, I will cooperate fully." His big clawed hands clenched at his sides. "My wish is to stop the person responsible whoever he may be. If we work together I'm certain we can put an end to these attacks."

Lily tightened her hand around the figurines resting in her palm. She hadn't been able to save Kiq, but maybe she could save some of his people. Maybe then she'd be able to banish the guilt and panic that paralyzed her with constant second-guessing. In her work, hesitations got you killed. Until she'd come to peace with Kiq's ghost she'd be unable to go back to the job.

The only way Lily could get access to Metro's case would be through Bradley. Just the thought of him made her head hurt, but she had to do this. Hell, maybe she was turning into a masochist.

"Okay," she said. "I'll call my contact at Ormney Affairs in the morning and start reviewing the case files as soon as possible."

Jolaj dipped his chin in a brief nod. "Thank you, Agent Rowan."

Lily shrugged off his gratitude and walked over to her mini-chiller, desperately needing some space, some sense of normalcy. "In the meantime, tell me about the first attack."

He followed her over to the meals bar, but kept a careful

distance as if he understood her need for a space.

Lily pulled out two boxes of lyte-water and set them out.

"It happened several weeks ago," he explained. "As I said, they found the bodies in a container near the docks. Fresna worked there loading cargo."

Jolaj took the water she offered, but opted to stand across the bar rather than sit on one of the stools.

"He never returned from his meal break," he continued. "They went in search of him after their shift. They found the container locked from the outside."

"They started looking in cargo containers at random?"

"No. They tracked him. Our sense of smell is very keen."

Lily's hand tightened on her drink. "So, they found the bodies. Did they recognize the woman?"

"Yes." He made a slight back and forth motion of his head that might have been a subconscious nod. "They had seen her in one of the restaurants near the docks, but they had no other information."

Lily took a long sip of the cool water. When Metro had found the body in the river, they would have questioned everyone at the docks and the businesses nearby, looking for any witnesses, but she'd have to work it through herself. With better information, more details, she might do better. Find someone who would remember something. "You said the container was locked, but why didn't he *slip* out? I wish there was some way we could be sure he died inside. Maybe he was moved there."

"If he'd been drugged as we suspect, he may not have been able to think clearly enough to *slip*."

"Your friend Lanyak didn't have any trouble *slipping* when he was drugged."

"We don't all have the same level of skill, Agent Rowan." His voice transmitted a trace of disappointment, as if her generalization bothered him. "Lanyak's natural abilities were keen and he had trained for many years."

"And the other victim?"

"I do not know what his natural talents were, but he had no training beyond the basics we all learn as children."

Lily took another sip of her water and watched Jolaj do the same. As he tipped his head back to drink, his eyelids twitched. The lighting bothered his eyes. She wasn't wearing her com-lens so she had to use voice commands to adjust them. "Lights seventy-five percent.

The room dimmed to a more comfortable level for them both. He blinked several times and his pupils widened. "Thank you, Agent Rowan."

In some crazy way, his few weaknesses reassured her. But, he knew her darkest secret and that wasn't reassuring at all.

"If we're going to be working together, you should call me Lily."

"Lily." He said her name like he was tasting it.

An unexpected ripple of pleasure buzzed up her spine. She decided not to think too hard on that surprise. "Okay, so your guy couldn't get out of the container. That doesn't explain why he went inside in the first place and why the woman would have been there."

"I'm not certain why they were there. The men who found them said she seemed to have died quickly, but he bled to death after tearing the flesh from his body."

Kiq had done that. Torn at his own flesh. It was the reason she'd gone into the chamber with him. To stop him from hurting himself. She'd been so sure he wouldn't hurt her. That she could reach him. Stupid.

Thinking of Kiq it was impossible not to make a mental comparison with Jolaj. The patterns of the Law Keeper's face reminded her of cat, with the stripes on his forehead curving up from his eyebrows and disappearing into his hair. There was the strip across his eyes and parallel lines that crossed his cheeks. All of his stripes were more subtle, less vivid than Kiq's.

Lily shivered, still wet from her shower. "Is there anything that ties the two men together?"

Jolaj hesitated. "Aside from the circumstances of their death, being found with a human woman, no. Nothing."

"I'll want to speak with the workers who found them."

He nodded. "I can arrange it for tomorrow morning."

"Make it afternoon." Lily took another sip of water. The accelerants used to rapidly heal her injuries always dehydrated her and she could feel the effects setting in. "It will take me some time in the morning to get cleared to work on this." She also wanted time to go over the evidence reports.

Jolaj walked slowly around the bar and stopped beside her.

"You should still be in the med facility."

She knew the fatigue had to show in her face and she'd been leaning against the bar more than she might have otherwise. He stood too close, eyes full of concern, looking every inch the strong, protective male, and despite the panic he could so easily trigger, she wanted to step into his warmth. "I don't like med facilities," she said, suspecting that she was starting to sound whiny and hoping she was too tired to panic again. "You should be in The Zone." It was hours past curfew. "You want to tell me how it is that you're not?"

"No," he said. "I don't think I do." He smiled at her for the first time and her stomach flip-flopped. He took a deep breath and his hand hovered near her arm as if he wanted to touch her but didn't dare. "I should probably get back."

"You probably should."

His hand fell back to his side. "I'll be in touch tomorrow. Good night, Lily."

A slight vibration disturbed the air and rippled across her skin like a caress. Then he disappeared.

CHAPTER 9

Lily decided to meet with Bradley in his office at the Federal Building downtown. She could have used her secure link and handled everything from the comfort of her apartment, but she wanted to keep their association formal and professional. The seven-block morning walk to the nearest glide-rail station had helped her work out the aches and soreness left over from her most recent injuries. By the time she stepped off the train into the fifth floor lobby, she was ready to face whatever the day would throw at her.

A brief detour through security to clear her weapon and a quick trip up the express elevator landed her in the sleekly modern interior of the Ormney Affairs office. In an effort not to look too out of place, she'd paired her Dad's black leather coat with black wool trousers and a black turtle neck she'd dug out of the back of her closet, but the familiar weight of her pulse pistol, nestled under her left arm, made her feel more comfortable in her own skin than she had in months.

A twenty-something man in an expensive suit greeted her from behind the reception counter. "Good morning." He smiled warmly. "Mr. Rubeiro's in the conference suite at the end of the hall on the left. I don't think he's expecting you, but I'm sure he won't mind if you go on back."

Lily nodded, not bothering to tell the man he'd mistaken her for her sister. At least she hoped he had. She'd hate to think

Bradley had been so sure of her that he'd sent her identification to the receptionist. She made her way to the conference room. The far wall was all glass and a barely discernible door led out onto a patio covered in foliage.

Bradley stood as she entered, as did the Ormney Elder seated across from him at the triangular conference table. The design should have eliminated the appearance of seating opposing forces and yet it was clear that she'd walked into a meeting between adversaries.

The Elder was dressed in formal robes and completely gray. His stripes were so faded she couldn't tell what his original coloring had been. Acknowledging her with a curve of lips, he clasped his hands behind his back. "What an unexpected pleasure, Mrs. Rubiero."

Mrs. Rubiero.

It didn't matter that Lily hadn't wanted the title in years. His mistaken greeting wriggled through her like termites exploring the newly discovered convenience of old, long abandoned tunnels twisting through her foundation.

Bradley rounded the table and stood beside Lily. "Councilor Vaj, this is Agent Rowan. She's my wife's twin."

Amethyst eyes studied her, full of curiosity. "Ah, yes. I see the differences now. Forgive me. It has been some months since I last saw your sister." Vaj dipped his head with a polite nod.

She wanted to ask him about the differences he saw. She hadn't seen Rose in *years*. She'd made a few trips to DC to see her mother, her brother...but she'd avoided her sister, and Rose had made herself easy to avoid.

"It's an honor to meet you, Councilor." She made her best effort at a polite smile then switched her gaze to Bradley. "I came to discuss the request you made yesterday, but I didn't realize you were in a meeting. Is there somewhere I can wait?"

A satisfied, closed-mouth grin snaked onto Bradley's face. "You've reconsidered, then?"

She agreed with a quick nod.

"Excellent news." Bradley's exuberance grated and his explanation to Vaj didn't improve the situation. "Agent Rowan is going to help us with the investigation." To Lily, he said, "Vaj and I both feel this is our top priority at the moment."

Vaj's expression seemed open and relaxed, but he made

her uncomfortable on many levels. Being Ormney was enough to keep her on edge, hyper-aware of his size and the claw-tipped hands he clasped behind his back.

She took in a calming breath and focused for a moment. She'd killed one of his people yesterday. Someone who'd probably been as much a victim as the woman he'd attacked. That made two Ormney men she'd terminated. Possibly two good men she'd removed from the Ormney gene pool.

Bradley had introduced Vaj as Councilor, one of a council of six, the Ormney governing body. She didn't know if he knew Jolaj had enlisted her aid or if they even knew each other. Jolaj had said he couldn't be involved officially. He'd also said the Council had been given all the details of Kiq's death.

Lily's hand moved to her stomach as if she needed to hide the scars. "It's an honor to meet a member of the Continuation Council."

"Ah, you're well informed," said Vaj. "Few humans show an interest in our governance."

She shrugged. "I can't claim to follow Ormney politics, Councilor. But the medallion." Lily indicated the symbol on the pendant Vaj wore on a thick cord around his neck. "It's a Council symbol, right?"

Kiq had kept a small leather bound book embossed with a similar symbol.

"Ah, yes. The Perpetuation Medallion symbolizes our commitment to the Principals of Perpetuation. A reminder that we must always represent the good of our descendants. Each member of the Council wears one."

Vaj pointed to the broad top end of the first triangle and traced his finger down to the center circle, only the tips of his claws showing. "Many contribute to the making of one—" he drew his finger from the center to the broad base of the bottom triangle, "—and the one contributes to the survival of the many." He wrapped his hand around the medallion in a gesture that looked habitual.

Bradley smoothed a hand down his suit jacket. "The Council negotiated the treaty allowing the Ormney to make a home here. And it's up to them to ensure the terms of the treaty are followed to the letter."

"Or to renegotiate terms when needed," Vaj added.

Lily got the distinct impression the conversation had drifted back to whatever they'd been discussing before she arrived. The Ormney Affairs office had a reputation for being ultra-pro-Ormney, so the undertones between Bradley and Vaj struck her as odd. "I don't want to interrupt."

"No problem at all." Bradley put out an arm as if subconsciously corralling them all to the door. "Vaj, perhaps we could continue our discussion later this afternoon."

Vaj inclined his head in a stately manner. "Certainly." He met and held Lily's gaze for a heartbeat. "It was a pleasure to meet you, Agent Rowan."

The Councilor left the conference room and Bradley led Lily a few steps down the hall to his office. In under a minute, he had Deepwater Regional Field Director Marjorie Gardot on his office-com.

"Marjorie, good to see you again. Thanks for taking my call."

The image of the short, fiftyish woman with a cool smile and assessing eyes loomed large on the video display wall. "I see Agent Rowan is there with you. Can I assume you're calling to officially request her reassignment?"

Bradley's smile tightened beneath the weight of Gardot's scrutiny, but he didn't hesitate. "Yes. Precisely."

The woman gave away nothing of her thoughts. "Agent Rowan."

"Director Gardot," Lily acknowledged.

"Bradley, you'll excuse a moment." Without waiting for a response, Gardot turned her back to the screen and her voice switched from the office com to the com-link in Lily's ear. "I'm clearing you for reassignment to this case, but I'm not clearing you to divulge any further information related to your last assignment."

Despite the director's unremarkable tone, Lily accepted it for the stern rebuke it was. The director wasn't pleased she'd shared information about the possibility of negative Ormney drug reactions with Metro.

"Understood, Director."

"And, Agent—" the director paused as if she wanted to make sure she had Lily's full attention, "—I expect you to keep your responsibilities to this office clearly in focus in this matter."

Lily measured Gardot's words and the possible meaning

behind them. "Yes, Director."

With her acknowledgment, the director turned back to face the vid and Bradley. "Always a pleasure, Mr. Rubiero. Close com."

The screen went dark abruptly, leaving them standing side by side in front of the quiet com station.

Bradley sucked in a breath as if he needed to reset after the director's abruptness. He turned to face Lily. "You're looking a lot better this morning, but you still look tired. You okay?" He reached over to Lily and tried to slide his hand into hers.

She stepped away, to put some distance between them. "I'm fine."

"Okay, then, can you tell me what that sidebar was about?"

Lily lifted a shoulder to her ear in a less than subtle deflection. "Nothing for you to worry about."

Bradley laughed. "You in trouble?"

"Maybe I was a little too forthcoming with confidential information yesterday."

"About the drugs?"

"Yeah." That was definitely part of it, but she thought there was something more. The director must be worried that the course of the investigation could tempt her to repeat the mistake.

"I'm sorry," said Bradley. "I probably got you in more trouble when I spoke to her about the drugs."

"No, I reported in when I got to the med center yesterday." She'd requested Deepwater's science division share details of all known Ormney chemical vulnerabilities. She'd already told Metro that Deepwater had the info so they were pressed to transmit the details."

Bradley stared at her silent and doe eyed.

Lily shifted on her feet, uncomfortable. "Did you tell Director Gardot about the earlier case? The woman found in the river?"

"No," said Bradley. "No need to tell her about that at this point."

Lily wouldn't argue the point. "I'll need that file as soon as possible, and clearance for the new Metro case."

While Bradley went to work getting her what she'd need, Lily took in the office. The decorative mini-vid screen on one corner of his desk flicked between professional portraits of Rose and Ambassador Rubiero, Bradley's father.

A display curio held several pieces of Post-Crossing Ormney art. There was no Pre-Crossing Ormney art. Not in Bradley's case. Not anywhere. They'd lost every physical representation of their culture. She tried to imagine losing even a small fraction of Earth culture. What if the Louvre were destroyed? The pyramids in Egypt? The works of Shakespeare, Beethoven, Roberts? If the only thing remaining of them were memories? She wondered what Jolaj had left behind, what memories of home he held precious.

"Lily?"

"Yeah." She turned to see a Metro file pull up on the vid display.

"Here's the case we think is related to yesterday's attack."

"I'll want a complete copy of this sent to my data account." She stepped closer to the display and listened as Bradley read.

"Ginger Simon, age forty-two. Unemployed. Picked up repeatedly for petty theft, vandalism, vagrancy. Her address is in The Mixer."

There were two images on screen, one of a lump of flesh that looked vaguely like a rib cage and another of Ginger, looking serious, ivory complexion, coal black hair.

"You said they found her body."

"Enough of it to get a DNA identification."

So a lot of poor Ginger was still eddying around the bottom of the river or had found its way out to sea.

A silken artificial voice interrupted her thoughts. "Urgent com from Secretary Lupcke."

Bradley engaged privacy mode, pulled the ear-tuc from his com unit, and slid it over his ear. He listened for a moment then ended the call with a brief yes-sir, thank-you-sir.

Lily waited, curious. "Everything okay?"

"Ah, no." Bradley slipped off the ear-tuc, his face sober and empty. "There's been another attack."

CHAPTER 10

A crowd had already gathered outside the boxy, multi-story building when Lily and Bradley arrived at the crime scene. Officer Ferguson escorted them up to the apartment where Mary Santini had been murdered. Sean met them at the door with a day's growth of blond whiskers not quite covering his tempered scowl. Lily understood. Two murders in two days changed things for Metro. They'd thought they were working a one-time incident with the perpetrator already out of the picture.

"You got the com with our clearance?" she asked.

"I got it." He nodded at Lily then he turned to Bradley. "Brad."

Sean joined them in the hall, forcing them away from the door. "Forensics should be through with their sweep in a few minutes. I can fill you in out here until they're done."

Lily stepped back, noticing the door next to the crime scene was also open. The sound of weeping spilled out.

Sean sucked in a lungful of air and flexed his shoulders in a stretch. "This was called in as a *stringer* attack based on the damage done."

"Ormney," Bradley corrected.

Sean shrugged then pulled Lily to the far side of the hall. "The victim is ripped up a lot like the one yesterday. A neighbor downstairs saw an Ormney leave the building sometime before the victim's mother got home and found the girl dead. Bled out."

Bradley edged closer to Lily, clearly unwilling to be cut out of the conversation. "The victim is the daughter? Is this a younger victim?"

"Yeah, just turned eighteen a month ago." Sean jerked his head over his shoulder to indicate the weeping still coming through the apartment doorway. "The mother says the girl was top of her class and doing independent-ed to finish out her last year of high school, didn't have much of a social life. She worked at the grocery down the block during the day to bring in extra cash for the family and did her school work at night."

"Jesus," said Bradley. "An honor student and perfect daughter. This will explode in the media."

Bradley was probably calculating the additional damage that news would inflict on his public relations efforts, but Lily accepted the weighty news for what it was—another life lost to violence. "The neighbor hear anything?" she asked. "Give a description?"

"The one downstairs gave us a rough description for the guy she saw. There's no visual surveillance in this building, just basic security logs. According to those, she unlocked the door to the apartment in response to a buzz at 7:30 A.M. Someone opened the door again from the interior at 7:50 A.M. Door was left standing open."

"So, that gives you a timeline for the murder," said Lily.

"Yeah," said Sean, rubbing the bridge of his nose. The back-to-back murders had hit him hard. "The neighbor saw the *stringer*, ah, Ormney, leaving the building sometime before eight. Since curfew lifts at 7:00 A.M., he could have been here in time for the murder without raising any flags."

Lily held her tongue on the subject of curfew. She still didn't know how Jolaj had gotten clear of The Zone without tripping any of the curfew monitors. "Is it normal for the girl to be home alone at that hour?"

"She was the youngest child. Last one still living at home. The mother works graveyard shift and the father is in freight rail. He's on his way back from Boston Metro now."

Lily didn't envy Sean having to deal with the parent's grief. "Any suspects?"

"No obvious ones. So far no one in the building has specific ties to any Ormney, but we're still canvassing. She opened the door to her attacker so she might have known him. At the least she wasn't worried by his presence in the building."

"Kids are less cautious," said Bradley. "Especially teenagers."

"True," said Sean. "But the attack yesterday was only a few blocks away. The victim had to have heard about it. There are a few Ormney working stock and loading and unloading trucks in the store where she worked. So far that's looking like our best possibility for a connection. I'm headed over there next."

Bradley stuffed his hands in his pockets. "Are you doing anything to consider the possibility that this might be something other than an Ormney attack?"

Sean bristled. "We follow the leads and the evidence, Brad. So far the injuries, timeframe, and witness description, such as it is, points that way. If the techs find physical evidence pointing to something else, we'll pursue it."

Ignoring the posturing, Lily focused on the apartment where the weeping had quieted. She couldn't really see much. The techs appeared at the victim's apartment threshold and exchanged a few words with Sean.

"I'd like to see the victim," Lily said, raising her voice to be heard over the murmuring between the men. It was a lie, but Jolaj was counting on her to see something the others would miss.

Sean nodded and moved toward the door. Lily was relieved when he didn't hesitate. He didn't know the details of the work she'd done for Deepwater, but apparently he was prepared to treat her like a professional. "Brad, you might want to wait here." He didn't look back as he dismissed Bradley, maybe trying not to make it confrontational. Maybe, giving the guy an out. Lily was more than willing to leave Bradley in the hall. She doubted he'd ever even seen a dead body. Not in his job description. But she expected he would try to follow anyway.

"Bradley," she said. " Maybe you could talk to the mother. Use that charm of yours to get more info from her."

He nodded and Lily dismissed him from her thoughts. Inside the apartment, a tech sprayed her down with a light forensic sealant. An overstuffed semi-circle sofa faced an entertainment wall that had been muted. Images flashed across the wall in eerie silence. Like the apartment, the furnishings were serviceable, standard. The place showed all the signs of a family getting by and going nowhere. And that was probably okay by them.

Sean led Lily down a wide hallway lined with photos that testified to the family's pride in their kids. Portraits mixed with snapshots in a colorful jumble.

The smell of death spilled down the space, swelling as they got closer. The name MARY had been stenciled in green letters on the door that stood open at the far end. Sean stepped aside and let Lily go in first.

The copper tang of blood and the biting stench she associated with belly wounds lay thick in the air, squeezing her lungs like a horrid, blood-soaked blanket.

She took her time, looking past the gore and chaos to the pale green walls and feminine mint and white furnishings beneath. Feminine, yes, but not overly so. No ruffles or flounces.

An e-scribe tablet lay on the floor near the bed and basic secondary-school math formulas peeked out from behind the blood splattered across a work-display wall. There were no school banners. No stills of friends.

It looked as if the victim might have been a bit mature for her age, maybe hiding something, more likely a bit of an introvert, isolated, lonely. Not the kind of kid to draw the attention of a random attacker, but exactly the kind that might be targeted by a more methodical predator.

Lily half-listened to Sean's all-business explanation of cast-off patterns and the preliminary ME report.

She let her eyes see the victim, slowly. As she'd done with the room, she tried to look below the obvious offense of blood and torn flesh.

Mary's face was surprisingly untouched, her pale blue eyes open and unseeing. Wisps of baby-fine hair spread around her head in a shade of red almost too perfectly uniform to be real, but the delicate eyebrows, arching thinly over her eyes, were the same carroty color, suggesting it might be natural after all. The sprinkle of freckles decorating her nose and cheeks clinched it. No teenager had ever wanted freckles.

"No sign of a struggle till we get in here," said Sean. "She fought. Defensive wounds on her forearms."

His flat, cop delivery of that detail sparked along the scars of her own arms like electrical current along a glide-rail. Lily took in the deep grooves carved into Mary's arms then moved on to the girl's torso. She couldn't tell what color the shirt had been before the attack. Lily clutched the edge of her coat and squeezed the leather tight in her fists. She wouldn't look away. Not yet.

Focusing on the details, she saw that the tiny flower buttons than ran down the edge of one side were all free of the matching button holes and all still intact. They hadn't been fastened when her abdomen had been ripped open.

Lily pointed to the perfect edges. "She must have opened it for him before the attack."

Sean leaned forward and made an hmm noise in the back of his throat. "It's possible he threatened her and she went along until she reached her breaking point."

"Maybe." Or she knew her attacker and went along until he got too rough. But that was a stretch, wasn't it? If this attack was related to the incident yesterday, they were looking for a drug-crazed Ormney. Not someone likely to be successful seducing a seventeen-year-old girl. But why would the victim let an Ormney she didn't know into the apartment. It didn't make sense no matter how Lily looked at it.

As she stood over the body, she let herself see the whole—the victim rather than the details. So much destruction. Tears welled in her eyes, but she refused to let them fall. Suddenly, the room seemed too small and she couldn't slow her breathing, now coming in shallow, hitching pants.

Lily strode out of the room. She didn't stop until she found a closed door halfway along the hall. With a shaky hand she twisted the knob, pushed it open, and stepped inside. She pressed her back against the nearest wall and let it take some of her weight. Her head fell back against it as she stared at the ceiling and sucked in a few deep breaths. She'd had to get away from the smell, the blood.

All that blood.

She heard Sean step into the doorway and hated that he'd seen it get to her. She'd seen worse; before the accident she'd been able to distance herself. She didn't know if she'd ever get that back.

Sean stepped inside and closed the door. "Lily, why are you doing this?"

She couldn't give him an answer when she wasn't sure she knew.

He handed her a plastic rectangle that was cool to the

touch. "Put that on the back of your neck."

Lily did as instructed. The cool sensation spread through her at turbo speed and her thoughts cleared. The room she'd picked must have belonged to another child at some point. The room was small on the bed was the right size for a teenager. Most of the personal positions had been stripped and the bedspread and curtains were generic blue and brown stripped that suited a guest room. There were a few things, a soccer jersey had been framed and hung on one wall. A baseball sat on the dresser.

Sean eyed her without any judgment. "Lil, I don't know what you've been doing for the past five years, but I'm pretty sure it wasn't this. You were meant to be a cop, but that doesn't mean you have to work this case. Hell, I wouldn't work it if I didn't have to." He sighed. "And butting into a Metro investigation won't win you any friends in the division. We want you to come home."

She said nothing. JAX Metro hadn't been home for a long time, but she knew he was talking more about family, the O'Leary family.

Sean stood beside her, calm and relaxed. Green eyes cool and measuring. "I can't believe you'd screw yourself this way for Bradley."

The accusation whipped through her like a jolt of electricity. She focused her full attention on him and leaned into his space, her jaw locked so tight she could feel the muscles in her face twitch. "Is that what you're thinking?"

He held his ground and grinned, but his eyes were still serious, worried. "Feel better now?"

Lily's body sagged as the anger left her and she moved back and shook her head. "Jerk."

Sean bumped her with his shoulder and they smiled at each other. A moment of silence passed easily between them, then he rifled a hand through his blond hair and slid back into cop mode.

He took a deep breath like a swimmer preparing for a dive. "Anything about this victim seem familiar or connect back to you in any way?"

Lily shook her head. "No. Why?"

He walked over to the dresser and grabbed the baseball, squeezing it tight in his fist. "There was one thing I had the techs bag and remove from the body. I wanted to let you see the scene without the distraction, first."

"What…"

"There were lilies pressed into her hand, post mortem."

Her stomach twisted painfully. Hell, by the time they got through this investigation her insides would be pretzel-shaped. "You think that has something to do with me? That whoever's behind this knows I'm on this case?"

He tossed the ball from one hand to the other and shrugged. "It might be a message for you. Maybe a threat."

"Or it might not have anything to do with me. Maybe it was remorse. Lilies are used for funerals all the time."

Sean's eyebrows shot up. "Ormney funerals?"

Lily had no idea, so she lifted a shoulder in answer.

Sean set down the baseball and tugged at his collar. "According to the mother, the flowers aren't from the house. If he brought them then we're talking premeditation."

"Premeditation doesn't fit with the last attack. What does this mean, Sean?"

"I don't know yet. But whatever this is, I think you should stay as far away from this case as possible."

Lily frowned. "I can't do that."

"At least move in with Mom and Dad for a while. Get out of this neighborhood. Damn it, Lily. Your apartment is under a mile from both crime scenes."

She let the implication soak in for a moment. Of course she'd known, but hadn't considered it significant. Sean's statement made it impossible to ignore. It was getting harder to ignore the coincidences. "Did you find a connection between the attacker and the victim yesterday?"

He glared at her for a ten count before he answered, "Nothing, yet. Jennifer Richards was a licensed sex worker. Mary Santini was just a kid. I doubt we're going to find much to tie those two together. Maybe the canvas will turn up something, but I'm still putting my money on finding answers at the grocery where Mary worked."

Lily removed the strip from the back of her neck as she straightened, leaving the support of the wall. "I'd like to tag along."

Sean's jaw clenched before he spoke. "Can't say I'm shocked."

"If you find a way to ditch Bradley, I'd be thrilled," she

added.

A hint of an honest grin tightened his lips for a moment and lit his eyes. "Can't say I'm shocked by that either. There is still the neighbor to interview."

"Didn't one of your men already take care of it?"

"Yeah, but he didn't get much. You'll probably want Bradley to talk to her, anyway."

"Good idea." Lily smirked. "He'll need to be able to tell OA we were thorough."

He stood at the window and watched her walk down the street with her cousin. Once again, she was leading those idiots in the right direction—exactly as he planned. He wanted them close. Wanted to see their futile efforts to identify him. Wanted to see the moment when they understood his cleverness—the rightness of his actions.

No, he didn't expect them to come right out and applaud his actions, but quietly, in whispers in the locker rooms, in hushed glee at the local cop bar, they'd acknowledge he was doing what had to be done. What they, with their rules and policies, could not. When they knew what was happening, they'd start looking for opportunities to join in, shooting first and asking questions later.

He looked back to the old woman sitting in her medi-chair in front of the built-in entertainment wall. Stupid cow probably didn't even remember he was still in the room. By the time he was done, his crusade would make him unforgettable.

CHAPTER 11

Lily had always liked the irony of The Corner Grocery's location, center of the block, sandwiched between a hov-board repair shop and a community med clinic. She'd shopped there occasionally to supplement her standing weekly order of Ready-Meals. Like the crime scenes, it was only a few blocks from her apartment.

Word of Mary's death had already made its way to the store. Despite the bright, open space and cheery décor, the atmosphere inside felt heavy and close. The shop owner moved slowly, her features devoid of expression, as if all the vitality had drained from her body.

Sean took the lead in questioning the fiftyish woman with short blond hair and kind eyes. Lily stayed close enough to listen but let her gaze wander. A reed-thin boy stood at the scan point near the doors, viewing a training program and looking grateful for the nearly empty store. He'd probably been recruited from some other task to fill in when Mary hadn't shown up for work.

A young Ormney male came out of the storeroom carrying a stack of large boxes. He didn't bother with a hov-pallet and showed no signs of strain under the heavy load. His claws were extended, piercing the cardboard to secure a steady grip on the bottom box. When he noticed Lily watching him, his eyes narrowed, almost disappearing in the dramatically colored black and red bands of his face. He swept the room with a slow glance, catching on Sean then returning to the aisle where he sat the boxes and began unloading the contents, filling the shelves.

"I knew something terrible had happened when she was late," the owner was saying. "Mary is never late. I told her a million times to be careful. This can be a dangerous neighborhood for a pretty young girl. That's why I asked Oz to start walking her home in the afternoons. She—"

"Oz?" Sean interrupted.

"Yes. He's very reliable. He started going by and walking her to work last week." She made a small choking sound. "He...h-he's not dead too, is he? I thought, I mean, isn't he the one who found her?"

"No," said Sean. "This Oz, you haven't heard from him?"

Lily wanted to turn more of her attention to the shop owner, but couldn't take her eyes off the stock boy. His movements had become sharp and choppy, pushing and shoving the boxes instead of placing them carefully on the shelf. He didn't look their way but he was definitely listening.

"No," said the owner. "I can't imagine...I hope he's okay." Her voice broke on the words, sounding unsure, hesitant.

"What can you tell me about Oz?" Sean's tone was all compassion and sympathy, the kind of voice that could charm fleas off a hound.

"Oz is a good young man. A hard worker. He's been working here about a year. Keeps to himself mostly, but friendly to the customers. If it weren't for the curfew I'd have made him my evening manager."

Her reference to the curfew could only mean one thing. "Oz is Ormney?" Sean prompted her gently.

"Yes," she said. "That's why I trusted him to be the one to walk with her. They're very trustworthy, and everyone knows they don't look at our girls the way a normal boy would. He'd never take advantage of Mary. Not *that* way, you know?"

"Yeah, I know," said Sean.

The shop owner huffed with exuberant relief. Relief because Sean understood? Or did she take his statement as agreement and absolution from any guilt?

The stock boy had stilled completely, one hand resting palm down on the top of a box, the other at his side, frozen.

As Lily watched, his claws slowly dug into the top of the

box. The sound of the shredding cardboard left her sickened. She felt again that terrible moment when Kiq's slashes had slowed and become a desperate digging. She'd been too weak to fight then. Too weak to lift her arms to block and push. Too weak to scream at the pain.

She closed her eyes and focused her thoughts back before the fear. Memories of Kiq's Ormney-eyes laughing even when his wide thin lips hadn't seemed to know how to shape a proper smile. Gentle, clever Kiq.

She silently counted until her pulse rate and breathing were perfectly normal. The Ormney had more acute senses than humans and she couldn't let him notice her fear. She opened her eyes and studied the stock boy more thoroughly. Calmer, she saw that he was a few years younger than Kiq had been. Despite his more than human strength he was small, underdeveloped in comparison to the more mature Ormney men.

Like Kiq, he'd have been born on Earth. Grown up in the same world Lily had. As she slowly stepped toward him she was aware of Sean's eyes on her, but he made no move to interfere.

The boy watched her approach, his expression guarded in that slumped shoulders, chin up way only the young can pull off.

"*Glin eli dossry.*" Lily watched his face carefully as she spoke the words, stopped just out of arm's reach, then introduced herself.

His eyes widened in surprise, making them stand out against the mask of his facial markings. The rest of him stayed still, ready, cautious. "Where'd you learn that?" he asked.

"A friend," she said. Kiq had explained that the greeting translated roughly as *friend of your descendants*.

"We don't use the old language anymore."

"Only to tell your history and to speak your prayers. I know. But my friend told me if I ever needed to gain the trust of any of the Ormney, I should use the greeting. Said it would make it clear that he'd been convinced I was a friend of his people."

He frowned, then relaxed subtly. "To teach you this greeting he must have respected you a great deal. I'm called Ajak."

"Do you know where Oz is?"

She watched him struggle with his answer. He'd acknowledged her trustworthiness as required by his culture's protocol, but he didn't yet feel that trust in his bones. She hadn't earned it and a kernel of guilt ate at her for putting him in that position.

"I only want to talk to Oz," she said. "A young girl is dead. One of your coworkers. Wouldn't he want to help us find out who hurt her?"

His scowl deepened. "He's not a suspect?"

Lily took a deep breath. It would be easier to lie, but she couldn't do that. Not when she'd invoked Kiq's trust. "I'm sure Metro will consider him a suspect. But I'm not Metro. I'm a civilian contractor working for OA."

"You came in with the Metro detective." The boy was smart and cautious.

"Yes, Metro has orders to cooperate with me. The OA wants to make sure this doesn't cause the Ormney any trouble."

Ajak darted a look to Sean then back to her, clearly unsure what to do.

"Until I see him, speak to him myself," she continued. "I don't consider Oz anything but a potential witness and possibly a potential victim."

"Victim?"

"Yes. I think whoever killed the girl might also have tried to harm Oz."

"Mary?" His posture softened at the mention of the girl.

"Yes. Mary."

"I don't know where Oz is, but I think he'll be in The Zone. If he found her, found her dead, he'd have gone to—"

Ajak's nostrils flared then he looked to the door.

Lily followed his line of sight to see Jolaj filling up the entryway. His gaze swept over her, and touched on Ajak before moving to Sean.

Why was he there? He'd said he couldn't be involved officially, so it made no sense. There was no Ormney dead to deal with here.

Returning her attention to Ajak, Lily prodded him to continue. "He would have gone to..."

The muscles bracketing the boy's mouth tightened and twitched. "I have to finish this now, Agent Rowan. If you truly want to help Oz, the Law Keeper will help you."

"Ajak, this is important. I need to know where Oz—"

"Where would you go?" he interrupted. "Who would you go to, if you found someone dead?"

"I'd call Metro, to—"

"Metro. Your Law Keepers, yes?" His eyes shifted to Jolaj and Sean. They were walking over, weaving around the fresh vegetable bins. "Who better to call when there's trouble?"

CHAPTER 12

Jolaj wasn't surprised to see Lily with Detective O'Leary. He'd asked her to become involved in this dangerous situation and she'd agreed. Committed to a course of action. Not all Earthers understood duty, but he suspected this one had it knitted in her bones.

He was more surprised that she'd managed to get Ajax talking. The boy's slumped shoulders and tight lips broadcast guilt or maybe worry that he'd said too much. Hoping Lily would understand he too had a duty to perform, he met her gaze as he stopped far enough away to give her plenty of space. An illusion, the small gold and green display of boost-drinks between them wouldn't stand in his way if he wanted to get to her. But he didn't want to see that fear in her eyes again and he knew she wouldn't want to be forced to fight her panic in front of her cousin. "I must insist you do not question any of my people without a Law Keeper present."

Her head tilted as she measured his words. "We were only talking."

Jolaj would have preferred if he could talk to her without so many ears around. He didn't know how to make her understand the situation without saying more than he wanted Detective O'Leary to hear. "If you violate our agreement, the Ormney will no longer cooperate in Metro investigations."

Lily's eyebrows shot up. "I wasn't aware talking was

forbidden in the treaty." Her remark seemed aimed at the detective so Jolaj let his gaze linger on her as they spoke. She looked stronger than she had the day before. She'd worn her golden hair down, twisted in one loose curling bunch down her back. Her ivory skin glowed with a healthy pink tint and the purple tinge beneath her eyes had lightened, leaving only a slight shadow to draw attention to het wide green eyes.

The detective's voice cut smoothly into his scrutiny. "Not the Ormney Accommodation Treaty, Lily. Law Keeper Jolaj is referring to an agreement Metro negotiated with the Ormney about ten years ago."

"O-kay." She drew the word out, letting it vibrate in her mouth. She clearly hadn't been aware of this. "Well, Sean," she said, looking directly at Jolaj. "Please explain to the Law Keeper that I'm not Metro. I'll question whoever I think will help me get to the bottom of this." The light in her eyes told Jolaj she was angry, but not overly so. She seemed to enjoy the confrontation.

Standing nearby, Ajax started glancing toward the bright red stockroom door as if calculating the distance and the likelihood that he could get away with leaving the conversation.

A muscle in Sean's jaw ticked. Lily's attempt to gain the detective's support in such a manner seemed destined to fail. This was akin to the insincere banter he'd seen other humans engage in to take each other's measure. But Lily and the detective were cousins, family. There should be no need for such things between them.

"Even Deepwater is bound by the treaty," said Detective O'Leary. He breathed in deeply, expanding his chest as if trying to assert dominance. "But there is no reason we can't all cooperate to get through this. We all want the same thing here."

Lily's eyebrows drew together over those intelligent green eyes. "So, you called him in to..."

The man blew a noisy puff of air. "It's standard procedure to call in a Law Keeper when we need to question Ormney witnesses."

Ajak edged around a stack of boxes and closer to the door at the mention of questioning.

Jolaj decided it was time to end their bickering, before the boy resorted to a *slip* to get clear of the two Earthers. They all tried to avoid slipping outside The Zone. It made the Earthers uncomfortable. "Since you've already questioned Ajak, I would like a moment to speak with him as well."

"Ajak isn't under any suspicion here," said Lily. "He hasn't given me any reason to think he knows anything about Mary's death."

Jolaj felt certain that was not entirely true. Strange that she'd protect the boy. She was all contradictions, this small, troublesome woman. An unexpected need to pull her close and breathe in her scent unsettled him. No woman had troubled him so much in a long while.

Ajak shifted, from one foot to the other. "I'd like to go back to work. I have morning deliveries to prep."

"First," said O'Leary, "I have some questions. Last I checked I'm still the cop here."

"Fine with me," said Lily, holding up her hands in a gesture of submission that didn't match the mischief in her eyes.

Jolaj stood patiently by the drink display and listened as Ajak answered the detective's questions with discretion. He didn't reveal the true nature of the relationship between Oz and the human girl despite O'Leary's expert interrogation.

When all the questions had been asked, Ajak turned to Jolaj. "Sir, Agent Rowan believes Oz could be in danger."

Jolaj weighed his words carefully. "I will do my best to ensure his safety."

Ajak nodded his acceptance then looked to Lily. "And will the friend of my descendants be a friend to us all?"

She stepped closer to him. "I will always be a friend to those who would honor all that I honor."

Jolaj was shocked to hear her use the translation of the formal pledge of his people.

She stretched out her right hand. It was steady, but Jolaj wasn't fooled. She was wound tight in expectation of touching the boy. "I hope to always call you friend."

Ajak returned the greeting, loosely gripping her hand. Jolaj wanted to move closer, to be there to hold her if her fear overtook her. It was a foolish notion. He was only likely to frighten her more, so he stood still and silent as the boy's retracted claws pressed lightly against her skin.

She kept a smile on her face, but she shivered at the touch. The sight heated his blood with a territorial hunger he had no right to indulge. Despite his best efforts he couldn't stop himself from going to her. Stepping clear of the gold and green display, he wrapped his hand around her arm, needing to urge her away from the younger male.

Her breathing changed, stalling in her chest as her cheeks washed palest white. Jolaj released her instantly and took a step back. For a single moment, he had forgotten her needs and remembered only his own.

Some humans feared the Ormney instinctively as any predator fears another larger, stronger predator. As any person feared the unknown. But he knew her fright was all the more powerful for the real knowledge she kept of his people. He had seen the silver/white scars covering her belly and splashed across her breasts and arms. She knew too well of their primitive natures. Their bodies and instincts had been meant for a more primitive environment, just as his heated reaction to the sight of an unmated female touching an unmated male belonged to a less civil society.

Damn the inappropriate genetics. May their descendants avoid such unseemly struggles.

"Lily?" Detective O'Leary stepped squarely between them. "You okay?"

"Yes." Her voice shook with the single syllable.

Sean cleared his throat. "Ah, I'm going to head back over to the crime scene. You want to walk over with me?"

"No," said Lily. "I'm going to visit the shop lav then I'll catch up."

"I can wait." A threat meant only for him, lay beneath O'Leary's clipped response.

"Go on. I'm fine." Lily waved her reluctant cousin away.

The man didn't budge. "Do what you need to do, I'm not going anywhere without you."

Lily grabbed O'Leary's arm and led him toward the door. "I'm fine and so is the Law Keeper. I'll explain later."

They argued a minute more, the detective glancing his way at every break in the conversation. Jolaj hid his hands behind his back and did his best to look unthreatening. He was tempted to grab a few of the drinks and juggle them like a street performer. He hadn't heard her desire for him to leave in any of her words. When Sean did leave, Lily waited for the store staff to wander back to their tasks and Jolaj encouraged Ajak to make his deliveries. They would talk later.

Lily caught Jolaj off guard when she appeared in front of him and reached up to grab a fistful of his tunic. She yanked hard, pulling his face down close to hers.

"Now, you want to tell me where in hell Oz is?" Anger flashed in her eyes even as her words shuddered under breathless fear.

"I don't—"

"Wrong answer," she snapped. "Let me make this easier for you. You do want to tell me where Oz is and you do want Sean to interview him. If he had nothing to do with Mary's murder there is no reason he shouldn't cooperate."

Jolaj wrapped his hand around her wrist where she still clutched his tunic. The softness of her skin beneath his touch threatened to distract him. "What did Ajax tell you to make you so angry."

"He didn't say anything, our conversation just made me realize that the boy would go to you. I'm not exactly sure how, but you are in the middle of this as much as I am. Why are you making things more difficult now?"

Her hand shook more the longer she spoke.

He breathed her into his lungs, but her fear had eased, not deepened. "We've learned we cannot count on fair treatment from Metro. Now let go, before your arm gives out."

She released his tunic, allowing him to straighten, but Jolaj kept a light grip on her wrist. Her bones felt delicate, fragile, but he knew underestimating her would be a mistake. She had a strong survival instinct, something that only made her more desirable to a man who'd lost a mate as he had.

Ignoring his touch she met his gaze levelly. "Sean will be fair."

She could ignore him all she wanted to, but he had to believe she wouldn't have let him continue to hold her wrist if some part of her didn't want his touch.

"Was your arm injured when you fought Lanyak?" The thought brought back the primitive need to assure himself she was all right, but he controlled it ruthlessly. He would *not* scare her again.

"Just wrenched it, but the muscles of that arm aren't fully recovered from…" Her lush mouth opened and closed twice before she shrugged away the obvious fact that she was referring to the damage Kiq had done to her. Something she seemed unready to discuss with him.

Jolaj took them both back to the original conversation. "Sean's authority is limited and your people tend to look for someone easy to blame."

"He's in The Zone, right?" Her question emerged breathless, but this was neither the fear she'd been unable to hide nor the desire he longed to hear in her voice. She waited for him to decide. To trust her judgment.

He weighed his need for her help. His confidence in her commitment to see justice done and nodded his answer to her question. "I will arrange an interview."

Her breathing relaxed, deepened. "We'll meet you at Metro headquarters."

"No. I cannot risk Oz's safety. I will escort you into The Zone. You may interview him there."

He met her gaze as she contemplated his offer.

"All right." She tugged her wrist from his grasp. "I'll tell Sean."

He watched her walk away, captivated by the fluid grace of her body. She enflamed his desire without purpose, without knowledge or intent. As long as she remained blind to his need for her, he'd be able to maintain his control. He could use her to aid his people and they could focus on the very real need to keep the others safe.

He would ignore the mating instincts waking inside him. He couldn't afford to frighten her with his wild hunger. He needed her trust as much as she needed his.

CHAPTER 13

Lily had thought the wall seemed enormous from her blocks-away rooftop. Standing in its shadow with Sean and Detective Newman, the wall seemed unreal—like something from a nightmare. It didn't seem to intimidate the crowd of protesters gathered around the main gate. So far they'd been non-violent, but an entire squadron of Metro officers stood ready to intervene if things turned ugly.

Sean had been pissed when she told him she'd arranged for Jolaj to take them into The Zone to interview Oz. He'd issued Jolaj a warning about withholding information from Metro in a tirade peppered with more explicit language than she'd ever heard from her easygoing cousin. He hadn't spoken to her since.

Lily pressed a hand to her lower back and stretched the still sore muscles from her encounter with the alley wall the day before. On the other side of the gate, flat-roofed buildings lined the streets. The grass covered, pedestrian-only lane that served as the main thoroughfare into The Zone lay empty. She didn't know if the decision to clear the street had been made by the Council or if the residents had chosen on their own to stay out of sight of the crowds.

Jolaj, flanked by two other Law Keepers, appeared from a side lane. He was tall even next to his own kind. All three men moved quickly, but with athletic grace.

Lily elbowed Sean. "Here they come."

Sean turned his attention from the protesters to the Law Keepers approaching the gate. "They didn't bring the suspect with them."

Lily stopped short of rolling her eyes. "I told you they wouldn't bring him. They don't consider him a suspect and even if they did, he's under their jurisdiction. They're not going to turn him over."

"Exactly." Detective Newman's whole body moved with the single word, like a corner bully bouncing on the edge of a brawl. "Even if he confesses we won't be able to arrest him."

Sean silenced Newman with a stern look. Newman's heavy jowls made his frown even more severe. He wore an ill-fitting suit and shiny shoes—classic detective style. Lily looked over her cousin's plain slacks and synth jacket, grateful that he at least looked like he'd come from the right century.

Lily led the way toward the gate with Sean quickly reaching her side. His jaw flexed as they crossed the line into The Zone and met the Ormney.

"Law Keepers," Lily greeted.

One of them should've extended a hand for a shake, but Newman kept his hands stiffly at his sides and Lily shoved hers in her pockets. She couldn't afford a panic attack and it was going to be hard enough just being inside The Zone. It landed on Sean to take up the slack and his O'Leary manners seemed to get him through.

Jolaj assessed them then waved an arm up the lane. "Everything is arranged. Please follow me." With that he strode ahead, leading them deeper into the village that had been built on a more human scale than the city surrounding it.

They walked up several blocks, bypassing the side lane she'd seen them use earlier. She could see no building above three stories, but ladders built into the adobe-like walls provided a direct, if low tech, route to what upper levels there were. The buildings were a uniform off-white color. Foliage topped every roof and trailed down the exterior walls, filling the street with the fresh smell of green growing things and buffering the sounds of life in The Zone. The muffled whoosh of the monorail line overhead was barely audible. There were no auto-carts to disturb the quiet notes of voices, music, and laughter.

Jolaj led them to a one-room neighborhood center. The

building sat on a large public square. The entryway consisted of a wide arch. No door or barrier of any kind. The windows were also absent any glass.

She studied the young Ormney standing in one corner of the sunlit room as she walked past the two Law Keepers posted at the door. The young man's body language broadcast grief and devastation. Hard to say if there was any guilt in the mix.

Jolaj introduced them to Oz. Lily couldn't keep a sad mile from her face as she noted his white and orange coloring—almost the same shade of orange as Mary's hair. They would have made quite a colorful pair walking through The Mixer. Unfortunately, his coloring also matched the neighbor's description of the Ormney she'd seen leaving Mary's building that morning.

Sean and Oz sat in two large wooden chairs that had been dragged to the center of the room while the rest of them gave them some room. Lily picked a spot along the wall to the side, not far from where Newman stood to provide a secondary recording to go along with the one from the camera on the badge Sean wore around his neck.

Jolaj chose to stand opposite Oz, where the younger Ormney could easily look to him for comfort or approval. It surprised Lily that Sean didn't voice an objection. She hoped Jolaj had time to prepare Oz for what was about to happen. Sean had explained that he would have to be tough on Oz. Going soft would do the boy no favors if they couldn't clear him immediately. Lily had passed it along. Despite trying to be objective, her gut told her Oz hadn't been Mary's attacker. They didn't know how long the drugs would have lasted, but she suspected he'd never have made it back to The Zone without incident if he were the one.

Sean sat straight in the chair with the toes of his short boots tucked beneath. "Oz, you know Mary Santini is dead?"

Oz dipped his head in a gesture that moved his shoulders along with it, as if the air had been sucked out of him, causing him to collapse in on himself.

The Law Keepers frowned at Sean's blunt tone, but they didn't move.

Sean went on in the same frank way. "How long had you known her?"

Oz straightened and met Sean's gaze. "In the summer, she moved to day shift at the store where we work. Maybe five months ago. Before that, I'd seen her around, coming into work."

Sean nodded at the young Ormney's equally direct answer. "Would you consider her a friend?"

"Yes, sir."

Lily couldn't see Oz's eyes well enough to know if he glanced to Jolaj, but she saw the older man's slight nod of approval. Approval of what, she couldn't be certain.

"Do you know," asked Sean, "if any of the other Ormney ever showed particular interest in her? Held a grudge against her?"

Oz's hands gripped the chair as if he might slide to the floor if he let go. "No, sir. Everyone likes Mary. She treats everyone with respect."

Sean fired off his next question like he didn't want to give Oz time to think. "You've been walking Mary to work for several weeks?"

"Yes, sir," said Oz. "Some of the boys on her block were harassing her. Shouting. Being crude when she walked past." His jaw tightened as he bit off the words.

"And it was your employer's idea for you to make sure she got to work safely?" Sean pressed.

Oz nodded again, a short, jerky motion, but he didn't meet Sean's eyes.

"Did anyone else ever walk her to or from work?"

"No." Oz's answer was almost a bark, fast and sharp.

Lily saw Sean take note. His posture changed, sitting taller, alert, and watchful. "Tell us what happened today."

"I arrived at her building at the usual time. I took the stairs..." Oz looked to Jolaj and some silent communication passed between them.

"And," Sean prompted.

"I stopped on the first turn. I smelled...death." He studied his feet. "I knew it was her."

Sean leaned forward, crowding into Oz's space "You knew?"

The youngest of the three Law Keeper's fists clenched at his sides, but Jolaj and the remaining man remained stoic.

Oz shrugged, his shoulders burned with grief. "Her apartment was close to the stairs, it had to be her place."

"You didn't go up into the apartment?"

The young man shook his head. "Not today."

"But you've been there before."

If he'd been there, ever, forensics would find some trace of it.

"Yes."

"So, you smelled her blood and you ran?"

Oz heaved a big breath and let it out slowly. The sigh caught in his throat, sounding broken and painful, then he nodded again. "I guess you could put it that way. I did. Yes.

"You didn't check to see if she was alive?"

The question garnered another simple shake of his head.

"The attack didn't stop her heart," Sean continued, "didn't stop her brain function. The ME said she bled out."

All three of the Law Keepers scowled at Sean. If looks could kill, her cousin would have been obliterated. Oz wrapped his arms around himself and rocked in his seat. Lily looked away from the distraught young man to find Jolaj's gaze boring into her. He didn't understand this was an approved interrogation technique for Metro investigations. Lie to the victim, scare him into saying more than he planned. She was surprised to see Sean use the tactic, but she'd tried to warn them it could be rough.

Lily mouthed an "it'll be okay" in his direction, but doubted that would be good enough for Jolaj.

Sean hadn't let up—adding a dose of outrage he said, "You couldn't go to her? What, ten meters too far?" He leaned forward into Oz's space again. "You couldn't call for help? You left her there to bleed to death, Oz. Maybe you wanted her dead. Maybe you ran because you killed her?"

Oz surged up out of his chair, scraping it back across the floor behind him with a clatter. He made a terrible, mournful growling noise as he scrambled toward Jolaj and threw himself against the Law Keeper's chest. Oz clutched at Jolaj's biceps as the garbled growls died into whimpers.

"She was dead." He wept, his chest heaving. "I swear. I know the smell of dead. I wouldn't have left her there, if there was any chance."

Lily studied him as his sorrow poured out. He pressed against the larger man for comfort and his fingers dug into Jolaj's tunic.

His fingers dug into Jolaj's tunic.

The significance of that thought crashed over her like a

wave, stiffening her spine.

"He didn't do it," she said. "Couldn't have."

Sean scowled. "Lily, I—"

"He couldn't have ripped her up like that, because he doesn't have claws." She reached for Newman's arm and tugged. "His hands, zoom in on his hands for the record."

Sean said nothing, his expression went blank.

Jolaj cleared his throat as he moved closer. "After our people arrived here, we banned further use of genetic engineering. Some of our engineered traits will recede naturally through the generations. A few in this generation were born without claws."

Sean leaned forward in his seat to study their hands, then sighed back into his chair. "I'll be damned."

Lily took in Jolaj's face, back to his stoic façade, and kept her questions for him until later.

Oz turned back to face the room. "Please believe, I would never have abandoned Mary."

His eyes were wide and earnest against the bright orange band that crossed the bridge of his nose, from temple to temple.

"I believe you," she said easily.

He made a gruff huffing in the back of his throat that seemed to convey his gratitude.

An Ormney couple appeared at the door. The woman stood with her arms wrapped around her body as if she held herself tightly under control.

Jolaj laid a hand on Oz's shoulder as he spoke to Sean. "Would it be acceptable for Oz to speak to his parents for a moment, Detective?"

Sean made a low noise of acceptance and then one of the Law Keepers led Oz through the open doorway, where he walk into the open embrace of his parents.

When Lily turned back to Sean, he was shaking his head. "Everyone give us the room, please."

Everyone did.

When they cleared out. He waved her into the chair Oz had vacated. "How do you know so much about them?"

This had been simple observation, but there was enough truth to his supposition that she faltered before answering. "There are thing I can't explain right now. I know you don't really know me enough to trust me, but I promise you I'm not holding back anything that would help you."

Sean's face scrunched into the expression of a man forced to drink sour milk. "I don't know you? Lil, we grew up together. You slept at my house as often as your own. I backed you up at school and damn-it Lil, after you got in that fight with that girl from two blocks over, I even helped you ice your knuckles and braid your hair so you're momma wouldn't find out. You were every bit as hard headed back then as you are now." Sean scrubbed his hands over his face and rubbed at his temples then shook his head at her. "I know you've been through some things. I can accept that you aren't ready to talk about them just yet. I just wish *you* trusted *me* enough to let me back you up in whatever you're involved in now."

Lily gripped the arms of the chair, hoping to prevent the shaking feeling inside her from making her shake on the outside too. She didn't know how to react to all of that. Didn't know what to say. The words that spilled out weren't anything she'd thought over or planned. "I don't trust anyone anymore."

Sean got to his feet forcing her to look up at him. "You trust him."

She followed his pointed finger to see Jolaj filling up the doorway. She looked back to Sean. "He already knows all my secrets." She pressed her lips together tight to prevent anything else from escaping.

Sean nodded. "Okay." Disappointment and maybe even pain cracked in his voice. "Then let him back you up for now. He's a good man, even if he is pissing me off at the moment. When you're ready, I'll be waiting. We all will."

Back straight, he strode to the door. A look she couldn't interpret passed between the two men and then Jolaj moved out of the way and Sean went outside.

Lily didn't know how long she sat in the chair, hollow and numb. At some point Jolaj crouched down in front of her, keeping his hands out of sight. The position should have been awkward for a man of Jolaj's size, but instead he looked like a cat, balanced comfortably, waiting for something to happen.

"I'm all right." She said it because she couldn't think of anything else.

He seemed to be searching her face for something. In the end he just said, "I know."

CHAPTER 14

Lily stood with Jolaj in the shade of the Law Keepers' neighborhood center. Sean was finishing up his questioning inside. Now that Oz was no longer a suspect, everyone was much more relaxed. Newman had even taken off his suit jacket.

The square had grown more crowded while they'd been inside. A mix of adults and children filled the open space, playing or relaxing in the late afternoon sunshine. Grass covered most of the square but one area was covered with colored stepping stones.

It occurred to her that this was the first time she'd seen an Ormney child. They were all educated in Ormney schools. Many Ormney never left The Zone. Only those who left for work regularly spent time beyond the wall. The requirements of the Ormney Accommodation Treaty had served to keep the Ormney isolated. There had been little attempt to integrate them into Earth society.

"Why did Detective O'Leary lie to Oz?" One shoulder braced against the curved exterior of the building, he studied her profile as he asked the question.

She could only see him out of the corner of her eye, but there was no forgetting his presence. Lily pressed her upper back to the cool surface of the white-washed, adobe-like center. "Sometimes the detectives have to lie to convince a criminal to admit to what they've done." She smiled to herself. "Our legal system is hard to explain."

"It would be easier for him if Oz had been Mary's attacker."

"Sean would never go after Oz because it's expedient." Lily shook her head. "There might be some who would, but not Sean."

"My role as Law Keeper is very different from that of you Metro officers. We don't focus on catching and punishing law breakers. We are charged to teach and guide our people in how they must fulfill their duties and responsibilities in The Way." His voice had sparked with enthusiasm when he turned to the subject of guiding his people. Sincerity painted his features. He might not have the same methods as a cop but he had the same passion she'd seen in her cop-grandfathers, uncles, and cousins. It was something she respected.

He turned to face the square full of Ormney of all ages as he continued, "Our laws, the Laws of Continuation were written to ensure the perpetuation of our species, not to ensure order and civil society. We do, and help others to do, what is required for our survival."

Lily angled to take her own turn at studying his profile. "You sound more like a priest than a cop."

"We do not pray to a god as you do." The plains and angles of his face didn't change.

Relieved she hadn't insulted him, Lily shifted her attention back to the square. The children that would be the future of his race. "No. I know. You call on your descendants—"

"To help us see The Way."

On the surface, it seemed beyond odd to expect guidance from some future generation, but she suspected the Ormney understood time differently. Or maybe it was just the consequence of fighting so hard to have a future.

Jolaj's arm brushed hers and she realized he'd moved closer, but she didn't feel threatened. Didn't feel the panic. Something about watching the children play soothed her edgy nerves. Standing side-by-side, not looking at him, she could almost believe he was just like any other man.

Jolaj pitched his voice low. "You understand our ways better than any other human I've met." His words sounded almost reverent.

Lily resisted the urge to turn and face him. She couldn't

allow the conversation to shift from safe territory to the personal. She slipped off her jacket and adjusted her feet so that more of her body rested against the wall. The cool of it soaked through the fabric of her turtleneck. She considered taking off her boots. It had been awhile sense she'd felt grass beneath her toes.

"Your people haven't exactly tried to help us understand your ways. The programs you run in The Mixer are the only ones I've heard of that try to help people understand."

"The Council doesn't want us to be seen as invaders, conquerors, or missionaries."

"Or do anything that could turn public opinion against you, like promoting your beliefs over ours." Lily could see the logic. "But there are plenty of people who would like to learn more about the Ormney culture."

"Nor do we wish to be seen as subjects for study." Jolaj said the words, but they sounded empty. No outrage. No humor. No sparks of passion. Just rote recitation of prepared answers. "The Council has chosen to share the facets of our culture slowly, gradually, over time."

For the Ormney, the good of the children and the children's children was the measure of every decision. But she supposed that didn't necessarily mean they always agreed. It was a logical conclusion, Lily had never thought through before.

Lily pressed her shoulders back and pressed her hands together in the small of her back. The movement brushed her arm against Jolaj again. "I met Councilor Vaj this morning."

"He's one of the more progressive councilors. He favors faster integration with Earther society."

In the square, kids played a game involving sets of colored shapes painted on the ground. The shapes had been arranged with each color group following a basic *slip* pattern. The children *slipped* from one colored shape to the next within a color pattern, then ran to another color and *slipped* into the pattern of children moving along the new group of shapes. Standing with Jolaj she became part of the scene, despite being very aware that she didn't really belong. Not in The Zone. Not in Jolaj's life.

She cleared her throat to get rid of the inappropriate regret. "Human children would be playing some kind of game with a ball."

"Our children also enjoy such games. But learning to

master *slipping* is as important to us as eye-hand coordination. It's a natural ability and children will *slip* whether or not they are taught. They play this game to learn control."

"Kiq taught me about the basic *slip* pattern," she said.

He turned, putting his shoulder against the wall again, but this time he was much closer. "That's how you were able to defeat Lanyak?"

"Yes. But you don't seem to follow the pattern." She glanced at him them away. "I've seen you make impossible *slips*."

"As the children master their abilities, they learn how timing and control allow them to expand the patterns," he explained. "The more skilled children can move from one pattern to a related pattern in the field. With enough practice and talent it is possible to make nearly any *slip*."

"Even into another universe."

He made a murmured sound of agreement. In her peripheral vision she saw him lift his hand as if to touch her then let it fall away. "And everything we found in this universe has been beyond our expectations."

Shifting from one universe to another. Lily thought about that for a long moment. She'd only been a child when the Ormney arrived, so she didn't know how much people then understood about how the refugees had gotten to Earth. There had been a lot of talk everywhere about the refugee's ability to *slip*, mostly worried people fearing how easily they could get through a locked door. What good were locks when these strangers could bypass them? But, the fears had faded, at least in her kid-world. She'd been taught in school that the Ormney abilities were limited. The Crossing had been a dangerous, once-in-a-lifetime event for them. It was the whole reason people trusted The Zone wall to enforce the curfew. It was supposedly taller, thicker than they could safely pass through. The more she learned, the more that rationale seemed laughable.

Lily and Jolaj stood in silence for several minutes, but she couldn't ignore the problem that had brought her to this place. Not for long. Things were growing more and more tense outside The Zone. She needed to solve the puzzle of the murders before anyone else got hurt.

She turned to match his pose, wanting to see his response to what she would ask. They were closer than she should have been comfortable with, but his hands were out of sight and his pupils had widened and rounded in the shade. "Why didn't you just tell us Oz doesn't have claws?"

He hesitated. "It was best you saw this for yourselves." His words were almost a whisper.

That couldn't be it. He hadn't even wanted them to know where Oz was. "We could have wasted a lot of time looking for him."

A frown pulled his eyebrows together. "I wouldn't have let that happen."

Usually a skeptic, Lily realized she believed him. Sean had claimed that she trusted Jolaj. Why? He'd slipped into her apartment. He'd tried to keep information from her. She shouldn't trust him, but in this she did. She held his gaze. "Okay."

His frown lifted and the tightness that had been building in her chest eased.

He glanced up to the sun, narrowing his eyes to slits then quickly looked back to her. "It's past the time when I had arranged to meet with the two men who found Fresna and the woman. Should I make arrangements with them for later tonight? It would have to be here, in The Zone. They cannot be out after curfew. Especially now."

"Curfew doesn't seem to stop you?" She made it a question, unable to curb her curiosity.

He didn't look away, but he didn't respond either. He couldn't or wouldn't answer.

"No," said Lily. "Tomorrow morning is soon enough."

"I'll walk you to the gate, then."

A smile slid onto her face. "Thanks, I'm not sure I'd find my way back."

They stopped by the entrance to the center and asked the Law Keeper there to let Sean know where they'd gone.

They walked comfortably together. In the short time she'd been there, The Zone already felt more familiar. Less *other*.

Jolaj broke into her thoughts. "And what will you do next?"

"I need to go to the Forensic Arts building and see what I can find out." Mary Santini's death gave them a fresh crime scene with new evidence. The answers could be in the science.

"I should accompany you." She might not have noticed

the small change in his tone before, but she knew him better now.

"You have responsibilities to deal with here. I'll be fine."

"Take an escort then. You must be careful," he warned, voice going stern. "Many people saw you come into The Zone today. If the person behind these events is doing this out of a hatred of the Ormney, becoming involved could put you in danger."

Lily decided not to mention the lilies found on Mary Santini's body. They had no way of knowing what the flowers might mean. "I can take care of myself."

"That's one of the things I like most about you, Agent Rowan." This time his voice warmed like mulled wine when he met her gaze, approval softened his features. The heat in his look started a tingling low in her belly. The man was dangerous. Thank God there was nothing behind that warmth but protectiveness. The Ormney didn't see Earthers in a sexual way. Everyone knew it.

She kept walking. They didn't speak again until they reached the gate. She avoided his gaze as she promised to be careful and took her leave. With a Metro escort.

CHAPTER 15

Lily stepped off the cross-town glide-rail and onto the platform. A brief afternoon sun-shower had left puddles dotted across the uneven pavement and brightened the central plaza just beyond it to a carpet of radiant green. With her destination in plain view, she'd left her escort on the train and on his way back to crowd control.

The walkway skirting the edge of the square provided a convenient path to the third building on the eastern side of the plaza. The Forensic Arts Building, with its vaguely medieval style, seemed to shun the technology it housed. What did it signify that the city's best medical examiners and scientists spent their days in the shadows of gargoyles and gothic arches?

Her official ID code got her through the auto-secure door and allowed her to access the building's automated manager. She requested the location for Sara O'Leary and waved to the lobby guard as she walked toward the elevator.

Despite the ancient feel of the architecture, the building was fully modern. The doors slid shut and a twenty-four-hour news feed appeared on the side vid-wall. Seconds later the vid faded to black and the elevator opened.

The locate request must have alerted Sara that Lily was on her way up. Her favorite cousin stood waiting in the corridor. The white lab coat she wore hung loosely around her reed-slender body and hung lower on her thighs than the silver-blue skirt beneath it.

Sara had twisted her hair into a knot high on her head. Since the last time Lily had seen her, she'd dyed it a cotton candy blue a few shades brighter than her eyes.

A tight smile tugged at Sara's lips and her hands tapped restlessly against her thighs. "Hey, stranger."

"Sara..." Lily didn't know what to say. She certainly owed her cousin an apology for not staying in touch, but somehow a simple "sorry" didn't seem adequate. She could tell Sara she'd missed her. It was true...and still not enough.

Before Lily could work it through in her head, Sara sighed, a gesture that managed to involve her whole body. "I *would* kill you," she said. "But this is my best lab coat and my laser scalpel is in the autopsy surgery."

She stepped forward and embraced Lily tight enough to squeeze the air from her lungs. She didn't smell like peppermint anymore. Lily clung to Sara and let go of another little piece of her childhood. Sara smelled of the forensics sealant all the evidence handlers wore to prevent contamination. A powdery, not unpleasant scent.

After a long minute, they shifted apart and Sara shoved her hands into the large pockets of her lab coat. "You'll be here about the Ormney."

Lily nodded. "Among other things."

"Well, whatever you want, you've got the clearance. There was a priority one message waiting on my office unit when I reported in. OA? Bradley? I can't believe you're working with that jerk."

"Believe me, I'm avoiding him as much as possible."

Sara made a short, sharp *hmm* noise at the back of her throat. She led the way down the hall. "Come on. Let's talk in my office."

Lily followed her past the large semi-sheer wall panels lining one side of the corridor. Deepwater med and research facilities used similar partitions. A touch on any control pad could engage a full privacy mode or provide a clear view into any of the lab stations on the other side.

Sara's office boasted a sophisticated com and data system, two comfortable-looking chairs, and a mini fridge with a large old-fashioned chain and padlock.

Lily eyed the fridge. "You keep specimens in your office?"

Sara grinned. "Nope. My lunch, drinks..." She waved her hand. "Stuff like that."

That didn't explain the padlock. Lily lifted her eyebrows and waited.

"You'll understand when you meet my staff." Sara sat in the oversized office chair behind her desk. "It's a stellarly bad idea to leave food out where those pranksters can get to it."

Lily opened her mouth to speak, but Sara cut her off. "Don't ask. Trust me, you don't want to know. Now, spill. I know you didn't come here to check out my fridge."

Lily sat opposite Sara. "So far there have been three women attacked that we know of. In each case it looks like an Ormney ripped them up with brute force."

"So far? You're expecting more."

"Yes and soon. Two attacks in two days is pretty damn accelerated and frankly, alarming."

"They brought your latest victim in a couple of hours ago. I've got my best forensic pathologist working the case now."

Lily processed that, glad they were making it a top priority. The Medical Examiner served the entire Metro area and probably stayed backlogged.

Sara studied Lily from behind her desk. "Where does Bradley fit into this?"

"He asked me to get involved. Some double-talk about not believing Metro could get cooperation from the Ormney."

"You say it's double-talk, but you agreed to help."

"Not to spend time with Bradley, if that's what you're thinking."

"I know you're not stupid enough to fall for his crap twice, but I couldn't blame you if you wanted to get a little payback for what he and Rose did to you. He wants you back." Sara looked thoughtful. "Has for a while."

"I could never do that to Rose. Never."

Sara huffed a laugh. "And here I thought working for Deepwater would have stamped out all those nice ideals of yours."

Lily didn't find it funny. "You know damn well, service to country and community was bred into our DNA." Part of being raised in a family of cops was believing in doing the right thing. At least it had been for Lily.

"And yet you dropped out of the DC Metro Academy to

go into civilian service."

"Yeah, and now they want me to pretend to be a cop. How am I supposed to do this, Sara?" She groaned out a sound that was half laugh and half frustration. "I have no idea what I'm doing here. I don't have any training for investigating murder." She acted on intelligence, she didn't collect it. Didn't investigate beyond what was necessary to plan an op. "Why does everyone think I can do this?"

"Of course you can do this. Leave the tech to my team and you handle interviewing suspects and following the clues we turn up. Hell, if Sean can do it, it can't be that hard." Sara flashed Lily a quick grin. The rivalry between brother and sister had always been a superficial one, more for form than heartfelt.

Lily eased back in her chair. "Sean's brilliant and you know it."

"Runs in the family, cuz."

"Not on my side," said Lily. "If I had any brilliance I wouldn't have let Bradley drag me into this mess."

Sara stood and came around to lean against the front of her desk. She looked Lily right in the eyes. "I'm betting why you're doing this has a lot more to do with a dead Ormney man and a critically wounded woman than it has to do with Bradley-the-Bastard."

They shared a long moment of silent understanding. Lily wasn't the only one in the room who tended to take on a little too much personal responsibility. It felt good to be there with someone she understood. Someone who understood her. She'd been a fool to forfeit her family for her pride.

"Come on." Her cousin straightened and turned to the door. "Let's go look at your dead Ormney." She glanced over her shoulder with a grin. "I'm dying to show off all the research I did on this one."

Lily laughed.

Sara led her down the hall to a secured door, then entered a code and swung the door open wide. Recessed lights glowed softly against the walls of the cavernous lab. Pinpoint spotlights lit the three stainless steel tables that dominated the center of the room. Square silver doors lined one wall.

The opposite wall ended about shoulder height, giving way to a plexi-divider, that separated the room from a balcony-style seating area. It reminded Lily of the box seating at the downtown sports arena. The third wall was one of the semi-transparent walls and she could see several white clad figures moving around through the misted privacy panel.

Lily tilted her head toward the shadowy techs. "Mary Santini?"

"Yes, but you'll have to wait for those results." Sara flipped a switch as she talked. "Leno is a genius, but compulsive. Having strangers in the theater will only throw him off his stride."

"Genius? High praise."

"Well deserved. I recruited him in from the Chicago Metro number two spot." Sara flashed another of her quick smiles. "Said he'd rather be number two to someone who was at least in his league, even if I was an infant."

She pulled a small cube from the pocket of her lab coat and slid it into the unit mounted at one end of the nearest shiny silver table. A pinpoint light expanded and blended with several new beams of light, emanating from lenses positioned around the table. A blurry image formed, then slowly sharpened, almost solidifying, into a perfect hologram of the dead Ormney. Fascinated, Lily stepped forward. The burn marks directly over his heart were clear and distinct.

"You okay with this?" Sara asked.

Lily nodded. She'd be okay with looking at the results of her actions if it would get her closer to whoever had engineered the attack.

"Your second full blast stopped the heart immediately."

Again, Lily nodded, then returned her gaze to the hologram. The fist-sized mark high on the man's chest caught her attention. "What's this?"

"Many of the first generation immigrants are tattooed in exactly this position," Sara explained. "The tattoos invariably reflect their role. Elder, Law Keeper, Science Tech…"

"Like the medallions and insignia they wear?"

"Exactly." Sara shifted her position—a subtle outlet for that endless energy of hers. "You know they can't take non-organics with them when they *slip*. Apparently, they knew the trip into our dimension would be so arduous they wouldn't be able to bring clothing with them. They tattooed the insignia on their flesh."

Lily memorized the inked lines. "What's this one mean?"

"Not sure. I poured over gigs of data to prep for this autopsy, but I didn't see one exactly like this. It looks a little like—"

"The Perpetuation symbol," Lily finished for her.

"Right. But the triangle is off."

Lily studied the mark. The tips of two scalene triangles pointed together and overlapped a circle. She recognized the larger triangle as the probability pattern Kiq had used to teach her the most likely locations for any *slip*.

Her cousin stepped closer. "Does it mean something to you?"

"Maybe."

Sara waited.

Lily pointed. "This triangle is tied to their *slip* pattern, but I don't know if it's tied to any specific role. They all have the ability to *slip*. They all use the patterns." Lily thought of Jolaj and his explanation of the differences in their abilities. Some used the patterns with a great deal more skill than others.

Sara dipped her head to indicate the hologram. "Well, he's not telling."

"Give me a still vid and I'll ask around."

Sara nodded, then pointed to the Ormney's thick neck muscles. She rattled off a quick series of coordinates for the controls and the hologram altered, virtually simulating peeling away the layers of tissue to create a cross section. "This is a void in the tissue," she said. "It's deep and the related damage indicates a projectile. We matched it to a dart picked up in the sweep of the female victim's apartment. The kind fired from a close contact animal tranq gun. One of our forensics teams is working on pinning down possible type matches."

"And what about the drug?"

"It matched closely, but not exactly, one of the artificial compounds on the list you provided Sean. A little digging tagged the origin, control, and use of the substance on your list as military—bio-weapons related. We're still searching for data on this exact substance."

"Send what you have to my data-com and I'll work on that too." Lily paced slowly around the image. "Any idea how far away the shooter was?"

"At least ten yards."

That caught her attention and brought her to a stop. "That wouldn't be an easy shot with a dart gun."

Sara grinned. "See. You're doing pretty good, so far."

Lily tossed her back a rueful frown. "Sean will have picked up on that. He'll have Metro looking at vets and looking for similar MOs, tracking possible buyers, checking out practice ranges. Someone practicing with a dart gun would be memorable."

"He's got the boots on the ground, to follow up on that stuff," Sara agreed.

"I'll concentrate on the drug, the symbol, and this particular Ormney." Lily had to look away to collect her thoughts. "Can you tell me anything else about him?"

Sara tapped the hands against her thighs as if there were music in her head. "Sure. Age, about sixty. He's definitely from the Crossing Generation, but that's still in his prime for them. They have a longer life span than we do. This guy led a tough life in the first half of his years."

Lily had already noticed the hairline scars on his chest and shoulders. "Any idea what kind of hard?"

"All kinds, I'd say. Signs of early years' malnutrition and every kind of injury, from projectile wounds to *slip* trauma."

The list made Lily's head spin, but her attention focused on the one thing she'd never heard of. "*Slip* trauma?"

"Here's where Bradley's OA clearance and my dedication to thorough research paid off." Sara waggled her eyebrows. "According to Medical Examiner records back in the arrival days, lots of Ormney died when they reached Earth. Nearly a third *slipped* into our universe and ended up colliding with solid objects, falling from crazy heights, or buried alive. The military took some of the corpses, of course. But there were so many bodies taken into custody by the Medical Examiner's office they had a backlog for a year."

"Jesus. I had no idea."

Lily needed time to consider that, but Sara was on a roll. "The Ormney wanted the bodies back, but they didn't have much pull back then." Sara grimaced then went on. "When the MEs examined the bodies they found some unusual tissue damage. A sort of degrading of the cellular structure. Most often found near the area where flesh had merged with a solid object, but not always.

They speculated that the damaged areas, that were not directly associated with areas where solid objects merged to the flesh, were caused when the subject started to *slip* into *sync*, realized the problem, and managed to hold the *slip* long enough to get that area of tissue clear of the object."

"And this guy had *slip* trauma?"

"Right. That means he must've had some close calls with *syncing* into solid objects."

"But survived." Lily had no idea how that might be related to the case, but it was certainly interesting. "Sometimes, I'm blown away by just how little most of us know about them."

Sara raised her eyebrows and tilted her head. "Given the curious nature of the average human being, seems a little unlikely, doesn't it?"

Lily agreed, "Damn unlikely." It could only mean the Ormney had made an effort to discourage that curiosity and it to have been the technology exchange agreement that had given that power.

CHAPTER 16

After reviewing the data on the dead Ormney, Sara insisted on taking Lily out for a little personal time. They both needed dinner and there wouldn't be any results from Mary's autopsy for hours yet. Lily needed time to let everything she'd learned soak in, so she agreed without much fight.

Sara took her to a night club one rail stop up the line, assuring her the place was well equipped to feed them. The neighborhood was upscale, trendy, the short walk from the station to the club well lit and well trafficked. The club's interior was sleekly minimalist. Gently pulsing patterns of colored light softened the plain white surfaces and drew attention to the only decoration, life-like robotic figures that stood on pillars near a dance floor. Light splashed color across the figures as they moved in rhythm, matching the synth-music pumping through the club's sound system. An enticing designer scent drifted in the air.

Sara led Lily to one of the privacy booths ringing the main room and engaged the screen, leaving them with an obscured view of the dance floor and complete privacy. Inside the small space the music pumped in at a more comfortable level and the soft, plush seating invited relaxed sprawling.

"Worth the extra expense," said Sara as she settled onto one of the mini sofas.

Lily sat opposite her and waited while her cousin ordered edibles and beverages.

"So," said Sara, leaning back into the cushions. "How long are you in town before you head back out to some lawless land to distract yourself with offing bad guys?"

The question caught Lily off guard.

"Don't look so surprised," said Sara. "We're family and family's allowed to ask the awkward questions."

"It's been a while since I spent any time with family," said Lily. "I'm rusty."

"Entirely your own fault. We've been here all along."

"Yeah. I see that now." Lily eased back into the cushions. The O'Learys—she should have known, but hadn't. Her father had been buried less than a year before her mother remarried, moved them to DC, and left behind the O'Leary ways. "When Rose and Bradley got married..."

"The family had to accept it, didn't mean any of us had to like it."

"I had to get a little distance and Deepwater provided a good opportunity. My work didn't give me much time for trips home."

Sara tapped her fingers against her lips, then waved those fingers in the air between them as if she could wipe away Lily's answer. "Excuses. But let's move on. Or, more precisely, back to the question."

How long was she back for? "I'm not sure."

Sara frowned. "Or you can't or won't tell me because it's all bound up in Deepwater secrecy?"

"Something like that."

"So, while you're here…" Sara let her voice rise and fall with the questioning lilt of a gossipmonger. "What are you planning to do about Bradley?"

"As little as possible," Lily deadpanned.

Sara slipped off her shoes and pulled her feet up onto the seat. "Oh, he isn't going to be easy to ignore if you're working with him."

"I suppose not."

Her cousin grinned. "Do you honestly think his reason for getting you involved in this case is anything less than personal?"

"I do have knowledge of the Ormney—"

Sara laughed. "Get real. If anyone has access to the Ormney, it's Bradley."

"You have a point." It didn't add up for Bradley to get her involved. "What can he possibly want from me?"

"Honey, you have to face facts. What Bradley wants is to get back in your pants."

The thought dredged up bitter memories and turned Lily inside out with remembered anguish. "You forget there is nothing special about my pants. I'm one of an identical pair. He proved years ago that Rose would serve just as well. Better, in fact."

"Hardly." Sara humphed. "You don't even talk to Rose, do you?"

Lily shook her head.

"I don't suppose your mother would say anything. But Brian... hasn't he told you anything about Rose and Bradley's marriage?"

Lily propped an elbow on the back of the seat and let her head rest on her hand. "Not a favorite topic of conversation."

"No, I suppose not. Lil, Bradley hasn't been...satisfied...with Rose for years. Haven't you ever wondered why those two don't have any kids?"

Lily shrugged. He told me their marriage is in trouble."

Sara's expression turned from amused to condemning in an instant. "I bet he did, that lowlife scum."

Lily laughed. "Aren't you the one that suggested I consider doing him again for old time's sake?"

"That isn't exactly what I said. Besides, being a lowlife doesn't mean he isn't sexy man candy."

Lily chuckled. Laughter was something she'd let fade from her life and now that she'd found it again, she wanted to savor it. Together she and Sara laughed their way through the edibles and a second round of drinks. Then Sara dragged her onto the dance floor and Lily gave herself permission to take an hour to ignore everything and swallow the dose of medicine her cousin was prescribing.

He watched the two women emerge from the privacy booth, struggling to control his anger. She had no right to hide from him. They'd picked their club well, the latest tech, no possibility of overriding without planning.

He'd followed them from the Forensic building, of course. Had to cool his heels while they hid themselves away. He took another swallow of his whiskey, letting the burn fire his anger. Had they spoken of him? Had Lily mentioned him to Sara?

His vision tinged green as he watched her dance. Men couldn't help noticing her athletic body, even hidden away beneath her conservative clothes, and it didn't take them long to be maneuvering for a turn, bumping their bodies against hers. Quick, vague touches. Sensual slides.

He would have to punish her for allowing it. She was his. The thought made his dick hard. He'd punish her then he'd show her the glory of being touched by someone who held life and death in his hands.

CHAPTER 17

Lily keyed in her code to the side entrance of her building and headed up the interior stairwell. She was halfway to the first switchback before she heard the slight rasp of husky breathing. Her hand went instinctively to her weapon. She kept it there as she hugged the wall, taking the steps slowly. Heart pounding. Her pulse loud in her ears.

She leaned around the corner...

Relief washed through her. "Damn it, Bradley." Heart settling back to a normal rhythm, she eased her hand away from her pistol. He sat on the top step, listing slightly to one side.

He made an effort to get to his feet, leaning heavily on the banister. "Hey, beautiful. 'Bout time you got home."

"You're drunk, Bradley."

He grinned. "Well. Yes. Yes, I am. But not too drunk." His expression turned sober, even though *he* clearly wasn't. "You ditched me today, Lily." His bottom lip stuck out in a pout.

Lily stepped around him and onto the landing, well aware Bradley followed in her wake. "You're saying you went out and got drunk because I didn't spend my entire day holding your hand?"

"Strictly speaking, you didn't hold m'hand a'tal. Mebe if you did I might not've minded getting ditched."

Once she cleared her door's security locks and wedged it open, she faced him. He was just a step behind her and their bodies collided. He wrapped his hands around her arms to steady himself.

His fingers squeezed gently as he held on to her and pressed closer. He smelled like expensive whiskey. She brushed him away.

"Come on, Lily. Ask me in."

"You're drunk. Why would I want a drunk in my place?"

He swayed on his feet. "'Cause I might not make it home safe if you don't let me in. After all...I am drunk."

For several heartbeats they stared at one another. His stupid grin softened and turned wistful.

"I remember the first time I saw you. You looked so... beautiful... and so lost. God, what were we, thirteen?"

Lily sighed. "About that."

"Your stepfather brought the family t'our homecoming reception. We'd been in some godforsaken African country for two years and you looked like a fairytale princess in your green party gown."

Lily's fingernails dug into the doorframe. "I hated that dress"

Bradley laughed. "I know. Knew it then. That's why I took you up t'the games suite. Knew you'd rather thrash me at foosball than dance."

He'd rescued her from excruciating boredom. He'd made her feel comfortable, put her at ease, when she hadn't felt comfortable since her father had died. When her mother remarried, they'd gone from back yard barbeques and tag football to cocktail parties and art galleries. He was right, she had been lost.

She looked into his familiar gray eyes and saw the lanky teenager who'd made her laugh and helped her escape from a countless number of her stepfather's stuffy social engagements. "Come on in." She swung the door wide. "I'll get you some coffee and call for transport."

Lily wasn't surprised when Bradley went straight toward her bed. He sat on the edge and fell back, arms stretched wide. She used her com-lens to turn up the lights and engage the locks then slipped out of her coat and holster. She heated a carton of coffee then carried it over to him.

He looked up and smiled. "I could stay here."

"No," she said. "You couldn't."

His position on the bed accentuated the lean lines of his body and left him looking vulnerable, playful.

"Sit up and drink your coffee."

He stretched a hand out, palm up, asking for help. She set the coffee down then put her hand in his, prepared to steady him. She should have known better. With a firm grip he pulled her down and she ended up sprawled across his hard body. "Bradley, you idiot."

He cupped her face gently, stroked her cheek with his thumb. "You're always wound so tight. Le'me help you relax."

The heat of his body beneath her and the look in those gray eyes tugged at long buried memories. She moved her free hand up his rib cage and watched his eyes close and his breathing change. There was little to stop her from leaning in and pressing her lips to his soft, sensual mouth. Loyalty to a sister that hadn't given her the same consideration? Pride? Were they worth more than the physical pleasure, the satisfaction a vindictive indulgence might provide?

She moved her hand to the center of his chest and pushed her shoulders up and away from him. His eyes fluttered open and he reached up, wrapping an arm around her waist. The move aligned their lower bodies in a more intimate way.

"Luv me," he whispered.

That was the problem. She didn't love him anymore. She had once, but not now. Pulling free of him, she clambered off the bed. His arm fell away and his eyes drifted shut again.

She stood over him and watched as the drink dragged him down into sleep. He was her past. She wasn't the same person she'd been when she'd loved him. The person she was now needed a stronger man. A man who understood loyalty. A man who understood there were things that couldn't be fixed with charm and pretty words, no matter how sincere. A man who understood the woman she'd become. She didn't expect love in her future, but that was no reason to hang on to her past.

Lily put the coffee back in the mini-fridge and slipped back into her coat and holster. With one last look over her shoulder she lowered the lights, stepped into the hall, and reset the security.

Everything that had happened in the last forty-eight hours rattled around in her head. She needed time to think, to put things in perspective. And there was only one place guaranteed to reestablish her priorities.

CHAPTER 18

The mechanical noises, beeps, and hums of the med center pecked at Lily like a hungry woodpecker. She concentrated on her com-link and the building's subnet feeding her directions deep into the med center labyrinth.

She recognized the bulldog-faced Detective Newman standing at the nurses' station down the hall from Jennifer Richardson's room. He acknowledged her and waved her past. The two men sitting by Jennifer's bed were more of a surprise.

The bigger man was instantly aware of her. His hair was military short but the open-throated poet's shirt and tight black pants tagged him as an alt. It took her a moment, but she recognized the guy kneeling between his thighs and wrapped in his arms as the other victim from the hallway outside Jennifer's apartment. He was wearing a lot more clothes, a lot less blood.

They stood in a single graceful motion as she entered the room. Her pulse sped up a bit in appreciation of the agility it took for a man to go from kneeling to standing without anything in-between. The victim from Jennifer's apartment stepped forward, pulling free of the other man's supportive embrace. *"Mais*, you, you're the woman from ..." His voice carried undertones of old Louisiana, maybe Cajun, that she hadn't caught before. His skin was pale, setting off blue-black hair that hung to his collar and eyes so true blue they could inspire sonnets about azure pools and moonlight. He wore a tight blue T-shirt and well-worn jeans.

Narrow silver bracelets ringed his wrists.

"That's right," she said. "Lily Rowan. Glad to see you're okay."

He reached a hand down to squeeze the muscles of the injured leg. "*Oui*. Lucas, he made sure of it. Me, I'm Tie LeRoue. I live next to Jen. This is Lucas Delaponte."

"A pleasure." Delaponte stepped into place beside LeRoue. "I'm in your debt, *cher*. Had you not dealt with the Ormney, my Tie would have surely gotten himself into even worse trouble." There was a touch of scolding mixed with tender indulgence in his tone. A more cultured version of the younger man's patois laced his accent.

Lily let her gaze drift to the woman in the bed. A machine breathed for her, pushing air into her lungs. Aside from the artificial rise and fall of her chest, she lay still. "How's she doing?"

Tie spoke softly, as if he didn't want the patient to hear. "She's dying, her. Docs say her intestines, spleen, and liver were all shredded and she lost too much blood. The damage is too severe and she ain't strong enough to take the regeneration fast enough to recover." His voice trembled. "*Oui*, she's dying. Oughtn't die alone, I say."

Lily turned back to him. Lucas had wrapped his arms around Tie again as the two men stood back to chest.

"Were you close to her?"

"We were friends," said Tie.

"All three of you?" Lily asked.

He started to answer, but Lucas quieted him, tightening his arms around his shoulders. "Is there a reason for you asking, *cher*?"

"Another girl was killed today. I think there's a connection and I want to find out what's going on."

"Tie already answered Metro's questions."

But Lily doubted Lucas had answered any questions. And she doubted Tie had been completely forthcoming. Not out of any wrong doing or complicity, just to protect the girl. She hadn't come to the Med Center for an interrogation, but she suspected Lucas would be the key to getting the truth about Jennifer Richardson.

"I'm not with Metro, but it would help if you could talk with me about her. I can promise you I'll protect her privacy." She met Lucas's intense scrutiny, wearing her sincerity as plainly as she could.

Finally, he answered. "She's Tie's friend, but we did play together a few times. The three of us. She liked to be bound."

"Not by her clients," said Tie. "And she wasn't in the life. Just adventurous. She wanted to play with people she felt safe with, so I introduced her to Luc."

"That was over a year ago, now," said Lucas.

Lily studied Jen's broken body. There was still the question of why the Ormney, Lanyak, had been in Jennifer's apartment. She remembered the way Oz had grieved over Mary. They'd been more than coworkers. More than friends. She'd bet her favorite pulse rifle on it. She turned back to the two men.

"You said Jennifer was adventurous. Had you ever seen an Ormney visit her before?"

Tie looked instantly uncomfortable.

"It's all right, *beb*," said Lucas. "I think Lily will keep her word to protect Jen."

Tie kept silent for a full minute. Until Lucas commanded him to "answer her" in a firm masculine tone that made the smaller man shiver in his arms.

"I'd seen the Ormney in the building before. She talked about him."

"Was he a client?" The very idea went against everything the public had been led to believe about the Ormney.

"*Non*," said Tie. Lily breathed a little easier for a heartbeat, then Tie added, "They were lovers."

CHAPTER 19

Jennifer Richardson had taken an Ormney lover.

The idea should have shocked Lily. It would have disgusted or terrified many Earth-natives. But not Tie LeRoue or his dominant partner. They had known and they'd kept that knowledge quiet to protect Jennifer from ridicule.

"Please," said Lily. "Tell me about it."

Tie and Lucas shared a silent exchange and Luc excused himself to go get drinks from the cafeteria. Lily and Tie settled into the two guest chairs. Tie leaned forward, hands clasped, forearms braced on wide-spread knees.

"She met him about six months ago. She thought he was sweet. A gentle giant, that's what she called him."

"Did they become lovers then?"

"Not at first. He met her in the market, carried her things home for her. He didn't like her being a sex worker. Normally, Jen wouldn't have put up with that, but he didn't mean no harm with it. Just didn't understand. They don't have nothing like it, I guess."

"No," Lily agreed. "Procreation and family lines are very important in their culture. That would make sex work almost sacrilegious to them."

"Not so much he didn't want to do it with her, though," said Tie. There was no malice in his voice. "Took a few months. She offered, I think. Said he seemed lonely. She's a kindhearted soul."

"So it was a pity thing?"

"*Non*, not just that. She was sweet on him." His cheeks pinked as he spoke. "Ah, she liked what he did for her too. He was a big mother f— Ah, a big fella. They say size don' matter, but sometime it do. Tie's grin was sin incarnate. "*Mais, oui*. Sometime it can be real nice."

An image of Jolaj, another big Ormney male, flashed into Lily's thoughts. She couldn't help wondering how his big body would feel beneath her hands. It was her turn to blush. Something she couldn't remember doing since her teen years.

Lily rubbed her palms along the tops of her thighs. "Did anyone else know that Jennifer had taken an Ormney lover?"

Tie looked at her through his lashes. "I don't think she talked about him to anyone but me. *Non*, she didn't want anyone to know. Some folk may have seen him in the building, but I don't reckon they would've known anything for sure."

"But he came and went often?"

"*Oui*, often enough."

"Did she mention anyone who might have started treating her differently?"

"*Non*."

Lily thought again about Jolaj. He'd said he'd been friends with Lanyak. Did he know what his buddy was up to?

"Did she ever mention Lanyak frightening her or becoming violent?"

"*Non. Mais oui*, he bit her once, enough to leave a scar. But she said it was a love bite. Nothing that scared her. She went to the clinic to have the scar removed, that's all."

Lucas appeared in the doorway and handed them each a carton of flavored water. He and Tie both looked tired, like they carried weights around as they moved.

"Thank you for talking with me." Lily shifted her focus to Jen. "I'm going to sit with her awhile." She didn't want to go back to her apartment where Bradley was sprawled across her bed. "You should go home and get some sleep. I won't leave her alone."

The two men made appreciative noises and left her to sit with the broken woman. Jennifer lay pale and lifeless. She didn't, however, look ill. No fever, no sweating, no toxin setting her body on fire.

She showed no sign of the terrible reaction Lily had

suffered from her claw wounds. Hopefully, her warning to Sean had allowed them to stave off that battle for her, but it seemed odd there would be no sign at all.

No anti-toxin was one hundred percent without side effects. No, it didn't seem likely Jennifer would have been spared all of the effects of the toxin secreted with the Ormney claws.

Jennifer should have been dying much faster.

CHAPTER 20

Lily sat curled in the chair next to Jennifer Richardson's bed when a subtle change in the tones and lights on the med displays jerked her out of a light doze. She pulled herself to her feet and hurried into the hall to see several of the white-coated med staff already headed her way at a relaxed pace. She stepped away from the door, clearing the way for them to go in, and watched through the viewing panel as they moved around the room in a methodical pattern.

She'd spent more time than she cared to in med facilities over the past year, but she had no precedence for what she saw. The lack bugged her. She wanted to know what was going on but she didn't want to disturb the med team. Detective Newman, who'd been sitting in the hall, had also gotten to his feet, but he shrugged, clearly no more in the know than Lily. When she turned toward the nurses' station, looking for someone she could tag to explain, she saw Timothy Perry in his tailored hospital scrubs straighten and turn toward her.

"Hey, Lily. How long have you been here?" The Timmy she remembered from down the block when they'd both been kids had been awkward and reserved, but he seemed to have gained grace and confidence with age.

"A few hours, I guess. Can you tell me what's going on in there?"

He stepped over to the view panel and watched for a

moment, eyes following the quiet pattern of movement in the room. "This is the patient you asked about, before."

"Yeah."

He finally turned to face her. "I'm sorry, Lily, they knew she wasn't going to pull through."

Lily nodded, swallowing down an unexpected lump of sadness.

"Her metrics finally fell below legal requirements for life sustaining care." Tim studied Lily's face as he continued, "They're turning off the machines, freeing her from the ventilator and IV. The on-duty MD will call it and record the time of death for the records."

There was no fight left in Jennifer as she died. She didn't show any reaction to being deprived of the mechanical aids that had kept her alive. Lily, Timothy at her side, stood sentinel at Jen's bedside as her body simply gave up.

He finally glanced at his wrist-com, as if checking the time, then back at Lily. "You look beat, you should go home."

She wondered if Tie LeRoue would beat himself up for not having been there when his friend died. "If you can point me toward the nearest cafeteria, I think I'll grab some coffee before I go."

"I can do better than that," he said. "This way."

He led her around a corner and down a hallway to a nearby staff lounge, where he cleared the security door and ushered her inside. The room went quiet as he closed the door behind her, shutting out the constant background noise of the terminal care unit. A full-size sofa, a fridge unit, several lockers, a tiny table, and two chairs crowded the cramped space. Timothy stooped to dig through the fridge unit and came up with a supplement-bev.

"These are great for energy when you're running on empty." He tossed her the carton and watched in silence as she opened it and took a grateful swallow. It had a mellow fruity flavor that went down cool against her parched throat. The bev and edibles with Sara had been nearly eight hours earlier. She tipped the carton toward Timothy. "Thanks. I needed this more than I realized."

He nodded and waited for her to take another long swallow. "The other night, you didn't say anything when I assumed you were a cop." There wasn't any heat in his observation.

"Sorry about that."

"Hey, it's none of my business. I'm just surprised. You were so determined to be a cop like your dad."

"After he died a lot changed."

Timothy nodded. "You left the neighborhood."

"Mom wanted a clean break from the past."

"She wanted a husband who wouldn't be killed in the line of duty," said Timothy.

It was an astute observation.

Lily swallowed another gulp of the cool beverage. "You know they never actually declared his death as being in the line of duty. He'd logged out right before."

"They never caught the guy?"

"No. Since they couldn't determine if Dad had been responding to a crime, they ruled it a random homicide." That had made her father a victim instead of a hero. It didn't matter to Lily, but it had made a difference to her mother, who'd felt cheated. If she had to lose her husband, she had at least expected to be a hero's widow.

"Losing a parent changes things," he said. "No matter the reason."

"Yeah. Your mother?" Lily vaguely remembered his mother had been out of the picture, but she didn't know how or why.

"Mom officially went missing when I was about nine. The cops didn't find any evidence of foul play so they assumed she just left us. But Dad and I knew she wouldn't have abandoned us. She had to be dead."

They shared a quiet moment before Tim shook himself and straightened from where he'd been leaning against the fridge. "I have to get back to rounds. You can stay here as long as you need."

"Thanks. You're a life saver."

He smiled then left, pulling the door closed behind him.

Lily took advantage of the privacy to use her com to link into the Deepwater data-engine and do a multi-source search on Tie LeRoue and Lucas Delaponte. She was relieved to see they had no history of connections to any anti-Ormney groups. No public criminal record, but without going through Sean, she couldn't access Metro's internal files to make sure they hadn't been tied to any investigations or had any complaints filed against them.

She had to find time to go over things with Sean. God willing, there wouldn't be another attack and she could spend the day digging into the information from the earlier cases. She had to find out more about the first two deaths. An Ormney male and a human female. Could they have been lovers like Jennifer Richardson and Lanyak? She needed some answers.

The Ormney didn't carry personal coms, instead they used a system of community coms. Lily put in a message for Jolaj to meet her at the entrance of the S&H dock district as soon as curfew lifted for the morning. She wanted to get a feel for the first crime scene and interview the dock workers who'd covered it up.

CHAPTER 21

Lily could get through the next twelve or so hours without sleep, but she'd spent the last twenty-four alternately at the scene of a murder, in a morgue, and camped out at the terminal unit. She refused to face the day without washing all of that away. Her apartment wasn't far from the dockyard where she hoped to meet Jolaj and she wasn't going to let the fact that Bradley was passed out on her bed keep her away from a hot steamy shower.

As she expected he was still there when she arrived. At some point he'd woken up enough to pull off his clothes and crawl under her comforter. She propped a knee on the edge of the bed, grabbed his shoulder and shook hard. "Get up and go home, Bradley."

He groaned and buried his face under her pillow.

She leaned back and considered her options.

She could shoot him. Maybe with her pulser on stun. But that seemed counterproductive.

He started to snore softly beneath the thick bedding.

Damn.

She could pull him off the bed. Hitting the floor would certainly wake him up.

She flexed her shoulders and decided she was too damned tired for that. A quick check of the time confirmed she needed to meet Jolaj in ten minutes. Waking Bradley now would mean dealing with him and she was already going to be late. Better to do it on the way out of the door.

Lily headed for the shower, pulling her clothes off as she went. She wasn't particularly modest. That didn't mean she wanted Bradley to see what a mess Kiq had made of her body.

If she was quiet and quick, she'd be done and dressed before time came to drag him out of bed and leave him in her hall wearing nothing but whatever he'd kept on under her comforter. Liking the idea more and more, she showered with the speed and efficiency born of on-the-job practice.

She'd stepped out of the shower and was rubbing Dermamend into the scar tissue across her abdomen when a com tone shrilled. She pulled a wrap around her body and stepped clear of the privacy screen to get a better view of the room. Bradley hung half out of the bed, digging through a pile of his clothes on the floor. He came up with his com and opened an audio link before he noticed her.

"Morning, sweetheart," he said. Then, "shit," as he quickly switched to his ear-tuc, but she'd caught a word or two from the other end. Enough to know it was her sister.

"Ah, sorry, Rose," he said. "Just realized I overslept."

At that moment Lily hated them both for dragging her into their screwed up lives.

"No," he said. "I'm not at the flat. I had to work late and I crashed on the office couch."

Anger had her dropping her wrap and striding toward the storage unit next to her bed. She jerked open a panel, pulled out a pair of undies and a white SafeSkin tank top then yanked them on. She faced him as she was tugging the bottom edge of her tank down to her hips.

"You shouldn't lie to your wife, Bradley. I know I don't have any practical experience on marriage, but I'm sure that's not a good thing."

"Damn, Lily."

He really was an idiot. She'd been careful to keep her voice too low to be picked up on the com and he'd gone and said her name. From the look on his face, he'd caught a glimpse of her scars. He stared at her as if he'd never seen an injury before, but she didn't give a damn. The scars didn't embarrass her and maybe if he saw them, he'd realize he really had gotten the better model with Rose and stay the hell away from her.

His attention snapped back to whatever Rose was screaming into his ear while Lily pulled out a pair of gray trousers then stepped into them.

"You have to leave," she said. "I have some place I need to be."

She went to the bed and yanked the covers back. It turned out he was wearing boxers these days. He was still pretty to look at, but she felt only contempt for the way he conducted his life. She grabbed his arm and pulled him to his feet as he continued to try to calm Rose on the link.

After scooping his clothes off the floor, Lily dumped them in his arms then shoved him toward the door.

Focused on Rose, Bradley let her guide him across the room. She opened the door and pushed him out about the time she spotted a startled-looking Jolaj coming up the stairs. He was there and then gone—*slipped* toward *out-of-sync* in an instant.

Lily shoved Bradley farther into the hall then pulled her door closed and pressed her back against the smooth carbonlite surface. She waited as Jolaj *synced* into view in the middle of her apartment. "I thought we were meeting at the docks."

Jolaj thought she looked worse today and every bit as fascinating. The purple crescents beneath her eyes were darker again. They made the green of her gaze shimmer a deep emerald.

Thick, steamy air from the shower she'd obviously just left filled her home. Her bed was a rumpled mess and reeked of the mostly naked man she'd just pushed into the hall. He'd recognized the man as Ormney Affairs Liaison Bradley Rubiero.

Lily leaned against the door looking like a cross between warrior woman and vulnerable female. She wore a tight sleeveless top that hugged her breasts and abdomen, emphasizing her toned, athletic build. The faint white scars that wrapped her arms added to the image of a seasoned Defender.

Her golden hair hung wet down her back and her tiny pink feet peeked out from under loose fitting trousers. Jolaj wanted to take those feet in his hands and press against the arches to see if she would squeal with laughter or moan in pleasure. He wanted to trace the delicate pattern of blue veins visible through her pale skin. He wanted to shake her until she swore an oath to stay away from Bradley Rubiero.

"Liaison Rubiero has a mate," he said, unable to stop the growl that rumbled unwanted from deep in his chest. "A wife."

Her golden eyebrows rose. "Yes, he does. She's my sister, actually."

She walked toward him, stopping with only inches between them. He had to crane his neck down to look into her upturned face.

"Bradley is a jerk," she said. "He stopped by last night drunk and passed out. I have no interest in sleeping with him, if that's what's rattling around in that big, thick skull of yours." When she paused, he could see a quick mind turning behind those remarkable eyes. "I'd sooner sleep with you," she said at last.

When he didn't respond, she took a small step forward, the soft swell of her breasts pressing against his chest. "And don't give me that *Ormney don't do sex with humans* line," she told him, her voice low and fierce. "I'm not buying that crap anymore."

He held himself very still. She was angry and didn't realize how her taunts sent fire roiling through his body. How her aggressive stance only made him want her more. She had learned some piece of the truth behind the horrible deaths he'd asked her to investigate and she was testing him.

"I wasn't going to say that." He reached out to wrap his hands around her arms, carefully pressing against her soft skin while keeping his claws as retracted as possible. Her breathing quickened and her fist clenched compulsively. The smooth tracery of her scars beneath the pads of his fingers mad him want to shake her and make her promise never again to take such risks with her life. Gently, he forced her back, putting space between them. "I was going to tell you I've arranged for you to meet with the men who found Fresna's body before they begin their shift at the dock. It might be best if we leave now."

Lily studied him in silence for several heartbeats, her breathing still fast, then bobbed her chin in agreement and started to pull away.

He tightened his hands on her arms and her gaze snapped back to his. She was nothing like the sweet, simple mate he'd once valued so highly, but everything about her called to him. Her words and actions had shaken his control of the mating instinct. He needed to warn her away.

"You should know... my mate didn't survive The Crossing.

I haven't shared the pleasure of mating with a female since that time."

He released her arms in favor of wrapping a hand carefully around her throat. She trembled at his touch and her pulse beat a rapid tattoo beneath his hand, but she didn't struggle. He bent down to put his face very near hers, letting her breath brush his lips and her scent fill his lungs.

"Do not offer sex again, unless you mean it."

CHAPTER 22

He stood at a flower cart near the North entrance of The Zone—the place where his mother had sinned. He selected an elegant bunch of purest white calla lilies, while keeping one eye on the steady stream of Ormney animals pouring through The Zone gate. He humphed under his breath. Some predators the bastards were. They couldn't even smell his hate for them. His absolute loathing. The flower stems squished in the crushing grip of his gloved fist. Fuck.

A quick glance told him the vendor was busy with a dorky suit type buying roses for his wife. Plenty of time to slide the ruined flowers back into the cart's holder and select another bunch for Lily. Content to study the faces of the filthy beasts walking past, he waited. When the vendor finally got to him, he paid using a *borrowed* com link. He had to work at keeping a smirk from slipping across his face. The owner didn't need it anymore.

The vendor put the flowers carefully into a silver box then passed him the e-card. With an easy smile, he thanked the man and stepped over to a bench and sat, watching the steady flow of foot traffic as he considered what message to enter. His gaze caught on the animal he'd been waiting for. Slipping the e-card in his pocket for now, he rose and headed down the street, stepping into the wake of the big ugly male. If he had any luck he'd find where the animal had stashed the little slut he was fucking.

And somewhere along the way he'd find a private locate-

and-deliver drop for his lilies. Remembering how tired his own special Lily had looked this morning, he pulled out the e-card and tapped in the perfect message.

Don't lose sleep over the lost girls. They made their beds and they deserve to die in them.

CHAPTER 23

Kuna and Shev, the two men who'd found the earliest known victims, were waiting at the diner where Jolaj had arranged to meet them. One tall but slim, the other stocky with noticeably large ears, both wore identical grimaces. After quick and painfully polite introductions they went inside. The diner was low tech but clean and smelled of real bacon. Her stomach rumbled, drawing the notice of all three Ormney.

Lily slid into the booth seat opposite the dock workers, taking slow, careful breaths. Despite her earlier show of bravado, their big clawed hands, resting on the table, still had the power to flash her back to panic mode. Jolaj slid in beside her and the press of him against her shoulder and thigh ignited a completely different sort of panic, distracting her when she should have been concentrating on the men she was there to interview.

Twenty years. Jolaj's mate had died twenty years ago.

Lily had tossed out the line about sleeping with him out of anger. Anger that he'd thought she'd sleep with Bradley. That he hadn't told her Jennifer and Lanyak had been lovers. That she found herself attracted to a man who had seemed completely unreachable.

The server, a middle-aged man with a round face and a ready smile, poured steaming coffee into their mugs then went back to restocking supplies at the other side of the near-empty diner.

Lily focused her attention on the men seated across from her. "What can you tell me about..."

"Fresna," Jolaj supplied.

The one called Kuna, the stockier of the two, cleared his throat then met Lily's gaze. "Fresna worked with us at the docks."

The other man, Shev, tapped his claw tips against the scarred table top, sending a shiver across Lily's skin. She wouldn't let the panic out today, she promised herself. Shev repeated the little staccato tap. "We ought to be getting to work ourselves. Shift starts soon."

Lily kept her focus on Kuna, who seemed more willing to talk and had, god bless him, moved his hands beneath the table. "How long had you known Fresna?"

"I knew him from when we all got jobs at the port about fifteen years back."

Lily took a sip of coffee then slid her hands around the warm mug. "Did he have a beef with anybody? Anybody who'd want to hurt him or cause him trouble?"

"No." Kuna's voice didn't falter and he didn't fidget or give any sign he might be lying.

Lily did see him glance at his coffee, but his hands remained out of sight. "What happened the day you found Fresna dead?"

Kuna looked down as he began his answer. "It was a normal work day to start out. We, ah…" He peeked up at her. "We didn't notice he was missing till end of shift."

There was some regret there, Lily thought, but still no deception.

"We usually walk together," he continued. "Back to The Zone, but he never came in from the yard. Never came to scan off shift. So we asked around as everybody was leaving. Couple of guys said they'd seen him headed to the long-term container storage lot earlier in the day."

"We went out looking for him," Shev added. "Thought he could have fallen or gotten hurt."

Kuna nodded. "When we got to the lot I scented him and followed that to the container. Knew he was dead inside. It was locked from the outside. When we opened it we saw him and Doc both dead."

"Doc?"

"The woman," said Kuna.

The woman they'd had a nickname for... and still thrown her dead body in the river. "Could you tell how they'd died?"

"Doc, she was broken," said Kuna.

"Her neck, for sure," Shev said.

The uncomfortable twist of dread tightened in Lily's stomach. Jolaj chose that moment to shift in his seat, pressing his thigh more firmly against hers. "Any other visible damage?"

Kuna hesitated, eyes unfocused as if remembering. "Some gashes across her face and arms."

Lily took another sip of her coffee. "That's all? Just her face and arms?"

"That's all," he said.

"The others were all eviscerated," she explained.

"The broken neck may be the reason," said Jolaj. "If he was drugged and acting blindly, instinctively, he might well have broken off the attack when she stopped fighting."

Or she might have been dead before he arrived. A dead body would have drawn him into the container.

"Fresna had done a job on himself," said Kuna. "He was covered in gashes and torn up real bad."

Shev shivered. "The inside of the container, there was blood everywhere."

Jolaj made a noncommittal noise. "If she died quickly and most of the blood was his, it's possible that he threw himself against the container trying to escape."

But of course, they would never know, because the two men in front of them had covered it all up. Lily fought to suppress her anger. "Did you scent anyone else?"

"No one in the container," said Kuna. "Some of the other crew, the supervisor for that area, all in the yard around it. Those were all pretty old scent trails."

"I scented the woman outside too. And another human." Shev had cupped his mug with his hands and that seemed to have stopped the claw tapping. He took a sip of coffee before continuing. "Male I think. But I didn't recognize him."

A human male—Lily filed that bit of info away for later consideration. "The woman? You called her Doc. You recognized her?"

Both men nodded.

"Who was she?"

When the both kept silent, Jolaj leaned forward. Putting her hand on his thigh, Lily stopped whatever intimidation he intended. Beneath her palm his thigh turned to stone. A muscle in his cheek twitched.

Kuna and Shev watched them like gawkers at a hov-board exhibition, waiting for a spill.

Lily withdrew her hand and focused her attention on Kuna. She smiled. "How do you take your coffee?"

His big eyes, blinked once, twice, a third time. "Two sweeteners." His confusion made it sound like a question.

The sweeteners came in little packets in a holder at her end of the table. She plucked two from the stack and tore them open. She turned them over, letting the thin slivers of sweetener tip into his mug. The melted instantly to disperse through the warm liquid.

Lily leaned back against the seat. All three men stared at her openly. She dipped her chin at Kuna. "It's okay. Go ahead. I'm fine."

He pulled his hands from beneath the table in smooth, slow movements. His eyes never left her as he sipped.

As he set the mug back on the table Lily gave him another half smile. "Now, you were going to tell me about the woman."

Kuna nodded. "We only knew her as Doc. Doc Smith. I saw her a few times at the after-shift dives near the docks."

The woman pulled from the river had been DNA-identified as Ginger Simon. Doc Smith was obviously an alias, but why? "Any idea why she hung out there?"

Kuna darted a glance at Jolaj then shrugged. "Said she was doing some kind of medical research. Used to ask lots of questions."

So Doc was a nickname because Ginger had been playing doctor. According to her record, Ginger had been into petty crime. She might have been running a con. "What kind of questions?"

"She asked some of us for tissue samples, blood, stuff like that." Kuna frowned. "We all told her no, but she kept coming around. Said she just wanted to get to know us better."

Shev fidgeted with his mug, twisting on the table. "Some of the guys would talk to her."

Kuna's frown deepened. The faded brown stripes of his face followed the brackets around his mouth, failing to camouflage the expression. "Many from our generation lost their families in The Crossing. Sometimes they get lonely."

Mention of The Crossing made it impossible not to think of Jolaj. How lonely had he been? He should have found a new mate in twenty years. He would have to have loved his dead wife very much for his grief to keep him celibate so long.

Lily didn't think Shev and Kuna were holding anything back, but they were clearly nervous. "Anyone you can think of that might know more about her?"

Shev shook his head.

"No," said Kuna. "But she gave me a com code where I could contact her." He rattled off the code, then repeated it back when Lily used her com-lens to do a data search.

Lily slanted him a look. "You just happen to remember the code?"

"We don't carry com-units much. I learned to memorize."

The data search returned a dead end. She ran it again with the same results. The com address had been wiped from the data. Very curious.

Shev scooted free of the booth and stood at the end. "We must get to work now."

Lily curved her lips into a semblance of a smile. "Okay." She blew out a frustrated breath. "I appreciate your help."

Jolaj walked them to the door then came back and slid into the booth across from her, lifting an eyebrow.

"The record was removed from the public data."

Jolaj took advantage of the extra space, sitting in the middle and stretching his arms out, hands slide along the seat. "What does this mean?"

"I have no idea." The com code was the only lead they had. "A Metro search might turn something up, but I'd have to tell Sean where the information came from."

Lily only had to study his face to confirm that option was off the table for now. "There might be another way." She tagged her brother's com. She didn't like bringing him into it, but she could count on him to keep it just between them.

"Hi, sis. You should've called." Hurt hid under Brian's scolding and she hated that she'd worried him. She should have known one of the O'Learys would have told him.

"I'm fine, Bri. Truly. But I need your help. No questions,

okay?"

There was a pause and she could almost hear him thinking across the link. "Sure, as long as you swear we'll make time to talk soon."

"Swear," she said and made a mental note to call him when things settled down. He was her little brother. He shouldn't have to worry about her over every little thing, but he'd been the one to locate her in the med center after the accident with Kiq. She had given Deepwater instructions not to call her family unless she was dead and they'd complied. Brian had found her anyway and been furious.

Jolaj watched her conversation intently.

She mouthed the word "brother" before continuing. "I just need a data search."

Background voices drifted over his com. "Okay, send me what you have."

Lily sent the code and planned to ask him to tag her com when he turned up anything, but he didn't give her a chance.

"I've got it," he said. "No individual name, but it's linked to a midtown flat that's owned by The Corporate Leasing Company. Sending the address now."

"Thanks, Brian."

"Anytime. Gotta go. Love you," he said then closed the link without waiting for a reply.

"The address doesn't match what was in the victim's case file," she told Jolaj.

"Is that bad or good?"

"It might be our first solid clue to what's really going on."

"Good, then," he said.

"Maybe, yeah."

CHAPTER 24

The address tied to Doc Smith's com code was upscale. Nothing like the efficiency room deep in The Mixer, listed on Ginger Simon's case file. Lily was very aware of the barely concealed curiosity all around them as she and Jolaj entered the high-rise building located at one of the midtown transport hubs. It was a good location for getting anywhere in the city quickly. The area was largely residential with a few retail and service businesses to meet the needs of the people who lived there.

The treaty required the Ormney to live in an approved zone. Many worked among the human population, but their work was concentrated in specific areas. An Ormney in midtown stood out. If Fresna or any other Ormney visited Doc Smith there, someone would remember.

When they reached the level for Doc's flat, the hallway was empty. Probably most of the residents were inside working at their remote terminals.

The locks were high security. Lily crouched down to get a better look. "I'll have to go back to my place and get my kit to hack this."

When she looked up to Jolaj, she saw decision flash in his eyes and knew he would *slip* at any second.

"Wait!" She grabbed for his wrist and his skin tingled against her as she made contact. As she held him the tingle faded to be replaced by the hyperawareness of his claws that could lead to panic. She acknowledged it and decided not to let it rule her. Not today. Not this moment.

Lily kept her grip tight on his wrist. "It's too dangerous. You've never been inside before." He could *slip* to just inside the door. Odds were good the area would be clear. She'd seen Kiq do the same thing dozens of times, but she suddenly didn't want to rely on the odds when it came to his life.

He wrapped his free hand around hers and gently pulled it away then used his grip to draw her to her feet. She could feel the dangerous pressure of his claws pressing against her skin. They stood very close together.

He slipped his hand slowly free of hers, carefully brushing along the edges of hers with the soft pads of his fingers.

"Thank you for your concern, Agent Rowan. This is well within my abilities."

"But—"

"I'm able to make partial *syncs*. It allows me to determine the safety of the surroundings before I *slip* fully *in-sync*. I'll be able to avoid any obstacle."

News to her, but his posture was all confidence. He believed it was safe. She nodded.

He *slipped* toward *out-of-sync* and was gone. Seconds later the door clicked open and he urged her into the cool interior of Doc Smith's flat.

They'd entered into the main living area, Lily just steps inside with Jolaj at her back. An arch in the wall to the right led to another area. Privacy tinted glass took up the whole of the far wall. The décor was monochrome, very sleek, very modern. A pricey audio-visual display wall glowed softly, providing ambient lighting in subtly shifting hues. "A lot of square footage in a high rent district for a woman who hung out with dock workers and kept a low-rent apartment in The Mixer."

An incoming call blinked in the corner of Lily's com-lens. Rose's name flash across the display as she put it in focus. "Damn." Her sister hadn't spoken to her in years. Now she was calling?

Jolaj moved up to stand beside her. "Problem?"

"My sister." Until that moment, she'd completely forgotten the incident with Bradley. Shoved it to the back of her mind to make room for the dead who needed justice and the innocents probably already targeted by the killer. They were a hell of a lot more important than Bradley and Rose.

She blocked the com and went back to studying the room. She walked over to the sofa and lifted a throw pillow and squeezed it in her hands. A lavender additive drifted up from the compressed material.

Jolaj moved to the archway and glanced through then turned back to her.. "What are we looking for?"

"Anything that will tell us who *Doc* really was." Lily tossed the pillow back on the plump seat cushions. "It's been cleaned recently." She ran her finger tips over the surface of a café table positioned in front of the window. "How would a small time street criminal be connected to a place like this?"

Jolaj had propped a shoulder against the arch, choosing to watch her rather than moving on to the next room. "It would seem unlikely that such a character would live in this home. Perhaps you were given the wrong file. Another woman who died in the river at about the same time? Doc Smith's body might not even have been found."

"Possible, but I'm pretty sure Doc Smith is an alias. This place is scrubbed clean. No personal possessions. If someone had reported her missing, Metro would have tagged this address. Why isn't anyone looking for her?"

Jolaj shrugged. "I don't know."

They shared a long moment of silence as they studied each other more intently than they'd studied the elegant flat.

Lily pitched her voice low. "Were they lovers? Doc Smith and Fresna?" She was more uncomfortable with the subject than she cared to admit. It wasn't the general idea that bothered her. It was Jolaj. In the space of a few hours he'd gone from being an untouchable, Ormney quasi-priest figure, to someone who might want her. Someone she might want right back.

She'd never thought of Kiq that way and they'd worked very closely. She'd liked him. Cared for him. But she'd been his Training Agent. That made him off limits even if she had been attracted to him. She hadn't been. Not to Kiq.

But Jolaj? Oh, yeah. Undeniably.

Jolaj tipped his head in thought. "I honestly don't know if they were lovers. I didn't know him. It was Shev who told me what had happened."

"But Lanyak and Jennifer Richardson were lovers, and Oz and Mary?"

Jolaj held her gaze as he answered, "Yes."

Lily twisted the length of her hair around her hand and lifted it off her neck. The temperature in the room suddenly seemed too warm. "How common is this?"

Jolaj shifted his weight back to both feet and took a step toward her. "Not common at all. It is forbidden by decree of the Council."

Lily frowned. "Why?"

"Many reasons," he said. That decree didn't stop his gaze from drifting over her breasts, stoking the heat making her perspire.

Hastily, she knotted her hair at the base of her neck and dropped her arms. She let the vague answer go for the moment. "Well, if they were breaking the rules, that could point back to an Ormney behind the attacks."

"If the Council learned of this, they wouldn't deal with it in this manner."

"I wasn't thinking of the Council." Though Lily didn't have any reason to rule them out.

Jolaj's stare followed her as she went looking for a household interface and adjusted the thermostat. "Most of the individuals involved," he said, "have been very careful to keep their relationships a secret. I don't think there are many who know."

When Lily turned back to face him, Jolaj had drifted back under the arch. It only took a few strides to reach him. Just being close to him had the power to send her senses into overdrive. Not at all like the panic that had swamped her in the past. "But you knew about Lanyak and Oz. Do you know of others?"

"Yes." The single word dropped softly into the conversation, despite the weight it carried.

She matched his tone. "They'd fit the pattern, then. We need to warn them of the danger."

His pupils were wide again, almost round in the dim light. "I already have. They're being as careful as they can, but I can't keep the men away from their mates and they can't bring them into The Zone."

Mates? That seemed like a really weighty word. "Why just Ormney men? Aren't there any females who have human lovers?

Or were you generalizing?"

"*Slip* talent is often stronger in males than females. Many more females died in The Crossing, leaving many unmated males among us. We have not yet overcome the deficit."

Lily had to take a few steadying breaths. He answered her questions completely without feeling and she suspected that lack hid some very big, bad emotions that he'd prefer to keep hidden.

She wanted to lean into him. Press her palms against the heavy muscles of his chest. Foolish considering her personal experience and her tendency to panic at the least contact. "That first night, when you showed up in my apartment. This is the secret you wanted me to keep, isn't it?"

"Yes."

Lily nodded. She would keep his secret as long as it didn't put more lives in danger.

She moved to edge past him into the space beyond, but he turned sideways keeping them from brushing together.

Lily stalked through the two bedrooms feeling like a voyeur. One bedroom seemed to be a spare. No clothes in the storage. No sundries in the lav.

The main bedroom gleamed, spotlessly clean, but there were clothes neatly folded and hung in a well-organized walk-in dressing room. There were office clothes, evening gowns, a few casual things, and lab coats. This couldn't be Ginger Simon's. Lily was abruptly certain of it. The question was, had there been a mistake in identifying the file or had the identification been intentionally falsified?

In the corner of the room, an area had been set up with a data port for a professional grade com unit, but there was no unit connected to it. If a relative or someone who knew the woman had gone through the apartment after she went missing, why would they take a com unit and none of her personal effects? Or had they? Maybe they'd taken mementos that just weren't noticeable as missing and left the wardrobe?

"Lily," Jolaj called out from the living area. Lily followed the sound of his voice and stopped at his shoulder, facing the large media screen.

"I found a memory strip laying on the top of the screen edge."

He stood, watching faces play across the scene. Smiling

people played to the vid capture in a collection that seemed to catalogue the dead woman's family or friends.

"Freeze frame." Lily studied the average features of the woman on screen. "I've seen her before."

He complied then looked at her over his shoulder. "Do you know her?"

Her brain had been snagged by the image but the answer didn't immediately come. "I don't—damn. Yeah."

"The image from Ginger Simon's file?"

"No. She worked at the Deepwater med facility. I don't remember her name, but I remember her. She was one of the damn vampires, always running checks, always wanting blood."

"Deepwater." Jolaj's voice went even and emotionless again. Lily remembered him telling her he wanted her help because of her Deepwater contacts. He'd suspected the investigation might turn back to them.

It made perfect sense. The flat was owned by a corporation. Probably one of Deepwater's sister companies.

"Don't worry," she said. "I'll look into it. I told you I would."

He turned, bringing them face-to-face. "I fear I am putting you in even greater danger."

Lily wanted to wipe away the worry lines on his brow. Instead she shoved her hands in her pockets. "I'll be discreet."

He didn't seem satisfied, but he said nothing as she pocketed the memory strip and opened an audio only com line to Director Gardot at Deepwater.

Despite the fact that Lily would normally have to go through several admin levels to get to the director, Marjorie Gardot's voice snapped across the line. "Agent Rowan. Problem?"

"Yes, ma'am. Sorry to bother you, but based on your last guidance I didn't want to involve anyone else at the company without your authorization."

"I took your call, Rowan, spit it out."

"I'm standing in a midtown flat I believe to be a Deepwater duty-flat and I think its most recent occupant was one of my victims." Lily rattled off the address.

"And?" The director replied without hesitation, admission, or denial.

"And, I'd like to confirm these facts without involving

Metro." It was akin to a threat. It could get her fired, but she didn't think so.

"I can confirm the address is Deepwater owned." Gardot's voice was granite. "And I can confirm that the assigned Agent disappeared two weeks ago. We were unaware of the reason for her disappearance. We will *not* report her missing status to Metro. Is that understood?"

"Understood." Lily made a conscious effort not to clinch her jaw. "But I need to know who she was and what she was working on."

"Most recently, we'd been keeping her close, working as a research tech in our med lab. No covert or field assignment authorized."

Lily's brain spun. Nothing authorized. Director Gardot chose her words carefully. Nothing authorized didn't rule out something unauthorized.

Lily decided to push. "A name, Director."

"I can't give you a name at this time, Rowan. Find another thread to pull. This one isn't going anywhere. End com."

Lily slid a finger over the com-link tucked over her ear and met Jolaj's gaze. She'd left the line audible so he could hear the unfiltered conversation. Gardot would be pissed if she knew. That thought only amused her. She was less amused at Gardot's half helpful answers. "Deepwater suspects *Doc Smith* was doing unauthorized research. But research on what?"

Jolaj drifted closer. "According to Kuna and Shev, she was researching the Ormney."

"Yes, but what specifically and why? And does it even matter here. If it was her research that kicked things off, how do the others tie in?" Lily's shoulders slumped under the weight of too many answered questions.

Hands tucked behind his back, Jolaj crowded into her space. "If the person behind these attacks truly despises my people, just spending time with Fresna might have been enough to get her killed."

"Maybe." They had learned a lot, but had more questions than ever.

Together they walked back to the apartment's front door, but Lily's com signaled again before she could get the door open.

She laid her hand over his on the handle. "Hang on

another minute—com."

"Your sister again, Agent Rowan?" Concern flickered in his eyes despite his deadpan expression. She'd had to look up to see it. That close he towered over.

"Yeah, an alternate profile, but it's here." Even as she said it she used her com-lens to decline the call and block the new profile.

"Family is a valuable link to the continuation of your line."

"Yeah." She lifted her hand off of his. "Believe me, my line is doing plenty fine without me." She fought for nonchalance and failed.

They were face-to-face, bodies only inches apart. He eclipsed her view of everything but him. He wrapped one hand around her arm. "Lily…" There was no panic, no fear. She wanted to press into him. The fire banked in his eyes said he wanted that too.

"I'm fine." Lily found the strength to step back far enough so that he could open the door. "We need to poke around this building a little more, then I need to go back to my place. I can dig into Deepwater DataCore from there, run some probabilities, look for ties."

He'd dropped his hand when she'd moved back but his body angled toward her, leaning in, as if he wanted to fall."I'll accompany you."

She didn't need his help to do data mining. She should send him away, but she didn't want to. She liked his presence. His deep voice. The heat he made her feel.

Lily's com signaled again. "Damn it." She glanced toward the message and relaxed when she saw Sara's name instead of Rose's. She opened an audio channel, this time leaving it in privacy mode. Sara's voice came across the link.

"Lily, I am so going to kill you, slow and painful."

Lily laughed. "What did I do now?"

"I can't believe you didn't tell me about the lilies found on Mary Santini's body. You need to be careful, cuz."

Beside her, Jolaj growled low and angry. He shouldn't have been able to hear that.

"I'm being careful. I haven't been alone since then."

Sara let out a shrill of outrage. "You walked me home after the club last night then walked home alone in the middle of the freakin' night, Lil."

When Lily ventured a look at Jolaj, his eyes had narrowed and the rest of him had turned to stone. She suddenly wished she'd taken the call in another room. "Oh, right. I forgot about that. But I spent the night at the med facility surrounded by lots of people. Besides, all of the attacks have taken place during the day."

Sara groaned. "So far. You idiot. That doesn't mean the bad guy can't change his MO. What about today? Are you wandering around out there in the open? Making yourself a target?"

She gave Jolaj her best innocent grin. "No. I've had backup at my side all day."

"Your pistol doesn't count, Lil."

Lily forced her eyes closed and set a mental *la, la, la* playing in the back of her mind in an effort to block out the man standing beside her. "Not my weapon. A person. I haven't been alone, except to pee. I swear."

Sara made a humph noise. "I have that data you wanted on the toxin found in the Ormney's blood."

"Great. What've you got?" Her lids popped open and her gaze immediately went to Jolaj, hoping to find him brighter at this news. He wasn't. And she was stuck in his deep-sea eyes again.

"Not over the com link."

Lily wanted to pound her forehead against the door. Sara needed to give her something to appease the mighty beast. "My link is secure."

"Deepwater encryption, right?" Sara elongated some of the syllables, clearly calling attention to the subtext.

"Yeah." Lily huffed.

"So," said Sara, "maybe we should talk face to face. We have a lot to go over. We've finished up the autopsies on Mary Santini and Jennifer Richardson."

"Okay, I have a few things to finish up then I—" Jolaj changed the angle of his head and his lips parted as if he might speak. "I mean, we'll be over."

Sara didn't miss a thing. "We?"

"Yes. Now, anything else before I close this link?"

" Lil," said Sara. "I went over the autopsies with Sean a while ago. Before he left, he said our reports are sending him back to The Zone."

Jolaj heaved a sigh and leaned against the door. "Oz."

"But why would he be going after Oz? We ruled him out." Lily had been asking Jolaj, but Sara answered.

"If you're talking about the Ormney male without claws, there's something you should know."

"What is it, Sara?"

"The preliminary report was wrong."

The preliminary cause of death had been exsanguination. How could that be wrong? "I don't understand."

"I'm saying, the murder weapon wasn't what we expected."

Lily shook her head at Jolaj, still confused.

Jolaj frowned. "What she means is that the fatal injuries were not made by Ormney claws," he offered the news completely calm. No shock or even mild surprise.

"You knew?"

He nodded. "I suspected."

"Who are you talking to?" asked Sara across the com-link.

"Sara, we can talk more when I get there."

"Sure, but who—"

Lily closed the com link and glared at Jolaj. "You want to tell me how you knew it wasn't claws?"

"I didn't know. But no Ormney are missing. If the killer wasn't one of us, the weapon couldn't be claws."

Lily swore. "This is why you didn't point out Oz's lack of claws yesterday. You suspected it wouldn't eliminate him anyway."

He nodded. "I thought Metro would have this information sooner."

"Damn, damn, damn." Lily paced to the center of the room and faced him with a bit more space between them. "You can't keep holding out on me this way."

"I'm sorry, Lily." He followed her across the room and stopped a breath away. "I couldn't be sure of anything."

Lily held her ground. "What else aren't you telling me?"

His fist clenched and unclenched at his sides. He sighed, his spine sagged then hardened again so fast she almost missed it. "Many things."

CHAPTER 25

Jolaj wanted to tell Lily everything. The realization twisted him in knots. "We should speak to building security before we go."

Standing in a dead woman's home, he watched fire flash in Lily's cool green eyes.

"That's it? You as much as tell me you're holding information back, then say let's go talk to security?"

His regret and frustration bubbled up to fray his control. He fought to keep his hands off her. Standing so close to her while she spoke to her cousin had been a trial. Even now he could hear her breath move in and out of her lungs. His head was full of her sage and honey scent. "I will tell you what I can, when I can."

Her breathing hitched and her body trembled. An Earther wouldn't have heard that hitch. Wouldn't have seen the tremble. But he wasn't like them and that was the problem. Would he ever get past that damn fear of hers? Damn, he shouldn't want to. But he did. He needed her tremble from want.

He eased back to wait for her to recover, but she followed his step, pressing her breasts against his chest and tipping her head back to look into his face. "You asked for my help. People are dying, you damn arrogant jerk. If that doesn't mean any damn thing to you, why did you pull me into this?"

His hands came up, hovered inches from touching her. Her bravado tugged at his heart and pushed aside the edge of anger, leaving raw, tender lust. He needed to put his hands on her.

"You don't know how to do things the easy way, do you?"

"I'm not afraid of you." Her voice steadied as she spoke, as if the words gave her strength.

Despite his will, his hands skimmed down the arms of her heavy leather jacket, searching for some hint of the heat beneath. "Liar."

"Fuck you."

The words were spoken low and harsh between deep, heaving breaths. His head knew how she meant them, but his body longed for a more literal meaning.

He fit his hands to her waist and lifted her pulling her against him. She reached for his shoulders to steady herself, but she didn't fight him. Her body was tender, lighting fires across his torso, from chest to hip. Sliding a hand under her ass, he encouraged her legs to edge around him. The heat of her curves fitting to his body brought his need to a boil and he thought he might find release just from pressing against her. He lowered his head to rest his forehead against hers. "I would like nothing more."

Her trembling hands lifted from his shoulders and settled along his jaw, urging him to look at her. Her eyes met his then slipped down to his mouth. Her tongue darted out to spread moisture along her pink lips. He took a deep breath, enjoying the press of her soft breasts as his chest expanded, then exhaled. Her thighs tightened against his hips.

She wanted him.

Her hands had stopped trembling and her breathing was heavy but no longer panicked.

Slowly, giving her time to stop him, he dipped his head down to taste her lips. Soft and plumb, they tasted him back.

He wanted to take her, right there in the middle of a dead woman's home. Lust rode him hard. He pushed his tongue into her mouth. The wet heat surrounded him as he pressed his tongue along hers. He pulled her bottom closer, letting his hardness find the sensitive parting between her legs.

She moaned. Then pulled back leaving them both panting. Her hands slid down to his shoulders and squeezed his tight muscles. Her breath heated his skin just beneath his jaw line, making him want to purr for her.

"Please, Jo. Put me down." Her voice was soft and seductive, but the meaning of her words splashed cold water over the flames and called his reason to the fore.

He waited until she looked up to lock her gaze to his, then he carefully lowed her to the floor. As her toes touched the ground he watched for her reaction, regret, or worse—fear.

Lily stood silent and still for several seconds before trying to speak and when she did, nothing came out.

Jolaj wanted desperately to hear what she would say, but he couldn't force her to speak when she wasn't ready.

"We have work to do." He nodded to encourage her agreement.

She dipped her small chin then turned on her heel and strode to the door.

Jolaj followed her into the hall, watching her walk away. Knowing he should let her go and wondering if he could.

Together Jolaj and Lily took the elevator down to the security office. Her Deepwater ID got her access to the security vids. Fresna had been there. Walked in with the mysterious Doc Smith on several occasions, always staying for a couple of hours.

Lily glanced his way with the weight of understanding in her eyes. But Jolaj didn't see the same thing she saw on the vids. Or rather he focused on the difference between the two on vid and the couples he'd known. Lanyak and Oz had both been in love with the human women they'd broken Council decree to bed. Fresna hadn't been in love and neither had the woman. There was no sign of it in their body language. Even when they were alone in the elevator or the hallway. If Fresna had fucked the woman, it was all he'd done.

Security could filter the vids based on the flat number. Each time the flat security was keyed a record was logged. What they couldn't or wouldn't do was give them the woman's name. Just the lease holder and that led back to the Deepwater front corporation Jolaj and Lily already had. A little more checking showed that no other Ormney had visited the woman or the building in recent months. That made it simpler when they confronted the building's doormen.

There were two doorman stations, one on ground level and another on level six where the glide-rail ran through the building. They tried the ground floor station first. Lily asked the attendant to recall any Ormney visitors and flashed the vid-com display they'd downloaded from the flat's display wall. The first man remembered the woman with a little prompting, but didn't have a name. They had better luck on the sixth floor.

The attendant there recognized the woman immediately. He was a short, round man, buttoned into a solid gray uniform. His eyes were lively and his mind seemed sharp. "That's Doctor Rawls. Simone Rawls. Nice lady."

Lily turned off the vid and thanked the man. Jolaj followed her to the glide-rail platform to wait for the next train.

"Simone." Lily rolled her shoulders then looked at him. "Not far from Simon. Ginger Simon."

He hated that he'd added to the pressures that plagued his little fighter. "The woman whose remains were pulled out of the river?"

"Yeah. That's the identity that popped for the DNA." She rubbed the back of her neck, still rolling one shoulder. "It could be an alias, but why does a research tech need an undercover flop and ID?"

Jolaj didn't know enough about Deepwater to help, so he remained silent and let her work through her thoughts.

"Doctor Rawls." Lily spoke, eyes unfocused. "A company med tech who hangs out at the docks. Known there as Doc Smith. Maybe floats another identity as Ginger Simon. Ginger Simon. Simone Rawls."

Jolaj watched her talk it through, fascinated until she turned icy pale. Worried he moved closer.

Her eyes flicked as they sometimes did when she was using her com-lens. "Damn me. Doctor Simone Rawls." She looked up to meet his gaze. "Doctor Simone Rawls texted me the day Lanyak attacked Jennifer Richardson." She sucked in a breath and exhaled, her body shuddering, but she didn't look away. "Two weeks after she died."

It didn't make sense, but their com's were capable of many things he had no interest in. Perhaps it was a prerecorded message. "What did her text say?"

The grin that graced her lips was anything but happy. "She changed my damn evaluation appointment. Ensured I'd be going toward the glide-rail station at exactly the right time to hear Jennifer Richardson scream."

CHAPTER 26

Lily had been in the killer's sights from the beginning. Or at least from the time of Lanyak's attack. That thought created a coil of fear deep in Jolaj's gut.

Had he played into a killer's hand by dragging her deeper into this horror?

The glide-rail pulled to a stop at the platform and together they stepped into the train. The small car overflowed with people. They'd hit midday rush. Standing room only. Charged by his instinct to protect her, his fear became an electromagnet drawing him closer to her side. The crowd gave him a good excuse to press his body to hers as she held on to a center pole. Their hands rested inches apart on the cool metal. An unnatural silence cocooned them amidst the mass of people until Lily startled and opened her link to answer the call coming in on the com-link over her ear. She engaged privacy mode but he had no trouble hearing and from the look she gave him she'd expected that.

"We just got a report of an Ormney attack in progress." Detective O'Leary's voice sounded breathless and rushed. "I'm on my way there now. Sending you the locate data, if you want to swing by. Closing com."

Lily over her shoulder to him. "It's at the South Regional med center, fifteenth floor, research and development unit. This line will get us there in fifteen to twenty."

He shook his head. "Too long. In progress. He said in

progress. I might be able to stop it."

He didn't want to leave her alone. Not after what they'd just learned. He couldn't let any more of his people die either.

He wrapped his palm carefully around her jaw and lifted her chin. "I have to go."

"I'll meet you there," she said.

"*He* could be there," he warned. "He could be watching. To see what he's set in motion." He waited as she took his meaning and accepted his assessment. "When you come into the building be on guard. Be ready for anything."

"I'll be careful." She clutched a fistful of his tunic. "You too."

He nodded, lowering his hand. He saw the worry in her eyes as he began to *slip*. She would know *slipping* from a moving glide-rail to the fifteenth floor of a building, blocks away, could be deadly. She rarely showed her emotions around others, but just then they were as luminous as clouds lit by a crack of lightning in a night sky.

They lingered, clear as purpose, even as the world around him slid out of focus. There was a moment of feeling torn apart before he *slipped* toward *out-of-sync* and his surroundings fell away completely. Then he could no longer feel his body. There was nothing, no light, no warmth, no air. Only the familiar tug of Earth's gravity, could reach him in the space between. It comforted and steadied him as he concentrated on the time, the pattern, the destination. No longer did he have to face the terror of pushing past the tug of safety, slipping endlessly through the deep dark in search of something, anything.

Time ticked through his thoughts and slowly, carefully he *slipped* toward Earth's pull. Adjusted. Studied the eddies and currents created by the denser matter of roadways and buildings. As he neared *sync* the tearing collision of walls and floors battered against him until he snapped to a halt, *slipping* to *in-sync* in the med center hallway. A crowd of metro and security formed a solid wall of men a short distance away.

He pushed into a run, *slipping*, as a startled security officer turned to face him. The brief *slip* carried him past the men and planted him directly in front of a wide-eyed Kabel. He knew the man. Knew him as a man of quiet strength and reason.

"No one is dying today, friend."

Kabel roared and charged toward him. He took Kabel's weight center mass, latched on, and took him into a roll.

Lily watched Jolaj *slip*. There one minute. Gone the next. She keyed in her com with a priority link to Sean.

"O'Leary." The short, sharp bark probably meant he hadn't taken the time to see who was on the line.

"Law Keeper Jolaj is en route to the scene."

"Lily?"

"Yeah. Let your men know, Sean. We don't want him dropped accidentally." He wouldn't hear her fear in her voice. She had it under control.

"Right," he said. "More?"

"No. Be safe."

"Close link."

The line went silent, leaving Lily out of touch. Out of the action. Alone. It didn't sit well.

Outside, the superscrapers of midtown gleamed in the afternoon sun as the glide-train rocketed past. There were three stations between her and the med center. No freaking way did she intend to twiddle her thumbs and wait for the train to load and unload for each of those stops.

She used her com link to order up a premium, piloted jet-hop to meet her at the next station. When the train glided to a stop, she pushed her way through the crowds. She ignored the long bank of elevators directly across the platform and jogged over to a side door that led to a wide glassed-in staircase and an access to the exterior emergency glide-poles.

She could see her jet-hop waiting at the taxi stand one level down. She took the stairs at a fast clip and picked up speed as she ran the length of the stand. The driver stood next to the open door of the vehicle. She motioned him to get in and dove for the opening as he fired the engine.

He'd already punched vertical when he spoke without turning his attention away from the readouts and controls.

"We're in a hurry, Madame?"

"A big one. I need fifteenth floor of the South Regional Med Facility, five minutes ago."

The hopper was tip-top. She barely felt the change when he leveled off and shot them in the right direction. "Taxi stands are at ground level, fifth floor, and top of the building, Madame. I believe the roof puts you—"

"I said fifteenth."

"But—"

"Just find me an emergency access, I'll manage."

"That is against safety—" He cut his standard safety warning short when he caught sight of her. She'd donned her best bad-ass agent face. "Yes, Madame."

He got her there in under three minutes and managed to sidle up to a likely emergency access. He went eggshell white when she threw open her door, wrapped her hand around the exterior emergency grip and leaned out to the access panel. Fourteen stories of empty space loomed between her and the street below. She suspected he was thanking God that he'd gotten her account details in advance.

"Hold her steady." She had to shout over the noise of the hop's engine.

It took a stretch, but she managed to touch the panel's exterior override. The panel slid open providing a narrow entrance, but plenty of vertical space. She turned to the driver. "Tag my account for double. You did good."

He gave her a shaky smile, but kept his eyes on the controls.

She positioned herself in the hopper's hatch, then pushed off, jumping for the entry. When her boot heels connected with solid flooring, she pushed into a run. She could hear the commotion so she followed her ears.

A crowd of uniforms—Metro, security, and medical—ringed a square of space at the juncture of two corridors. Most of the medics pressed against the walls or hunched over the injured. Security looked on, ready, alert, and clearly irritated that the Metro cops had pushed ahead of them.

Sean was there and his men formed a protective ring to keep the others out. A tumble of chairs and tables littered what had probably been a waiting area, now devastated by the two Ormney males rolling on the floor, locked in combat.

There was blood. Her gut twisted at the sight of it smeared on the floor. Jolaj pinned the man tight, arms keeping the man's back pressed to Jolaj's chest. The position kept him mostly clear from the wild man's claws and teeth. But it couldn't have been that way from the beginning. The blood made that much clear.

Jolaj held his opponent steady. Probably trying to tire him out as the man tried to shake Jolaj off. The drugged Ormney flailed as he made a sound, half growl, half keening wail.

The pinned man jerked and spasmed then threw his weight to the side. The two men crashed into a chair. The back of Jolaj's tunic had soaked through with blood. A human would have been stripped of flesh, but the Ormney had thicker skin to go with their lethal claws. Still the sight kicked her breathing up above where it should have been.

She had to help him. But how?

Jolaj forced them into another roll, ending back as they'd been before, with Jolaj on his back and the other man squirming like an overturned bug. She had to help them before one of the men ended up dead.

Lily pushed her way around to the first tech she could find and fisted her hands in his scrubs. "We need something to knock him out."

The startled man squealed. "Hey!"

Lily pulled him off the wall and shoved him toward the nurses' station. "Now."

He started jogging down the hall and Lily followed.

The man stopped at the locked pharmacy cart. His hands shook as he punched in a code. "We can't do this. We don't know what he's already on." His voice turned pleading. "We could kill him."

Damn! He was right, but a part of her didn't care. The part that needed Jolaj to be safe. "Restraints, then."

The tech gulped air and held his hands out in a surrender gesture. "Okay, but nobody can get close enough and—"

"Just do it!" Lily shoved him toward the nurses' desk. They had to have an emergency stash of that sort of thing. She'd worry about how to get close when she got there.

The moment he pulled out the bundle of safety restraints, Lily sprinted back to the waiting area. She shoved past Security then Metro to work her way around behind the two men on the floor. The wild one had worked a leg free and was thrashing again.

She unwrapped the restraints. Soft and wide, but sturdy. Still unsure exactly what she was going to do, she edged closer.

Jolaj growled. Not for his opponent. For her. His way of

telling her to back off.

Like hell. He had the man's arms pinned, but that meant he couldn't get an arm around his neck. Lily held a length of the restraint out where he could see it. "If we're careful we can restrict his airway without killing him." She hoped she sounded confident.

Jolaj nodded then spoke soft and calm into the man's ear. "Steady now. Control. You're stronger than the drug. I've got you. We're going to sit now. Stay calm." A constant litany of reassurance.

Jolaj worked the man into a seated position but he would have to pull his upper torso away at least enough for her to get the restraint over the man's head. Jolaj would have to trust her to get it done right. And fast.

She worked her way closer, watching the wild man's claws. She had to take a couple of deep breaths to chase away the blackness that hovered just out of her vision. When she looked up to Jolaj, he was watching her, waiting calmly as if he had all day. Wildman, as she was coming to think of him, let out a mighty roar and jerked all three of them to the side. Jolaj moved him back into position then nodded and she moved around behind them. Jolaj leaned his head away as she slipped the wide bandage like material around the man's neck. She checked the placement then slid to the ground, letting her ass hit the floor and her boots find purchase against the struggling males. She reared back with all her strength and held the pressure steady.

A woman screamed. Lily craned her neck to see a woman wearing the silver of the technology exchange program being held back by med center security. Horror and fear played across her face in turns. She matched the security techs for height, tall for a woman. Leanly, athletic build. Cinnamon brown hair neatly tucked into a bun.

Lily hoped security would hold the woman clear. She hoped her strength would hold. Time dragged. Her muscles burned.

With dozens of eyes on her, the sensation of being watched was skin crawling. *He would be there.* That's what Jolaj had said. She scanned the crowd. Bradley stood directly across the space from Lily. She didn't see anyone else acting out of step for the situation. Among the faces, she recognized Timothy Perry and one of the nurses she'd met during her brief visit to the center.

Both tending to the injured.

If the killer was there he wasn't letting his interest show.

It took twice as long as it would for a human, but eventually the Ormney's limbs went limp and his body turned to dead weight.

She released the restraint and crab-walked away from him. "Medic! We need a medic here."

Everyone seemed frozen. Hushed.

"I said medic. Now!"

The circle of blue, white, and silver surged forward, lapping over Metro and Security like a wave spilling over a sea wall.

Lily put her feet under her and managed a crouch as she helped Jolaj get the man off of him. She found Sean at her shoulder. Caught and held his gaze. "He's a victim."

Sean nodded without hesitation. "We've got civilians down here though. We need him restrained before he comes to."

She let hands pull him away from her, freeing her to move to Jolaj. She clutched her fists in his tunic and pulled his face toward her. "You were supposed to be careful."

He was moving too damn slow for her liking. "The woman," he ground out.

Lily twisted to locate the woman in silver. She hunched over the Ormney male, checking his wounds. Lily reached out for Sean's arm. His attention snapped back to her. "That woman in silver, she needs to stay with the Ormney. They worked together." It was a guess She hoped it wouldn't bite her later. "She might be able to help keep him calm if he comes around. She needs to stay close and you need to put a protection team in place."

Sean's eyes flashed. "Telling me how to do my job?"

She was just happy everyone was alive this time around. She couldn't hold back a grin. "Only a suggestion...Detective, Sir." She gave him a mock salute then turned back to Jolaj. Behind her, she heard Sean assign several of his men to protection and ask the woman to stay close.

She helped Jolaj stand then stepped around behind him and tugged at his tunic. "Damn. Medic. I need a medic here!"

"Lily? Are you hurt?" Timothy Perry appeared at her side.

"Not me. The Law Keeper. The big dumb jerk, here. We need to stop this bleeding."

Timothy held up a tube of liquid healant. "This will

staunch it until we can do a thorough exam. Help me get his shirt up."

Lily edged in front of Jolaj and tugged at his tunic, sliding her hands up his torso. He lifted his arms and together they got the material over his head.

She pulled his long auburn braid forward and out of the way, then used the shredded tunic to hold pressure against a gash on his left shoulder. He breathed evenly, a steady rise and fall of his chest while Timothy sprayed the healant across his back. No sign of pain or discomfort. She looked up to find his gaze making a slow, relentless scan of the room. Like a panther with his catlike eyes watching, observing, waiting for his prey to make a telling move.

When Timothy worked his way around to Jolaj's shoulder she left him to it, then crouched down to gage the seriousness of the wounds on Jolaj's thighs. Not as much blood there. His hand settled and tightened on her shoulder. She looked up the line of his body.

He grimaced as he met her eyes. "I'm fine. See to the woman."

"But—"

"Not now, Agent. See to the woman. Help Sean." His voice lowered and his eyes pleaded with her. "Step away from me. Please."

She realized then how her position would look. At his feet. Her hands wrapped around his thighs. *He could be watching*, he'd warned. The one responsible for all this could be watching.

All around her, people were in motion. Working. Not paying any attention to them. But somewhere in the room, one pair of eyes might be fixed on them.

She moved her hands, slipping them up his thighs to settle at his hip bones. That left her face even with a part of his anatomy that was perfectly happy with her position, despite his injuries. She pushed to her feet, keeping her body close. Slipping her hands up the sleek muscles of his chest. "Let the bastard come."

He watched Lily Rowan put her hands all over the filthy animal and his blood boiled. He'd brought her into this. Made her what she was. Bitch. Had the animal made her his whore?

He'd wanted his hands on her. Wanted to stroke her.

Reward her for her role in his little public service activities. Now he'd have to use his hands to punish her. Bring her pain. Make her realize her humiliation.

Not only did she touch the animal. The Law Keeper. She'd helped him save the other animal. She should have pressed her pulse pistol to both their foul *stringer* heads.

He'd heard her words to her cousin. She'd as much as told him to protect the animal and his little silver-suited slut. Protective custody. Well, that road block left his evening free.

Free to punish Lily Rowan for her betrayal.

CHAPTER 27

"Hey, babe." Bradley's casual endearment grated across her nerves. She was close enough to Jolaj to feel the rumble stifled in his chest. No, Jolaj did not like the Ormney Affairs Liaison.

Lily faced Bradley. "Why are you here?"

He frowned, looking her up and down. "Damage control. Third day in a row. All holy hell is going to break out when it gets out and it will. You okay?"

Lily slipped an arm around Jolaj, ostensibly to help him support his weight, but he wouldn't lean on her. Wouldn't shove her away either. Lily used that ruthlessly to drag out her play to rile the bad guy. "I'm fine. Jolaj is the injured one."

"Quite the hero. I need to ask for your help, Law Keeper."

There was something cruel under the slick polish in Bradley's voice. The kind of double speak Lily had come to associate with corrupt officials around the world. As angry as she'd been with him through the years, she'd never before doubted his belief in his work and doubting him in this, now, undermined another small wedge of the solid ground she'd been left to stand on. Lily let her newly heated anger show. "Jolaj needs medical attention."

"I'm all right, Agent Rowan. I'll do what I can to help."

"You need to be patched up," she insisted.

"Actually," Bradley said, "the injuries could work to our advantage. Media's on the way. We're going to make a statement before the security vids leak to the press. If you're okay to stand on your own, the injuries will look good on camera. The heroic Law Keeper, willing to put himself in danger to keep the rest of us out of harm's way."

Bradley turned to Timothy Perry who'd just finished applying healant to Jolaj's shoulder. "Will he be okay for twenty minutes?"

"Sure." Timothy's answer was sharp and short. "The bleeding's stopped. The damage is mostly superficial."

Bradley focused on Jolaj, hands buried in his pockets. A gesture Lily knew meant he was uncomfortable with the situation, she just didn't know why.

"We need to put a trustworthy Ormney face on this incident," said Bradley. "Standing side-by-side with Sean. Law Keeper and Metro working together to address the problem."

"We need to keep everyone together," said Lily. "Law Keeper Jolaj will want to keep an eye on the Ormney victim."

Sean walked up. "He's secure and with the medical team. I've put two men on the door. I don't much like talking to press either, but Bradley's right. We need to keep the public calm."

"I'll do what I can." Jolaj shrugged his massive shoulders, drawing her notice to the broad expanse of bare, muscled chest and to the fist-sized tattoo over his heart. A tattoo identical to the one she'd seen on Lanyak's autopsy hologram.

"We need to find you a shirt."

"No," said Bradley. "We need him in the uniform and the blood can only help."

The degree of callous calculation behind his words disgusted her, but she knew what he suggested was the best thing under the circumstances.

Lily acknowledged Timothy's help with a simple thank you. He nodded and turned away, looking annoyed at the implied dismissal. She would have to try to soothe that over later. Timothy had been nothing but helpful.

"We're setting up in the lobby." With a hitch of his head, Bradley indicated the direction. "I'll wait for you at the elevator banks down the hall."

Lily waited as Jolaj pulled the blood stained tunic over his head. The stretch and play of muscle tempted her to touch and stroke, but the blood served to douse that need. When Jolaj had the tunic on they all headed down the hall together. She let Jolaj put a little distance between them, since he hadn't tried to exclude her completely. He seemed to want her close, if not as close as she'd been playing it.

Lily watched him walk, his movement stiff. He needed a better exam. There could be internal injuries. And she was being stupidly protective, when moments earlier, she'd made them both a target.

She was torn in two by the knowledge that she wasn't only putting herself on the line. Ten minutes earlier she'd been concerned that he was putting himself at risk and now she'd put him there herself.

Lily hung back out of the circus as the press briefing got started. It had been set up in the hospital's sixth floor lobby. Sean was doing his best to protect the crime scene and slow down the hackers that would be looking for internal security vid showing the incident.

The army of reporters fanned out in a colorful array facing the microphone where Sean, Bradley, and Jolaj stood ready to take questions. After Bradley made a short statement, the press took turns shouting questions. They started simple and safe, but all it took was one difficult question and they all started in, like sharks scenting blood in the water. "Law Keeper, how were you able to subdue the attacker?" The reporter's tone relayed suspicion even as he smiled, showing shiny white teeth.

Jolaj spoke calmly and clearly. "The man was a med tech working in the technology exchange program. Not a trained fighter."

"Are there many trained Ormney fighters?"

"We're always told the Ormney are a peaceful race." Another reporter mocked. "Do you consider yourself a trained fighter?"

"I'm a Law Keeper. Trained to serve and to protect, much like the human Metro Law Enforcement Officers."

A short, pixyish woman shouted out the next question. "Why is it that what we seem to need protection from lately is you Ormney?"

"All Ormney are saddened by these incidents."

Bradley stepped forward. "It's important to remember the

Ormney men involved are as much victims as the women who've been injured."

"Injured? Two women have been murdered, Liaison Rubiero. Are you discounting those who've lost their lives?"

Bradley took on a grave, funeral parlor expression. "An Ormney life has also been lost and another Ormney citizen has been hospitalized as a result of today's incident."

"Was the Ormney involved today drugged, like the one who attacked a woman in The Mixer two days ago?"

Sean leaned over to the microphone. "The details of today's incident are being investigated as we speak. We can't say more until we have all the facts."

Lily's com signaled. Her mother's name glowed on the display. Leaving the crowded area behind, she found a room down the hall, stepped inside. She tapped her com-link. "Mom? Is everything okay?"

She couldn't remember the last time she'd heard from her mother.

"Your sister is hysterical. Heartbroken." Her mother's voice hadn't changed. With a little more thought she remembered that her mother had been scolding her then too. "She says you're having an affair with her husband. Lily, tell me this isn't true."

"Of course it isn't," she said automatically.

"Then how is it, she called him and caught the two of you in bed together?"

Lily didn't need to see her mother's face to know her jaw was clenched tight. Her elegantly arched eyebrows would be drawn together and her eyes would be flashing with that how-can-you-do-this-to-me look.

"We weren't in bed together. We're working together, that's all."

Carts and boxes of supplies littered the room around Lily. She paced her way around the obstacles and her mother lectured. "Lily, you can do better than that. Working together doesn't require you to spend the night together."

"Mom, have you seen the news lately? We have a crisis going on here. People are dying. No one is working regular hours on this." Lily kicked a rolling cart, sending it crashing into a stack of boxes. She hated having to cover Bradley's tracks. Having to make explanations when she'd done nothing wrong.

"You need to talk to your sister," said her mother. "She's devastated. She hasn't answered my calls since before breakfast."

"I've got a lot going on, but I'll try to get in touch with her."

"You do better than try. Rose and Bradley are working through some difficulties. This is not the time for you to be intentionally hurting your sister over things that should have been forgiven and forgotten long ago. Bradley is her husband now, Lily. That might not mean anything to you, but—"

Lily closed the com-link, leaned against a cart, and let her head fall forward. Marriage, family, it all meant more to Lily than her mother could guess.

It didn't surprise her when Jolaj walked into the room. She turned her head enough to watch him close the door and move closer. She'd known he'd come looking for her. Yeah, he'd left her on the glide-rail to try to save a life, but he'd hated doing it. That had been clear in his eyes.

He approached her slowly, cautious. He reached for her, like a fascinated boy reaching for a bird that might fly away. His hands settled on her shoulders, the heat of his big body a single step away. She took that step, fisted her hands in his tunic and pressed her forehead against his chest.

"Your mother didn't believe you?"

She tipped her head back to look up at him. "You heard that from the hall?"

He nodded and she studied his broad face.

"You believed I'd slept with Bradley too.

His nose scrunched then flared. "I smelled him in your bed. I wasn't thinking clearly in that moment." His hands squeezed gently. "You are an honorable woman. Your integrity is clear in everything you do."

She couldn't stop the grin that tugged across her face. "Thanks. You're a good man." He was a goddamned boy scout. Trying to take care of everyone, even her. But his loyalty to his people would always come first. It was part of who he was.

She pressed her cheek against his chest, closed her eyes, and slipped her arms around him. She clung to his strength and solidity for just a moment then stepped back. He let her step out of his arms without protest.

She straightened her spine, stretching a little, standing

straighter. "We should get you upstairs. You need med treatment."

She started to turn to the door but he stopped her. "You need to make Sean understand the danger you've opened yourself to. Tell him whatever he needs to know and let him watch out for you, Lily."

"I wouldn't break the confidences you've shared with me for the sake of my own safety. I can look after myself. But you're right. I'll have to give him what he needs to put an end to this before anyone else dies. I'll try not to drag out any details that won't help him."

The strain in his face didn't ease, but he didn't argue.

When they stepped out of the room, they found Sean waiting for them in the corridor. She tried to gauge Sean's reaction to seeing them together, but his cop face was in full effect.

Lily returned her own blank face. "The press conference?"

Sean tipped his head toward the press, now crowded a short way down the corridor where some of Sean's men were keeping them back. "Broke up a few minutes ago. Got a lot less interesting for them after the Law Keeper ducked out."

She eyed the crowd of reporters, a blockade between them and the elevators. "Is there another way off this level?"

"Staff elevators," said Sean. He waved a hand to indicate the direction.

She nodded and headed that way. Jolaj and Sean were at her side before she rounded the corner. "Where's Bradley?"

"He had to head downtown," answered Sean. "Some folks are calling for a full lock down. Keep the Ormney in The Zone until everything is resolved."

"Hell, I guess it was inevitable," said Lily.

Together she, Sean, and Jolaj stepped into the elevator and Sean called for the fifteenth floor. They all backed off against the walls and turned toward the center so they could talk.

Sean pinched the bridge of his nose. "We aren't getting this figured out fast enough."

"No," said Jolaj. "The situation grows worse every day."

They weren't going to get anywhere with a conversation the length of an elevator ride. "Brian told me he came down to help you and Uncle Patrick update the old war-room last summer."

"Yeah. All the latest," said Sean. "Your brother is gifted with the tech. Would have made a damn good e-cop."

"If Mom hadn't dragged us all to DC after Dad was killed."

"Yeah," said Sean. "You're thinking it's time to call a meet, get the whole team together and see where we are?"

Lily darted a glance at Jolaj then nodded. "Will your dad let us use the room?"

"Dad's in UT Metro." The elevator doors slid open and together they walked down the hall. "Got a call that Grampa Will was causing trouble in the retirement community again," Sean continued. "Dad and Junior went down and now he's joined Gramps in some damn crusade to break a hov-cart theft ring."

Lily made a face.

"Don't laugh. This is downright big time for Gramps these days. Last Christmas he dragged Dad out there for the great mistletoe caper. Anyway, I have all the pass codes and Mom won't mind." Sean's face had softened as he'd spoken of their family. "She'll insist on feeding you."

"I could eat." It was a simple thing. A meal with family, but it wasn't simple at all.

They left Sean at the lobby where the investigative unit was doing interviews and overseeing the evidence techs. Lily and Jolaj made their way to the corridor where the Ormney victim had been stashed. It was deep in the research and development wing. Silver uniforms everywhere, both races represented in almost equal measure. The technology exchange programs were the biggest areas of employment for Ormney outside The Zone.

Several uniformed Metro officers stood outside the secured room and across the corridor two Ormney techs stood their own watch. When Lily and Jolaj stepped inside all eyes turned to them. The drugged Ormney lay on a bed, restraints secured his limbs and torso to the frame. Two med techs, one human and one Ormney, studied the bio readouts. The silver-suited woman with the cinnamon hair stood nearby, arms wrapped around her middle, she rocked forward and back in a subtle movement. Subtle, but there. Another woman who'd become involved with an Ormney.

A silver-suited Ormney woman stood with her, six inches taller with a straight and proud posture. Her chocolate brown hair had been pulled back into a twist, emphasizing the broad, Ormney features of her face.

Two women, two species, wearing a single uniform. It clearly wasn't a problem for them, but had it driven someone to an anger hot enough to take lives? Or was this Deepwater meddling for some unknowable reason?

The room wasn't a private stay room. It was some part of the R&D program and had several beds. The human med tech led Jolaj to one of the empty beds and engaged a privacy screen. Lily turned to the two women standing together. "How's he doing?"

The Ormney woman answered, "We haven't been able to sedate him for fear of a drug interaction, but he's fighting the drugs. The restraints seem to be helping him focus."

The Ormney man in the bed pressed against the restraints, but more as if he were flexing and testing them, not truly trying to get free.

"Kabel is strong." The human woman's eyes stayed on the man that had to be her lover as she spoke.

Lily introduced herself as a Deepwater Agent, investigating on behalf of the Ormney Affairs Office. "It would help if we could talk. I have a few questions."

"I've already answered the Metro officer's questions. I can't leave him right now. You understand? You're also working with Father Jo, right?"

Lily nodded, surprised how much she disliked the nickname for Jolaj. She'd heard the kids in The Mixer use it, but now that she knew him it didn't fit. "I understand. But we can talk down the hall. We won't go far or be gone long."

The woman nodded, reluctantly. She glanced back at the restrained Ormney then at the woman who'd been standing with her.

"I'll stay here until you come back," said the Ormney woman.

Lily found an empty office a few doors down, the door in sight of the cops and Ormney standing in the hall.

"What will happen to him?" The woman wanted to know.

"I can't say. That's up to Metro. And their Council."

"I don't know what you could need to talk to me about. I told the officers, I didn't see anyone inject him with anything. If someone darted him, he didn't seem to have noticed. We were sitting together talking when he started acting strangely. Told me to get away from him." She wrapped her arms around herself and began to rock again. "I knew. I knew what was happening, but I didn't know what to do about it. I couldn't leave like he wanted me to."

"I understand and for what it's worth I think you did the right thing." It was the right thing to say. The woman stilled, straightened, and met her eyes. "The person who drugged him—"

"Kabel," the woman provided.

Lily flashed a quick smile. "If the person who drugged Kabel was there and you ran, he would probably have followed you. Whoever is behind this seems to want to hurt both the Ormney men and the women who associate with them."

The woman's eyes drifted away then returned. "Why? Why would anyone do this?"

Lily didn't have an answer. They had only the roughest of theories built on a foundation of unanswered questions.

"Who knew about your association with Kabel?"

"Everyone in the R&D department knows we work together. Anyone in the med center could have known."

"I'm talking about your personal association, not your professional one."

The woman studied her toes. "I'm sure most of our coworkers know we're close."

"Anyone seem to have a problem with that?"

The woman met Lily's eyes. "No. No one."

Frustration, frayed the limits of Lily's patience. Once again they had nothing. No suspects, no leads, no way to find the person behind the attacks before someone else ended up dead.

CHAPTER 28

Lily and the woman walked back down the hall together
and stepped into the room to find Kabel straining wildly against his
bonds. The woman visibly stopped herself from rushing to his side.
She stood just inside the door, breathing hard. "I'm here," she
whispered. "Be strong."

Kabel seemed to ease, instantly. His muscles remained
tense but he no longer thrashed against the restraints.

The privacy screen that had been engaged around Jolaj and
the med tech wavered and Sara stepped through. "Hi, cuz." She
smiled at Lily then came to stand in front of her. "He told me you
had come back into the room." Her eyes went wide. "He caught
your scent. That is so wowser."

Lily should have been thrilled to see Sara there. Her cousin
had a way of putting things in perspective, but the sight of her
coming through that screen had only ramped up Lily's tension.
"What are you doing here?"

Sara pulled a sample square from her pocket and waved it
in the air. "I wanted to do an analysis on the new victim's blood."
She put the little square back in her pocket. "And Sean wanted me
to give you a ride to Mom and Dad's place."

Lily tilted her head toward Kabel. "You do know he's the
one that was drugged?"

Sara's smile widened. "Sure. But I am an MD. I thought
I'd see if there was anything I could do for the Law Keeper while I

was here. Problem?"

Lily shook her head. "No. No problem."

Across the room, the privacy screen wavered again then
disappeared. Jolaj had changed into borrowed scrubs. His eyes
seemed to see straight into her soul. As if he knew it did indeed
bother her that Sara had been behind that privacy screen with him.

He thanked the med tech then stepped closer. "I must see
to Kabel's security. I would ask you to stay close to your family for
your own safety."

Lily nodded. "Sure. Ah. Maybe you can get a ride over to
Aunt Jane's with Sean later?" She hated feeling awkward about a
simple invitation. It made sense for them to all work together. The
war-room had always been family only, but for this, he should be
there.

"I'll come if I can." He trusted her to keep her promises.
He trusted her judgment about what to share with her family. It
was there in his, for once, open face.

The commotion in the hallway startled Lily and had Jolaj
slipping past her and Sara to stand between them and the door. They
all relaxed a little when Sean appeared in the opening with hands
out in front of him in a whoa-there gesture.

Sara was first to recover from the tension that had swept
the room. "Well that was totally iced." Sara looked to Lily, grinning
like an idiot. "I've never actually seen anyone *slip*."

Lily lifted her eyebrows. Sara had been living in the same
city with the Ormney for twenty years. How could she have never
seen one *slip*?

"What can I say?" Sara shrugged. "I spend most of my
time at the MEs office." Sara lowered her voice. "Does he do that
a lot?"

"Sorry to interrupt your moment, sis," said Sean, "but we
have a situation here." He focused on Jolaj. "The Council has
demanded we turn over Kabel. They say he can be better cared for
in The Zone." Every Ormney in the room seemed to bristle at the
statement, but Sean didn't give them time to respond. "There are
several Law Keepers in the hall and a jet hop waiting at the patient
exit." He turned to the med techs. "Can you get your patient ready
for transport?" He'd infused his words with enough command that
no one mistook the question for one that needed an answer.

The Ormney woman spoke softly to Kabel's lover. The

woman had gone two shades paler, draining her color to a near translucent white.

Jolaj turned to face Lily. "I will be unable to meet you at your uncle's home, but it would reassure me to know you'll be safe in their company."

His concern for her safety reminded her that Kabel's lover would no longer be safe either. With him being taken to The Zone, the others couldn't stay and protect her.

"Sara will want to swing by her lab first." She stepped to the side where she could clearly see Kabel's lover. "Maybe you could come with me and Sara. I'm sure we have more to talk about and I'm sure Sara would love to have another take on her tests. You work medical technology exchange, right?"

"Yes. That's right. I'm sure I could help."

With that settled, they quickly had Kabel ready to go. Secured to the huv-stretcher they took him out into the hall. Jolaj and Sean went first, speaking to the two uniformed Law Keepers, then the techs with the stretcher, followed by Kabel's lover and the Ormney woman. The police officers and tech personnel lingering in the hallway, watched in silence as they passed.

Lily and Sara followed behind, keeping pace with the procession, eerily like a funeral march. As they moved down the corridor toward the patient lifts the rhythm of the med center seemed to return to a more normal pattern. A mix of blue-and-white uniforms replaced the sea of cops and silver-suited exchange techs.

Lily let the rhythm wash over her, running through the unanswered questions in her own head until something tripped her instincts. Something off.

A blue-suited tech walked calmly down the hall toward them, passing the Law Keepers without a glance. He didn't glance at Sean or Jolaj. Unconcerned.

No, not unconcerned, she realized. Focused.

His eyes raked across Kabel, strapped to the stretcher. The man wore a white lab coat over his medical scrubs, his hands stuffed in his pockets. Lily pushed forward, shoving the woman walking in front of her out of the way. It startled everyone and created instant panic.

The blue-suited tech whipped his hand out, the laser scalpel gripped tightly in his fist flashed silently as he sliced through

Kabel's restraints then slipped his hand under the stretcher and lifted, tipping it over and dumping the drugged Ormney to the floor.

The man pushed into a sprint, attempting to barrel past Lily, but she snagged him and took him down to the floor. He ended up on top, trying to dig the scalpel into her. She fought and blocked to keep from getting cut up, but she registered the commotion filling the hallway as Kabel got to his feet, wild and confused.

Lily managed to smack the man's hand against the floor hard enough to render it useless. The scalpel fell free.

Over her head, Kabel swung a wide arc, connecting with the Ormney woman. The thud of the blow knocked her into the wall and her scream kept Kabel focused on her. He wrapped a clawed fist around her neck and threw his head back in a ferocious, shouting, growl.

Blood arced across the hallway.

Not the woman's blood.

Kabel fell to his knees as blood gushed from the wound in his neck. Soaking his life into his tunic. The Ormney med tech who'd been caring for him moments before, shoved his body aside, claws still dripping blood, and wrapped the Ormney woman in his arms.

Lily managed to shove her knee into the balls of the man still trying to reclaim the laser scalpel. He groaned and tried to pull back. Lily used the momentum to roll him over and land her knee in his groin again. His eyes rolled back in his head and he collapsed into a ball of anguish.

Sean was suddenly there, putting cuffs on the man. Lily got to her feet and took in the situation.

Sara was clear, standing well away. The only injured were the man Lily had subdued and the Ormney woman, being seen to by the male. Kabel was clearly gone—down in one blow—his human lover wailing over his lifeless body. Jolaj stood over them, grim and silent. There had been too many people between him and the commotion for him to do anything. The corridor too small for easy maneuvering, not even with one of his incredible *slips*. Lily knew this loss rocked him. He'd fought so hard. They'd both fought hard and thought they'd saved Kabel only to have the brief success snatched away.

"I had to stop him." The Ormney male turned to face Jolaj and the tableau of grief. "I had to protect my mate." His voice shook as he looked down at his blood-coated claws. "I had no choice."

The idiot in cuffs had taken the choice away, leaving them only grief and more death.

CHAPTER 29

Beneath Sara's jet-hop the midtown residential buildings stretched on for miles. Glistening with the silver of reflective glass, they twisted upward.

Her cousin cleared her throat with a noise clearly meant to drag Lily out of her thoughts. "Are you being all maudlin because the outcome is damn dreary, because you're bummed you won't get to pal around with the Law Keeper anymore, or are you just afraid of facing Mom?"

Lily considered the question carefully, but given the choices there was only one of the three she could safely discuss. "It doesn't sit right, Sara. Everyone is acting like this is over, but it doesn't feel over."

The man who'd cut away Kabel's restraints had turned out to be a member of *Earth For Earthers*, one of the extremist anti-Ormney groups. It made things fit neatly into the theory that the crimes had been committed to stir up trouble and make people afraid of the Ormney.

Sara sighed. "It won't be over until they find everyone involved, but the arrests will calm the public and likely curtail EFE from instigating any further attacks."

When Lily didn't respond, Sara went on. "Sean said Metro is already questioning the EFE members who lived in the buildings where Jen Richardson and Mary Santini lived."

"It doesn't feel right. So far, Metro hasn't found any sign

of the drug in the homes of any of the EFE members where they've searched." Lily shifted in her seat to watch Sara. "Tell me about the drug."

Sara glanced toward her then returned her attention to the sky and the heads up instruments display. "I have to agree, they need to figure out how EFE got the data on the drug. It was so close to the core formula on the Deepwater list, it had to be a direct derivative."

Lily told Sara briefly about Simone Rawls, leaving out the part about how the Ormney had found and disposed of her body. "She was doing unauthorized research. Director Gardot wouldn't tell me any more than that."

"Maybe Rawls was freelancing," said Sara. "Maybe she was EFE's source for the drug. She could have sold the info to them. That would explain a lot."

"Yeah." But it didn't explain how a dead woman had arranged to put Lily in the vicinity of one of the attacks or why. Lily couldn't rest easy until that was cleared up.

She'd wanted to continue the investigation but no way was Sean letting her in on the Metro interrogations. Kabel's death and the arrest of the EFE member had effectively eliminated the threat to Kabel's lover and the Ormney had taken his body back to The Zone. Jolaj had gone with them, but Lily suspected he was no more certain that the situation had been resolved than she was.

"Metro is doing a sweep of the EFE headquarters," said Sara. "Maybe they'll find the answers there."

Lily's stomach did a flip as they cleared midtown and Sara dipped the jet-hop down closer to the tops of the shorter buildings of The Fringe. A smile flashed across Sara's face and Lily breathed easier, knowing Sara would drop the grim topic for the moment.

"On to number two on our list." Her grin widened, lighting her face as she spoke. "The Law Keeper."

Lily's belly flipped again, but the jet-hop remained steady under Sara's hands. "What about him?"

"My amazing power of deductive reasoning tells me he's the person you were hanging with before this latest round of badness."

"And?"

"And he is a majorly iced exemplar of male hotness."

Lily laughed. She and Sara had been school girls together,

but Sara's open sexual curiosity never failed to surprise her. "He's Ormney. They don't do sex with humans." Lily fell back on the common fallacy trying to keep things light.

"Oh, honey. I'm sure you could convince him to give it a try." Sara speared Lily with a wide-eyed look. "Take it from me, based on anatomy, I'd say there isn't anything physical getting in the way." She laughed at her own thoughts. "Well, he is seriously hung and that could be uncomfortable, but...worth a try."

Lily shook her head. "You are completely insane."

Sara did her best imitation of a mad scientist's maniacal laughter. They laughed together and it felt good...until Lily realized they'd dropped into the Old Duval Street neighborhood. If it had changed, she didn't remember the details well enough to notice.

Single family homes sprawled on lawns that were narrow but deep and dotted with trees. The family would never have been able to afford the luxury of land if the house hadn't been paid off decades earlier. Sara parked on the street and Lily climbed out of the hop then leaned back against the side and stared at the house, a sprawling two level poly-board with gingerbread trim. The Azaleas wrapped around the foundation were quietly green. The trees in the back towered over the house now, waving at her with their red and gold leaves. The pavers up to the door were shiny-new. Recently replaced.

She didn't look down the block to where the house she grew up in probably still stood. She never did. She'd visited for holidays only a few times over the years. Had never gone any farther down the block.

More than a dozen years earlier, her father had stopped his auto-cart three houses down from where she now stood. He'd stepped out of the cart, and died.

That's all they knew. Not why he stopped, why he got out, or how his body had ended up in the overgrown backyard of the neighbor's house without the residents noticing a thing.

An entertainment unit turned too loud.

A blown circuit in the outdoor security system.

That's all it had taken to allow the killer to hide the body and leave the scene without being noticed.

The front door of the O'Leary house swung open and Aunt Jane stood there, her arms wide. Lily straightened then jogged up the walk to cling to that warm embrace. The smell of baking bread permeated Aunt Jane's sweater. She hugged her Aunt tight and savored the scent a moment before she blanked her mind, pushing the memories aside.

Aunt Jane pulled her inside and tugged her toward the kitchen.

"Rosalee's here with the boys. Pat Jr. is in UT Metro with my Patrick and your grandfather. You think they would all have had enough of law enforcement without having to run off and play cops and robbers in the retirement community."

The hallway led into the bright open space of a kitchen almost identical to the one she'd grown up with. She'd stood at the big center counter side-by-side with her sister, Rose, learning to make homemade bread, peel and mash real grown-in-the-dirt potatoes, and bake anything edible into a casserole fit for a family of five.

"We're here, Mom." Pat Jr.'s voice rang out from the vid-display located against the wall.

Rosalee, his wife, stood at the counter, smiling at the vid of her husband with a look both indulgent and deeply satisfied. She and Pat Jr. shared the kind of love Lily had always wanted. That I'll-be-there-for-you-forever kind of love. Their boys, Connor and Mathew, giggled as they pressed cookie cutters into the dough that had been rolled across the floured countertop. Connor looked so much like Lily's younger brother had at that age it brought another wave of nostalgia, like stepping back in time and finding Brian in Aunt Jane's kitchen. Behind Rosalee and the boys a wall of windows looked out onto a green carpet of grass, spread beneath the shade trees, the old storm shelter just beyond.

Half-halo images of Junior and Uncle Patrick smiled and waved, the hint of a hov-cart interior ghosted around them. "We're on a stakeout so we had time to check in."

Connor glanced up from his cookie making with curious eyes. "Aren't stakeouts supposed to be at night, Dad?"

"Stakeouts have to be when the criminal is likely to come out. Everyone here is Gramp's age."

Mathew elbowed his brother. "He means they all go to bed early."

Connor pressed a flour-coated hand to his face and giggled. Rosalee wiped his face with a towel, ignoring her son's pained "oh, Mom."

Sara nudged Lily in the back as she moved into the room and Lily was drawn into more hugs and greetings. On the halo-vid, the image bounced as her grandfather climbed in to the hov-cart and her uncle and cousin slid over to make room. Gramp's face came into view and seemed to track directly to her. "Is that my Lil-Bit?"

"It's me, Gramps."

"'Bout damn time you turned up."

"I know, Gramps."

"You're not going to disappear on us again, are you?"

"No immediate plans to, sir."

His bushy eyebrows drew together and she could see him consider grilling her further. In the end he let it go. "Good enough," he said, then repeated, "Good enough." The familiar words accompanied by a few sharp nods of his head signaled a return to casual chatter.

Lily was pushed to a work area and given salad greens and vegetables to toss together. The warm easy banter of the family wrapped around her as she worked, but her grandfather's frown stuck in her head.

Lily stayed through the meal preparations and the dinner, served early to accommodate Connor and Mathew, then hugged Rosalee and the boys as they headed home and promised to visit. Sean hadn't made it in time for the meal and wouldn't be there until late. They made a plan to meet into the night then crash there so no one would have to head home late and exhausted. Sara needed to go back to her office to meet with her staff and she offered to bring back things for both of them to sleep in. That left Lily sitting with Aunt Jane in her parlor, eating cookies and sipping hot cocoa.

The house hadn't changed much through the years. The furniture was a mix of textures and fabrics, all old and well made. The gold velvet recliner Jane had once threatened to set on fire, had been recovered in a more sedate whiskey color—no velvet. A collection of vintage family photography still hung on a wall near the entryway. The entertainment display had been upgraded.

She and Aunt Jane shared the sofa with the plate of treats between them. Lily nibbled at the edge of a chocolate chip cookie, savoring the sweet mix of vanilla and chocolate flavors on her tongue. "These are delicious."

Jane smiled. "They're my mother's recipe. Your dad and I loved them when we were growing up. I wish you could have known your Rowan grandparents."

Lily wished so too. "Dad used to talk about them, but I've forgotten the stories."

"That's not your fault, Lily." Jane's smile dimmed. "Stories have to be told often to be remembered."

Taking a sip of her chocolate, Lily turned sideways in her seat and leaned back against the armrest. "Mom's not one for remembering the past. She likes to look forward."

Jane shook her head. "I should've found a way to spend more time with you. Maybe then you'd have come to us when…" A tear escaped the corner of her eye and tracked a wet line down her cheek.

Lily had never even considered that her decision to break ties would hurt anyone else. She set her drink on the end table. "Aunt Jane, please don't…it isn't… I made my own decisions."

Jane wiped the tear from her cheek then set down her own drink and moved the plate. She scooted closer and reached for Lily's hands. "It's never too late to make new ones." Jane squeezed her fingers. "Whatever is next for you, we'll be behind you. Okay?"

Lily nodded, her heart aching like an overused muscle. Regrets were hell—and just one of the things trying to fit inside the shriveled muscle in her chest.

"Good." Her aunt released her hands and leaned back. "Can you tell me what's been on your mind all evening? Or do you need to give Sean a call?"

"Sean?"

Jane got to her feet and grabbed the plate of cookies . "I know that look, sweetie. Your worrying about that case."

Lily took a cookie from the plate when her aunt offered it. "The case is wrapping up. Everything is settled."

Heading toward the kitchen, Jane stopped and met Lily's gaze. "Something is worrying you and if you don't deal with it you won't be getting any sleep tonight. Now finish your cocoa and think it over." Jane gave her a half smile then left the room.

It didn't take her long to admit her aunt was right. Lily had said as much to Sara earlier. The case didn't feel over. Until it did she couldn't believe the danger had passed. There could still be women at risk. Tomorrow she'd get Jolaj to share names with her but tonight she knew what she needed to do.

Tugging on her holster and coat she joined her aunt in the kitchen long enough to kiss her cheek and let her know she wouldn't be sleeping over after all. She promised her aunt she'd be careful then headed for the nearest glide-rail stop.

CHAPTER 30

He kept to the shadows as he moved down the street. He knew where the neighborhood watch cameras were. Knew the angles. Knew how not to be seen.

He wore a woolen scarf wrapped around his head and neck, obscuring most of his face. His coat covered him down to the gloves on his hands and down to his thighs. If the cameras caught him, they might get his height. They'd peg him as heavier than his own trim physique. The bulk beneath his clothes served as more than a disguise. It included the latest urban-amour available on the civilian markets.

He expected her to fight.

She was, after all, trained to defend, to attack, to kill.

A simple override-jacker, purchased from a street grifter, cleared him through the building's side entrance so his entry wouldn't be logged. A change in the setting disrupted the secure-cams. He quickly pulled sealant out and sprayed himself down with a second coat, a refresher to the more thorough job he'd done earlier. He shoved the tube back in his pocket.

His heart pumped fast and eager as he scaled the stairs. Blood flowed fiercely through his veins, fueling the deadly strength he'd trained into his muscles.

He stood at her door and took a delicious moment to go over the perfect fantasy of how the next few minutes would play out. It could have been different, but she had made her choice.

She'd sided with the animals and it was time for her to die like one.

Gripping a pulser firmly in his hand he signaled for a response. Waited. Ready. The door slid open and she stood there.

"Hello, Lily." He squeezed the pulser's trigger panel as he spoke, then watched the shock play across her features.

She fell to the floor as she lost control of her muscles, her head slamming softly against the smooth polymer floor. After a quick scan to make sure she was alone, he stepped over her and into the room, dropping his bag by the door. He reached down and dragged her farther into the room, letting the door slide closed behind him.

The box of flowers he'd sent her sat on a table unopened. He shook his head at what could have been. He slipped the pulser into his bag and pulled out his real weapon. The polished silver of the metal-alloy claws he'd made himself shone with lethal beauty. Kneeling beside her, he looked into her brilliant green eyes and pulled it onto his hand. "It all could have been so different."

Fear widened her eyes and her body stilled. No doubt, she was beginning to regain control of her muscles. Quickly, he wrapped one hand around her neck, leaning in with all his weight and crushing her larynx. He threw a leg over to straddle her hips. She struggled beneath him like a kitten pinned on its back. Her hands beat against his arm and shoulder, but the armor did its job, softening the blows. Her body rocked beneath him. Her golden hair lay like a cloud around her face. Her cheeks and lips had been tinted a pretty shade of pink, feminine.

Had she been waiting for the animal?

He rested the razor sharp blades against her rib cage. He didn't want it to end too soon. He pressed down and across, putting the weight of his body into the slash.

Bright red blood welled up through the gaps in her ruined sweater, but she didn't stop struggling. Her struggles were weak. No strength behind them. Unskilled. He'd expected better.

A flash of intuition stopped his heart for a single breath.

Releasing the hold on her neck, he struck a blow calculated to stun her without knocking her unconscious. He'd had plenty of opportunity to practice. To gauge his punches. She stopped struggling for a moment as if her brain tried to recover from bouncing around inside her skull.

Gathering a fistful of her sweater he widened the rips. The

delicious rending sound caressed his senses, drawing a shiver like feathers on bare flesh. Before the oozing flow of blood coated her belly he had time to see what he'd been looking for. Or rather to not see. No scars marred the soft perfect skin. Only the shallow gashes he'd dug against her ribs.

Rose.

He met her eyes again. Hers were full of tears. She had done nothing to deserve the pain he still ached to inflict on her. Control. He was in control. He decided who suffered. And she had suffered enough. She had been the good sister. The good girl. But she was a pale reflection of the stronger, bolder sister.

Her tears welled over, bathing her temples and soaking into her hair as she tried to speak.

He used a single finger to wipe them away. "Sh, I'm sorry, Rose. Don't cry."

No, she didn't deserve to suffer. He'd make sure she didn't suffer any longer.

CHAPTER 31

Lily stepped off the elevated glide-train and onto the well lit platform in front of the elegant midtown high rise. Heading for the elevator banks, she debated whether to buzz the apartment where Kabel's lover lived. She could stand guard in the hallway with no one the wiser, but someone might have already gotten inside. If they hadn't stopped the killer, all the killers, the woman could be bleeding out while Lily hesitated.

A scuff against the pavement behind her spun her around, her pulse pistol in her hand. Jolaj stood at the edge of the platform where the train had just rocketed on to its next station.

"You're supposed to be in The Zone." Lily looked up and down the platform, grateful to find it empty. It was well past curfew. "You can't be seen here." She slid the pistol back into its holster.

"You were supposed to be with your family." His words rolled out on an angry rumble.

"I thought she might have been left unprotected." She didn't have to explain who. He would know.

"She's heavily sedated and under the care of several people I know can be trusted with her safety."

The quiet settled around them comfortably, as if a silent hand wrapped a length of fabric around, a warm embrace of shared understanding, drawing them closer together. Dangerously close.

Lily frowned. "You were on the train?"

"I went looking for you at the O'Leary home and when I realized you were not there I followed your scent to the rail station. From there I was able to *slip* up the trains until I caught up with you."

"I'm not sure I like the idea of you following me around."

He moved toward her. Slowly. Cautiously. When he stood inches in front of her he wrapped his hands around her arms as if he couldn't not touch. "I will see you safely home."

His statement left no room for discussion. No room for refusal. But Lily bristled at the thought of allowing him to dictate to her.

"No," she said.

She heard the whiz of an approaching train whisper along the rail.

"Get on the train and go home, Lily." The command in his voice rang loud and clear even though his words had been little more than a whisper. Then he disappeared. The tingling sensation of his *slip* shuddered through the leather of her jacket and she shivered.

As the train came to a stop at the platform she saw him appear on the roof of the rail car. "Damn." She hated his arrogance, but there wasn't any reason to remain if the woman was already being protected. Reluctant, she strode forward and stepped inside.

She stayed on her feet, noting each face in the small compartment. Assessing threats. It was part of who she'd become.

When she stepped off the car at the Clinton station, she looked around for Jolaj, but didn't see him. That didn't mean he wasn't there. She knew, because she was coming to know him. She strode over to the stairs that led from the platform to road level and leaned over the railing. She spotted him waiting in the shadows at the bottom. "You're just lazy." She whispered the words for her own entertainment, too low to be heard on the street level. "That's why you *slip* so often."

She smiled despite her frustration with him.

Instead of heading down the steps, Lily stepped onto the catwalk that ran along the edge of the rail.

Jolaj frowned, scanning the area for some trouble that would have sent her along the dangerous raised walkway intended only for emergency access. He listened to the sounds of the night and picked out the trace of her movements. Relaxed. Unhurried. Her sage and honey scent drifted to him on the breeze. He could find no sign of fear.

She'd called him lazy. Could she be taunting him? An odd lightness stirred in his chest. Inappropriate, considering the circumstances of the last several days. Despite that, he couldn't keep the smile from curving his lips as he watched her movements. It was a game. She was playing with him.

He kept to the shadows, keeping her in sight as he moved down the street below her. The rail line crossed just above a building three blocks down from hers.

The crosswalks between the rooftops had been painted to obscure their presence, day or night, but his vision was too keen to be fooled. She could easily reach her home without ever coming down to the street. With a thought he *slipped*, worked the patterns, calculated, marked time, and *slipped* cautiously back in to *in-sync* on the roof of her building.

His heart tripped in his chest as he saw how narrow the crosswalk actually was. She moved across it like a shadow, graceful and effortless. He waited, leashing his restlessness, wanting to move to where he could reach out to take hold of her waist as she reached the edge, but worried her fear of his claws might startle her into a fall she would have otherwise avoided.

She jumped down onto the sturdier surface of the building and he allowed himself to breathe. He breathed in the garden spread out around them, covering the expanse of the rooftop. His heart expanded as she brushed a lavender plant with the tips of her fingers, releasing its scent on the breeze. She knew the garden well. Perhaps spent time there. She would enjoy his home, the top level covered in foliage and open to the sky.

She didn't head to the stairs, leading down from the roof. Instead she looked out on the neighborhood. He moved behind her, shuffling his feet a little to avoid startling her.

"I'm not lazy," he said.

She looked over her shoulder and shook her head, but there was something soft and peaceful in her eyes. Something he hadn't seen there before.

"*Slipping* requires as much exertion as climbing stairs."

She grinned and turned back to look out across the

rooftops and he reached for her. She shivered a little as his hands found her shoulders and slid down her arms, then under to reach around her waist. He stepped close and wrapped himself around her, glorying in her acceptance.

He slipped one hand inside her jacket and let his claws rake across the SafeSkin top she wore beneath it. He could hear the change in her breathing, but he could not make himself pull away. When she lay her arm across his, pressing her hand against him, keeping his hand firmly in place, his body hardened. Every muscle tensed in anticipation. His cock stretched to aching proportions.

He pulled her more tightly against him, wanting to feel her ass against his desperately eager flesh, but the damn coat dulled the sensation.

He bent to press his lips to her temple. Her skin tasted sweet. She turned in his arms and looked up into his face.

"Jo..."

"Please, Lily." His hand shook as he wrapped it around the back of her head. "Be with me in this moment."

He feared she would deny him if he asked for anything more. She was spirit weary and he wanted to give her solace. To take solace in her body. In his soul, she already belonged to him. Her scent filled his head and her sadness tore at his heart. He needed to protect and care for her. She had called to his mating instinct from the moment he'd seen her in the alley. Sick with grief, he'd still been drawn to her.

He reached up and worked his fingers through her hair, freeing it from what remained of the knot she'd twisted it into that morning. The soft golden color shimmered in the moonlight as it fell loose around her shoulders.

Slowly he lowered his head. Pressed his lips to the soft plumpness of hers. He slipped his tongue out to taste her.

Damn, how he wanted her.

His entire body throbbed with wanting.

He thrust his tongue past her lips and lifted her in his arms. Her legs wrapped around him. The edges of her coat slid out of the way and he pulled her to him, fitting them together as they were meant to be. He thrust his hips forward, glorying in the heat of her pressed against his cock, only a few thin layers of cloth between them. She moaned and arched her back, pressing her breasts to his chest.

"I need you, Lily." He needed her more than breath and shamelessly let his urgency color his words. "Mil'nal lij li." It rumbled up from deep in his chest. "I need to fuck you."

She laughed and buried her face against his neck. "It sounded prettier in your language."

His lungs heaved. Fear squeezed like a fist around his throat. Fear she might grow angry or afraid, but she hadn't pulled away. He could still feel her breath on his skin, feel the heat of her pressed against him.

"It will not be a pretty thing." Not this time. It had been far too long for him. Lust clawed at his control and he hadn't even gotten her out of her damned clothes.

She leaned back and met his eyes, her hand cupping his jaw. "I don't need pretty."

He growled, unable to speak. He would give her his need and hope it would be enough.

He strode over to a large, pillow-like cushion positioned amidst a stand of potted trees. He pulled her down and shifted her above him. Ever careful not to trigger her fear, he pushed the coat and holster from her shoulders. She helped him, wiggling out of the soft leather. Her movements above him stroked against his erection and he ground his teeth together at the sparks of need, licking along every nerve ending in his body.

He filled his hands with her breasts, both frustrated and grateful for the soft, SafeSkin top that clung to her curves and kept him from scratching her in his haste to get inside her. He wanted to see her breasts again as they'd been when he'd found her in the shower, tight nipples tipping the full firm flesh. Wanted to feel their texture against his tongue. But that would be for another time, when he had more control.

Twenty years since his mate's death and in all that time he had never truly been tempted to take any particular woman. Had turned down the opportunity to take a new mate. His body hadn't pressed him to claim a female he didn't feel eager to bind to him for all time. Not until this woman did his body shake and throb with lust and the undeniable need to thrust his cock into her soft flesh.

He wrapped his hands around her hips and rocked her against him. She threw her head back, arching her body above him, exposing the long line of her throat. He couldn't wait much longer.

He tried to free her from her trousers but the fastenings were beyond him.

"Off." He groaned out the single word close to her ear as he pushed her hands toward the offending clasps.

Praise Perpetuation, she rolled to her back beside him and freed herself as if by magic and allowed him to pull the soft material of her slacks and under things down her thighs.

Again he growled in frustration. He wanted to taste her, but he could not take the time he should. Wanted to touch her, but feared hurting her with his claws. Wanted to pleasure her, so she would let him fuck her again and again.

He surged up to his knees and pulled her under him on her hands and knees. Wrapping his arms around her, he pressed his hand over hers and moved her fragile fingers to where he needed to touch her. He pressed her hand against her own flesh, urging her to touch herself as he wanted. As carefully as he was able with his arousal riding him hard, he pressed her hand against the soft folds between her legs. His other arm held her tight against him. He couldn't allow her to change her mind. She had to need him as he needed her.

The cool night air brushed across their skin like an erotic caress, doing nothing to cool the urgency rushing them forward.

Lily couldn't think straight. She could only feel the heat of his body pressed against hers. She let him guide her hand. The realization that he wanted her to touch herself only inflamed her already overheated body. His hand pressed her fingers against the closed folds between her legs building a slow, undeniable need for more.

He was so careful with her. Gentle but determined. Impatient and demanding, but unwilling to risk hurting her with his sharp claws. She had been hurt so often and in so many ways, she had never even entertained any thought that he wouldn't hurt her. She'd allowed him to touch her knowing she could be hurt.

The motion of his hand on hers changed, working hers to press between the folds, to open her body to his demands. The erotic thrill of touching herself at his urging tightened something low in her belly. The first touch of her own finger against her swollen clit flashed sharp pleasure through her, bowing her body back against him.

"Again," he growled. "Do it again."

His fingers urged her to slip along the moist folds and stroke repeatedly across the sensitive spot. Her hips moved of their own will and his matched her rhythm.

"Inside." He urged her hand farther down to slip into the slick channel where she needed to be filled, but her own finger wasn't enough.

"Please," she begged shamelessly.

A low rumble was his answer and the sudden withdrawal of his hands. She moaned at the loss of his touch, but then he was back and she could feel the hot length of his cock against her ass. He slipped between her legs, his broad tip bumping against her fingers where they still played between her legs. His rumbling groan vibrated along her neck as he raked his teeth across her pulse point then lifted his head away.

Jolaj ached to sink his teeth into the warm sweet curve of flesh where her neck and shoulder met. Lust and instinct warred with reason. He didn't need to bite her. She'd already been exposed to the Ormney toxin she didn't require the antitoxin in his saliva.

Resisting the temptation, he pushed her forward urging her face and shoulders down to the bedding. She had to put her hands out to catch herself as he pushed eagerly against the opening of her channel. He thrust tentatively at first then slowly but firmly thrust inside. Pushing past her body's defenses.

Despite the slick wetness that readied her for his cock, getting inside her wasn't easy. His size stretched her. She moaned and gasped, breathy sounds that sometimes seemed to indicate pleasure and at others may have meant discomfort, but he couldn't stop until he was lodged firmly inside her. She yelped and rocked forward. He eased back, but moved with her not allowing her to draw away. He needed to giver time— Then she pressed back, pressing him deep inside.

How could he hope to be worthy of such a woman? She was strong and fierce and... so very damaged. Why did she let him inside when she had been so viciously attacked by one of his kind?

He wrapped himself around her and pressed his jaw to her temple. His chest rumbled softly with the contentment as he savored being inside her. His woman. In the distraction of experiencing her velvet heat gripping his cock, he let a growl escape the back of his throat.

The inhuman sound should have frightened her, but she arched her body and pushed back against him, letting him know she wanted more. Needed more. He needed more too. More of her heart and soul, more of her flesh and body.

He pushed at her top, baring her breasts. He traced his hands over them, brushing firmly against her nipples, then pulled her to him so that they knelt together. The scarred flesh of her belly beneath his palm reminded him to go slow as he'd promised. He had to avoid triggering her fear. Had to be careful not to hurt her in his eagerness.

He blew hotly against her cheek then closed his mouth onto her shoulder. Only the SafeSkin kept him from biting into her. The undeniable power of instinct and the mating urge pushed him to make sure she could feel the firm pressure of his jaw. She clenched around his cock in response and he started thrusting. Slow, deep, and hard. Wanting to fill her up with pleasure before he filled her up with his seed.

He moved her hand back in place between her legs and changed to quick thrusts that slapped against her, driving her clit against her own fingers, driving her hard toward release. He drove her through the first wave of her orgasm, dragging out the pleasure until he joined her. He reared back still keeping their bodies locked together as they moaned their satisfaction to the stars overhead.

Somehow, he promised himself, he would find a way to hold on to this woman.

CHAPTER 32

Lily lay in Jolaj's arms. Their clothes a heap beneath them. The jungle of rooftop plants blocked her view of the city around them, creating an illusion of secluded safety. Languid satisfaction turned her muscles to jelly and urged her to stay there all night.

She rolled onto her back and Jolaj moved with her to keep her firmly in the shelter of his embrace. Lying under the vast openness of the star lit sky with him seemed surreal. He didn't even come from any of the constellations flickering and winking overhead. He came from a different universe, a parallel dimension, or some such crap she didn't fully understand.

The world that had created him, shaped him, was inconceivable to her. Unreal.

But he was real.

The heat of him warmed her even in the chill night air. His big palm rested on her belly, spanning across the exposed surface. She squirmed at the reminder of the scars beneath his hand and tugged her top down across her breasts. She turned in his arms to face him and found him watching her intently with those Ormney eyes. His elliptical pupils were wide and near round in the darkness.

She let her gaze travel down the length of his bared body. He was a magnificent male. The glorious length of his hair lay trapped beneath him. Heavy muscle stretched across his chest and roped down his arms and thighs. She trailed her hand along the multicolored patterns that splashed lightly across his abdomen and watched the play of muscles bunch and flex beneath her palm. A handful of silvery scars shimmered grimly in the moonlight. She traced the tips of her fingers across one scar, close to his heart.

"You told me the role of Law Keeper was more like a priest than a cop. Why the scars?"

Jolaj captured her hand. "I wasn't always a Law Keeper." He pressed her hand to his lips and kissed her knuckles then returned her hand to the center of his chest.

The muscled expanse of his chest begged to be stroked and she did, following every contour. She traced the tattoo that seemed to verify his statement about not always being a Law Keeper. A *slip* pattern similar to the one Kiq had taught her. Like the one she'd seen on Lanyak in the autopsy halo.

"This has something to do with why you're so good at *slipping*," she mused.

"Yes. But nothing to do with the scars." He tucked a lock of hair behind her ear. "I was recruited as a Searcher after serving as a Defender for two years."

Lily had suspected he might have been a Searcher, but thinking of the courage required to *slip* into nothing, hoping to find a new world, awed her. Lily didn't recognize the term Defender beyond the literal meaning of the word. She'd never heard of it as an Ormney role or classification.

"You became a Law Keeper after The Crossing?"

"Yes."

It made sense. They wouldn't have needed Searchers anymore after they found Earth. "What did you do as a Defender?"

"Not all Ormney chose The Way. As conditions worsened, some areas of our planet became lawless. Outlaws and organized raiding bands regularly attacked our territory. We protected the people from those threats."

"I didn't realize not all Ormney followed The Way."

"Can you imagine every nation on your planet choosing the same path?"

"No. I guess I can't."

He was such a gentle man it was hard to imagine him as a Defender. A soldier. But she could easily imagine his sense of duty leading him to serve in any way his people needed. Lily let her fingers drift over to where his hand lay low on his belly. She stroked her hand across his, carefully avoiding the clawed tips.

Jennifer Richardson had called Lanyak her gentle giant, but he hadn't been gentle under the influence of the drug that had been used to turn him against her. "Lanyak was a Searcher too?"

"Yes."

"What did you think of his relationship with Jennifer?"

"I thought it ill advised, but I understood his need." Jolaj slipped his hand from under hers then pushed her hand lower toward his erection. It had never fully subsided, but now it had hardened to tempting proportions. She wrapped her hand around him and stroked slowly. "The need to be held." His breath caught on the words. "The need to be touched. It is a very...human...need, is it not?"

"Yes."

He deliberately deepened his breathing as if he needed to focus to control his response to her touch. She studied his face as he watched her hand slide up and down in a firm caress. Stark need etched across his features even as he held himself tightly in check. Recklessly, she wanted to crash trough his control.

Her eyes still on his face she leaned over and circled the tip of his cock with her tongue. Her heart thrilled at the sight of his head thrown back in pleasure. A rumbly moan escaped the back of his throat as she slipped down taking as much of his cock in her mouth as she could manage. The tip quickly bumped the back of her throat and she held him there, relaxing her throat and swallowing against the firm luxurious length of him.

His hand tightened in her hair and urged her up. His hands on her waist easily lifted her astride him and urged her down. His cock slid tightly, deeply inside her eager sheath. She felt full. Full of his cock, full of him. His need, his desire filled the empty achy places inside her. His hands on her hips guiding her in a shallow rocking motion that stroked his cock across her most sensitive spot kept her connected to that need and to his gentle, unyielding spirit. Together they rode from the slow currents of pleasure to the wild swells of passion until they both lay boneless and sated.

CHAPTER 33

As her body cooled in the night air, Lily snuggled closer to Jolaj. His warmth seeped into her muscles like expensive brandy chasing away her worries and regret. She resisted fatigue to trace her fingertips lazily down his torso—across the rippled stretch of his ribs to the taut plains of his abdomen.

Beneath her hand, muscles that should have been relaxed or tightening with response were instead taut as stone. The discovery made her draw her hand back as a weight crushed down on her chest.

He'd broken curfew. He'd broken the Council prohibition on sex with humans, but more important to Jolaj, he'd broken his own moral code. Lily was all too aware she wasn't a potential mate in his eyes. Cold seeped through her, making her shiver. Giving in to temptation with her was probably some kind of sin. The sure knowledge that now or later he would regret what they'd done lodged like a cancer in her belly.

Knowing his rejection would come didn't make it any easier in the moment he began to pull away. Tugging his clothes into place, he got to his feet and moved to the edge of the roof. He crouched there on the edge, studying the alley below.

Lily pulled on her own clothes and felt better, stronger, more grounded with the weight of her pulse pistol at her ribs and the familiar safety of her father's coat.

She moved closer to where he crouched. "I'm going in

now. You should get back to The Zone."

"No." He stood and looked over his shoulder at her.

"Jolaj—"

"The air is tainted with the scent of death."

Lily's heart skipped and skittered before she managed to pull the threads of her training back into place. "A rat in the alley, maybe?"

"I don't think so."

"Close?"

"It is faint, but yes. I think so."

He began to blur and his voice echoed in the alley, urging her to wait there.

Like hell.

She spun in a circle, trying to spot him on an adjacent rooftop. Nothing. She leaned over the edge of the roof line and caught a movement in the shadows below. His familiar form stalked along the alley toward the front of the building. She took the emergency glide-pole down into the alley and reached for her pistol as she caught up with him at the main entrance.

He disappeared in a tingling rush. She keyed in to open the door and slipped inside. He was already there, waiting.

"It is a little stronger inside, but still faint." He spoke as he moved quietly along the corridor. "The scent has escaped from one of the apartments to the corridor and then outside as the door was opened."

Lily still didn't smell it. She knew it could be anything. People died. Sometimes naturally. But they were both very aware that a death in The Mixer could also mean the killer had struck again. Most of the attacks had been within a few blocks of Lily's apartment and the killer had probably used Simone Rawls' com-unit to pull Lily into his twisted little games. She looked back to the door, wondering if the killer might still be close by.

"Do you think he just left the building?"

"No." Jolaj's attention fixed firmly on the stairs leading up to the second level. "The scent would have taken time to disperse this widely. And I heard nothing from the rooftop. No door closing, no footfalls nearby."

Lily followed as Jolaj took the stairs at a steady, unhurried pace. She was alert but not worried.

Not until he led her directly to her own door.

CHAPTER 34

On edge, mind racing, Lily checked the security measures on her apartment door. Brian had upgraded the circuits and programming and he was the best with anything programmable. No one should have been able to get inside.

Sean could have brought in one of Metro's e-teams, but why and how would that lead to a dead body in her apartment. Bradley? Lily didn't think he could hack her security without trashing it in the process. Unless he'd somehow rigged a bypass routine when he'd spent the night alone in her apartment. Damn. Could he have gotten inside then opened her door to a killer?

Lily keyed open the lock and slid the door slowly open, pulse pistol still in her hand. As soon as the door opened the smell of death assaulted her senses. She jerked back, an involuntary response to that awful, unmistakable scent that Jolaj had caught all the way up on the roof. The sound of a familiar old jazz number registered, but she didn't allow herself to consider it. She took two paces into the room and Jolaj followed.

Her gaze swept the single room apartment, noting the body, sweeping past, refusing to see the detail. She had to be sure the room was clear first, but there was something about the size and shape of the body. Not Bradley. A woman. And familiar.

Lily's gaze jerked back to the body. The woman lay on her side, facing away from the door. A mass of blood-matted hair obscured her face. A dark stain marred the back and shoulder of her winter white sweater and blood pooled beneath her. There wasn't a great deal of it anywhere else. It was all there as if she hadn't resisted. Simply laid down on the floor and allowed her attacker to kill her. As if she'd bled out from a single wound.

Everything about this murder was different. The victim had died too clean. The timing was all wrong. And how had the woman gotten into Lily's home, past her security?

Realization slammed into her as she stepped closer, the pistol suddenly heavy in her hands. Oh, God. It couldn't be.

"Lily, the woman is dead. You should alert Metro." Jolaj stood next to her, but his voice seemed miles away. A shadow sound, receding into the distance as the jazz swelled to fill the room and memories filled her head. The sultry rhythm of her father's favorite late twentieth century tune competed with the sharp staccato pants of her own breathing. She hadn't heard that music in over a decade.

Somewhere far away Jolaj called her name as she knelt by the body. She could see now that the woman's hair had been a pale, champagne blond and her perfect manicure had been princess pink. The inescapable truth lodged in Lily's chest as she reached out with a shaky hand to push the hair out of the woman's face.

Her voice shuddered as she breathed the name. "Rose."

CHAPTER 35

Jolaj had stood by uncertain as Lily approached the body. The woman was clearly dead and he'd expected her to caution him not to disturb the scene—she might not be a cop but she thought like one—but Lily had touched the dead woman. He recognized the name Rose, but he wasn't prepared for the shock of seeing a slightly softer version of Lily's face when she pushed back the mop of blood-soaked hair.

The sight tore at him, but he knew his shock was nothing compared to Lily's horror. He picked his way carefully around Rose's body and squatted down, pulling Lily into his arms. He drew her around, pressed her cheek against his chest. "I'm sorry."

Jolaj looked down into the dead woman's familiar green eyes. They were wide with the fear that had gripped her as she lay dying.

It could have been Lily.

The woman who had touched his soul and given him back hope for his own future could have lost her life, facing the same terror. She could still be in mortal danger.

Before that moment, he'd been afraid for his people. Afraid for the men who'd chosen human mates and afraid for the women they loved. He'd even feared for Lily, but she was a strong, smart woman who could protect herself better than most. Now the fear had become more personal and more terrifying. More real. He couldn't lose her now. His soul couldn't survive it.

She was quiet in his arms, but the dampness of her tears soaked into his tunic. He stroked the back of her head and bent low to fill his lungs with her scent. "You must call Detective O'Leary."

"Sean?" Her voice shook as she attempted to speak through short, shallow breaths. "I should call Sean."

She didn't move and it became clear she'd only repeated his suggestion without any real understanding. Her grief had left her disoriented and vulnerable. It clawed at his heart to see her so shaken.

"Lily, you must call Sean and tell him your sister has been murdered. You must make the report."

She lifted her head from his chest and nodded, straightening her spine. She looked down at her own hands as if they were strange and unfamiliar. They were shaking. He steadied her hand as she touched the com-link over her ear.

"Rowan. Activate. Link to Sean O'Leary."

It took only four seconds before O'Leary's sleep slurred voice came over the link. "Lil? Damn, what time is it? You okay?"

"I'm fine, Sean. I just arrived at my place and found Rose here. She's been murdered."

Jolaj watched as she spoke in near-normal tones. He doubted O'Leary would hear the lingering traces of pain affecting the pitch of her voice.

"No," he denied. "That's not... Fuck. Damn it Lil, are you secure?"

"The scene's secure. I'll wait here for your team."

"I'm not getting a fix on you." A thread of panic wormed through his voice. "I've never been to your place."

She took a deep breath and spoke clearly. "Activate locator." Her posture softened as she continued. "You should have my coordinates now."

"Yeah, got 'em. Hang on. I'm sending units. I'll be there. Just hang on."

"I'll be here."

"Wait, Lily—"

"Close link."

As Lily's head dipped downward, Jolaj cupped his palms along her jaw line and urged her face up. Despite calm demeanor her cheeks were wet and shining with tears. He pulled her toward him and bent his head to press his forehead to hers. He made the low rumbling sound of mourning and comfort in the back of his throat, willing her to understand. Among his people the sound of mourning served as a shared release of grief, their way of strengthening each other and their identity as a people through generations of harsh and often deadly times.

Lily listened to the comforting sound of Jolaj's rumbling bass and pressed her hands over his, held them for a moment then pulled his hands away. She turned back to her sister's body, whispered her goodbyes, then wiped the tears from her cheeks with her fingers, hands still shaking. The years apart only sharpened her grief in that moment. She would never be able to tell Rose how much she'd loved her. Rose had died angry and thinking Lily had betrayed her. God, how had she let this happen? How had she screwed up so badly?

If only she'd answered Rose's call that morning. If only she hadn't taunted the killer. If only she'd been home.

Lily pushed the self-recriminations aside and tried to look at her sister objectively. Rose's hair was a snarled mess around her head. A small purple shadow marred her temple. From this close she could see what hadn't been visible from the door.

She had to wipe fresh tears away. Rose's sweater had been ripped open. Blood soaked the material and coated the bared flesh. She could see several parallel slashes beneath the dried blood. Like a single slash from a handful of claws. But Mary Santini's injuries had looked like claw wounds. There had been more. Many more. "Something stopped him."

"He attacked her with blades to imitate claws." Jolaj stroked a hand down Lily's back as he spoke. "But the wound on the back of her head is the one that killed her."

"A stab wound, probably. Straight in." Lily paused to clear her throat and stop her voice from shaking. "A deliberate death blow."

"This is different from the other attacks."

"Yeah," Lily agreed. "But this guy hasn't exactly been consistent."

"He has used Ormney men as the weapon and he has used a bladed weapon to make a murder look like an Ormney attack."

Lily flinched as the music began again. She'd pushed it out

of her consciousness and hadn't noticed when it stopped. The sudden sultry jazz notes battered her. She found the music cube pressed into Rose's hand. Had Rose brought it with her or had the killer somehow known about her father?

"Music off," she commanded firmly and the cube went silent.

Lily pushed to her feet and Jolaj stood with her. Together they moved away from the body.

"Jolaj, you should go."

He reached for her, lifting her chin with the edge of his hand. "I won't leave you."

CHAPTER 36

Lily tried several times to convince him to go. The big stubborn bastard wouldn't budge. Did he think she couldn't handle herself? Especially on her own territory with Metro on the way? No, she realized, he thought she'd crumble again. Well, that wouldn't do Rose any damn good and Lily was determined to find justice for her sister. She had to hold it together, so she would.

Lily had expected trouble when Metro arrived. After all, Jolaj was out of The Zone during curfew hours. She hadn't anticipated they'd be impossible to reason with and on edge. She'd thought his Law Keeper uniform would afford him some professional courtesy. Instead, the officers ordered him face down on the floor. Something that wasn't going to happen.

The Metro officers were barking orders and pointing weapons in their direction. She could feel the aggression roll off of Jolaj in waves as he tried to edge between her and the officers. She stopped him with a hand on his arm.

"They're probably afraid you're drugged and dangerous." Every one of them had probably seen the vid of the attack at the hospital. She focused her attention on the officer who seemed to be leading the others, a stocky woman with silver streaks in her short cropped hair. "Look, Law Keeper Jolaj isn't under the influence of any drugs. He's here at my request. Please lower your weapons."

The woman kept her department issue stunner aimed at

Jolaj. "Sorry, Agent Rowan. We're not taking any chances. This Ormney is in violation of the curfew decree and at the scene of a violent crime."

"Damn it. This is stupid." She couldn't get Jolaj to go and she couldn't get Metro to stand down.

"I'm only going to repeat this once more," said the officer. "Law Keeper, get down on the ground. Hands and feet spread wide."

The room was so filled with tension Lily thought it a wonder they didn't all choke on it.

"Out of the way!" Sara's voice rang out from the hallway, capturing the attention of everyone in the room. "Oh, God." She pushed her way into the apartment and took in the situation so quickly Lily could almost see her thought process spinning in her eyes. "Jolaj, Lily," Sara acknowledged them then turned her focus on the Metro team. Dropping her ME's bag on the floor, She waved her credentials in front of her. "Chief Medical Examiner, Sara O'Leary. This is my crime scene. Everyone out."

Reluctantly, the cops backed out of the room. The female officer was the last to budge, her weapon still aimed at Jolaj. "Dr. O'Leary, we need to restrain the Ormney."

Sara tried to stare her down and when that didn't work she strode over to Jolaj to stand in front of him.

"Jolaj," said Sara. "Are you going to get scary on us?"

His eyes widened. "No, Dr. O'Leary."

Sara curved her lips in a grin that didn't reach her eyes and nodded. "Good enough for me."

The officer let out a huff of breath and lowered her weapon, and backer toward the door. "You people are insane."

The moment the woman was out of the room, Sara stepped away from Jolaj and pulled Lily into an embrace. "Oh, Lil. I'm so sorry." Her arms tightened then far too soon she released Lily and turned back to Rose's body, all business. "I was on my way home and heard the call go out. "How many people have been in here?"

"Jolaj and I found her. We checked her for signs of life. The four cops came a few feet into the room."

"You touched her?" Sara's attention snapped to Lily, clearly appalled.

"Her hair was in her face" Lily shrugged and her voice

tried to desert her. "I had to make sure."

Sara pinned her with a look full of sympathy. They both knew Lily was referring to being sure of Rose's identity, not life signs. Rose was unquestionably gone and had been for hours before they'd arrived.

"Okay," said Sara. "You two will have to wait inside until the techs get here and can process you for trace. Will you be okay if I get started?"

Lily nodded and had to swallow down the ball of grief in her throat before she could speak. "You'll take good care of her." It wasn't a question. More an acknowledgement between them that this would be difficult for Sara and her handling it meant a great deal.

Sara went back to the bag she'd dropped and pulled on white jumpsuit, perfectly tailored to her small frame. Sean arrived as she started her initial assessment and the forensic team wasn't far behind. The Metro officers fanned out through the building, each taking a tech with them. Doing it by the book, Sean said. And that also meant separating Lily from Jolaj and getting their stories separately.

Detective Newman led her back to the stairs and she sat on the upward staircase while he pulled out his e-notepad. When she answered his questions, she refused to be specific about where she'd been before she and Jolaj had stepped into the building. She said only that he'd been concerned about her safety and insisted on seeing her home. It would be interesting to see what they made of the rail and street view vids from the area. The rail vids would put them in the vicinity well before they arrived at her building, but the street vids wouldn't show them much.

Her lack of cooperation didn't win her any brownie points with him, but she didn't give a damn.

Lily's position a few steps up on the wide staircase put her eye to eye with Newman and he took advantage of that to level her with a look of contempt. "I'd think you'd want to make this easy, considering it's your sister dead in the floor of your apartment."

Lily stopped breathing as the pain of his blunt statement tightened her chest and throat. The disapproval in his stocky, compact body broadcast loud and clear he thought she was to blame. The hell of it was he was right. She forced herself to pull air into her lungs. To breathe in and out as if everything was normal.

"Look." She kept her voice steady and calm. "I know I'm a suspect, and as soon as we know time of death, I'll report exactly where I was at the time. So, let's worry about that when we get there." His disapproving scowl deepened the lines in his face and made his bulldog jowls droop even more than usual. "For now, can you focus on the fact that I'm the person who found the body and let's stick to that?"

They'd gone over everything twice when Sean appeared in the doorway of Lily's apartment and headed toward them. He and Newman exchanged a look and Newman moved away.

Sean sat down on the step beside her. "How you doing, Lil?"

She stuffed her fists into her coat pockets and widened her eyes, fighting off the tears his simple concern threatened to shake loose. "Stupid question, Sean."

He smiled sadly and nodded. "Okay. To the point, then." He dug in the pocket of his jacket and pulled out a clear evidence sleeve. "Recognize this?"

She studied the e-card, sealed inside the bag. "No. You find it on Rose?"

"It was tagged to a silver flower box we found in your apartment. The box hadn't been opened." He clasped his hands between his knees and propped his forearms on his thighs. "The flowers are lilies. The card seems to reference the deaths. At least the deaths of the women. *Don't lose sleep over the lost girls. They made their beds and they deserve to die in them.*"

Lily ran the lines through her head, playing them back again, looking for meaning. There had to be something useful there, but she couldn't see it.

"They're taunting us." Sean's hands tightened and he spoke through a clenched jaw. "Damn EFE lunatics."

"You still think this is EFE?"

Sean nodded.

She squinted at him. "I don't know."

"Has to be," he said, straightening and clenching his hands into fists. "I knew the guy in the hospital wasn't operating alone. I'll take down every last member of the EFE if I have to. They'll pay for this. Every last bastard who had anything to do with this is going to pay."

Lily shook her head. "It feels personal. Someone wanted

me involved from the beginning. I don't have any connections to EFE."

"Of course it feels personal." Sean turned his body toward her. "They tried to kill you."

"Yeah. And Rose is the one dead." She swallowed hard. "God. How am I going to tell Mom?"

"I'll handle it," he said.

"No." Lily pulled her hands free of her pockets and pressed her flattened palms down her thighs as if she could push away the pain. "I have to do it."

Sean eyed her thoughtfully. "No. We'll call Brian. She'll need him there when she hears the news." Sean but an arm around her shoulders and pulled her up against his side. "Trust me, Lily. I've done a lot of notifications."

Lily dipped her chin in concession and stared at the step beneath her feet. It felt wrong. She needed to take responsibility. But Sean was probably right. There would be time enough to face her mother.

"Sean, you need to know." She lifted her chin to face him. "They're going to find evidence that Bradley slept in my apartment last night."

"Fuck." Sean's arm slid free of her shoulder and his spine sagged with the added complication she'd dropped in his lap. He didn't deserve to be in the middle of this.

"I didn't...I mean, we didn't..." Lily pulled her jacket a little tighter around her. "There wasn't anything going on between us. He slept here and I spent the night at the hospital. We weren't having sex, but Rose believed we were. It's probably why she came. To confront me."

"Shit, Lil." He rested and elbow on the step behind them and dropped his head back then pinch the bridge of his nose.

"Yeah." They sat together in silence for several minutes. "What will happen to Jolaj?"

"That's up to their Council. We only have the authority to detain." Sean shook his head. "As if we could detain him against his will. Regardless, it's up to the Council to deal with him, but that won't be an easy out. They won't want to look like they can't enforce the terms of the treaty. And I think they're pretty tough on crime."

"They're all about discipline, duty, honor." Principles she

respected, but she'd somehow made them sound hollow passing across her lips.

"Right." Sean let a moment pass in silence. "What was he doing here, Lil?"

"He was seeing me home," said Lily. She and Sean shared a long look, but she didn't see the censure she expected. His look was searching and more accepting than she had any right to hope.

"Lil—"

The techs carried Rose's body into the hallway in a coroner hov-container and they both stood, whatever Sean had been about to say discarded. Sara followed the techs looking years older. When she saw them on the stairs she walked over, eyes red and cheeks pale. "I'm going to take her in. The forensics techs will be here awhile longer."

Sean acknowledged her, then they watched her follow the cart down the stairs.

"Okay," said Sean. "Time to call Brian."

CHAPTER 37

Her brother's face filled the small screen on Sean's com. Brian's expression went from carefree and happy to shocked and saddened before firm determination settled in.

"Yeah," he said. "I'll tell Mom and then head down."

To collect the body. Mom would want Rose back in DC. The funeral would be a big social event. The idea sickened Lily, but Rose probably would have wanted it that way.

Sean's arm wrapped around her and she realized she'd hunched over the multi-com like an old woman. Grief had layered upon grief, loss after loss, until she could no longer support the heavy weight.

"Lil, you have to be strong." Brian's voice resonated with determination. "You remember what Dad used to say? It gets worse before it gets better."

She laughed grimly. "God, Bri. I don't think it could get any worse." And she wasn't sure she could take it if it somehow did.

"It could get worse for me, sis. I could lose you too. I'm counting on you to make sure that doesn't happen."

She nodded. Unable to acknowledge any of the feelings roiling inside her. Gratitude that he didn't seem to blame her. Love for him. Guilt for being alive when Rose lay dead. And terrible loss.

"We'll make them pay, Lil. Every last one of them. Just

let's focus on that."

She nodded again, a little surer. She let his confidence and resolve fill her up and rebuild her will to fight. "Sara and Sean are on the job already. I want to go back over everything. Try to see what I've missed."

"Good idea. I'll come by Aunt Jane's when I get there. We can all go over it together. And in the meantime I'll touch base with my contact in The Pool."

His simple statement threw her off balance. She knew Brian was deep into his tech, but he had to be deeper into the tech culture than she thought to have developed contacts among the elusive and aloof members of The Pool. The implications worried her, but for now they could use it. "Do you have a white-hat contact that might be able to use The Pool to back door into Deepwater?"

"Maybe with your ID."

"I'll transmit the codes." She'd be fired for the security violation if the hack was detected, but she didn't give a damn. "I want every scrap on Simone Rawls they can dig up."

"How does she connect to this?" Brian asked the question but Sean had grown more intense at her side.

"I think she's somewhere close to the beginning of it, but I can't be sure."

"Okay. See you soon, sis." Brian's gaze remained steady on hers. "Love you, Lily."

Tears again threatened to spill but Lily fought them. "Love you too."

She transmitted the codes then closed the connection.

Sean cleared his throat again. "Sara dug up the file on Simone Rawls and sent it to me. I wish you'd brought it to me earlier. The first victim is always the most likely to tie back to the killer."

"I'm sorry, Sean. I was going to talk to you about it but things have been so hectic."

"These damn bastards haven't let us catch our breath."

"You think there's more than one killer?"

"There has to be. We have the EFE guy from the hospital locked away, he couldn't have done this. And it explains the different methods used for the murders and the attacks. We haven't been able to find any documentation of a plan at their headquarters, but that doesn't mean anything. I've been interviewing these people all night and some of them are smart enough—"

"Detective O'Leary." Newman's voice interrupted on Sean's com. "You wanted an alert when the *stringers* showed."

Sean glanced to Lily, but spoke to Newman on the com. "Tell the Ormney representatives that I'll be down in a sec." He closed the link and got to his feet.

Lily stood and kept pace as he headed down the stairs. "I guess the cultural enlightenment training didn't take with Newman."

Sean shook his head. "These attacks have drawn out the ugly side of a lot of people."

When they stepped out of the building, pink tinged the sky, but the morning sun hadn't yet risen above the horizon.

Jolaj, Newman, and an officer she didn't recognize stood between a half a dozen cops and another half dozen Ormney Law Keepers. Lily went to Jolaj while Sean spoke to the Law Keepers.

"Will you be okay?" With so many people around she couldn't say the things she wanted to say. How much his sticking around had meant to her, how worried she was for him. She wanted to slip her hand in his—longing for the reassurance of his touch—but even that small gesture could cause him more trouble.

He dipped his chin in answer. "Lily, I know you're strong and smart and capable of many things, but anyone can be harmed if the attacker is determined enough. This killer has proven he's determined. There's safety in numbers. You must promise to stay with your family until I can come for you."

"Then you'll be back?" Her heart thumped hard. She shouldn't have been surprised. He was constant. Reliable. And a lot of other boring words that meant the world.

"I must answer to the Council, but I'll return to you." He waited for her to meet his gaze. "Now promise."

He stood close, his heat and his scent teasing her senses, tempting her to lean in and wrap her arms around him. For both their sakes, she remained still. "I promise."

Lily watched Jolaj turn and walk away, flanked by the other Law Keepers. It was like watching the sun dip below the horizon. Sure, it would return, but until it did all of its warmth and light were gone too.

"You two made friends fast."

Lily looked over her shoulder to where Sean stood. "Is that a problem for you?"

"My only problem is the information you're holding back. How is he involved in this, Lily?"

She turned to face him. "He wants to help us stop it."

"Seems more personal than that."

She turned to face him and nodded. "He knew most of the victims."

"And you don't find that odd?"

"He wasn't involved in the attacks, I'm sure of that." She tried to sound firm but it came out more tired than anything.

"No," Sean said. "I can't say I see him for this either. But there's something else going on here. And being in the dark, that pisses me off."

She studied his face. "Yeah. He told me to tell you everything."

Sean scowled. "Everything?"

There were still cops everywhere. "Not here."

"Come on." He tossed the words over his shoulder as he walked toward a duty auto-cart.

Lily had to jog to catch up. As he slid behind the controls she got into the passenger seat. "Where are we going?"

"Mom and Dad's. You told Brian you'd be there. You need a ride and maybe you'll feel like explaining when we get there."

"I don't want to take you away from the investigation."

"I'll have everything forwarded to my com. I can coordinate the investigation remotely. Sara will join us there."

After, Lily thought. Sara would join them after she'd finished autopsying Rose's body.

CHAPTER 38

Jane O'Leary met Lily with open arms. In the warmth of her aunt's arms, guilt swamped her. Her aunt had lost a niece. One that had spent holidays and shared vacations. One that had probably called and kept in touch. Lily wanted to do something, say something that would ease her aunt's loss. She knew what Jane wanted, needed—someone to grieve with her. But Lily couldn't afford to grieve. Maybe she didn't even deserve it. If she let herself feel she might fall apart.

She could be hospitalized again, she might *need* to be hospitalized.

When Lily tried to speak her voice stuck in the back of her throat. When she finally broke it free, she barely managed the words. "We'll find him. It won't bring her back, but she'll have justice. They all will."

Aunt Jane pushed Lily away, just far enough to look into her eyes. She wrapped her warm hands around Lily's face then slipped them down to squeeze her shoulders.

"I know," said Jane. "You're going to catch him. And my Sean and Sara are going to help you."

Lily tightened her lips in what she hoped would pass for acknowledgement of her aunt's words.

Jane pulled Lily to the kitchen and pressed herbal tea into her hand. They sat at the kitchen table in silence while Sean paced up and down the hall, directing the investigation via link. Lily wanted to ask him about Jolaj, but she had no idea how long it would take for the council to decide what to do with him. Concern for what might be happening to him ate at her, but asking Sean to look into it seemed wrong. His focus needed to stay on the case, on the killer.

Lily passed the morning with her aunt, helping around the house. Relieved to have the mind numbing tasks while Jane contacted members of the O'Leary side of the family to relay the news. Sean didn't break contact with his team until Sara arrived. She looked pale and tired and perfectly comfortable crying into her mother's apron. Lily envied her cousin the freedom to indulge her grief. Lily would never want her mother to see her so vulnerable. Her mother would call it weak and improper. That was the lecture Lily had gotten when she'd balked at moving to Washington. The last time she'd cried had been at her father's funeral.

No. She *had* cried. In Jolaj's arms.

She'd shed her tears in front of him. Fallen down more than a little and trusted him to pick her back up. He made her feel safe for reasons she didn't understand and didn't want to question.

When Sara pulled it together she left her mother in the kitchen and led Lily and Sean to the family war-room. It sat in the back corner of the house. Two walls of dark tinted windows looked onto the backyard and the trees and bushes beyond the lush carpet of the lawn. A simple vid-screen stretched the length of the opposite wall. A large media display table dominated the room, positioned in the center and surrounded by a half dozen comfortable chairs. The table's surface gleamed an unrelenting black, slick and empty like a blank slate waiting to be covered with grim crime scene vid-captures, clues, and bread crumbs that might lead them to the truth.

Sara sank into one of the faux-leather work chairs and touched something beneath the table. The surface was still black, but the quality of black was different—a hint of glow brought the black to life as Lily settled into a seat.

Sara started with Rose's preliminary autopsy results. "The head injury was the cause of death. We're estimating the time of the attack at around six thirty last night."

Images from the crime scene and autopsy flared into being along the smooth surface.

"Before curfew?" Sean who'd been standing by the

windows came over to sit in one of the chairs. "Interesting. They're still trying to shift the blame onto the Ormney."

"The light would have been fading, but there would have still been people on the street." And plenty of Ormney heading back to The Zone.

"The attacker stunned her with a pulser," Sara continued. "Standard strength. Could have been an off the shelf street model. She suffered blows to her temple and to the back of her head. Blunt force." Sara's fingers moved expertly over the table surface, tapping relevant pictures to highlight or enlarge them.

The last image was a split. It included an x-ray, showing the conical fracturing. It also included a still of the corresponding injury—Rose's blood-matted hair pulled aside to show the damaged tissue of her scalp. Lily ignored the growing ball of cold forming in her belly. She couldn't allow herself to give into the useless temptation to imagine how her sister had suffered and slip into selfish grieving. Deliberately, she laid her hands on the top of her thighs, keeping them relaxed, then leaned back into her chair. "Why stun her then hit her?"

"She could've fallen and hit her head," Sean suggested. "Or the killer might have hit her after the stun started to wear off."

Sara sat deep in her seat as she continued in a tone that was solid and crisp and practiced. "There were four parallel lacerations across her chest. Looks like the same weapon used to kill Mary Santini." Despite the objectivity in her voice, her grief weighted her limbs and managed to make Lily's vivacious cousin seem almost still. "If you find it, we can match it to the wounds. We collected trace from the body, but I'm not expecting much. Our initial scan picked up sealant. Not from our lab either. We add a chemical tag to ours. The killer probably sealed up before entering the apartment."

Sean riffled his fingers through his blond hair. "That could mean we're looking for someone who works in a lab, or medicine, or just someone who's been killing for a while."

"There are signs she was held down while she struggled to get free." Sara's voice softened and she held Lily's gaze. "To corroborate that, there was evidence of a heightened state of fear before death. So the stun, the blows, the lacerations, she was probably conscious through all of that."

"Awake and terrified." Lily shivered at the thought of Rose

fighting for her life. She pulled her lip between her teeth to stop the foolish babbling that wanted to tumble out. No, she couldn't think about that. Lily forced her mind to focus on her cousin's report.

"Yes. But it wasn't enough to label as torture. The blows seem more like rage." Sara paused, sucking in a breath. "She would've survived them. We could've saved her." Sara slid her hands across the smooth surface of the table then turned her palms up with a shrug. "Then for some reason the killer switched tactics. The injury to the back of her head, a perfectly placed, single deep penetration, severed her spinal cord. Instant death."

Lily dug her fingers into her thighs, using one kind of pain to stave off another. "He figured out he had the wrong person."

Sean and Sara both watched her, silent, waiting for her to continue. "He realized it wasn't me. Her sweater was ripped open. More than the slashes account for."

"He could have done that before he cut her," said Sean. "He wanted her terrified."

"No," said Sara. "The slashes came first. I found fibers in the wounds."

"Something tipped him off," said Lily. "He ripped the sweater to confirm what he already suspected. He was looking for my scars." She ran one hand lightly across her abdomen.

"Scars?" Sara turned in her chair.

Lily moved her hand back to the arm of the chair and resisted the need to dig her fingers into its surface. "From the training accident."

Sara leaned forward in her chair. "Lil—"

Lily held up her hand to stop Sara from expressing the concern filling her eyes. "The point is, who would know to look for that? How would someone from EFE get information that can only be found in my Deepwater secured file?"

"The same way they got the formula for the drug they've been using," Sara surmised.

"Simone Rawls." Lily wished very much she'd paid more attention to the woman when she'd been alive. If she could go back in time, she'd kill the R&D tech herself just to prevent the devastation the woman had unleashed.

Sean leaned forward too, watching as Sara touched one of the table's control surfaces. The grisly photos of Simone Rawls' remains appeared on the table's surface.

With the touch of her finger, Sara dragged the images to spread them out. "Simone Rawls, AKA Ginger Simon."

"What's left of her," Sean observed.

Lily linked her com to the room's private network and pulled up the images she and Jolaj had lifted from Simone's flat. "Jolaj and I searched her duty flat and found these photos. They'd been overlooked. Everything else had been cleaned. Nothing helpful there. Director Gardot confirmed she was a research tech for Deepwater, but implied whatever Simone was up to was off the clock."

Sean dragged one of the images of a happy smiling Simone closer. "Any chance of getting a file of her latest assignments, known associates?"

Lily thought back to her conversation with the director. "Director Gardot was clear she wouldn't be providing any more info."

Sean looked up from the images. "That's why you asked Brian to dig into their files?"

Lily nodded. She wanted to tell him how much it had meant to her to have him at her side for that conversation, but decided to wait. They all needed to focus.

Sean tapped his thumb on the table. "Rawls is a victim, not a suspect, so it'll be tough to get a warrant."

Lily let her eyes drift to the back yard. "Through Jolaj's contacts I was able to find out that Simone was poking around the docks. She'd been trying to get the Ormney workers to participate in a research project."

"Drug trials?" asked Sara.

"Not that we can verify. Definitely, trying to collect physiological data."

Lily leaned forward and propped her arms on the table. "There's more. She was on staff in the Med Center where I was treated after the training accident."

"If she did sell the drug to EFE, she could have also told them about your accident." Sara rubbed her eyes and leaned back in her chair. "But she's been dead for weeks. Since before you got involved."

Lily steadied her nerves. There was one small detail that hadn't seemed important at the time, but it now seemed as big as the sky. "That may not be true."

The guilt of all the clues she'd missed weighed heavily. "The killer's interest in me isn't new. The day Lanyak attacked Jennifer Richardson, I received a message from Simone Rawls changing the time of my evaluation appointment."

Sean leaned forward and slapped a hand against the table's flat surface. "Setting you up to be on the street when it went down."

"But Simone was already dead by then," said Sara. "It must have been our guy."

Sean added a note to the file open in front of him. "First, while working at Deepwater, Simone Rawls learned about a drug that turns Ormney crazy along with the details of your accident."

"And the scars," Sara added.

Sean nodded. "Next, Simone started doing independent research on Ormney physiology in her spare time. Somehow she connected with EFE and gave them info on the Ormney and on you."

Sean reached out, taking her hand. "You're not just a part of this. You're right there at the beginning."

His palm was large and warm, but it didn't make her feel safe.

"I know you don't want to talk about it and may even be under orders not to divulge any Deepwater shit," Sean continued. "But I think it's time you told us about this accident and how it's related to this drug. There has to be a connection."

Lily weighed the value and consequences of telling them about the classified program that had changed her life. She didn't think the information would help, but it wasn't fact that made her decision. It was the patience in Sean's face. He could have blamed her for the mess she'd made of things, instead he held her hand and waited.

Lily pulled her hand free and stood. She paced to the window and stared out at the well- tended green lawn. She would tell them but she didn't want to see their reactions. "A year ago I was assigned to train a new recruit. An Ormney. We'd been working together for several months when a routine resistance exercise went badly wrong. He was exposed to a gas commonly used to provoke panic in trainees. The exercise is supposed to provide practical experience staying in control during a biological or chemical attack. He reacted badly. I was injured." It was factual to the point of understatement, but she saw no reason to tell them how close she'd been to death or how terrified Kiq had been or what it had been like to press her stunner to her friend's heart and take his life.

Lily took a deep breath. Concentrated on her heart rate. On staying calm as the memories rolled through her. "He attacked me. I survived. He didn't."

Sean made a noncommittal hmm sound. "I take it that gas is the one this drug is derived from."

"It has to be."

"It would make sense, then," said Sara. "That Rawls would mention you in connection to this drug."

"And maybe they wanted you involved," added Sean. "Thinking you'd be sympathetic. After all, you'd been attacked yourself."

"The flowers." Lily turned her back on the serene view of the backyard. "When were they delivered?"

Sean touched the table surface and text scrolled by as an image of the flower box and the e-card message appeared on the vid-wall.

"Before the incident at the medical center. Rose must have picked them up and carried them inside."

"They weren't a taunt." Lily settled into a seat and studied the message. *"Don't lose sleep over the lost girls.* Somehow, he knew I'd spent the night in the med center the night Jennifer Richardson died."

"He was expressing concern for you." Sara pulled up an image of the lilies that had been left on Mary Santini's body. "I can run this past one of our forensic psychiatrists, but I think he was courting you. Drawing your attention to his work like it was some perverse gift."

Sean ran a hand through his short cropped hair. "Then why the fuck did he try to kill her?"

"I pissed him off." Lily's insides turned to ice.

Sean sat a little straighter. "What? How?"

"I helped Jolaj try to save Kabel—at the medical center." She'd taunted him. Knowing he might be watching, she'd deliberately antagonized him.

"Yeah, maybe," Sean said. "If Sara's right and this guy was

courting you, that means we've got one guy behind all of the attacks. One who isn't the EFE guy that slashed Kabel's restraints."

Air rushed into Lily's lungs making her feel lightheaded.

"The EFE guy could have heard about the attack," Sara suggested, "and seized the opportunity."

"That means our tie to EFE is shaky. Shit." Sean slapped the table.

Lily leaned forward. "Think about it, Sean. You said you'd been interviewing EFE members all night and got nothing. You swept the headquarters and picked up members who lived in the area of the attacks, but you got nothing."

Sean's fists clenched tight with nothing to hold on to. "Where the hell does that leave us? Who else could Simone Rawls have told and why?"

"Or," Sara began. "Who else knew about the drug and your history, your scars? Who knew you spent the night at the med center?"

Lily thought back. "There was Tie and Luc. Hospital staff, Officer Newman." And one other person. "Bradley." She said the name before the impact of it really reached her. He knew because he'd spent the night in her apartment, in her bed. Bradley, who had made every attempt to convince her that he no longer wanted Rose. And now Rose was dead.

Lily drew her thoughts back to the moment and realized the whole room had fallen silent.

Sara visibly shook herself and sat straighter, pressing back in her chair as if she needed the few extra inches separation from what Lily might say next. "Bradley?"

Lily shifted in her own seat. Her brother-in-law was the last thing she wanted to be talking to her family about. "The Council knew all the details of the training incident," she explained. "Bradley is close to one of the council members. And he saw my scars in the morning after I got back from visiting Jennifer Richards." Of course it hadn't really been much of a visit. She being more of a witness to the woman's death. Death at the hands of her lover.

Simone Rawls had also been killed by a man that had very likely been her lover. At least young, sweet Mary hadn't had to face being ripped apart by the man she loved.

Sean pushed back from the table and stood. "Bradley was there yesterday too. During the initial attack." Sean strode over to the wall screen and drew Bradley's name with his finger then started a list beneath it."

Sara twisted in her chair to get a better view of the screen. "Are we seriously considering Bradley a suspect?"

Sean's eyebrows lowered as he continued to write. "We follow the facts and the fact is that Bradley had motive. We all know he wanted Lil back. And if Lil is right about the hospital…" His shoulders hitched and he turned away from the board. "He would've seen everything that went on there."

Lily couldn't see Bradley as violent. His trademark had always been as a diplomat, a talker, not a man to anger quickly or act in violence. Why had she even suggested him? Did she want him to be guilty? To be evil enough to kill his own wife? Just so she wouldn't feel as guilty for whatever her part in all of it was? "Where the hell *is* Bradley?"

"Did anyone contact him?" asked Sara.

"Damn it." Sean tapped his com-unit. "I was too worried about Lily and Brian and Aunt Karen. But he should have gotten a call about the attack from HQ."

Sean shook his head indicating he wasn't able to get through.

Lily used her com-lens to tag Bradley's com, but got no response. "Nothing for me either."

Sean tapped his com again and paced back to the windows Turning his back on the room he requested a link to the Metro response net.

Lily turned her focus to Sara. "What about the physical evidence? Bradley can't really be a suspect, can he?"

Sara reached over and put her palm over the fist Lily had unknowingly melded around the chair arm. Lily forced herself to release her grip and Sara slid their hands together.

"Hun, I can't rule him out. What are your instincts telling you?"

Lily licked her suddenly dry lips. "It isn't Bradley. He isn't a good person sometimes, but he doesn't have enough hate in him to sustain such an elaborate plot." Lily glanced to Sean to reassure herself he was still talking on his link. "And murders this brutal have to be based in hate, right? No amount of wanting or dissatisfaction could lead a man to something like this." She said it as a statement but heard the question in her voice. When she'd been working hostage recovery, she'd seen greedy men do terrible things to get their way. But not this. She couldn't bear to be the motivation for all of this.

Sara squeezed her hand. "I agree. This isn't Bradley. He's an ass, not a monster. The shadows ringing her eyes seemed even darker than when she'd first arrived home from the autopsy. Lily wanted to wrap her arms around her, but she couldn't move. Couldn't risk breaking down.

"We have a trace on his com unit." Sean's voice so close made Lily start, but he didn't seem to notice. He dropped back into the chair he'd vacated earlier. "Bradley's at a midtown residential address. I sent a team to pick him up."

"Good," said Lily. "That's good." But her cousins didn't seem to agree or maybe they were all too tired to react—good or bad.

They would all have to find their reserves, because she had a bad feeling that Bri had been right. Before things got better, they were going to get worse.

CHAPTER 39

Jolaj stood silent and on edge in the small Council Room. It wasn't the prospect of facing the Council's censure that bothered him. It was the familiarity of the darkened room. The Symbol of Perpetuation glowed pale against one wall. Five round fixtures directed luminous beams down to the unadorned seats where the Council members would sit behind a narrow curved table. The rest of the room was hidden away in a darkness that had always suffocated him with memories of the great black emptiness of *out-of-sync*. So much was different on Earth but this room had been remade in the image of those final years on the home-world when they'd been forced to live underground, out of reach of the increasingly toxic atmosphere.

On Earth they'd chosen to make their homes as open to the sky as possible. They'd reengineered clean biotechnologies, relying on native Earth plant species to green and power their community. The things they'd worked to preserve from the old world were the social order, their customs, and their devotion to The Way.

The Council Room here looked much like the one where he'd given hundreds of Search Reports. Week after week of *slipping* into the black, searching for a phase to stabilize in, desperate to *sync*, to breathe, to rest. Only to return and report failure. To stare into the grim faces of the Council again and again.

The tall, thin Councilor Chak and his diminutive mate

Councilor Tayp were the first to enter. Jolaj's muscles tensed and twitched instinctively as he met Chak's dark, intense eyes. Tayp did not bother to meet his eyes at all.

Jolaj was prepared for the wave of guilt that further tightened his body when his longtime friend Tasst and his graceful mate Zee found their places and sat. Tasst had been his mate's brother.

Councilors Vaj and Relerin stepped into the room last, moving close to one another. The two seemed always to be touching and offering comfort. This eldest couple of the Council remained a mystery to Jolaj. Their motives so often steeped in complex reasoning that went beyond the interests of a warrior like him.

Vaj spoke first, calling the session to order. "We're here today to address the actions of Law Keeper Jolaj, beloved hero of the people, honored warrior of the Council's Defenders, brave Searcher with hundreds of high risk search *slips* to attest to his dedication to Continuation and our beloved descendants."

The introduction, blatantly intended to remind the Council of his past service and sway them toward leniency, surprised Jolaj. He might have expected such a tactic from Tasst, but Vaj seemed an unlikely ally.

Chak with his close-trimmed hair and distinct peach-and-ivory coloring, lifted his hand in the air and patted the air as if to tamp down Vaj's praise. "Yes, we all recognize the valuable contribution of the Law Keeper, but we must deal with the matter at hand. This breach of the treaty comes at an inopportune time, now, when the humans' fear of us grows stronger each day."

Tasst clicked his claws aimlessly against the tabletop. "Perhaps if we allow the Law Keeper to explain what has happened in his own words?"

The Council members all nodded their agreement.

How would they react if he simply told them that Lily Rowan had become vital to him? In his way of thinking, there was nothing more important. He shelved his defiance for later and removed all trace of anger from his tone. "Honorable Councilors, the one responsible for the recent murders has not only targeted our people but also those who have accepted us, made us welcome, and befriended us. While our people are safe here in The Zone during curfew, our human friends are alone and vulnerable. I remained out of The Zone to offer my protection to these humans."

Tayp cleared her throat and met his gaze for the first time. "It was my understanding that these attacks have been occurring when curfew is not in effect."

Her colors were a rainbow of warm ginger hues, but her eyes were black as the emptiness of *out-of-sync*. Jolaj had faced the black many times in the *Search* years, but never did he welcome the cold.

He met her stare with no hint of the chill she visited upon him. "Until tonight that was true, but I feared that might change. Despite my efforts, a woman was murdered last night and others remain in danger." Jolaj paused a moment to ensure he had the full attention of each councilor. "I believe the Council must allow those of us with human companions to bring them into The Zone for safety."

There were several long moments of silence before Councilor Relerin spoke in a voice softened by age, but clear with purpose. "I agree, Jolaj. It would be irresponsible to leave these humans unprotected."

Several low grumbles followed her statement.

Tayp's fist struck the table in front of her with a thump. "You say companion, but don't you mean lovers? Isn't this all a result of our males giving in to the corrupting influence of the human culture?"

Her mate, Chak, sat taller in his seat. "It hasn't escaped our notice that only human females and our males are being targeted."

Vaj, hand tight around the medallion against his chest, frowned. "The desire to unite with a mate is not a human corruption."

Chak leaned forward to look across her mate and pin Vaj with those cold eyes. "Indulging lust with humans has little to do with the sacred union of mating."

Jolaj would once have agreed with the arrogant Chak. But he could not think of what he felt for Lily as mere lust. It had not been lust that had made it impossible to leave her alone with her sister's corpse. Nor had it been duty.

"With respect, Councilors, your opinion means little to those of us who feel it is our duty to protect those we have put at risk."

His friend pinned him with questioning eyes set in a too familiar arrangement of golden stripes. "There are others?"

Jolaj nodded, refusing to give in to the guilt that came with the anticipation of Tasst's disapproval.

Tasst shook his head, disappointment rippling in every movement. "You count yourself among them? You have a human female—" Tasst hesitated then ground out the final word "Companion?"

Jolaj spoke carefully, not in defense of his friend's feelings, but out of respect for Lily. "I've been working closely with agent Rowan. I believe she is known to the Council."

"Yes," said Chak. "We're familiar with the Deepwater Agent's role in Kiq's death."

Jolaj wanted to roar at Chak's accusing tone. It could be argued that it had been the Council's hesitance to share information with Deepwater that had created the tragedy. But those thoughts wouldn't serve the situation before them. "What you might not know is that Agent Rowan has ties to Metro law enforcement and the Ormney Affairs Office, as well as Deepwater. I believe her to be the most likely person to be able to quickly uncover the truth behind the murders. I also believe her tie to Kiq makes her someone we can trust to be fair to our people."

"You trust the woman who killed Kiq?" Tasst scowled his disapproval.

Jolaj's restraint slipped and he snapped out his reply. "I trust the woman who allowed him to nearly *kill* her before she would defend herself."

"Let him finish," said Vaj.

Jolaj was grateful for Vaj's interjection. It gave him a moment to calm. He could not let it appear that his affection for Lily clouded his judgment. "I have enlisted Agent Rowan's assistance to solve these murders and with her aid I believe the murderer will soon be uncovered."

Chak huffed. "Under whose authority did you involve yourself in this matter?"

"I've acted without your consent," he conceded. "But I have done what I believed best served the descendants."

"And how does breaking curfew, breaking the treaty, serve our future on this world?" asked the long-quiet Zee.

Jolaj did his best to look humble and full of remorse. "I

sincerely regret the difficulty caused by my actions."

Chak huffed again. "But you'll continue to do what you think best?"

Jolaj remained silent, as his answer would only anger the Council further. Despite his caution they broke out in an incensed and discordant jumble of voices.

"What gives you the right…?"

"Who do you think you are to make such a decision…?"

The councilors talked over one another, until Vaj boomed above the din. "Jolaj is a hero of the eta-War, the Searcher responsible for the *continuation* of our race. He is the citizen who has dedicated his life to our people—"

Relerin interrupted. "And sacrificed the perpetuation of his line that others might survive. How dare we question his service with this ridiculous proceeding?"

Silence filled the darkened chamber.

"No one is above the advice of the Council," said Chak.

"You're quite correct, Councilor, but I believe this fine hero of the people would not have acted without our consent if he'd held faith in our fairness and wisdom." Relerin got to her feet. "Perhaps it is time we direct our attention to our own actions and consider how we've failed in our duties that Jolaj should be forced to act alone." She stepped clear of her chair and paced slowly around the table. She stopped in front of him, looking up to him with wide, clear eyes, her tiny hands clasped together in front of her body. "You've so often faced danger alone on our behalf. Do you once again affirm your actions serve the descendants of the people?"

Jolaj considered her question and his own heart. Had he let his personal feelings color his judgment?

Relerin lifted one slender hand and held it palm up, waiting until he placed his larger one in hers. She covered it with her free hand and spoke low for his ears alone. "Sometimes, the needs of the champion are the needs of his people. A warrior has no time for doubts. Your instincts have been true ever before. Why do you question them now?"

Jolaj saw only confidence and belief in her face.

He spoke clear and loud to be heard by every member of the Council. "I affirm I serve our descendants now as ever I have."

She smiled, released him and turned enough to address the

others. Her voice rang through the darkness. "I take upon my own head, responsibility for all the actions of this man, past and present, and will bear any consequence required. I grant to him my full support in all matters before the Council this day."

Jolaj registered the shock on the faces of the Council at Relerin's words, but they each acknowledged her pledge and authority.

Tayp stood to speak to Relerin. "Your support—past and present—a strong statement. One we must acknowledge. However, law is law. Any infraction of the law disqualifies this man from service as Law Keeper."

"Agreed," announced her mate, the peach-toned Chak.

Tasst slowly got to his feet, moving as if his years had doubled during the brief session. He pressed two palms against the table and leaned forward. "Chak speaks true. Law is law. Despite Relerin's statement, you cannot be allowed to continue as Law Keeper."

"Agreed," echoed Zee.

Tasst's words had creaked across his lips with such regret that Jolaj almost believed his old friend suffered more over this inevitability than he did. His duties as Law Keeper had been all that had given purpose to his life since *The Crossing*, but he could not regret his decision to stay by Lily's side.

Relerin's support had lightened his biggest concern. He would be able to bring the human women into The Zone. He would have Lily safe in his home.

Tasst cleared his throat and Jolaj realized he hadn't responded to Tasst's statement.

"As the law requires." Jolaj had become a Law Keeper to serve the descendants, not to serve the law. With brisk efficient movements, he pulled his tunic over his head, removing the symbol of Law Keeper from his body. For one brief moment he felt lighter, freer than he had in years. Then he noticed the looks that lit the faces of Tayp and Chak. For them it was a victory and their expressions might be mistaken for satisfaction, but there was something more. Something larger and more devious.

He'd heard whispers that the council had discussed reinstituting the Searcher program with the goal of leaving Earth for a planet they could claim for their own. Could Chak and Tayp be behind such a scheme?

As he stood stiff and straight, bare-chested, he realized, by taking off the tunic he had exposed the tattoo that proclaimed him Searcher. A status and a symbol far more difficult to shed. They definitely had a larger plan and events had unfolded much as they wanted. A clever manipulation. A clever snare with him as the prey.

When had duty become a trap?

CHAPTER 40

A commotion in the hall turned everyone's attention to the doorway. Bradley walked in, looking like he wouldn't be vertical for long. His bloodshot eyes were swollen and deeply shadowed. His normally graceful walk had become a jolting shamble. He glanced at Sara and Sean then approached Lily. He pulled her into his arms, but Lily remained stiff and unyielding in the circle of his embrace. She wanted to be a better person, but she hated him in that moment. He smelled like liquor and perfume and she had to blame him for being a terrible husband to her sister. It was only fair—she hated herself for not having been a better sister to her twin.

Bradley eased back. "I'm so sorry, Lily."

She had no idea whether he meant it in a sorry-for-your-loss way or if he was asking for absolution for all of his sins. It didn't matter. She didn't have anything for him. Not absolution. And no desire for his comfort. No desire to offer any to him either.

Bradley went from sorrowful to angry in a lightning speed transformation. "What in the hell?" He was looking over her shoulder.

Lily followed his gaze to see the list Sean had made earlier. The one with Bradley's name at the top.

Sean walked over, no hurry in his pace, and wiped away the list. "Sorry, Brad. We have to look at all the possibilities. Most women are murdered by someone they know. The husband—"

"Don't give me that crap." Bradley's face reddened and he

threw up his hands. "You'd like that. If you could blame it on me." He stormed up to Sean and got in his face. "I did not kill Rose!"

Sean didn't flinch. "Relax, man."

Bradley gulped in air and outrage burst over his features. "Relax? You're accusing me—"

"I'm not accusing you of anything." Sean didn't move. Probably didn't want Bradley to mistake anything for aggression. "Seriously. Calm down. This isn't productive and we all want the same thing."

Bradley's shoulders slumped. "To find her killer."

Sara got to her feet and pulled out a chair for him. "That's right. Now have a seat and we can talk."

His focus shifted to her, clearly what she'd been aiming for.

Sean returned to his seat and Lily and Sara sat down. Bradley huffed in place for a moment, but finding no target for his anger he went over to the chair. He put his hands on the chair-back and leaned over it, but stayed on his feet. "Do you have any leads? Suspects? Besides me?"

Lily jumped when the war-room door swung open and Brian barged in. Something inside Lily shifted. How long had it been since she'd seen him in person? He was tall and too thin. His ash blond hair brushed against his collar and framed his angular features with a reckless abandon.

His long strides carried him quickly across the room. Lily met him half way. She pulled him into her arms and they both clung for a long minute. When he pulled back to meet her eyes she noticed the metallic glint of a neural implant near his temple. Another step toward joining The Pool? Her relationship with her brother had been strained—like all her family relationships had when Rose married Bradley. No, long before that—when her mother had moved them away. Now Rose was dead and Lily didn't know how to go forward.

His pale gray eyes seemed to see inside her. "We have a lot to talk about, but first we do this." He indicated the table with all its grisly images.

She nodded, struggling to find words.

Brian acknowledged Sean and Bradley with a shared glance and then went over and kissed Sara on the top of the head before settling into a chair to join them.

"Okay, bring me up to speed." Sean laid a palm on the smooth surface of the table. It came alive under his touch. The section around his hand lit with a series of symbols, boxes of running text, a narrow column of code, and a series of miniature views of live vid feeds.

Sean summed up their discussion while everyone listened.

Leaning forward, Brian tapped an image of Simone Rawls. "This woman—" A dozen more images of Simone appeared on the table as Brian spoke. "My contacts put her as a nexus point in the data they were able to get from Deepwater."

Lily grinned grimly. "So, you got in to their system?"

"In and out without tripping any alerts." A smile ghosted across his lips. "She came up on a list of people with access to information on Deepwater's Ormney research and development data, the Ormney training program." Brian turned his gaze on Sean. "And the aftermath of the accident that nearly killed Lily." He didn't look at her when he said it, but all traces of his smile had disappeared. "When we realized Rawls had disappeared weeks ago, that brought her to the top of our focus list."

Bradley snapped his attention from crime scene photos to Sean. "If it's data about the R&D you need, I'm sure I can apply pressure to get whatever you need. Part of our agreement with Deepwater was a full disclosure clause."

Sean shrugged. "Will take whatever you can get."

Brian pursed his lips. "It would be more helpful if you had and files already copied from them and stored on your own systems. Somewhere they couldn't have gotten to it to tamper with it in any way."

Bradley pulled his com out of his pocket. "I'll see what I can get."

Sara tapped one of her files and shot a look to Brian. "Were you able to find out if Deepwater is testing or manufacturing derivatives of the drug used in the training accident?" As she spoke, Sara pulled up a display of the lab reports on the various forms of the drug that had been used to instigate Ormney attacks.

"No." Brian shook his head. "As far as we can tell, Deepwater's only interest in the drug is in developing a countermeasure they could provide to any future Ormney agents they can recruit."

Sara leaned back with an exhausted sigh. "If Rawls was working on the chemical derivatives on her own, she'd need a lab. Was there anything like that in her flat?"

"No," Lily answered. "But Deepwater had already cleared the place out when Jolaj and I found it."

Lily had no luck keeping her thoughts from turning to the Ormney Law Keeper who'd broken a very important law for her. Where was he? What were they putting him through? What price would he pay for staying with her when she needed someone? Needed him.

Brian pulled up a copy of the Deepwater internal report listing the items that had been removed. "Nothing here."

Sara wouldn't back down. "Well, she had to be working on it somewhere."

Sean studied the list then glanced up at Brian. "Did you find any more data on Rawls?"

"Gigabytes, but so far, nothing relevant." Brian shrugged. "She definitely wasn't just a tech. Had agency training for clandestine field work. Real spy stuff. Fairly good at hiding her tracks. We've been looking mostly at her Deepwater activities, but I'll run a cross search with local labs and med centers, the university. See if I can find where she did her work."

Brian pulled up a file that Lily recognized as coming from her own notes. "Now that we know about Rawls's activities at the docks," he said. "I've put Snow on surveillance vid and security logs. We'll get more there, but it'll take time."

Sean shifted in his seat. "You've been in contact with your hacker since you got here?"

Brian frowned. "I have a line open, yeah. We need The Pool and Snow is totally legit and completely reliable. You have my word on that."

Sean raised a hand to Brian, in a calming gesture.

Brian had always been the quiet easygoing one, but time had given him more confidence. The changes in him reminded Lily of everything she'd given up when she'd joined Deepwater.

"How long," Lily asked, "before you get anything back from Snow?"

"Hard to say. Lots of data to sift through. Snow will start with the vid surveillance using facial recognition algorithms. Snow is crazy hooked into the metro grid. Once we narrow it down, it'll require eyes on hours of vid and that takes time."

Bradley leaned forward. "We have about a dozen interns at the OA office. Just say the word.

Brian frowned. "We can't distribute that work out unless we're prepared to go public with whatever we find."

Sean shook his head. "No, we can't afford to alert the killer."

Brian pushed a hand through his hair. "That's the conclusion I came to. Snow is on it for now and I'll pitch in when we're through here." Brian looked around the room. "What else have we got?"

Sean pulled up a map of the city highlighting the crime scenes and the known EFE related addresses. "Aside from the EFE member we arrested and the presence of other EFE members living in the area, we have nothing tying into anyone with a strong motive, no one with obvious opportunity, no one with connections to the drug. A lot of hours of cop work leading nowhere."

"Maybe we should walk through what we do know," Sara suggested.

Sean moved over to the timeline he'd started earlier and displayed the principal stills and stats for each crime scene and attack. "After Rawls disappeared," he started. "We have a few weeks of no related activity that we've identified. Then Jennifer Richardson was attacked. The only thing that marks her as out of the ordinary is her apparent friendship with the Ormney male who attacked her."

Sara pulled up an autopsy image of Lanyak. "The drug was introduced using an air dart to the back of the neck."

"We think through the open window of her apartment," Sean added.

Sara nodded. "My team has given Sean a list of possible darts and dart guns."

"I had our data techs look at her com and link logs," Sean said. "We're following the threads out from there. So far nothing pops."

Brian pulled up a refugee identification file for Lanyak. "What about the Ormney that attacked her? All I've got is an image and vitals."

"Lanyak was one of the Searchers before The Crossing." Lily carefully weighed what she could tell them that might help.

"According to the neighbor, Jennifer met him in the market and they struck up a friendship."

"Jennifer survived the attack initially, but died later." Sean added a note to the file he was working in. "Lanyak died on scene."

Lily let the guilt of that day roll over her then shoved it aside. "Not twenty-four hours later, Mary Santini was murdered by someone who tried to make it look like an Ormney attack. She let her killer in shortly before her Ormney coworker was scheduled to arrive to walk her to work. We don't know if he was targeted too, but it seems likely."

Sara shrugged. "The drug panel we ran didn't find any sign of the drug in his system."

Sean nodded. "He's not a serious suspect either. Without a chemical influence, he had opportunity but no motive."

Brian studied the files. "Any tie between Jennifer Richardson and Mary Santini?"

"Other than living in the same neighborhood, no," answered Sean. "They would have used the same glide-rail stops. They could have passed each other on the street or bumped into each other at the local market. Nothing that seems to pop as a real connection."

Sara pulled up stills from the autopsy vid. "I did notice both girls had recently had scar tissue repair. Jennifer on her right shoulder, Mary near her collarbone. The tissue repair didn't appear in either girl's med file."

Sean called up the contents file for Jennifer Richardson's apartment and scrolled to the lav. "An injury clicks with Dermamend found in her med supplies. Also quick-heal spray. Either she was accident prone or she let her clients get rough."

Or she was having sex with an Ormney. Lily remembered Jolaj's mouth on her shoulder. His claws scraping against her SafeSkin tank. "Tie LeRoue, Jennifer's neighbor mentioned taking her for medical treatment, said she'd been bitten. I think he said they went to a clinic."

The panels in front of Brian scrolled through data too fast for Lily to catch. "I don't see a record of it in any of the clinics in The Mixer or at the local med center."

"I can ask Tie for more info," Lily offered.

Sean lifted a shoulder. "Seems like a long shot but I can follow up with Mary's mother."

Brian looked to Lily. "Anything connect you to these women or the Ormney that are tied in?"

Lily shook her head. "Nothing."

Sean's thumb tapped the table as he spoke. "So far, this tissue thing Sara found and the fact that both women associated with an Ormney is our only link tying them together."

Brian said, "If the point was making the Ormney look like the bad guys maybe the women didn't matter."

"The attack yesterday took place in a public med center." Lily pulled up her notes from that incident. "No way they could be sure the damage would be limited to a specific human target. I definitely think making the Ormney appear threatening is a big part of this."

"So that takes us back to the anti-Ormney orgs," said Sean. "The team I assigned to work that angle has been drowning in possibilities and running short on solids. There are a few big orgs everyone knows about but they're probably our least likely bet. There are dozens of small orgs, on and off book. Beyond that we could be looking at an individual with a beef."

Sara made a hmm noise. "There are strong feelings over the limits in place on med tech exchange. Yesterday's attack might go more to the heart of it. Somebody with a loved one that had a medical issue that might have been saved if the Ormney would share more information."

Brian pushed back in his chair. "But how does any of that tie back to Lily?"

"Simone Rawls." Lily blurted it out. "She is the only thing that ties into me."

Brian looked grim. "Then that's where we have to look."

Sean's com-link trilled. He excused himself and stepped over to the windows to take the link.

Brian looked over to Lily. "When's the last time you slept?"

"There'll be time to sleep after we catch this bastard."

The argument she sensed brewing was cut short when the door slid open. Brian blanked the displays as a gasp brought everyone's attention to the woman standing in the doorway.

Lily pushed back from the table and stood. She had to swallow and focus on her breathing, but she managed to get out a single steady word.

"Mother."

Logically, she'd known Brian had brought their mother, but somehow she'd managed to push it from her mind.

Bradley scrambled to his feet. He straightened his clothes as he went to Lily's mother. He pulled her into his arms. "Karen, thanks for getting here so quickly."

She acknowledged him, but quickly shifted her attention to Lily—her features both watery and hard. She turned in a slow circle, taking in the space and staring Sean and Sara down in turn. "Well, the room has certainly come up a notch from the days when your fathers used to hide in here, drinking beer, and pinning grotesque photos to the walls."

"And solving crimes, Aunt Karen." Sara stood, the tips of her fingers touching the table. "They saved lives and put away grifters, rapists, and killers. Don't forget that part."

"Oh, I haven't forgotten a thing." Tears ran down Karen's face as she spoke. "They did great things for other people's families. But once again it's *my* family paying the price."

Brian got to his feet and pulled their mother into his arms. "You're upset. Maybe this isn't a good time to talk about this."

"Oh, Brian, how long do we have to stay here? I want you away from this. I can't lose you too."

Pent up sorrow, hurt, and anger churned in Lily's stomach as she watched her mother worry over Brian. She couldn't look away from them, longing to be included, afraid to see pity in the eyes of her cousins.

Brian drew back to look their mother in the face. "I'm sorry, Mom, but I need to be here, right now. If you want to go back to DC, I can make the arrangements."

She clung to Brian. "I'm not going anywhere without you."

Karen's tear-soaked voice sputtered and broke as she tried to speak her outrage. "I suppose you'll get what you've always wanted now." Being the object of her mother's venom didn't surprised Lily. It did catch her off guard when Bradley spoke up to defend her.

"It isn't like that, Karen. Lily didn't betray Rose. What was between Lily and I was over a long time ago. I just didn't know how to make Rose see that." Bradley moved back to her mother and took her hands in his. "Rose and I would have worked things out. I'm sure of it."

Lily carefully reined in her reaction. It had been the right thing to say for her mother at that moment, even if it did contradict everything he'd been telling her.

Her mother nodded, tears running down her cheeks.

Brian interrupted. "Brad, could you take Mom into the kitchen. I'm sure Aunt Jane will have tea and scones. Mom could use something in her stomach about now." His face was kind, generous, as he spoke to them. It turned deadly serious the moment they stepped out of the room. "Sean, Sara, could you give us a minute."

Sara opened her mouth to speak, but Sean put an arm around her shoulders and pulled her from the room.

Brian opened his arms and wrapped Lily in warmth. She wanted to burrow into his embrace and take the comfort he offered, but she was very afraid she'd shatter if she allowed any crack in her emotional armor.

Brian moved back enough to look her in the eye comfortably. "Lil, you can't do this all by yourself." Layers of meaning complicated the simple statement. *This* being all manner of things. The investigation. Dealing with her grief. Dealing with her mother.

"I'm fine." Lily shrugged. "And I don't intend to investigate alone." She held her hands out to indicate the room. "That's what all this is about. Working together."

Brian bit back the need to shake her. Despite her words, the inches between them became miles. She left everything important unsaid. He knew he had to find a way to get through to her. He reached out and captured one of her hands, breaking the illusion that she was out of his reach. "I know we haven't been as close the last few years, but I know you. You're about to bolt. Being here, this house, Mom, Bradley, even me. It terrifies you."

Brian could see the anxiety in his only remaining sister's eyes. She didn't squirm in her discomfort but the knowledge that he could read her so well had only thinned the veneer she hid behind.

"It isn't that," she said. "It's just that I need to follow up on Sara's lead. I need to talk to Tie LeRoue and find out which clinic he went to with Jennifer Richardson."

Brian watched her closely. The signs of her distress were

minute and well hidden. "Since I can't find any record of either girl getting those scars removed, I guess we'll have to do it your way."

"You should stay with Mom." She met his eyes and her jaw was tight.

She was trying to chase him away because she was afraid. He knew, but it still felt like she didn't need him, didn't want him in her life. That's the way it had felt when she'd joined Deepwater. It hadn't been him she'd been running from then either. But still it had hurt. He shook his head. "Are you going to break your promise?"

"Promise?"

She paled at the word. He knew what he was about to do would disturb her, make her even more uncomfortable, but he would do anything to keep her safe. With a thought, he activated the vid-wall and displayed a street vid that showed her talking to the Ormney Law Keeper in front of her apartment building that morning. There was no audio, but her words were clear on her lips. She'd promised the Ormney she would stick with her family. Brian was both grateful and annoyed. It was a vow no one had won from her since their father had died. So much had changed that day. What had this man done to hold such sway over her?

"No," she said. "I won't break my promise. Not if I can help it. I'll talk Sean into going." She watched the vid intently. "Your Snow dig this up?"

He knew she must be wondering what else Snow had found. Snow was just as amazing with satellites and surveillance vids, but Brian hadn't needed Snow's help to find the rooftop video. He'd been keeping an eye on Lily for weeks. Not spying. Not really. But he knew her *accident* had left her unstable and when he'd realized how much time she'd been spending high above the street he'd been compelled to keep an eye on her. The video most likely on Lily's mind had nothing to do with her safety so he saw no reason for a confrontation.

He popped another vid up on the wall. This one was far more important to both of them. It showed a stocky human approaching Lily's building the evening Rose was killed. "Snow thinks this is the guy that killed our sister."

Lily jerked straighter, face intense. "Is there a better angle?"

"No, and he never looks up."

Lily's hands balled into fists. "Have you cross referenced principal characteristics with the other attacks?"

"Yeah, but we didn't find anything significant. Based on the way he moves, odds are he took measures to obscure his identity. Padding, maybe prosthetics." The vid jumped forward and the man exited the building. "He was ready. He knew we'd try to track him. He used a scrambler in your building and another when he made it into a high traffic rail station. We lost him there."

Watching the killer walk across the vid display, Lily flushed even paler. Damn. She was going to lose it and Brian knew she wasn't ready to let him help her. He hesitated for a fraction of a second then with a thought he used his neural implant to send out a general broadcast com to The Zone: *Law Keeper Jolaj—immediate contact requested*. As Lily went for the door with long, ground-eating strides, the Law Keeper responded to his com: *Jolaj—awaiting message*. Brian flashed a silent text request. *Lily Rowan needs your assistance at the O'Leary residence*. He followed it with a locator bulletin.

He wasn't sure how quickly the Law Keeper would arrive. He'd stall her somehow.

Lily made it into the hall when she came face to face with their mother.

"What are you plotting now? You won't put Brian at risk too!" Their mom pulled away from Aunt Jane's hands. "It shouldn't have been Rose!"

At that everyone else seemed to start talking at once. Everyone but Lily. She went from pale to colorless—ready to bolt any second.

The pounding on the door silenced the room. Then the Ormney was there, inside, *slipping* to *in-sync* in a hazy blur. Lily pushed past their mother, Bradley, and even Sean, flying into the Law Keeper's arms.

The big Ormney male bent over her head and whispered something into her ear as he stroked her back. Brian had known they were lovers, but somehow the tenderness between them still managed to surprise him. Give him hope for his tough but damaged sister.

He looked around at the shocked faces and decided it would be better to avoid the barrage of questions poised to explode into the crowded hallway. Why wasn't the man wearing his uniform? Brian strode forward, edged past Lily and Jolaj and opened the front door. "If everyone will excuse us, the Law Keeper is going to help Lily and me follow up on a lead."

The Law Keeper's head lifted and he met Brian's eyes. They studied each other long enough to get each other's measure then headed to the door as if there had never been any doubt.

CHAPTER 41

Lily leaned against the jet-hop parked at the curb and took a deep breath then shivered as the after effects of the panic worked its way out of her system. Lily had needed air and the autumn breeze provided that. She'd also need to be away from her mother's eyes and the pain of her accusation. Her brother and Jolaj had provided that. Gotten her out before her heart exploded in her chest.

She met Jolaj's gaze. He stood close. There if she needed him again. Her brother had turned his back to give her privacy. God, she was thankful for the two of them. Guilt hovered over her shoulder, reminding her that, because of her, her sister had lost her life. It was no time to be finding her own. But every time she was near Jolaj she felt a little more alive. And her brother—he'd been trying to wake her up for months. Finally, she understood. Too late to make amends with her sister. Too late for them all to fit and be a family again.

The sky overhead was gray, promising stormy weather. It was mid-day, so the children were still in school and the street was quiet. Lily rubbed her hands on her thighs then realized her shivers just might be from the cooler temperature. Jolaj stepped closer and pulled her back into his arms. Sharing his body heat.

He rubbed a hand up and down her back. "You're cold."

She leaned into him and contemplated whether she might be able to stick close enough to him to stay warm through the coming storm. "I left my coat inside."

"I'll get it for you, but I may need your pulser to keep your family at bay." She allowed her lips to curve at the ridiculous picture in her head. She fisted her hands in his tunic and held him tight. "No, you won't.

She felt almost strong enough to head back inside herself when the door swung open and Bradley stepped out, her coat in his hand. Lily and Jolaj eased apart and Brian turned back around as Bradley approached. He squinted against the wind, drawing her attention to the red swollen rings that rimmed the dense network of angry blood vessels in his eyes.

"Thought you'd need this." He lifted her jacket and held it out for her. Lily took it and slipped her arms into the soft leather as he stepped back.

"Lily," rumbled Jolaj. "We need to talk."

It was an excuse to get rid of Bradley. But she didn't hate Bradley enough to send him back inside so quickly. He'd be facing some real heat from her mom and she couldn't wish that on anyone.

She reached for Jolaj and slipped her hand in his. For a moment she savored the peace that came with his touch and praised God there was no panic. Not for now. She squeezed his hand in silent signal. "It's okay. Give me a minute."

He frowned but left her side to stand nearer to Brian.

"Thanks," said Bradley.

She couldn't give him whatever he was looking for from her, but she owed him a moment for the coat. Unlike her family, he'd always understood her need to keep her father's things, her need to have something more tangible than memories to hold on to. As teenagers, they'd talked for hours about everything under the sun. He listened to her talk about Dad endlessly, without complaint.

She wished she could feel comforted that he'd noticed she'd stepped outside without the coat, that he'd braved the others' censure to bring it out to her, but she just wished he hadn't done it. Her mother would see it as further evidence that she was to blame for her sister's troubled marriage.

She wrapped the old leather more tightly around herself. "Thanks for bringing it out."

He nodded, face full of pain. He had to be running

through the what-ifs in his head. What if he'd been home? What if he'd been a better husband. Some small part of her wanted to use his obvious failures as a reason to blame him for Rose's death, but she couldn't. Her own guilt wouldn't allow it.

She could only blame herself and the killer. The damn image of Rose lying dead on the floor of her apartment had been burned into her brain. The horrible, sickening image... and the sound of her father's favorite jazz playing on the music cube in Rose's hand.

"Bradley, did Rose have a music cube with some of Dad's tunes?"

He didn't even have to consider her question. His eyebrows drew together, wrinkling his forehead as he answered, "No. You know she didn't hang on to any of your dad's things."

Still chilled, Lily rubbed her hands against her arms. "She started doing things differently after the two of you got married. I wasn't sure..."

His confusion turned to a full-out frown. "You mean because she started spending holidays with the O'Learys?"

"Yeah," said Lily.

Bradley looked away, suddenly finding the grassy yard more interesting.

"Bradley..." Lily tried to press him, but he wouldn't meet her eyes and she realized that Jolaj and Brian had edged closer, standing at her sides.

Brian held his hand out palm up. Lily slipped her fingers into his grasp and her heart sped with anticipation or dread of what he would say. "She did that to edge you farther out, Lil. She always worried you'd step back into the family and everyone would turn on her."

"It was my fault," Bradley said, studying his toes. "I never loved her like I should have." He looked up and finally met Lily's eyes. "I should never have given you that ultimatum about dropping out of Metro academy. But when you refused and I was spending all my time at the college. Rose was there. Sweet, giving, perfect wife material according to everything my dad had been preaching to me for years."

Lily so didn't need to hear any of that. Her stomach turned. "None of that matters anymore."

When Jolaj wrapped a hand on her hip, she welcomed the

connection they we're building. "Your brother said something about a lead?"

"Lily could have kissed him in gratitude for the change of subject. "Tie LeRoue, he might know what clinic Jennifer went to. It could lead to more info on Simon Rawls."

"Maybe I can help." Bradley was still trying to be helpful. "I have contacts—"

Brian released Lily's hand and edged between her and Bradley. "We've got it covered. Why don't you go back in and sit with Mom. She could use your support right now. She hasn't been comfortable with the O'Learys in years."

"Sure. No problem." He gave Lily one last sorrow-filled look then went back inside.

When the door closed behind Bradley, the knots in Lily's stomach eased. She activated her com-link and put in a call to Tie. She kept the com on audible. Brian leaned into hear, but Jolaj had no need. He stayed close, but gave her more room.

Tie's smooth voice filled the space between them. "Hey, *cher*. What's up with you? You *mebe* have news?"

"Sorry, Tie. No news yet."

"No worries. You'll catch this bastard, *oui*?"

"Yes." She didn't tell him she had more reason than ever to go after the killer with all her heart and soul. "But I need your help."

"Anything, *cher*. Anything at all."

"I need to know which clinic you took Jennifer to for the bite."

"The clinic? That would be the Clinton Street Clinic."

"Isn't that next to the Corner Grocery?"

"*Oui*.

She looked around and found Jolaj watching, listening intently. Brian frowned. He hadn't yet made the connection. "One of the other victims worked there."

Tie made a humming noise. "Anything else I can tell you, *cher*? I, ah, I'll be tied up for a bit after this."

"Working?"

"*Non*, *cher*. Playing." There was thick, sultry sin laced through his voice and with what she knew of Tie and his lover, Lily suspected his reference to being tied up had been perfectly literal. "Luc," he continued, "he has been doing his best to keep my thoughts off Jen and Luc's best is damn good."

"I have no doubt."

Brian touched Lily's shoulder to get her attention. "The doctor?"

Lily nodded. "Tie, can you recall the doctor's name?"

The com went quiet, then Tie answered, "*Non*, sorry, *cher*. I do remember it was a man, mid-thirties. Good-looking."

"Okay, Tie. Thanks."

"You be careful, *cher*."

Lily closed the link.

"Sounds like we need to make a visit to that clinic," said Jolaj.

Lily turned around to look directly at him. "You're not wearing a Law Keeper tunic." It had registered when he first arrived, but the realization of what it might mean seeped in bit by bit.

He put a hand out to cup her cheek. "The tunic never made me who I am. I still need to stop these attacks and prevent any more killings. That hasn't changed."

Her jaw clenched compulsively and she closed her eyes to fight the angry regret. They had stripped him of his role because of her.

He pressed his lips to her temple. "We'll talk about this later," he said, leaning back. "Now we go on the hunt for the killer."

CHAPTER 42

A check of the weather confirmed that a storm was approaching. Brian flew the Jet-hop he'd rented at the transport center. He complained about having to fight the wind but the hop rode steady. Lily teased him about being a baby and the moment felt good. She had no choice but to accept Jolaj's decision not to talk about what had happened at the Council meeting. He sat in the back while she sat in front with Brian.

Lightning flashed in the distance, but still no rain when they parked in front of the clinic.

Brian studied the street. "None of the victims are listed in the clinic's database."

Lily watched his eyes take in the neighborhood. "You hacked in?"

"The Pool did," he said.

"The Pool?" Jolaj asked.

"It is a community of people who spend their time connected to a network of computers," Brian explained. "They're in every metropolitan area and they have access to practically every networked system." Brian continued to talk as they walked up to the clinic entrance. "The people that make up The Pool use neural implants and biosensors to connect to the network. They can move through data streams as easily as we move from place to place in the physical world. Easier."

"The security for med records is typically pretty tight and

protected by tough privacy laws," Lily commented.

Jolaj frowned. "And these people, The Pool, they accessed the clinic's data?"

Brian rested a hand on the clinic door but delayed opening it. "That's right, but they didn't have to break any laws to do it. Some of my white-hat contacts have a contract to verify med record security." A hint of a grin lightened Brian's features. "I think the health department is going to be getting a recommendation to upgrade network security for neighborhood clinics this week."

He pulled the door open and they walked into the small reception area. A young brunette with plain features sat behind a wide counter. She looked up from her work screen, already asking for their health codes.

"Where not here for that. We need your help in an investigation." Brian stepped up to the counter and slipped a flex screen from his coat pocket and unrolled it on the counter top. He laid his hand on the thin, flexible material. "If you check your link, I just sent you Metro credentials. We're working with them on official business."

Lily had a feeling the credentials were a bit exaggerated. Jolaj stayed quiet behind her.

The receptionist looked them over and nodded. "How can I help you?"

Brian didn't even move, but vid stills of Jennifer Richardson and Mary Santini popped onto the screen. "Have you seen either of these women in the clinic?"

The woman's face twisted then her features smoothed into a professional mask. "I can't give out patient information."

"Both these women are dead and you have our credentials."

She glanced over to her work screen rechecking what Brian had sent her and nodded.

"I'm sorry," she said. "I don't recognize either girl."

Brian's eyes flicked away from her as he focused on something only he could see. His body language changed as if someone had dumped a power boost into his system.

His hand slid out to touch the screen again and the images changed. It filled with vid stills. Rawls on the street outside the clinic, Rawls keying in a door code, image after image of Rawls going in and out of the clinic with date stamps spanning months before her death.

The receptionist brightened. "That's Dr. Rawls. She volunteered here for a while. Haven't seen her in several weeks."

Jolaj moved closer to get a better look.

Brian and Lily exchanged a glance. "Snow found vid of Rawls at the docks and followed her here."

Lily smiled. "Give Snow a gold star."

Brian nodded but then he frowned as he focused on a point over Lily's shoulder. "We're having trouble getting details on staff and patient appointments. The victims aren't in the clinic list but if we can narrow it down to patients Dr. Rawls saw, we could try to verify identities and take a second look for anyone who might have registered under an alias." His gaze refocused then snapped back to the receptionist. "Could you provide us with a list of Dr. Rawls' patients?"

The receptionist wrinkled her nose. "Not for Dr. Rawls. She didn't see patients. She helped out with the lab work."

Lily's thoughts went back to their earlier discussions about Rawls. Could this be where she'd been doing her lab work? "Sara would want to see any lab notes."

Brian leaned into the woman. "What do you say? Notes?"

"That I can do." She tapped out a couple of selections on her screen. "You should have the file now. Not much there. She must not have been much of a note taker."

"Or she kept her notes on her private unit," Jolaj suggested. "Did you know Dr. Rawls well?"

The receptionist hesitated. "No, not really."

Lily remembered Tie's description of the doctor. "We believe Jennifer saw a male doctor, mid-thirties, good-looking. Sound like anyone you can think of?"

The woman frowned. "Could be. We have lots of staff here. Most aren't full time. They work shifts to meet the med board requirements for community care."

When Jolaj looked confused, Brian explained. "Medical staff are required to work a minimum number of hours annually in a neighborhood based med facility to keep their license. The med board's way of ensuring the neighborhood clinics can get good medical staff, since they can't pay as well or offer as many opportunities for advancement as the large med centers."

"So, where does that leave us?" asked Lily.

The receptionist said, "I can give you staff lists."

"Snow will be able to do a facial recognition scan on the same camera that picked up Rawls coming in to the building," said Brian. "If we can figure out what days the victims were here, maybe we can use that to narrow down a list of folks for Sean's team to check out."

To Lily, it sounded like they might finally have something to work with. "Maybe they can find someone who spoke to them, knew them, anything that might have connected the two girls."

"Is it possible that coming here for care of this injury is what made them targets?" asked Brian.

Lily nodded. "We should pay special attention to anyone who would have recognized the injury as a bite and might have understood its significance."

Brian frowned. "Significance? Do we know that already?"

The quiet that fell over the group seemed to be answer enough for Brian. Lily would have to explain later, out of earshot from the receptionist who was watching them with rapt attention.

"Okay," said Brian, directing his next question to the receptionist. "If I give you the dates, can you give me the staff that worked that day and the patient list?"

"Sure."

Lily stood back, feeling antsy and frustrated. She wanted something solid. Today. Now. She was tired of waiting. A loud boom rocked through her already revved senses. The glass storefront of the clinic shattered and the floor shook. She followed close behind Jolaj as he dashed through the door. She cast a quick glance at Brian. "You stay here and do this," she said. "We can deal with whatever is out there."

When Brian nodded, Lily turned her focus back to the street. A loud boom and a wave of heat flashed four meters ahead. She latched on to the doorframe. Absorbed the rumbling vibration of the explosion.

It rolled across the front of the building, originating in the little grocery next door. Fire licked out of the shattered front window, but the devastation barely reached beyond the storefront. Improvised explosive. A small crowd of angry citizens stood in the street shouting and yelling. They carried lit signs reading *Go home!* and *Employing Ormney funds murderers!*

"Damn." Lily reached for Jolaj's tunic but he was already

slipping and her hand met empty space.

She knew he hadn't left the area. He'd probably taken, what for him, was the easiest route into the building. He'd make sure the people inside were safe and that left her to deal with the rowdies in the street.

Lily activated her link to the emergency response net. "Reporting riot in progress, my location."

As she listened to the AI respond, she activated her locate beacon. She ignored the heat pulsing against the bare skin of her cheeks, despite the light mist starting to fall, and took a moment to search the half lit faces of the crowd.

She wondered if the killer was there, among them. Had he started this? Was he watching? Or was the riot just reaction, another offshoot of the violence he'd started? Ordinary folks shouted and hissed, some in jeans and sneakers, some in transit system uniforms, others sporting the caps handed out at the local welders union, all with faces twisted in anger or fear. No one seemed to be relishing the destruction enough to be the killer.

The market's fire suppression system kicked in, jetting chemical-laced water onto the fire with a hiss of steam, spewing a bitter waft of the flame retardant chemicals into the air. The excess water sprayed through the broken glass, splashing onto the pavement near Lily's feet.

A chorus of boos swelled up from the crowd. The noise jerked her attention to two women standing at the front. The open duffel bags at their feet tagged them as the fire starters, but they continued to chant, showing no signs of moving to reignite the blaze. Near the back of the mob, a man in a shiny, pea green bag-suit caught her eye. Something about his movements bothered her. He danced from foot to foot, arms held out in the rounded A-frame stance of street corner bullies. His dance took him more and more to the side of the crowd, but it didn't seem likely he was trying to leave.

Senses alert, Lily moved carefully toward him.

His eyes were on the storefront and his hands darted out, then in, toward the deep pockets of the suit. She lengthened her stride but not in time to reach him before he pulled out a boom-needler. Once clear of the crowd, he wasted no time in pointing the deadly, black market weapon at the store front.

He pressed his eye against the needler's sights, paying little attention to the people still shouting on his right or Lily approaching on his left.

Lily didn't draw her pistol. Not a good place to start a firefight. Instead she wrapped her fist around the pulser in her pocket. Thank God she'd carried both.

Pea-bag-suit guy shifted his hand, resting his finger on the trigger.

Out of time.

"Hey, peapod!" She shouted to be heard over the noise and she was ready when the barrel swung her way. She lifted her hands in the air in a classic don't-shoot-me gesture.

By the time he registered the pulser in her fist she was close enough to knock the needler's barrel downward with her left arm while stepping in to discharge the pulser. The charge, set to stun, tightened his body in an instant then dissipated. His muscles went limp in a wave that left him on the pavement like a wax figure left too long in the sun.

The noise of the crowd surging toward her from behind registered seconds before a blunt impact thudded through her shoulder and down her spine, spinning her around. The man toting an aluminum baseball bat was late fifties and paunchy, but he knew how to swing like a pinch hitter. She dodged the second swing, but a shove from behind sent her to the pavement in a grinding thump. She gave thanks for her dad's leather coat. She pushed through, turning the fall into a roll and coming up in a crouch.

"Lily, the gun!" Brian's shouted warning jerked Lily's attention to where he stood in front of the clinic then back to the crowd. A skinny teenager was scrambling for the boom-needler that pea-bag guy had lost in his fall.

Lily scrambled to her feet with thoughts of trying to kick the damn thing clear. No way was she reaching for it and leaving herself open for a more debilitating hit in the process. Even if she managed to grab it, that would just tie up her hands. Where in the hell was Metro?

Before the teen could close his hand around the needler, Jolaj *slipped* into *sync* next to him.

The boy went flying as Jolaj lifted and tossed him in a show of strength that left Lily grateful and a little breathless. The crowd scattered, clearing enough space for Lily, Brian, and Jolaj to close ranks and cover each other's backs.

"You were supposed to stay in the clinic," Lily scolded, as she rubbed shoulders with Brian.

"Lil, you were getting blindsided," grumbled Brian. "Besides, damn it, I'm a foot taller than you and outweigh you by fifty pounds. I can watch your back."

Luckily, the mood of the mob had already turned from angry to afraid. The grating wail of Metro sirens sapped the remaining will from them and they skittered away like strays headed for the alleys.

Lily faced Jolaj. "Everyone inside okay?"

He looked big and strong and invincible. Calm and steady. Studying her with soulful eyes. "The store owner has a broken arm, but she will recover. And you?"

"I'm fine."

He reached out to squeeze her shoulder. Expecting it, she didn't flinch or pull away, either from the pain or from any kind of fear of the claws that pressed into the leather of her coat.

"Lily—"

"Go," said Lily. They both knew his presence would make things overly complicated.

He squeezed her hand then released her. "I won't be far." Electricity prickled her skin and then he was gone. But not far, as he'd said. She'd bet he was within shouting distance and he probably could see her, wherever he was hiding.

That sense of his presence carried her through Metro's questions. She was standing alone outside the open back delivery bay of the Corner Grocery when he reappeared.

He reached out to wrap her hand in his. "I've convinced the Council to allow those of us with human companions to bring them into The Zone for their protection."

"That's probably a good idea, though it might cause more problems in the long term."

"We're getting them into The Zone as quietly as we can, using many different routes to draw less attention."

"Smart," she acknowledged, "but people will still notice."

He squeezed her hand and pressed his forehead to hers. "I want you to stay with me in The Zone tonight."

The heat of him, his breath against her skin and the low rumble of his voice drew her. Made her want to wrap herself around him. But it wasn't the time or the place.

"I can't. Besides, I'm not... I mean, I—"

"You should go, Lil." Brian's words rang out clearly from the doorway. "You'll be safer there."

She held tightly to Jolaj's hand as Brian walked out to join them. She wasn't certain how much he understood of her relationship with Jolaj, but he hadn't balked so far. "Mother—"

"I'll deal with Mom. I need you to be safe." He rested his hands lightly on her shoulders. "Just for tonight. Please, Lily."

Voices from inside grew closer and Jolaj leaned in to rumble in her ear. "We should go now."

"He's right," said Brian. "There's nothing else we can do tonight. Let Snow go through the vid and I'll go through the data. We can start fresh tomorrow."

Lily tugged her hand free of Jolaj's grip and stepped closer to her brother. She lifted her hand to cup his cheek. "I'll go, but you have to promise me you won't do any poking around on your own. You'll call. You'll wait for me."

"Yeah. I'll call if I find anything we need to act on fast and I'll wait for you."

"No matter what?"

"No matter what."

"Okay, then."

Brian smiled and his green eyes lit. "Okay."

CHAPTER 43

The gate in The Mixer would have been the closest route into The Zone, but Jolaj insisted they use the glide-rail line. Taking the train would allow them to get into The Zone without having to walk through one of the big, too-conspicuous gates. Lily walked onto the crowded train and stepped close to the safety glass window. Her thoughts raced over the data, the details. There was a killer out there. Her sister's killer.

Anger and guilt twisted together in her gut like the braids of a hangman's rope. Anger that the bastard dared to play God, passing judgment and dealing out death for perceived wrongs. Anger that the public would buy into his madness, uncaring of who got hurt. Guilt that she'd gotten involved and her sister had paid the ultimate price.

Lily jumped when Jolaj settled a hand at the small of her back. He'd been standing between her and the other passengers, but keeping a respectable distance. His touch was light through the barrier of her coat.

"Time to go," he said.

The train had been crowded when they got on, but no more than a handful of people remained by the time they rolled into the final stop on the line, The Zone's single glide-rail station. Lily was the only human left in the crowd that walked onto the rail platform.

She and Jolaj were last off the train and she hesitated at the top of the ramp leading down to street level, reluctant to leave the shelter of the covered platform. The storm had worsened, darkening the sky. Giving the illusion of night when it was only late afternoon. The wind smacked them in the face in rain soaked gusts.

The downpour seemed no obstacle to the Ormney. To a one, they stepped away from the shelter with their heads tilted back as if savoring the fat, wet drops that drenched them to the skin in seconds. No one hurried. No one ran.

The press of Jolaj's body behind her, urged her into the wet. She shivered at the warm caress of his breath against her ear as he bent close to speak above the noise of the rain.

"All but the young still remember the confinement of the final days of our home-world. We treasure all your world has to offer."

He moved around her, then. She stood alone under the shelter, as he stepped into the rain and lifted his face to the sky. His chest expanded visibly as he took in several deep breaths. He turned back to face her and held out his hand, waiting.

The rain kissed the broad angles of his face and darkened the cotton of his tunic as the soaked material clung to the curves and planes of his body. The huge expanse of The Zone stretched out behind him. A sea of green-and-white, like jungle topped dunes, lit in flashes by distant lightning strikes that arced across the sky. The wildness of the storm suited him, a stark contrast to the quiet strength of his indomitable will.

He waited there, claw-tipped hand stretched out, asking for her trust, her acceptance. Lily reached out, laying her hand in his and stepped into the storm.

The warmth of palm against palm zinged pleasure through her. His hand tightened and he tugged. She stepped close enough to press against his body. For a moment she was content just to be there in the storm with him.

Together they moved down the ramp and into the wide lane. Despite the waterproof finish on her coat, by the time they reached their destination, the rain had soaked her almost as thoroughly as it had him. She could see little of his home as he led her through the darkened ground floor but she got a sense of open space. The stairs to the second floor spiraled up through the ceiling.

When she stepped onto the second floor landing she could

see it was his sleeping area. A large platform bed took up most of the near end of the room. The other end had been left open, leading out onto a rooftop garden. Something in the design of the building ensured no rain licked in through the opening.

Jolaj walked straight through the room and back into the rain. In a move that was purely male and surprisingly intimate, he tugged his tunic off over his head and tossed it across a chair. The wind licked at the length of his auburn braid, wrapping it around his torso, drawing her eye to the way his muscles bunched and lengthened with his movements. Her hands tingled and her belly tightened at the sensual memories of exploring those muscles as they'd made love.

He looked over his shoulder, pinning her with a stare that had her speculating on whether he could somehow read her mind. God, she certainly hoped not.

Lily tugged off her own jacket and holster, hanging them on a hook she found on one wall. The single large bed dominating the space left little doubt he intended she sleep with him. Lost and unsure, she faced him but found his attention had returned to the storm-streaked sky.

His distraction only made it impossible for her to look away. It gave her tacit permission to stare. Just looking at him made her ache inside or rather forced her to acknowledge the empty ache that had become a part of her. She'd learned to ignore it but it never truly left.

A mirthless laugh bubbled up and escaped. The ache had become a more constant and faithful companion than any man had ever been. Jolaj wasn't like other men she'd known. His character. His make-up. He would be devoted to the mother of his children. But she could never be that. Even if she might be able to give him a child, the Council had forbidden it. And so even though he was different it would all work out the same in the end. His heart belonged to his people. He would serve them with devotion. Follow their laws and The Way and none of that included her.

She stared at him and wanted. Wanted him body and soul. If she couldn't have his soul she decided she would damn well have his body.

Lily strode into the rain, letting it soak into all the places she'd kept safe and dry. She shivered in the chill of the wind and pressed her breasts against his back. She slipped her arms around his waist and laid her cheek against the warm, smooth skin stretched across the heavy muscles of his shoulder.

He turned in her arms and, framing her face with his hands, brought her mouth up to his. He pressed cool, wet lips to hers in a kiss that burned hot. Hungry. Out of control.

She slipped her hands up his rain-slick torso to clutch at his shoulders. His kisses were drugging deep and tasted of the same terrible hunger he'd shown her the first time they'd made love. Need pounded through her body, demanding she give him more, take more. Refusing to be rushed, even by her own need, she forced her body to stillness, keeping distance between them when climbing him like a weedy vine seemed a finer idea.

Together they gasped for breath when he finally broke the kiss. His fingers slipped into her hair freeing it from the tangled twist. He dragged it down her back, clutching it in his hand, pulling her head back as he leaned over, sheltering her face from the worst of the downpour.

He held her gaze as he spoke. "You are the most beautiful creature I have ever seen."

He leaned down, pressing his forehead to hers then adjusted to trail kisses across her cheeks, dipping beneath her ear and along her throat. He worked his way down as if she were a feast he needed to devour until the edge of her SafeSkin tunic stopped his progress. He growled in the back of his throat.

"Take it off." The words rumbled, hoarse and full of need.

The SafeSkin was designed to stop a knife, slice or stab, the tunic was nearly indestructible. The thought of giving up that protection, terrified her. "No."

Her flat refusal drew another sound from him. This one more roar than growl. His hands dipped down to wrap around her hips, drawing her into the heat and solidity of his body. He lifted her. Positioned her against the emphatic length of his cock.

She thought he meant only to demonstrate the extent of his desire, but all thoughts of his intention evaporated as he pressed that hard length right where she needed it. He guided her legs around his hips, cupped her bottom, holding her in place as he worked her against him in a rhythm that sent need pulsing through her body as sharp as lightning, as expansive as thunder, as wild as the storm.

She clutched at his shoulders and pressed her face against

his throat as the sensations ripped through her. Long before she had any chance of getting her bearings enough to participate in the urgent exchange of pleasure her climax crashed over her. Her heart stalled in her chest as her lungs fought to take air into her too tight body. She rode the waves until the pounding pleasure eased and she became aware of the storm still swirling around them.

He carried her inside where the rain and wind stopped beating at them and the noise of the storm dimmed. She landed on his bed, boneless and too wrung out to move when he pulled her free of him and dropped her there.

She heard him move away, then return, and warmer air brushed across her rapidly chilling body. She forced her eyes to focus and tipped her head to where she could see him. He stood at the foot of the bed, stripping off his trousers. His cock jutted up, hard and long against his flat belly. He stroked his hand down the length and palmed the tip as his attention returned to her.

With a grunt his hands fell away from his cock and took hold of one of her legs. Squatting down he lifted her foot into his lap and pulled off one boot then the other. He used her legs to pull her closer to the edge of the bed. Still feeling boneless, she let him. His hands worked at her trouser fastenings for only a moment before he had them open and stripped them off her legs.

Lily finally forced her muscles to respond, to protest, when he pulled her legs wide and yanked her down to the edge of the bed. "Jo?"

He knelt between her legs and lowered his head to taste her. She dropped her question and threw her head back, closing her eyes to savor the warm, wet pleasure of his mouth.

The stroke and swirl of his tongue sent streaks of sensation spiraling through her belly. Her back arched and her legs widened in hungry eagerness. She was aware, but uncaring of the prick of his claws against her thighs. His tongue stroked aggressively against her. Need spiraled and tightened. Her hips rocked and her muscles tightened.

Then everything stopped and he stood between her legs, claw-tipped hands clenching and unclenching, chest heaving with a desperate need that matched her own. She lifted her arms, reaching for him. Needing him. Not only the pleasure he could give her, but the man he was. She needed him in her arms. Terrifyingly, she realized, he was already in her heart.

Bending down, he wrapped her in his arms and lifted her as he knelt on the bed and repositioned them both. When he pulled away again she tried to hold him but he pushed her hand aside.

He leaned in close, his face only inches above hers, his hands rested lightly on her abdomen. "Lily, my strong, fierce, Lily." He breathed the words on a sigh. "I cannot bear your fear. I cannot accept your lack of trust."

Her mind struggled to make sense of his words. Her thoughts were on, needing to be so close to him that she could forget anything existed beyond the passion she found in his arms and he was accusing her of not trusting him? She pushed away the haze that clouded her mind. "I trust you."

He pressed his forehead to hers. "Good," he breathed. "That's very good."

His claws scraped sharply against her skin as he worked his hands under her tunic. She grabbed his hands to stop him, pulling, but she couldn't budge him.

He lifted his head to look her in the eyes again. "I want to look at you. Need to look at you. All of you."

"Why does this matter? Why can't you just…"

His eyes widened. "Fuck you? Is that what you want me to do? Just fuck you?"

Her jaw clenched as an ugly mix of anger, frustration, and embarrassment flushed across her. "I thought that was what we both wanted."

He shook his head. "No. There is no *just* fucking for us. Just fucking isn't nearly enough."

"What the hell do you want from me?" She twisted against him as he continued to tug her tunic upward, exposing her belly, exposing the ugly white scars. The slashing traces where claws had torn her flesh. The scalpel straight lines left behind by the surgeons. She bucked, but he'd straddled her legs and she couldn't move him. He didn't stop pulling on her tunic until he'd lifted it over the swell of her breasts and then only to change his grip.

She stopped fighting him when he pulled the fabric up over her head. She knew she could only delay the inevitable. She knew she couldn't get free of him by fighting him.

She knew if she really wanted to be free, all she had to do was tell him.

But she didn't really want to win this battle.

She didn't want to hold on to her fear.

And she didn't want to be free of him.

She lay accepting as he tossed the tunic away, sat back and looked his fill. He traced his hands over her scars, much as she had done to him, but he quickly moved on to fill his hands with her breasts. His pupils widened even farther. His arousal reignited hers. This time when she rocked her hips, he moved immediately. Moved to kneel between her legs instead of sitting across them.

He pushed her legs wide and adjusted his position until his hardness stroked along the soft folds between her legs then he lowered himself onto her. She wrapped her arms and legs around him. Their rain-slick bodies slid together as they rocked, him poised at her portal but not yet inside.

He started over again, kissing her, kissing her cheeks, lingering over her mouth, and working his way to her aching breasts. He rocked against her, building her arousal until she needed to be filled so desperately she wanted to cry. The only thing that stopped her was knowing he was every bit as desperate for her.

"Please, Jo," she pleaded.

"Yes." He moaned as he surged forward. Filling her up, body and heart.

CHAPTER 44

Nerves prickled through Lily as they walked through the streets of The Zone. The savory smell of evening meals being cooked drifted through open windows. Something melodic and fluty accompanied the mix of talking and laughing. The music slipped over the windowsills to echo along the narrow walkways that wound through the neighborhoods. The sound of her hard-soled boots slapping against the wet pavement shouted that she didn't belong.

They were having dinner with Jolaj's family. They weren't blood relations, he'd explained. They were the relatives of his dead mate and the only family he had left. If that news hadn't been enough to chase away any appetite she might have had, he'd informed her they were also on the Council.

They reached the home of Councilors Tasst and Zee too quickly in Lily's estimation. She still hadn't found her equilibrium when the door slid open. A young girl with a wide smile and a zebra striped complexion welcomed them inside then dashed back into a crowd of children playing on the floor.

Lily had expected a sizable gathering, but the number of Ormney, all turning to look at her as she came in, made the boisterous O'Leary get-togethers look cozy by comparison. The ground floor of the home sprawled out to encompass a food preparation and dining area, several small seating areas, and the large, central area where the kids were playing.

"This can't all be one family." They ranged from pre-school age to teens.

"It appears Councilors Vaj and Relerin are also here with their children."

"Great." She smoothed her hands down the cotton of her borrowed trousers. Her whole outfit had been provided courtesy of Zee, Jolaj's sister-in-law.

A graceful Ormney woman glided toward them, navigating the obstacle course of children like a skater at a public rink. Her smile tilted in a more conservative, restrained angle than the girl who'd opened the door, but the resemblance was clear. The striping on her face had faded to a hint of light and shadow, giving her a haunting, ethereal look.

"Welcome to our home, Agent Lily. Our brother Jolaj has told us you have been a great help to him as he serves our descendants." The words were respectful but lacking any real warmth.

"As he always has." The man that stepped into place at the woman's side laid a hand on her shoulder, leaving no doubt they were a pair.

"Lily," said Jolaj. "Allow me to introduce Councilor Tasst, brother to my lost mate, and Councilor Zee, his beloved."

"Thank you for inviting me into your home," said Lily, dusting off manners she hadn't bothered with in years. "And thank you for providing the clothes."

Zee smiled thinly and led them to an area where the other adults were waiting on low seating. Lily recognized Vaj and the woman next to him had to be Relerin.

Vaj got to his feet and reached out for her hand. "I am so sorry for your loss, Agent Rowan."

Lily accepted his hand expecting to shake it and be released, but he clasped his other hand atop hers and stepped closer. He leaned down to touch his forehead to hers and made a soft noise in the back of his throat then stepped back.

"Thank you," she offered, not sure if she was meant to react in any particular way. Jolaj tilted his lips in a smile and dipped his chin in a small nod. Relerin looked on with no sign of disapproval. Tasst and Zee didn't meet Lily's eyes when she looked their way. They were suddenly very involved in the motions of sitting down.

Vaj settled in next to his partner. "This is Relerin."

"My pleasure, Councilor." Lily found the words easier with this woman who met her eyes easily and neither reached for her nor waited for anything from Lily. Relerin, waved to an empty spot as if she were the hostess rather than Zee.

"Sit for a moment, Lily," said Relerin. "You must be tired."

Lily sat with Jolaj, following his lead. She should be tired, but her heart rate was too elevated for any relaxation. It wasn't as bad as the scene she'd left at Aunt Jane's. Mostly because she didn't give a damn what any of these people thought of her. She was here for Jolaj, but she was under no delusion that they would approve of her. Civil was about as good as she could expect and they were doing civil well enough.

Lily's thoughts started to churn back over the puzzle pieces that might lead her to the killer while the councilors questioned Jo about the future of the Ormney understanding programs he'd started in The Mixer. She had no doubt they'd be grilling him about the case if it weren't for the houseful of children. Lily let her eyes drift over them. If they really wanted to improve relations between the Ormney and the Earth natives they'd start younger. Kids were less inclined to see the differences. They carried less hate.

A teenage boy snagged her gaze across the room. He stared hard at her eyes, but not really meeting them. His hands manipulated the small device in his lap and a message flashed in the corner of her com-lens. She checked the message and the text flashed across her vision. *Great com lens! Standard or secret Deepwater design?* The boy smiled and Lily smiled back.

She was sending him the specs when two younger children tumbled across the floor, landing in a heap at her feet.

One of the children squealed, an urgent, panicked noise, as the other shimmered half there and half not. Lily recognized the unstable child as the girl who'd opened the door for them.

The panicked boy kicked and pushed, trying to get free of her, but several of the other kids had been tumbling right behind them and two others had fallen to the floor in their wake. It was a tangled mess. The councilors breathed in a collective gasp. Vaj and Tasst had the clearest space in front of them. Both jumped to their feet and started clearing children away. The hazy girl panted in wheezy breaths and whined in an other-worldly way that had to be distorted from her not-all-there state.

Relerin bent down and began to murmur to the frightened girl. Zee sat frozen like a bystander at a train wreck as her son retreated into a shaking ball, thin arms wrapping around his legs.

Sara's description of *slip* injuries flashed through Lily's mind as the air around Jolaj filled with static and the tingly sensation she felt each time he prepared to *slip*.

Jolaj reached down and thrust one hand into the girl and laid another gently on the shoulder of her brother.

"Be calm, Daj," he said to the boy. The girl had already calmed and her form no longer flickered, though she was clearly not *in-sync*.

Daj's young face snapped to Jolaj.

"I'll help Estus remain as she is long enough for you to move free of her." Jolaj nodded encouragingly as he spoke, but the boy still seemed frozen and unsure what to do. Lily didn't know how long Jolaj could do whatever he was doing, but his jaw and neck were taut with strain and the others seemed to be planning to let him do it as long as it took.

She surged to her feet. "Jolaj, can I touch him?"

The effort of stabilizing the girl showed in his face as he met her gaze then nodded. "Please."

Lily carefully gripped beneath the boy's arms and lifted him free. Jolaj immediately altered his slip, pulling his hand away from Estus until it lay lightly on the girl's arm and he had settled into a matching half-there state. Together, they *synced* and the girl jumped to her feet and clung to Jolaj's leg, tears streaking her cheeks.

The adults exhaled almost as one. Tasst lifted his son into his arms and carried him into the crowd of small bodies, setting about calming them all. Vaj joined him.

Zee, free of her paralysis, leaned down to speak to her daughter. "It's okay, Estus." She gently pulled the girl away from Jolaj's leg. As she lifted the crying child into her arms, Jolaj brushed away the girl's tears with the back of a finger. "You're fine now," he said. "Your father tells me you have a new rail set?"

"Yes." She sniffed.

Lily saw Zee mouth a silent thank you to Jolaj.

The sentiment floated over the girl's head, beyond her

notice. "Would you like to see, Uncle Jolaj?" Estus's lips quivered as she spoke.

"I'd like that," he answered. He looked to Lily and she nodded then watched him walk away with the child and her mother.

"He has a special gift," said Relerin.

Lily pulled her gaze away from Jolaj to focus on the Councilor who moved to sit closer.

"I've never seen anything like it," Lily admitted.

"He's the best we have. Did you know he's the one who found Earth?"

Lily shook her head, too shocked to speak.

"Without his courage our people would have perished on the home-world. Without his abilities, many more would have been lost."

"I don't understand."

"Just as he was able to stabilize Estus, he was able to stabilize the weakest among us through The Crossing.

"His mate didn't survive." Lily cringed the moment the words left her mouth. She knew she shouldn't have brought it up.

"No," said Relerin without hesitation. "Her fear made her fight his control and she was lost. He blames himself."

"For not being able to hold her?"

"No," said Relerin. "For her fear. He believes she might have been less afraid, trusted him more, if he had been a better mate to her. His duties kept him from her a great deal."

Lily shook her head. "Why are you telling me this?"

Relerin smiled. "He has sacrificed much for us, but sometimes the needs of the warrior are the needs of his people."

Lily frowned. She didn't have the patience for riddles.

"You're a courageous woman, Lily Rowan. That is what he needs. I want you to know that you have my full support and that of my mate. We want Jolaj to have what he needs."

"I think you have the wrong idea. I'm working with Jolaj to stop the murders. After that I don't expect to see him again." The thought settled as a ball of sadness in her chest.

Relerin turned to watch the other adults as they played with the children. "Tasst hopes Jolaj will choose one of his daughters as mate. He's always wanted to bring Jolaj's bloodline together with his own, even before the ban on lab-based genetic engineering."

Lily's heart stuttered. "He introduced Jolaj to his sister?"

Relerin nodded. "And he worked on the genetic engineering program." She looked down at her hand. She slowly flexed her wrist and extended her claws. "Ironically, the things we engineered for were not the things to save us. It was our natural ability to *slip* that allowed us to escape our dying world. Tasst still has trouble allowing nature to take its course. Following the natural order often leads to The Way."

The room began to spin. Lily's vision blurred. She'd stopped breathing when those claws had captured her attention. Lily closed her eyes and counted the seconds in her head. When she could breathe normally again, it seemed hours had passed, but it had only been seconds. "I think I see where you're going with this. You think encouraging the natural attraction between humans and Ormney will lead to a better solution to your problems. A bit of a leap isn't it?"

Relerin folded her hands together in her lap. "Following The Way often requires a leap of faith. The concept is also common in human religions I believe."

"Yeah. I suppose it is."

Lily didn't know what to think of what Relerin had told her. She turned it over in her head, unsure if the councilor gave a damn about Jolaj or if she wanted to use him. Lily was still trying to figure it out when Zee returned to ask her to join in the food preparation. It was oddly like standing in her aunt's kitchen. She might not be much of a cook but she had lots of experience following instructions.

She stood, chopped vegetables to be served in a raw salad as Zee tossed the freshly chopped ingredients in an herbed dressing.

Zee tilted her head as she watched Lily. "You look as if you've done this often, yet you don't strike me as the sort of woman who would spend a great deal of time preparing meals for a family."

Lily hesitated before slicing downward into a ripe tomato. She briefly considered answering that her skills with a knife had little to do with cooking and everything to do with her job as a Deepwater agent. For Jolaj, she thought, she would wear her best manners, no matter how much they chafed. "You're right. I don't usually bother cooking for myself, but I grew up in a neo-trad household."

"Preparing meals together is one way we keep our families strong," said Zee. "We had hoped you would arrive earlier while everyone was working together." Her tone was cordial, but scolding lurked at the edges like a moldy crust on bread.

Zee allowed a small pause before continuing. Lily let the silence stand unwilling to explain or apologize for the precious time spent in Jolaj's arms.

"My son prepared a lovely strawberry and mint cake and Tasst allowed the younger children to help in preparing the meat and pastry dish so we could leave this simpler task for you." She smiled, seemingly unaware of the slight she'd delivered. "The children enjoyed the opportunity."

They both returned to their tasks for a moment.

This time Lily searched for something to say to fill the void, something conversational and appropriate. "My cousin's boys love to cook. They're a little younger than your youngest."

"Of course, Agent Rowan. You are closer to our eldest child's age than to the adults of our generation."

Was this a dig at her relationship with Jolaj and their age difference? Well, Zee would have to work a lot harder to get a reaction from her. She was far too used to her mother's less veiled insults.

"Your children are wonderful," said Lily, meeting her eyes. "Estus looks very much like you."

Zee looked away, absently stirring the dressing. "I owe you my thanks for helping Jolaj with her earlier."

Lily smiled and continued slicing.

"Jolaj is still young enough to father his own line," said Zee.

That thought did rattle Lily. It made her heart ache a little. "He would be a wonderful father."

"We've been trying to convince him to choose a mate for years. There are many young women of age now. Any family would favor his interest over one of the younger men."

Lily laid the knife to the side and wiped her hands, tamping down the mix of jealousy, sadness and anger that boiled like a noxious stew in her belly. "I'm sure you're right."

"We sent our own daughter away this evening. We still

have hopes he might choose her and it would trouble her to see the attention he pays you."

Lily glanced to where Jolaj played with the children. So strong, so patient. Zee was right. He was a catch. She swallowed, searching for a way to excuse herself with grace, but Zee forged on.

"There are others like Jolaj. Men who have gone long without a mate. He's a leader among them. Where he leads they will follow." She gave Lily a hard stare. "We can't afford the trouble this sort of behavior will cause. If you have any decency you'll—"

"Zee!"

Jolaj's strained voice startled Lily. She'd been like a soldier with one boot on a live mine, unable to move out of the line of fire.

Jolaj strode closer, moving to stand between her and the older woman. "I cannot believe you would speak this way to a guest in your home. A guest here at my request. A guest who selflessly serves our people at this difficult time."

Jolaj hadn't bothered to keep his voice down. She'd never heard him speak anything but softly. His tone now was not at all soft or calm. The angry rumble drew the attention of everyone in the room.

Lily rested a hand on his arm. "It's okay. I'm sure this comes from her concern for you. It's okay, honestly."

Jolaj reached for her hand and carefully intertwined his fingers with hers. "You are more gracious to my family than they have been to you. I'm sorry, Lily."

He held Tasst's gaze. "I'll take Lily home."

CHAPTER 45

When Jolaj had insisted they leave the night before, Lily had been embarrassed and relieved at the same time. She didn't want to come between him and his family, but she didn't want to waste a moment of what time they might have together either.

She lay, curled on her side, in the middle of Jolaj's bed. The sun was making an appearance along the horizon in a brilliant orange-and-red sunrise. Jo lay behind her, pressed close along her spine, his hands stroking her hip in a soothing caress. Less soothing was the sharp edge of his teeth as he scraped them across her shoulder. The sensation tingled through her, waking up all her nerve endings.

She shivered and stretched, rubbing against him. "You like space."

"Space?"

"You like to have a lot of room. Your bed is huge. Your bedroom is missing a wall."

His chest expanded and contracted against her back then the cooler brush of the air as he rolled away. "In the last years before The Crossing, the surface of our planet had become unsafe. We lived below ground."

"I can see how that would make you appreciate the open sky." Lily remembered how the Ormney had turned their faces up to the rain storm. She faced him.

"And space," he added. "The underground was always

meant to be temporary. The Council thought it best not to squander resources or time in the construction or expansion of private quarters."

"It must have been difficult to live under those conditions."

He'd been through so much. All of the Ormney had. She couldn't imagine it. Jolaj pulled her into his arms and Lily savored his warmth as she snuggled close.

"Those times are past."

There was something tense and anxious in his voice. Lily pushed up, resting a hand in the center of his chest, to look into his face. "Jo...?"

He frowned as he met her gaze. "There is talk among those who favor isolation as a means of keeping our culture intact."

"Talk?"

"Some say that we should build a city beneath your vast oceans. Others talk of reinstating the Searcher program."

A knot formed low in Lily's belly. "How serious is this talk?"

Jolaj reached up to push a strand of hair behind her ear. Her heart skittered a bit but quickly settled. He slowed the motion, letting his hand settle on her neck. His touch seemed to refuse to give any ground. He wouldn't let them take a step back and Lily was glad.

"The isolationists speak very seriously about such things," he said, "but they are a small minority. They had little influence until recently. The surge in anti-Ormney sentiment frightens many. They fear we will have no choice but to hide away or leave if things do not change."

The situation had been tenuous since the arrival of the Ormney. Twenty years and they were still forced to live behind a wall and subject to curfew. She'd never given it much thought before. It was just the way things were.

"I guess I can see why your people might be worried. The talk of restricting everyone to The Zone, day and night."

"It is a step back for us, but hiding away is not the answer."

"And the Searcher program? Would that mean you would have to go back to that?"

"It would be expected."

She laid back down, turning her head to lay her cheek on his chest. "Do you miss it? The adventure of it? The sense of doing something important?"

The muscles of his abdomen went taut beneath her hand.

"No," he said, his voice barely more than a whisper. "No. I hated it." He brushed the back of his fingers along her jaw. "The deep dark is a cold place, Lily. A man does what he must for his descendants but eventually the cold will take your life and steal your soul."

"It must have been terrible facing that over and over again."

The darkness that had shuttered his features lifted, desire warmed his eyes, and a slim smile tightened his lips. "Each time I touch you I know it was worth it."

But she couldn't give him descendants that meant everything to him.

He reached down, wrapping a hand around her thigh, and pulled her body over his. His hardening cock nudged intimately against her and she let her fears slide away. Her breasts pressed tightly against him. Every breath that expanded his chest sent a pleasurable spiral of sensation from her nipples to her womb.

He lifted his head and pressed his lips to hers. She met him eagerly. The passion and need in his kiss made her head spin. It went on and on as he tasted her in small sips and deep, mind-numbing gulps. She could get lost in kissing him, but the arch of his body beneath her made it clear he didn't intend to settle for kisses, mind-blowing or not.

Lily shifted then pushed back as he lifted his hips. His hands went to the dip of her waist, pushing her farther onto his cock. She stretched in pleasure, but he held tight, not allowing her to sit up or put even an inch of space between them.

Together they rocked in a shallow motion that created a delicious, ceaseless friction for both of them. It was a self-inflicted torture that would never bring them release. It was slow and intense and as much about his arms holding her close as it was about the orgasm hovering just out of reach.

She trailed kisses along his jaw and tasted the salty skin of his throat as he thrust into the wet heat of her again and again. His arms loosened and when she stayed wrapped closely around him, his hands began to wander across her body. He stroked the line of her spine, the curve of her hips. He stroked along the backs of her thighs, exploring the place where their bodies joined and trailed his fingers along the curve of her ass.

As his hands clutched at her, finally urging her to take him deeper and harder, she tightened her arms around him and held on. The future would have to take care of itself. For this moment he was hers and there was nothing but the pleasure. The pleasure building fast and intense until they flung themselves over the edge.

Curfew would lift in the space of an hour and Lily had to face reality. For a few hours she had allowed herself to set aside the grief of her sister's death, but it couldn't be set aside for much longer. Somewhere in the city, another person was waking up, free to go about his day. Another day of freedom for her sister's killer.

Jolaj got up and brought Lily her freshly laundered clothes. He kissed her gently then urged her to dress.

"We have company," he explained. "Friends."

Lily quickly pulled on her things as Jolaj pulled on a tunic and trousers of a soft jersey.

Jolaj made a melodic sound that wasn't quite a whistle and wasn't quite speech. In seconds, a half dozen figures solidified in his rooftop garden. They were all male. All from Jolaj's generation. Most kept their positions at the far end of the garden. One stepped forward. He wore a simple unmarked jersey tunic and trousers. Subtle shades of gray striped his features, but his eyes were a striking silver. He wore his shoulder-length dark hair loose around his face.

He dipped his chin to her then Jolaj. "It is true. You go against the Council to bring us closer to the Earth's children."

Lily suspected his statement wasn't far from what Zee had been dancing around the night before, but the way he said it sounded a lot more polite and there didn't seem to be any malice behind it.

"Kertu, my friend," said Jolaj. "This is Lily Rowan, a friend to the people and deserving of your respect."

Kertu stepped toward her and held out his hand. She took it, his claws pressing lightly against her skin. She was ready for it, making it easier to keep her panic at bay.

"I'm honored, Lily Rowan."

"Any friend of Jo's," she said. Then when he frowned she

finished, "is a friend of mine. Glad to meet you."

He released her hand and lifted his gaze to meet Jolaj's eyes. "There are many rumors whispering through the people. There is talk the Council will recall the Searchers." His gaze drifted to Lily then returned to Jolaj. "We love our people as ever we have, but..." Kertu dropped his chin to his chest.

Jolaj reached out and rested a hand on his shoulder. A gesture that drew the man's attention back from his thoughts. "My friend, I too feel the weight of service to our people and the sacrifices we have made. If the time comes, every man must choose his own path."

Lily watched the man study Jolaj, remembering what Zee had said. Where he leads they will follow. Jolaj might not want to be a leader, but Zee was right. He was the sort of man others looked to. The type of man who would know the right thing and do it, no matter how difficult. But if Kertu spoke for the others, these men were weary. Maybe Relerin was right. Maybe it was time for them to meet their own needs.

Lily had no idea what the answer was, she only knew she couldn't be any part of it. Jolaj had options. He could find an Ormney mate and father Ormney children. She had no right to get in the way of that. She had known from the beginning he could never be hers. It made her heart ache to think of it, but she needed to find a way to let go without sacrificing her dignity.

Kertu acknowledged Jolaj's words but his eyes still conveyed deference. If he chose to lead they would follow. One by one the men *slipped* away until only Kertu and Jolaj remained.

"Will you join us in the square?" Kertu watched Jolaj as if his response meant everything. The simple request carried the weight of a need for reassurance, a show of solidarity.

Jolaj squeezed Lily's hand. "It is our practice to begin the day with physical conditioning. I will only be a short while."

Lily squeezed his hand in return. "Go ahead. I have a few calls to make."

He nodded and the two of them *slipped* toward *out-of-sync* and disappeared.

Lily stepped to the edge of the garden and looked over the railing to watch as they joined the others in the square for an early morning session of a martial arts type exercise. The men who'd come to meet Jolaj were there, but they were joined by many others. Men, women, and children wandered out of their homes and moved into a loose formation below.

She watched from the rooftop mesmerized by their movements, their sense of community, and the respect they all seemed to have for Jolaj. The longer she watched the more certain she became that she needed to let him go before the letting go became so hard it would break her heart.

When her multi-com signaled with a message from Bradley, tagged important and asking her to meet him, she considered leaving, walking out of The Zone without Jo. It would be a big step toward letting him go. But she couldn't break her promise to him. And she'd promised not to go out alone. She took a deep breath and spoke in an even tone. "Jolaj, I need to go into town." His movements flowed to a smooth stop as he looked up to where she stood. Damn his hearing was spooky.

Another tag on her link caught her attention, Brian.

"Hey, Bri," she said. "Everything okay?"

"Fine." The one-clipped word spoke volumes.

"Mom being difficult?"

"Not intentionally. She wants to take Rose's body and go home."

A fresh wave of pain and guilt rolled through her at the mention of Rose's name. It wasn't that she'd forgotten. She just hadn't let herself think about it.

She heard Brian clear his throat. "But that's not why I called. I have a list of staff and patients names, prioritized by date. The ones who were in the clinic on the days when our victims show on camera are at the top of the list. I'm sending it to your com now."

Switching to data mode, she scanned the list of names as Jolaj came up the stairs, pulling clothes off on his way to the shower. To Brian, she said, "Have you given this to Sean yet?"

"Yeah. They'll run the list for connects with the victims or EFE, but remember we're also looking for something that ties back to you."

"Simone Rawls—"

"She might have been a key part of the connection to you, but she ended up dead. Something more than her made the killer pick you. Made the killer mad enough to come after you when things didn't go like he wanted."

"Yeah, okay. Maybe." Lily scanned the list again and one name popped for her. "Perry."

"Perry?"

"No. It can't be." Lily tried to pull up her recollections of Timothy Perry. He didn't seem insane enough to be their guy. "Timothy Perry is a Regeneration Tech. I've seen him at the Med Center a couple of times. He lived down the street from us when we were kids."

"Tissue regeneration would make sense. The victims were having scars removed. Snow's given me an address on him uptown. It is probably just a coincidence, that clinic has gone through more staff than a temp service, but I'll ask Sean to have his people prioritize him."

"Okay. You're staying at the hotel with Mom, right?"

He made a pained affirmative sound.

"We'll pick you up for breakfast in an hour. We have a quick stop on the way."

"See you then," he said, then closed the link.

Lily watched as Jolaj dried from his shower and pulled on his clothes. He was so there for her it made her insides ache. Nothing this good could last. "We need to go by the Federal Building to see Bradley then we're meeting Brian for breakfast."

His lips tightened at the mention of Bradley's name, but he nodded.

Lily prayed today would be the day they uncovered the killer's identity because every day her life was spinning more and more out of her control. She didn't know how much longer she could survive it.

CHAPTER 46

They made it to the Federal Building in twenty minutes. If she could deal with Bradley quickly, they could make their breakfast plans with Brian. Lily and Jolaj stepped into the elevator and requested a lift to Liaison Rubiero's location.

The elevator surged downward, Lily's stomach flipped. It wasn't a physical response to the barely discernible movement of the elevator, but years of training and experience manifest in the discomfort. Like an early warning system shouting *danger*.

Her hyper alertness must have tipped off Jolaj. He stood a little taller, bristling with energy. "What is it, Lily?"

"We're supposed to meet him in the Ormney Affairs office and that's up, not down."

Together they watched the numbers plummet. When the elevator doors slid open Lily had her hand on the grip of her pulse pistol. She stepped into a small anti-room, scanning for hazards. Jolaj *slipped* and the elevator doors slid closed behind her. He *slipped* back into *sync* across the room.

There was only one other way out, a single set of doors with a palm pad and voice activation unit. A small ID plate that read "authorized persons only" provided the only hint of where the doors might lead.

Even if the whole thing hadn't already felt very, very wrong, the multi-com lying on the floor directly in front of the doors would have tagged the scene with the unmistakable danger flag. She lifted her own multi-com to call for back-up and saw that the she had no signal.

She met Jolaj's eyes. "Jammed."

His gaze jerked to the small security cams mounted near the ceiling, standard in all the building corridors. "The building keyed to the location of Bradley's com-link when we were in the elevator?"

"Yeah." Lily understood Jolaj's line of thought immediately and eyed the security cams suspiciously. "If this area was being jammed his com locator should have been jammed too...unless someone stepping into the room triggered the jam."

"Or if someone watching engaged the jamming mechanism."

Her eyes tracked back to the multi-com lying on the floor, but every molecule in her body screamed trap. Jolaj had seen the com too, but neither of them had made a move toward it. First things first, she thought, they needed an exit strategy. She backed up, pressing her body against the elevator doors, knowing her proximity would activate the call feature.

She drew her pistol and held it low as she approached the multi-com. She crouched down and studied the unit before picking it up. Definitely Bradley's unit. A tiny smudge of blood disappeared under the closed doors.

She looked back to Jolaj and then the elevator. The indicator showed the lift remained at lobby level as if she'd never called for it. Lily reached out and pressed her fingertips against the smudge of blood. Her fingers came away with a sticky red residue. "It's still tacky," she said. "Not fresh, but not dry."

"Lily?" Jolaj's voice came from right behind her. He'd moved to stand closer.

If her senses were right and this was a trap, the blood trail leading under the doors had to be meant to lead her through, but how? And even if she could, should she? She looked back to the unresponsive elevator. Did she have a choice?

Lily pocketed the multi-com and pushed to her feet. She looked to Jolaj. "You should go for help."

"I won't leave without you."

She bit her lip. "I knew you'd say that."

His hands clenched at his sides as if he were working to keep them off of her. The thought made her chest tighten painfully. It was going to be hell when he eventually did leave her.

"You know, going for back-up is a really good idea."

He nodded. "Precisely why we should both go."

"I could try to hack the elevator," she said. "But it would take time. If Bradley or someone else is hurt they might not have time. I have to get through these doors, now."

"I can *slip*—"

"No!" Lily reached out and grabbed his arm as if the simple restraint could stop him. "You have no idea what's on the other side and this is obviously a trap."

"Obviously."

She studied the closed doors. "If I was meant to go through, shouldn't it have been left open?"

Jolaj stepped closer to the door tag and hand plate. "Bradley's offices are in this building and it was Bradley, or someone using his com, to call you here."

"Yeah."

"Perhaps he gave you the clearance you need."

"One way to find out." She laid her palm on the pad and felt the warm surge of the DNA scan. The narrow display flashed: *Rose Rubiero – Authorization Confirmed.*

The doors slid open with a swooshing pop and a heavy grinding noise. They were at least ten centimeters thick, the exterior surfaces coated in taf-steel, and fitted with a waterproof seal.

"It's a storm shelter," Lily said." Lots of the buildings constructed after the hurricanes of the first part of the century have them."

"It makes sense the staff and families of the Ormney Affairs Office would have access authorization."

"Of course. And Rose and I share the same DNA."

Jolaj stepped through the doors.

Light filled the wide corridor that led to another similar set of doors ten meters down the corridor. A trail of narrow bloody smudges urged her to move forward. Lily looked back to the elevator. There should have been stair access to this level, but she didn't see any sign of it. There would no doubt be an emergency ladder built into the elevator shaft.

Damn, damn, damn. She didn't like her options. Taking a deep breath she stepped over the threshold and listened to the sound of the door closing behind her.

For thirty full seconds the only sound was the pulsing thrum of her heartbeat in her ears and the deliberate even whisper of their breathing. There were no vents in the small space and the sensors would be set to ensure it was safe before opening the interior doors. Flooding precautions. She stood to the side holding her pulse pistol in a two-handed grip, waiting.

Another pop signaled the seal to the shelter had been released and the doors slid open letting in another whoosh of air. She didn't hesitate this time. She crossed the threshold doing a visual sweep of the next corridor. She could see smudges of blood trailing along the corridor, too regular, not to be intentional.

CHAPTER 47

Lily stepped out of the airlock, hyper-aware of the smudges of blood down the center of the corridor. Jolaj followed her and the doors behind them slid shut and sealed with a sucking noise. Lily's pulse revved and her muscles tightened as a surge of adrenalin dumped into her bloodstream. The walls shimmered and flexed, the belly of a malevolent monster had swallowed them down for its next meal.

She used her pulse pistol to take out the vid-cams mounted high along the hallway walls then moved up beside the first door. The blood trail led to a door farther up, but she wasn't moving forward without clearing the room that would end up at their backs. She hugged the wall on one side of the door and Jolaj took the other. With a clear verbal command— "Door 005, open"—the lock and seal popped. She pushed it open with the tow of her boot and slid inside. Neatly stacked supplies filled the inside.

"Storage," she said on a release of breath.

Together, she and Jolaj moved down the corridor, clearing each room methodically until they reached the door marked with a smudge of blood. When Lily gave the voice command the door slid open to reveal a near-empty room. Metal shackles had been bolted to the ceiling. The shackles hung low, about waist height. A metal table sat nearby with a small box positioned at the center of the table. Together they hovered at the doorway. She didn't know what she'd expected to find but this wasn't it. A shiver of unease slipped along her already too tight muscles and made her skin crawl.

More vid-cams were mounted high above a vid-wall. Lily lifted her pistol to aim for the cameras but stopped when the display activated. The picture that flashed into life sucked the air from her lungs. Her heart pounded wildly in her chest. "Oh god, Sara..."

The vid appeared to be a live stream. It showed her cousin, lying on an old mattress, hands and feet chained and bolted to a plascrete floor. She was gagged and struggling.

"If you shoot out the vid, I'll kill her now."

The altered voice boomed through the room, shocking Lily into gasping for the breath she'd been holding.

"Do you recognize the location?" Jolaj's gruff voice rumbled low and menacing.

Lily shook her head. The bare plascrete walls could be anywhere.

"Now, come inside." The words broadcasted over speakers were bitten off, angry, demanding.

Lily stepped inside and Jolaj followed her lead. Behind them, the door slid shut.

"Law Keeper, I'm glad you're here. Saves me a little extra effort and waiting." The voice barked a short laugh. "I'm tired of waiting."

Lily forced herself to look away from the vid, struggled to settle her heart rate She tried and failed to reach a state of calm, but managed to get enough air to speak normally.

"Now we're here, tell us what you want. Why are you doing this?"

"What do I want?"

Lily concentrated on the voice, trying to catch something to confirm the speaker's identity. Her brain was having trouble believing Bradley could be behind all this, but if not, where was he?

"I want the world to wake the fuck up and see what's going on around them. I want every last one of those damn animals to die." The voice had increased in speed and volume. She could hear the speaker panting for breath as he paused. "And, you, my pretty Lily, for your betrayal... I want *you* to suffer."

Lily kept her eyes on the camera as Jolaj paced the length of the room. She knew he was checking the door. She wanted to tell him again to go for help, but knew that was pointless.

"How did I betray you? I don't even know who you are."

He laughed, the sound sharp and ugly like a rusty knife. "Trying to get me to tell you who I am. Tsk, tsk. Did you think I'd fall for that? But don't worry. I do plan to tell you eventually and I'll even let Sara go. All you have to do is follow a few simple instructions. Cooperate and you'll have your answers. Your cousin will go free, unharmed."

"Why should I think you'll stick to your bargain? You never have before."

"Aaaannnn! Wrong answer!"

Lily flinched at the jarring buzzer-like shout.

"Wrong answer, Lily. I always keep my word. You're thinking I'm Bradley. I did use him to get you there. But I'm not lowlife Bradley."

"Again, why should I believe you?"

The camera panned to show Bradley slumped on the floor in another corner of the room where Sara was being held.

"Bradley is unconscious, but safe, for now."

"You could have recorded this earlier."

"My wicked little Lily, there are some things you'll have to trust me on. Besides, you don't believe that chicken shit could have executed such a brilliant plan."

Out of the corner of her eye, Lily saw Jolaj stop his pacing. The tension in his body was clear even across the room. He looked ready to pound on the unresponsive door, but instead he *slipped* toward *out-of-sync* and disappeared. For a brief moment she hoped he'd sensibly gotten out and gone for help. Too soon, he returned, *slipping* back to *in-sync* looking more frustrated than ever.

"Do that again, Law Keeper, and Lily will be dead in five minutes. I rigged the air vents with a lethal gas. Remotely operable, of course."

"Of course," Jolaj growled. He strode across the room to stand closer to Lily. He roared at the camera. "If she's harmed I *will* kill you."

"If you live another twenty minutes it will be because you were willing to let your precious little slut die alone."

Jolaj growled again, low in the back of his throat.

"You see what an animal he is, Lily? And you let that animal defile you, didn't you? Didn't you!"

Lily stood unflinching in the center of the room as their

host screamed at her, repeating the accusation, calling her names until the room fell silent.

She allowed herself one quick glance to reassure herself Jolaj was calm and alert. Her unflappable companion had gotten his anger back under control. They were good together, she reminded herself. They would get through this and so would Sara and Bradley.

When the silence had gone on several minutes, Lily decided to try to talk to the killer. The camera had been off of Sara all of that time and not knowing what was going on was tearing a hole in her gut. "You said something about a bargain."

"Good girl."

The condescending praise rankled, but Lily bit back her sarcasm. "I'm ready to listen, if you're ready to talk."

"Clever, clever, Lily. Things could have been so different." He sounded bleaker, as if the shouting had drained him. "But you've made your bed. Let's start by reviewing the rules."

Lily listened.

"First rule, the Law Keeper doesn't leave the room. Second rule, you take the power pack out of your pistol and smash it. Third, you put on the manacles hanging from the ceiling. Once you've completed these tasks, I release Sara and Bradley unharmed."

"And after that?"

"After that I give you one more task to do. If you complete it as I instruct I'll release the locks on the manacles."

It sounded a little too good to be true. Whatever he wanted her to do would have to be very, very bad. "Why give me a chance to survive this and come after you?"

"Not to worry, Lily. I'm not making this easy for you. The doors will still be locked. The gas will still go off on a timer. Once the manacles are released you'll have thirty minutes to get out of there before it does. You'll have a chance, Lily. A slim one. Fair, don't you think?"

"And if we don't comply?" Her gaze darted around the room, looking for something, anything she could use to get them out of there.

"I gut Sara like I did Mary Santini... while you watch. In thirty minutes the gas still goes off and you die."

"You know," she said, "I think you like killing."

"Oh, I do. I always do."

"So, why should I believe you'll let them go?"

"I only enjoy killing animals and the bad little girls who fuck them. Sara hasn't done anything wrong," he said. "She doesn't need to be punished."

"Rose hadn't done anything wrong, but you killed her."

"Your fault, Lily! You betrayed your own kind. You should've killed Kabel, like you did the others. Not protect him! You had to be punished. Rose took your place, but I didn't enjoy it. I made it as painless as I could for her."

Jolaj paced the length of the room like a caged tiger. If she could send him to help Sara she'd gladly put on the damn manacles. "I want to see Sara."

The camera panned to show Sara still struggling on the mattress. Lily looked hard at the image trying to think where they might be. She could see the wall from floor to ceiling and from one corner to another. Solid, plain plascrete. No windows. Artificial lighting. The only vent in sight—a small round pressure vent like the ones in the room where she and Jolaj were standing. Exactly like them. "It's a storm shelter," she whispered.

But there had to be thousands of shelters in the city. The one in the image was cheaply made. Probably private.

"No more stalling,: the voice boomed. "Time to decide."

"You're not expecting me to get out of this alive. Are you ever going to tell me who you are?"

There was silence for several seconds. "I think I like that you want to know who I am. Yes, I'll show you after you've put on the manacles. After I let Sara go."

His comment gave her more confidence that he would indeed let Sara go.

"All right."

Jolaj snapped his attention back to her. "Lily, no."

She met his eyes. "I have to take a chance." And if the masked bastard didn't let Sara go, but did reveal his identity, it might help her figure out where he might be.

Lily pulled the power pack out of her pistol and held it up in plain sight of the cameras. Then she laid the pack on the table and used the grip of the pistol to smash it. She left the useless weapon on the table and wrapped her hands around the manacles. The metal felt cold and terrifying in her hands. The locks were electronic, the only way to release them would be to cut power.

Or for the killer to keep his word.

Lily stepped into position and faced Jolaj. Her fingers shook a little as she placed one of the manacles around her wrist. He grabbed her hand before she could click the lock home. He spoke low. "I cannot let you do this. We will find another way."

"If you have a better one, I'm listening."

But Jolaj only stared at her, frustration etching hard lines in his face. "He may kill Sara the moment you close the lock."

A surge of panic made her heart thump harder, but she shook her head. "I don't think so."

Her eyes flicked to the vid as a movement caught her attention. A masked figure stepped into view. He stalked over to the mattress and dropped to his knees beside Sara. His right hand was encased in a glove with long taf-blade claws. Before Lily could react, his arm slashed down fast in an arc, scoring Sara's abdomen.

Lily screamed.

She screamed so loud the strain had already scratched her throat before her first cry died away. On screen, Sara sobbed and thrashed harder against her restraints. She screamed for him to stop, but another quick slash shredded Sara's blouse, leaving only her bright pink bra to cover her. Brilliant red blood oozed across the bared flesh, but the cuts were shallow. The man grinned into the camera. "Look what you've made me do. Are you going to let that animal tempt you into turning your back on innocent Sara? He's already cost you your sister."

Lily pulled her hand away from Jolaj. "I have to do this." She clicked the latch closed then held the other manacle out to Jolaj. "Help me...please." Her eyes swam with unshed tears.

He closed the other manacle around her wrist, then wrapped his big hands around hers. The warmth of him seeped into her and staved off the chill of dread gripping her with the feel of metal at her wrists.

"Good girl," said the killer. Lily watched as he sprayed something across Sara's wounds. The cream-colored gel of a liquid bandage formed over the slashes. He slipped a black hood over her head and tied it off behind her neck. He released the chains at Sara's hands, replacing them with zip ties that held her wrists tightly together in front of her then he released her feet. Sara immediately scrambled up on her knees, scuttling to move away from him.

The killer tapped a com at his wrist and a small inset image appeared on the screen. The inset showed the view of the killer from his wrist unit. He looked into the small camera, only his eyes showing through the mask. "Now don't forget you still have one more task to do." Then he went back to Sara. "I'm leaving you now, dear. Bradley's over in the corner. You should be able to wake him, if you care to help him. The door will be open."

Both views showed him leaving. In the vid, the door swung open, filling the room with a shaft of sunshine.

Lily couldn't see much on his cam when he left the room, but there were hints of sky, trees, grass. In the main vid, still gagged, hooded, and bound, Sara had found Bradley and was shaking him. There was no audio so he must have taken it with him.

Lily's attention was pulled away from the vid as Jo yanked on one of the chains. "They're solid," he whispered. "I can't get you free."

She cupped a hand around his cheek. "He let them go," she whispered. "He let them go."

"He hasn't gone far. They'll remain in danger for some time."

Lily could see now that Bradley was also bound and he looked too disoriented to stand. He was probably drugged and wouldn't be much help to Sara.

The killer could easily return and kill them. In his vid she could see he'd moved inside another structure and was climbing stairs. He stepped into a room and over to a window. She could see a bed covered by a comforter with pictures of baseballs and bats. The kind made for a child. He moved the wrist cam up and looked into it as he pulled the mask over his head.

Timothy Perry smiled into the camera. "Hello, Lily."

Jolaj tilted his head and frowned at the image.

Lily gasped. "Oh, God. Why?"

"I'm disappointed in you."

She jerked compulsively at the chains. "You were at the med center the day of the attack, you saw me the night Jennifer died." It fit. That much of it fit. "But why? Why would you do this?"

"The little sluts were sleeping with animals. When you lie

down with animals you get bitten."

"The bites. You treated them. Removed the scars. Mary Santini thought you were coming to see her to follow up on the treatment." That's why her shirt had been carefully unbuttoned. He'd been a medic and she'd trusted him. The outrage of it simmered in Lily's veins.

"That's right. Brainy Mary was very cooperative in the timing of her own execution. I volunteered at the clinic. House calls are common as vermin in that foul neighborhood."

"That's where you met Simone Rawls."

He frowned. "She was useful to me, but in the end she showed her true colors. She was a slut, just like you. But she was useful indeed. I never wanted to work in The Mixer, but my supervisor thought I needed to work with all kinds of people. Learn to play nice. But she's never understood that when I play, I like to make up my own rules." He laughed at his own joke.

Lily grabbed Jolaj's hand and leaned her head against his chest to hide her face. "He grew up in the neighborhood where I grew up," she whispered.

"Lily!" Timothy's voice boomed over the speakers. "You're supposed to be listening to *me*."

She ignored him, what she needed to say tumbled out in a rush. "The *same* street where the O'Learys live now. They had a house down the block. Most of those houses have storm shelters. They're on Old Duval. I *know* it."

Timothy screamed a steady litany. "Listen. To. Me. You. Whore."

Jolaj bent his head low and spoke though a clenched jaw. "I won't leave you."

Lily wanted to hold him close and never let him go. She wanted him to get the hell out of there. She couldn't tell him any of that. Instead she clenched a fist in his tunic. "Sara's still in danger."

He gripped her chin and forced her to meet his gaze—blue fire. "We get you free first."

Lily forced her fingers to release him. Hands shaking, she turned back to the vid-wall and studied the face of the man who'd killed her sister. "Why me? Why did you get me involved?"

His screaming had stopped. He looked at her like a bug he needed to squash. No—a bug he wanted very badly to pull in half. "The police weren't catching on." He spoke evenly, directly. "I saw you in The Mixer and knew you were the perfect person to bring my work to their attention. Clever Lily. Strong Lily." He layered the praise on like too sweet icing. The kind that left you with a stomachache after. Then a half smirk crept back onto his face. "Thanks to me." He nodded as if affirming his own words. "Yes, I knew you'd come through for me."

"Thanks to you?" Instinctively Lily braced as she asked the question. He'd set her up to ask. He was mad at her now.

The answer would be brutal.

"Yes," he answered, smirk deepening. "Haven't you figured it out yet? Tsk, tsk. Pay attention to me now, Lily. I'm the one in control. I'm the one who shaped you." He reached for something off camera. "Not *him*."

A still of her father popped into the corner of the screen. It had been taken at a distance. So young. So happy. The picture changed.

The poorly lit still made it easy to deny what she saw. At first. The glassy stare in her father's eyes. The grass beneath his head. The frothy blood at his lips.

Her knees buckled. Jolaj reached for her, but she jerked away.

Timothy hadn't finished. "If I hadn't killed your father, you probably would've grown out of your cops and robbers phase. You'd have ended up married to a cop instead of becoming a STU Agent for Deepwater."

She tried to speak. Her lips had numbed. Her whole body trembled. "You killed my father?" It couldn't be true. Lily shook her head as if the motion could negate his words. "You were a b-boy. When he was murdered."

Timothy laughed—the crackle of ice shearing away a glacier. "My first human kill." His chin jutted forward and he pulled the camera closer. "He caught me wringing a cat's neck. He'd already suspected I killed that stupid mutt of yours." His smile slipped away and his eyes froze over. "He would've tried to throw me in juvenile detention. Worse. He was going to tell my dad. My old man was plenty harder than yours, Lily."

Her mind reeled. She twisted her hands in the chains and jerked.

"You said you'd release her," Jolaj roared, voice sounding far away. The inside of her head had emptied, leaving an echoing hollow space where rational thought should have been.

Timothy barked at them. "Speak again, you ugly bastard and I'll end you both now. You're the reason she's chained up like an animal." Rage transformed Timothy's face into a terrifying mask. "Remember that."

"Timothy. Please." She needed it to be over, now. "Tell me what you want me to do."

"You see the box on the table?"

She blinked tears from her eyes and searched for the table, through the watery haze. "Yes. I see it."

"You should be able to reach it. I want you to open it." He spoke quicker. Anticipation tightening his syllables.

Lily reached for the box, hands shaking. She lifted the lid. A hypo-injector filled with a blue liquid sat inside.

"Good," said Timothy. "Now lift out the hypo. It can be used to deliver a contact injection. That's assuming the animal will allow it. He, after all, can *slip* at any time and leave you to die." He laughed coldly. "Time to see how devoted your lover is."

He couldn't mean for her to drug Jo. The tremors wracked her. Her hands spasmed. The hypo slipped, but it never hit the floor. Jolaj reached out and snagged it.

He mouthed the words "it'll be okay" as he pressed the hypo back into her hands.

"No." She pushed his hands away, refusing to take it.

Timothy chuckled. "It's your choice Lily. The hypo contains the same toxin I used on the animal that was fucking Jennifer Richardson. Either you inject your Ormney lover or the gas kills you both."

How quickly could Jo get to him? To Sara? Lily clung to the possibility. "Please Jo," she whispered. "Please go stop him."

But Timothy would use the remote for the gas and kill her if he did. She didn't want to die, but— "I'll die either way. Please."

Jolaj pressed the hypo back into her hands. "Trust me," he whispered back. "It'll be okay."

No, she couldn't do it. She'd rather die from the gas than to have Jolaj rip her apart.

"As soon as you inject him," said Perry, "I'll release the locks on your hands. You saved yourself before. You'll have a chance. Be brave, Lily."

Jolaj mouthed the words "trust me" again. She knew how

important trust, her trust, was to him. But she'd seen the effects of the toxin. She'd experienced it when Kiq had come damn close to killing her.

She took the hypo, hating the weight of it in her hands.

Jolaj stepped closer and tingling energy brushed against her skin. Yes, please *slip*. But he stood there looking as solid as stone. He pressed his chest up against the hypo shaking in her grip. He lifted his hands as if to steady her, but Timothy barked out a command for him to stop.

"She has to do this on her own," he said.

She pressed the hypo against the muscle of Jolaj's shoulder, closed her eyes and tried to force her fingers to tighten against the cool metal.

"I'm stronger than Lanyak," he whispered. "It will be all right."

Tears coated her cheeks.

Swallowing her fear, she pulled the trigger.

"Yes! That's it." Timothy's shout ricocheted around the room, leaving her cringing. Muscles locked. Terrified.

The drug worked fast.

The tingling sensation against her skin faded. Jolaj's pupils dilated. Filing his eyes with black. His chest expanded on a breath he never fully released. He swallowed in mouthfuls of air in short, shallow gulps that seemed to accumulate inside him like a lethal force waiting to propel him into a rage. A shiver swept over him and he flexed his hands like a street fighter ready for a brawl.

He lifted one of those claw-tipped hands toward her as icy fear flashed through her body, draining her strength and leaving her weak and nauseated. Lily swallowed down the bile burning her throat.

The palm of his hand settled against her cheek. The tips of his claws pressed lightly into her skin as his thumb brushed across her trembling lips. He leaned in close. "You trusted me." The words were a hot whisper against her face. His voice was steady and laced with wonder.

She managed a small smile through her tears.

The hypo clattered to the floor as she reached over her head and took a tight grip on the chains.

Jolaj threw back his head and howled, an animal sound that sent sparks of lightening sizzling through the blood in her veins. When his head lowered, his eyes were still glassy and he was breathing harder. His hands opened and clenched.

He stepped back, with a roar. He turned in a circle. Then he came at her.

In a flash of movement, one claw tipped hand arced across her vision.

There was a whoosh and her body jerked back without her ever feeling the blow. She tugged on the chains, letting them take her weight and kicked out as another whoosh of claws came at her.

Jolaj stumbled back, his arms swung out for balance and the warm, wet of blood splattered across her face. Horror pooled in her belly like a blazing fire. Lily looked down and saw blood oozing through her top near the bottom edge. Thank God she'd worn her own clothes. The SafeSkin had limited the damage, but one blow had been low enough to connect with the unprotected part of her torso. She knew it could have been much worse. But SafeSkin wouldn't protect her for long, given enough time, he'd bleed her and she'd die.

Lily railed at the camera. "Release me! Timothy!" She screamed it at him, letting the panic thread through her voice.

The shriek seemed to startle Jolaj. He backed away and threw himself at a wall, claws slinging her blood arcing high along the wall.

Lily looked directly into the camera and dug deep for the strength she needed to clear her head and find some angle to use. Beyond the camera she could see the salivating bastard's glee plastered across the vid-wall. "Timothy, please. Let me have the chance you promised." She jerked uselessly against the chains. "Don't you want to see me go down fighting? Don't you want to see me hurt him before he kills me?"

Jolaj moved toward her. Her heart pulled and hammered in her chest. Not again. Not Jo.

The locks clicked open.

Lily jerked free and grabbed the table. She held the thing up like a shield as she backed away. She had to think. Had to find a way out. Her eyes searched the room as she tried to keep Jolaj at a distance without sending him into another rage. He stalked her like a restless predator then leaped toward her. She held the table higher and braced for the impact.

She pushed as it shoved her back against the wall. Jolaj hit the table and went flying upward, nearly knocking her off her feet. He hit the wall above her. Blood sprayed around her again, but he hadn't touched her. The blood had to be his. He fell to the side and tumbled across the floor before springing back to his feet.

She stood stock still, unsure what had happened. If he'd meant to hurt her, she'd have been flattened. Wouldn't she? Lily stepped sideways and something crunched under her boot. She glanced down.

Glass and metal.

Part of a camera.

She looked to where blood arced across the wall. It reached high, near the ceiling. It covered one of the lenses.

She jerked her eyes back to Jolaj. He was coming again. She charged toward him, shoving the table and bouncing off him to end with her back against the opposite wall.

"Come on, Lily." Timothy's voice blared from the speakers. "You can do better than this."

Jolaj roared at the vid image of Timothy. God, Jo looked wild. He threw himself against the wall like a bull charges the matador's cape.

She smashed the table and came away with two table legs. They'd do just fine, if she wanted to kill him. Did she want to kill him?

He spun, ripping at the shoulder that had to be aching from that pointless blow. Kiq had done that. Ripped at his own flesh. The memory came to life in front of her as Jolaj beat his bloody fists against the wall then zeroed in on her. Cold dread churned in her stomach, threatening to empty its contents across the tips of her boots. She was ready when he barreled into her. Her thrust glanced along his side.

She'd pulled the punch.

She couldn't kill him. Couldn't even try.

He was on her then, knocking her to the ground, pinning her down against the hard floor. Beneath his crushing weight she couldn't drag in enough air. Each unseen touch of his hand landed like a pulser, firing panic through her nerves. A touch against her belly, her hips, squeezing tight enough to leave bruises...but no claws dug into her flesh.

He pushed up, putting a few centimeters between them. She gasped for air just as he slid a blood coated hand across her face. She choked and coughed and bucked against him, rolling to her side to spit the blood from her mouth.

She got an arm free then slammed an elbow back, connecting with his shoulder. Unfazed, he pulled her back under him. This time she had room to move her feet. She pulled them in tight and kicked out. At the moment of impact she knew it wouldn't be enough.

His body jerked and he rolled away. That wasn't right. She scrambled, kicking her feet, crawling out of his reach. The floor was slick with blood, but she didn't feel her life draining away. The slashes he'd made stung but they couldn't be deep. She ached all over from being shoved around and she had a hell of a lot of blood smeared all over her. It had to look bad. Maybe even fatal.

The low sound of Timothy's laughter echoed through the room. "I think you're going to die this time, Lily. But don't worry. He won't get out of that room alive. The other one I drugged and locked away tore himself up so badly he bled out. I'm sure your animal won't be any different."

Lily pushed and pulled, and tugged to get herself upright, doing her best to make the movements appear awkward, feeble. There was one more camera and Jolaj stood directly beneath it. She searched his face and found him panting and growling, eyes still dilated, but he wasn't charging.

He was waiting.

Her heart soared. Her mind sharpened.

Visibility beneath the camera would be limited. Lily pushed off the wall behind her and ran directly toward him. Her hands gripped the table legs as if they were baseball bats but she didn't swing or aim. She charged, stretching her arms wide. His hands clasped her waist and he lifted her off her feet and spun, slamming her high on the wall. She bent in to him, exaggerating the move, then reared back against the wall, arms reaching upward.

The sound of metal and glass smashing, the feel of it raining down over her head, loosened all her muscles. She sagged against his grip and he pulled her close.

His lips brushed her ear. "Audio," he whispered.

He threw his head back and roared.

Lily screamed. She kept screaming until her voice cracked and her throat ached with a fiery agony.

When she couldn't scream anymore he wrapped her in his

arms and pressed her face against his uninjured shoulder. One hand cradled the back of her head while the other circled her waist. He growled low and deep in his throat.

She dropped the table legs, letting them clank to the floor, and clung to him. His chest still surged with large heaving breaths. He'd fought off the effects of the toxin. Was still fighting them.

She'd been terrified. She should have been dead.

She slid her hands up and threaded her fingers through his hair. She clutched two big handfuls and pulled back to look him in the face. His eyes were still glassy but he was there in those eyes. Everything she needed from him was there. He hadn't left her. He had done the hard thing. For her.

He lowered her to her feet and framed her face with his hands. He bent down and rested his forehead against hers.

Then he *slipped* away.

Lily slid down the wall until her butt hit the floor. The slash low on her belly had started to throb. She pressed her hand to the gash and held it steady as blood oozed thickly around her fingertips. She was hurt worse than she'd thought. The sound of her father's favorite Jazz spilled from the speakers like a funeral dirge. Her funeral dirge. No. It would be Timothy Perry's funeral dirge.

Together, she and Jolaj would see to it.

CHAPTER 48

Jolaj *synced* in the Ormney Affairs office—the nearest place he could appear, coated in blood, and not risk causing a riot or being shot on sight. Even there, the receptionist screamed and ducked under his desk. A woman in a suit leaned out of an office down the hall. Jolaj strode toward her, wondering how in the deep dark he could manage to look nonthreatening. When Lily had injected him, he'd been able to make a partial *slip* to avoid most of the dose, but the rest was still in his system. He kept his hands low and spoke as calmly as his racing heart allowed.

"I need your assistance."

She swallowed then nodded. "What can I do?"

Slowly, Jolaj reached out, palm up. "I need your com-link."

The woman startled then dug hurriedly in her pocket. She came up with a shiny, slender rectangle. "Link activate," she said, then laid the device in Jolaj's blood smeared hand.

He'd hurt Lily. He'd made her bleed. The thought tied his guts in knots of pain.

Leaving her there had torn shredded him. He had to get her out before Timothy Perry's failsafe triggered, but he couldn't risk being seen on any of the surveillance cameras either. If his actions caused Sara's death, Lily would never forgive him.

"Connect Brian O'Leary."

After a pause, Lily's brother came on. "Hello?"

"Lily is locked in the storm shelter beneath the Federal

Building. I need to shut down all power and communication to the subfloors of this building immediately."

"Jolaj?"

"Yes."

"Give me ninety seconds, then go."

Jolaj barely contained a roar of satisfaction. Finally, he could breathe again. He could get her out in time.

He handed the link back to the woman. "Contact Metro Detective Sean O'Leary and tell him his sister Sara was kidnapped by a man named Timothy Perry. He released her, but she's still in danger and somewhere in the area of Old Duval Road."

The moment she acknowledged his request he *slipped* toward *out-of-sync* and *slipped* back into the darkened corridor outside of the room where he'd left Lily. Blindly, he felt for the door, then the wall near the control panel. Sinking his claws into the plaster, he dug for the security seal then yanked free the mechanism locking the door shut.

As the door opened, Lily's scent filled his lungs. The sound of her breathing filled up his heart. She jumped when he touched her, then she clung to him.

"My strong, beautiful Lily. Please forgive me."

"I'm okay. We're all right." Her hands found his face. Her trembling fingers traced his lips then she pressed her lips to his.

The primitive part of his brain wanted to take her, there on the floor, in the dark, but reason pushed the need away. He returned her kiss until her lips stilled. Rubbing his face against hers, he lifted her to her feet.

She moved stiffly, clutching his arm as he led her through the exit. He hated that he was responsible for her being battered and bruised. But to wallow in fruitless recrimination would be selfish. He had to be strong for her now.

He led her down the corridor to the elevator where he had to pry open the doors. Enough light sifted down the shaft from above that he could see the emergency ladder. With Lily's human eyes it was unlikely she could see anything at all. He pulled her forward and put her hands on the rungs.

She stopped and made him listen. "Sara. Please."

"I sent a message to Sean."

"You can be there faster."

He didn't want to leave her, but he knew she needed him

to see to the things she couldn't.

"I'll be fine," she said. "Please go."

He fisted his hand in her hair, careful not to pull, and brought it to his nose. He needed her scent in his lungs. "Brian is on his way here. He'll be here soon to take care of you."

"Good," she said. "I'll meet you there. Be careful."

Jolaj pressed his lips to her temple, then he *slipped*.

The Ormney Affairs office filled his vision again. This time the receptionist didn't scream. A small crowd had gathered in the hallway. The woman who'd been there earlier broke away and strode toward him. She held up the link and Jolaj reached for it.

"It's still active," she said.

Even if he found Sara, it wouldn't be enough. Not even close. He was going to make sure Timothy Perry didn't escape and he'd need help to accomplish all that must be done.

"Connect Zone Wide messaging. Kertu meet Jolaj, North Zone Gate, urgent. End."

Lily had trusted him, believed in him again and again and he wasn't going to let her down now.

Jolaj *slipped*, this time *syncing* at The Zone Gate. He had to wait only a heartbeat before Kertu appeared beside him. The man had been young at the time of The Crossing, yet even then Kertu's *slip* ability had nearly matched his own.

"I need your help. We'll have to *slip*. Will you follow me?" He hadn't made that request in twenty years. Hadn't believed he ever would again. Kertu nodded without hesitation and Jolaj initiated the transition. He reached out and laid a hand on Kertu's shoulder and together they *slipped* toward *out-of-sync*.

He welcomed the reassuring pull of Kertu's presence through the *slip*. When he began to *sync*, Kertu followed and they *synced* together in front of the O'Leary house. It was the only point of reference he had. The houses lining the street were quiet. A woman stood on the porch to the O'Leary home. She nodded as their gazes met. There was a weapon of some sort cradled in her arms.

Lily had said it would be a few houses up. He broke into a jog and Kertu kept pace beside him.

Together they worked their way into the backyard of the neighboring house. The fence gate already stood open, but they had to jump over the back fence line to reach the wooded area behind. Jolaj took in deep breaths, scenting the air. He had met Sara only twice, but each time she'd made a strong impression.

They threaded their way through the trees, parallel to the row of houses until he caught the scent. Kertu followed close, clearly alert and ready for anything.

They found Sara and Bradley huddled behind an oak tree. Bradley lay unconscious on the ground. Sara's blouse gapped open and what was left of it was drenched in blood. She gripped a broken branch in her hand as if ready to fight.

"Sara," he called, holding his distance. "It's Jolaj. Lily sent me. My friend Kertu is here with me. We're here to help you."

The branch in her hand dipped downward, her shoulders drooping as if the stick had transmuted to lead. Jolaj kneeled down beside her. She flinched but didn't pull away. Tears streaked her face.

She blinked up at him through swollen eyes. "Lily?"

Her tiny hands wrapped around his biceps.

"She's all right."

"Thank God." She closed her eyes on a sigh, but they sprang open wide after only seconds. "He can't be far." Her voice shook as her hands tightened compulsively on his arm. "You have to stop him. He's responsible for the deaths of all those people."

"I'll stop him." Jolaj looked over her head to Kertu. "Remain here and keep them safe."

Kertu nodded. "Keep your descendants always in your thoughts."

The old words sounded odd in Jolaj's ears. The Searchers had always parted with those words to remind each other remaining alive played an essential part in bringing their descendants into being. Those without mates had stopped using the saying when they'd realized they might never have those descendants.

"And you, my friend."

Kertu gently pulled Sara's hands away from Jolaj and drew her against his chest. Jolaj trusted his friend to care for Lily's cousin.

Jolaj back-tracked the trail Sara and Bradley had made. It led him to a plascrete storm shelter that had to be the room he and Lily had seen across the vid-link.

A house sat across a wide expanse of overgrown lawn. He

slipped across the space and into the house to avoid being seen. A fresh scent trail lingered inside the house. Methodically, he searched room to room. The house looked unlived in. Preserved from some time in the past. Dust coated every surface. Cobwebs hung in the out of the way corners. He found the bedroom Perry had been in when they'd lost the vid feed, but found no sign of the bastard.

Sirens wailed in the distance and he cursed the deep dark. His quarry would be on guard.

Giving up on the house, Jolaj *slipped* to a spot outside, circled the house in a quick jog and found a scent trail at a side door. He looked around for any cover Perry might be using to set him up, then jogged forward.

Perry had a wide variety of delivery mechanisms for his damned drugs. Jolaj had been ready for the injection Lily had been forced to administer, but he might not be able fight off the effects if he caught another dose now.

Lily pushed through the elevator shaft's emergency hatch on the ground floor and dragged herself through the narrow opening and onto cool beige tiling. She blinked at the bright light. Someone nearby shrieked, but Lily didn't have the energy to look for the source. She flopped onto her back and stared at the high arched ceiling. The exclamations of the people who'd been in the lobby had to mean she looked as bad as she felt.

The climb had been long, but not beyond her normal capabilities. She'd lost a lot of blood. Jolaj had bloodied her to sell his performance.

He'd bloodied himself, too. Dread shivered across her rapidly chilling skin as she realized he might be seriously hurt or putting himself in a dangerous position. If Perry... No. Perry didn't know Jolaj had survived his trap and even if he did, he couldn't realize that, even drugged, Jolaj could *slip* across the city in minutes.

She wouldn't lose Jolaj. Not now. Not ever.

Faces appeared above her. She should say something or do something, but her muscles weren't cooperating.

"Are you okay? We called emergency response. Help is on the way."

Sirens blared into her awareness then receded. Boots clattered across the tiled floor.

Someone was talking to her, pressing an insti-pressure pad against the slick surface of her abdomen. An oxygen boost mask appeared and slipped over her nose. The combination cleared her head enough that she could focus on faces.

A serious young woman in a med tech uniform leaned over her, pressing firmly on the pad. Lily reached for the woman's arm to get her attention. The pressure made it hard to inhale despite the oxygen. "Okay, now," she managed.

The woman eased back, leaving the pad in place. She grabbed a trauma scan bar and held it over Lily.

The other tech, a brawny blond with a crew cut dabbed at the blood on her face with steri-wipes.

He met her eyes. "There don't seem to be any injuries under the blood."

"No," agreed Lily. "Splatter."

"Should we be looking for another injured?" he wanted to know.

"No" Lily had to stop for a breath. "He left."

"Lily!" She recognized the shout as Brian's voice. He appeared at her side. She held a hand up and he clutched it between his palms. "You okay, sis?"

She pushed the oxygen boost away and nodded. "I have to get to Old Duval, Bri. I have to help Jo. Sara?"

"No word yet." Brian looked to the female medic. "What's her status?"

"Vitals strong," the woman reported. "She needs a trauma blocker and a transfusion. She's lost blood, luckily only one of the slashes is deep."

There had been nothing of luck in it. Jolaj had fought the drugs to keep her safe. Lily squeezed Bri's hand. "No med center," she said. "Just a patch job. Sara and Jo..." She had to blink away tears before she could continue. "I have to get there."

"Patch her up," he said to the medic. "I promise she'll get the care she needs as soon as everyone is out of harm's way."

Lily squeezed his hand in appreciation.

The medics cleaned her up and sealed the lacerations. Someone handed her an energy drink and a fresh tunic to replace her ripped top. With a little help from Brian, she got to her feet. Metro surrounded them. Lily didn't know when they'd arrived. She leaned heavily on Brian and let him convince the officers to let them leave as they walked to the jet-hop he had waiting.

In less than fifteen minutes, Brian set the hopper down in front of the O'Leary house. A small crowd stood outside and Metro units dotted the length of the road into the distance. A medic unit waited, ready.

Aunt Jane came up and engulfed Lily in a tight hug. "They found Sara," she said. "They metro officers are bringing her out now."

"I'm so sorry," said Lily. "I shouldn't have gotten her involved."

Aunt Jane pulled back and looked her in the eye. "None of that now. You're not to blame. My children don't need any help getting themselves in dangerous situations. It comes naturally." Jane pushed a lock of hair away from Lily's face. "They haven't found the man who did this. Your Uncle's back and he's out looking. Brian said it's Timothy Perry."

"That's right."

"Pat's been to the old Perry house. There's no one there now."

Lily nodded, thinking. She pulled out of her aunt's arms. She knew exactly where he'd be. "Tell him to go to our old house."

"It was sold years ago," said Jane.

"I know, but that's where he'll be."

"Okay." Her aunt pulled her com-link out of her pocket and slipped it over her ear. She activated the link and gave Lily's suggestion to her husband.

Jolaj followed the trail to the last house on the south side of the street. The scent of fear assailed his senses the moment he *slipped* inside. He found a young mother with her toddler locked in a closet and sent them out of the front door. Perry's stench led him to a second story bedroom. Ready for anything, Jolaj *slipped* through the door and *synced*. Perry stood by the window, watching the commotion on the street. He held an injector gun in one hand and a pulse pistol in the other. He faced Jolaj.

"I'm impressed," he said. "I thought you'd be dead. Tell me, is that whoring bitch still alive, too?"

Rage exploded through Jolaj, setting his nerves on fire and boiling his blood. This maniac needed to die. He panted, fighting for control. His racing heart drummed loud in his ears.

"This was her room, you know? I used to stand out there in the backyard and watch the house. Waiting for them to let their annoying little mutt out to piss." He smiled wistfully. "I enjoyed gutting that one. Enjoyed hearing Lily and Rose whine about him going missing even more. They looked for him for weeks."

Jolaj listened, biding his time, waiting for the bastard to step away from the wall. To give Jolaj enough room to *slip* in behind him, out of easy reach of the hypo.

"An animal." Perry continued. "They made all of that fuss over a stupid, dirty animal." His face flushed, the tips of his ears turned cherry. "My mother liked animals. All kinds. And when your kind showed up she started spending all her time volunteering at the shelter. That was back before The Zone."

Jolaj remembered. He remembered the cargo containers the Earth military had forced them to sleep in and he remembered the kindness of the humans who'd brought them food and donated clothing.

"Mom volunteered there right up until the day Dad had to put her down." Lips curled, he spit the words into the air, growing louder with each sentence. "She had a little half-breed bun in the oven. In the end, he buried her out back with the other animals we killed."

Shock almost cost him his shot at Perry as the man paced a little away from the wall. Clearing his thoughts, Jolaj *slipped* toward *out-of-sync* then *synced* behind the man. He pinned his arms, lifted him, and slammed him against the wall. The hypo dropped to the floor with a thunk.

Perry struggled. Jolaj slid one hand up and wrapped it around his neck, sinking his claws in enough to get the man's attention. "By The Laws of Continuation," he ground the words out between clamped teeth, "it's my right to take your life for what you've done."

He desperately wanted to end the bastard right there. Sink his claws in deep and rip the man's throat out.

Footfall on the stairs brought Jolaj around to face the door, a struggling Perry still locked against his chest.

A silver haired man with Lily's brilliant green eyes came through the door, pulser in hand. Jolaj growled and the man stopped short.

He lifted his hands in the air, one still gripped around the weapon. "Lily sent me," he said. "I'm her uncle, Pat."

Perry squirmed like the worm he was. "Help me!" he shouted. "He's gone crazy."

Jolaj's grip on Perry tightened until the man stilled, fighting for breath.

"Now hold up there," said Pat. "You don't want to do that. Get you in to all kind of trouble and I think our Lily's taken a shine to you. She'd be pretty mad if I let you do something to get arrested."

He edged a little closer.

Jolaj growled again in the back of his throat. "He kidnapped and hurt your daughter. Don't you want to see him punished?"

"Hell, yes. If I could, I'd rip him limb from limb, but we both know that's not the way it works."

Jolaj moaned, but he knew the man was right.

More boot heels stormed up the stairs. Lily and Brian came through the door. Lily was alive and whole and taking everything in with a glance of those beautiful green eyes. For her he would be strong. For her he would be civilized.

He retracted his claws but maintained his grip on Perry's throat.

His strong, fierce Lily pulled her pulser out of her pocket and changed the setting then stepped forward. She stood face to face with Perry.

"Why?" A frown etched deep groves across her forehead. "Why do you hate them so much?"

Perry laughed, a hoarse, ragged sound that garbled out of his bruised throat. "They're animals." His crazed features softened. "Animals who want to corrupt good girls like you. To steal mothers from little boys."

Perry's demeanor changed again in a flash of movement. He jerked in Jolaj's grip, kicking at Lily's legs. Her reaction was instant. She pressed the pulser to Perry's chest. She must have set it on low, because Jolaj didn't feel anything from the discharge. Perry went limp and Jolaj dropped him to the floor like what he was. Garbage.

Lily stepped over Perry and into Jolaj's arms.

A moment passed in silence. Brian and Pat studied their toes while Jolaj savored the feel of Lily safe and in his arms where she belonged.

"He's insane," she said into his tunic. "Thank God you're okay."

He breathed in her scent, gloried in her curves pressed against his aching body. He nodded into her hair. "Praise the Way."

CHAPTER 49

Lily closed the link, ending her conversation with Aunt Jane, and leaned against the railing surrounding Jolaj's rooftop garden. He had a great view of the lush landscape of The Zone. From the outside, The Zone, with its imposing wall, looked like a prison camp, but the people living inside had made it their home. Could they really want to leave?

Below, she caught sight of Jolaj and Kertu walking into the square. The council meeting had finally wrapped up. The men exchanged a quick embrace then parted. Jolaj looked up as if he'd known she'd be there watching. He blurred, then disappeared. The air behind her crackled with energy and she turned in time to see him *sync*. His skills were crazy good and he knew his own home well enough to make *slipping* there completely safe. Still, every time he *slipped,* a small knot of worry tightened in her gut.

Jolaj reached for her, capturing her face with his big hands and pressing his forehead to hers. The growling noise he made in the back of his throat rumbled through his chest, beneath the palm she'd placed there. The vibrations rippled through her, heating all the hidden and dusty corners of her heart.

She pushed back a little and looked up into his face. "Aunt Jane and Uncle Pat have Sara back at their place, surrounded by Junior, Rosalee and the kids. They're keeping Bradley in the med center to watch his head injury." She clutched a fistful of Jolaj's tunic. "Sean's still at Metro. Brian says Perry confessed to everything. The maniac bragged about how clever he was. What a service he'd done for mankind."

Jolaj smiled. "That information can't have been released. Has your brother been hacking into the Metro security cams?"

His humor chased away the anger she'd been hanging on to.

"Probably," she admitted.

Jolaj traced a thumb across her lips. "The Council has approved our request to allow all human companions to remain in The Zone indefinitely."

"That's good." She traced her hands down his chest and circled his waist. "It might take some time for the public to process all this. Despite the fact that a human was behind everything, it will be hard for them to get the images and fear from the attacks out of their heads."

He took advantage of the better access her movement had given him and slipped his arms around her, one hand at the small of her back pressing her closer. Lily moaned.

"Yes," Jolaj agreed. "It will take people some time. But the Council has also received many statements of support. The Mayor has promised to press charges against any employer who fires Ormney workers because of these events."

"Brian says there's good buzz on the Public Nets and in The Pool." She was proud that she managed to carry on the conversation. The way he was holding her was more than a little distracting.

His smile slipped, his face serious, but he didn't let her go. "Will your brother accompany you to DC for Rose's funeral?"

Lily leaned her forehead against his chest. Grief still fresh and raw. "Yeah. He's thinking of coming back here after. All his work is remote. He can live anywhere."

Jolaj worked his leg between hers adding a sweet pressure that made her want to arch her spine and rock against him. "And what of you, Lily?" One of his hands stroked her hair away from her face. "Will you try to run away from your family again? Go back to your position at Deepwater now that you're cleared for work?"

She didn't know how to explain that she wanted nothing more than to stay in his arms, in his life, as long as he wanted her. She didn't care whether their relationship could be formalized. She didn't need a marriage certificate. He was all she needed.

But what did he need? She let her love for him color her words when she answered, emotion making her voice husky and deep. "This is home now. I'm not going anywhere."

"Good." His perfunctory tone made it clear the she'd chosen the only answer he would accept. "Because I don't intend on letting you run away from me." Jolaj lifted her chin with his finger and she met his lips eagerly. The kiss was tender and full of longing. His mouth moved over her lips with an unspoken promise. He broke the kiss breathing heavily.

Lily struggled to hold him closer. "But I know how important descendants are to you. Even if what Perry told you about his mother's pregnancy is true, I still might not be able to give you children. And what if your people decide to leave?"

Jolaj cupped her jaw in his hands and lifted her face.

"I'm not going anywhere. I told the Council today that even if they restart the Searcher program, I won't serve. Several of the other Searchers were there. They all told the Council that they too wanted to make a permanent home here and would not serve in a new Searcher program. We asked the Council to reconsider the ban against taking human mates."

Lily's heart skittered and expanded.

"Your people have a saying—*home is where the heart is*. My people also have words about the heart. Words said between mates. *No matter where I slip my heart remains with you.*" His eyes demanded her understanding. "I won't deny I hope we'll have descendants, but even if I believed it could never happen, I would still choose you as my mate. I love you, Lily Rowan. I have no reason to search any longer. When I look into your eyes, I know I'm home."

A NOTE FROM THE AUTHOR

If you enjoyed reading *Deadly Lover*, I'd love for you to help others enjoy it, too. You can help other readers find this book by recommending it to friends or by reviewing it online.

To learn more about my books and get new release announcements, sign up for the "List" on my website: **www.charleeallden.com**.

Thank you for giving my books a try!

Charlee

ABOUT THE AUTHOR

Charlee Allden is a long time fan of love, adventure, and happily-ever-after. She writes sexy, intense, out-of-this-world romance and is a two time winner of the On the Far Side contest, sponsored by the FF&P chapter of Romance Writers of America®. She has also won the Golden Acorn contest and been a Reveal Your Inner Vixen contest finalist. She loves to hear from readers. Connect with her online at: **www.charleeallden.com** or find her on FaceBook, Pinterest, or Twitter.